The Exagggerations of

Peter Prince

Steve Katz

The Exagggerations of

Peter Prince

Steve Katz

Verbivoracious Press

Glentrees, 13 Mt Sinai Lane, Singapore

This edition published in Great Britain & Singapore

by Verbivoracious Press

www.verbivoraciouspress.org

ISBN: 978-981-11-2497-6

Printed and bound in Great Britain & Singapore

First published in the US by Holt, Rinehart & Winston (1968).

Note: Several of the original design elements from the hardback have been altered to accommodate this edition.

Introduction

W.C. BAMBERGER

It's no exaggeration to say that *The Exagggerations of Peter Prince* is unlike any other book that will open you today. Books, bound or, now, e-, are in the main done deals, finished products, areas firmly demarked, self-contained. *The Exagggerations of Peter Prince*, for its part, contains self-containment, but it is more. It will open you to new ways of not just reading, but of looking at things around—and within—you. And your experience of this perspectival retrofitting will feel as relaxed and sunny as a game of catch with the regular guy from up the block—right up to the point where it wrenches your heart almost out of your breast.

Exagggerations (the 'g' forming an elastic band in the middle of the word makes it infinitely expandable, and so it will serve herein as shorthand for the title entire) is a knot of energies, not an inert impress of letters and images on paper. Katz's novel novel—though there were hints and intimations, pages of plagiarism-by-anticipation as far back as Sterne, a scattering of models both to keep in mind and to ruthlessly banish, that had come before—was something entirely new; a rearticulation of the Form of the Novel to provide a channel for new ideas arising from new views, new needs and new crises. New ways, truer ways, of looking at words and matter and how words might matter were crackling in the noosphere (you read; you know what these were; let's just move along) when Steve Katz began writing. Givens—about the writing of fiction, as well as everything else—were no longer to be taken as such, no longer to be nodded at, but to be cut open and examined. It was a time of cleavage, and *Exagggerations* displays exceptionally dazzling cleavage.

Katz's skill as a novelist rose and converged with those energies, but his aesthetic sense, as appetitive as the best of writers' senses always are, had long roamed far afield from the novel-as-given. He has self-described some early work as having "Faulknerian" elements. His first published novel, *The Lestriad* (1962) shows the influence of film technique, both in its reflections—and variations—on Bergmann's *The Seventh Seal* and, I would hazard, Kurosawa's *Rashomon. Kulik in Puglia,* another novel written in this same early period, was a more traditional novel, while yet another he worked on at this time, *The Childhood of Marcus Morocco,* is a series of interconnected stories that shows Katz raising himself out of fiction's givens; it has structural similarities to *The Lestriad,* while tonally it is in places much like *Exagggerations.* (Neither of these early novels has been published in its entirety.)

Having surveyed the fictional territory and created a few reasonably-sized, if not entirely reasonably-organized works, he was ready to step up when the step-up moment came.

The Exaggerations of Peter Prince is a capacious, Nautilus-chambered book. The threads Katz weaves together on the first few pages, if tweezed out and separated, could be described by turns as "surrealism," as "fairy-tale-like," as "parody," and more. But Katz coaxes these disparate tones and stances, words and ideas into flocking together. They come straight at us, filling our depth of field for a startling moment, only to veer off and be replaced by another, just as vivid and just as alive. These quick, beautiful changes begin on page one and continue on through the length, the heights and the depths of the novel.

Exagggerations, again, is less a book-as-finished-object than a structure—and an exceptionally generous authorial attitude of acceptance—for friendly grapplings with the givens and other forces that surrounded Katz at the time of its writing—from a rumination on the fluorescent lights under which he writes (a passage that Robert Burton would have been pleased to include in his *Anatomy of Melancholy*), to friendship (Ted Berrigan suddenly steaming through the book, for one brief photoplay page), to self-realization, gender roles and more (some explicitly so, some implicit and surrounding), as well as literary theory itself—to flow through and become visible in a unique setting, even as they retain their own character. We might think of Buckminster Fuller's image of a knot as a pattern of force rather than an entity (he spliced together several kind of rope and slipped a knot along its length, so the knot was by turns cotton, nylon, etc.—the knot being the pattern not the physical object), and so recognize that the truest *Exagggeration* is that capacious openness, Katz's knot of intertwined attention, language, orthography and humor—and humor here is omnipresent, cropping up in every shade, the lightest to the darkness, extremes often presented as being as close together as piano keys—that flows through all the subjects of his attention, even as they, reciprocally, flow through it.

Those (too few, in my view) critics who have turned their attention to *Exagggerations* have tended to focus on the formal innovations—the side-by-side columns, the typographical zaniness, the graphic diversions and crossed-out pages (which we of course carefully read), rather than the content and the insistent, relentlessly stirred and stirring, emotional mix. Peter Prince's conflicted yearnings are front and center from the first page: he loves his Jingle, but tests and threatens that love with the reek of cheese, a disdain of cats (with a whisker of culpability in their demise), and a conflicted heart. Just as clearly as Peter Prince struggles in the first few pages here to find a stance toward Jingle he can live with, Katz's narrative voice openly struggles to find a stance toward his text that he can live with. Thus his exasperated, oft-quoted self-interruption:

> Enough! Katz, you're making this all up. It doesn't make a
> bit of sense. It's not a promising beginning. Why can't you
> follow instructions? You can't write whatever you want:
> Peter Prince Peter Prince Peter Prince. Where's the story?
> (p.4)

And exactly *there* is where the story is, of course, in that contradiction:

because he *can* write whatever he wants, and not following instructions (from whom? From "good writing," we can assume) is an important part of the delights of the story, of *Exagggerations*. One moral of this story is that if some feeling is important to us, we are likely to be (and if we are honest with ourselves, admit to being) conflicted about said feeling. Such scene-captures of the doubts that are the truth of our reality, of our lives, as lovers or as writers, are present at all levels of the book. (*Exagggerations* is, yes, fractal in this sense.)

To be clear: The novel elements in *Exaggerations* are not signs of a capricious nature; not presented just to be novel elements. That kind of self-aggrandizement is inimical to Katz's approach, and to his protagonists, as well. His hero here, Peter Prince, is stubbornly as stubbornly individual, as true to his own nature as each wordy passage and page here is true to its own.

And this, I would suggest, is one of the elements that so consistently mark Katz's protagonists as "regular guys." There is nothing nose-up intellectual about *Exagggerations*, nor about any of Katz's work. The deepest and widest ideas and events are presented to us as simply as a ball landing in a glove. Peter Prince, for (and because of) all of his conflicts, the unimaginable things that happen to him (at one point he is captured, stripped naked and his penis is . . . enlarged by force—we certainly didn't see that one coming), remains the rumpled epitome of the regular guy:

> He likes the simple stuff, can polish off a good liter of wine
> with a meal, and then seal the feast with a slug of *grappa*:
> that stiff burn of raw booze always sets him on his feet,
> gnashing his teeth. He . . . stands up, pulls the napkin from
> his belt, and wipes the big moustache that curves into his
> mouth like a pushbroom. "Deeeeelishus," he says, and
> slaps his gut in satisfaction. One tail of his workshirt flops
> out in front. (p.203)

This describes not just Peter Prince, but Dusty Wier in *Wier & Pouce*,

Nathan in *Antonello's Lion*, and many another, each an individual variation on this rumpled ideal.

The "simple stuff" referred to in *Exagggerations* includes not just 120-proof Italian liquor, but deep emotion and compassion, as well. Some of America's rawest nerves in the late 1960s, the time of *Exaggerations'* writing and publication, are touched on in the episode of Peter Prince, Bebo and Thwang-Nuc (called Teresa). At this point Bebo is Peter Prince's girlfriend. She was disowned by her family for marrying a black man (with whom Peter Prince has a very difficult, racially-blocked conversation), from whom she is separated. Peter Prince does not much care for Bebo, but has attached himself to her largely because he loves and pities her adopted Vietnamese daughter, Teresa. (It should be noted that Katz wrote the passage below three years before the publication of the unforgettable photograph of 9-year-old Phan Thi Kim Phuc running from the napalm that is horribly burning her nude body.)

> The experimental use of napalm for psychological warfare by American advisers in her native province only half-maimed the child . . . one side of her was roasted and slightly paralyzed, her fingers gone, her body thick with scar tissue like callus. Because her cheek was destroyed and her mouth partly seared shut she had difficulty speaking her native Oriental dialect, and could manage only a little whistling, like small sirens, out of the side of her mouth that would open, which she took to be the American language. (p.87)

The episode ends with Peter Prince, like many another American of good conscience confronting the cruelties and futilities of the time, being tempted by nihilism (the word "nothing" appears again and again on the last pages of the story) when the little girl smothers under a plastic garment bag (which, as is pointed out in passing, is a petroleum product—

as was the napalm that maimed her):

> "No," he said, and tried to tear the plastic membrane from her face. It stuck to her hands like oil. It was a plastic cleaning bag. . . . It tried to smother his arms. Nothing was there. She had been dead. Right. That was it. Nothing had come in a plastic sack and had roosted on her face. (p.120)

This is *Exaggerations* at its best—where it clearly shows us that it really doesn't exaggerate at all.

Katz trusts that there are other honest, intelligent souls, that they (shall we say "we"?) are among his readers. When Katz writes of/for himself, he is writing of/for us, as well. As we read *Exagggerations* one of the most pervasive feelings we have, page after page, is that Katz trusts us, his unmet readers, trusts us to "get it," to understand, to know, to feel, with him. And it is a sign of this trust that *Exagggerations* didn't become the Big Daddy of Katz's work, neither did it become the Sheep Dolly, spawning shorter-lived clones. Elements of this book, discoveries made during its writing, truths shoveled up out of the deep ash that passé fiction leaves behind, make further appearances, less or more insistently, in much of Katz's later work—in the story collections *Creamy and Delicious* and *Stolen Stories* (for my money the finest collection of short fiction published in the last half of the 20th Century); the unclassifiable *Moving Parts*, the novels *Wier & Pouce*, *Swanny's Ways* and *Antonello's Lion*—but never again does he address himself in such blunt-edged, hectoring terms as "Enough! Katz, you're making this all up." He doesn't nag, doesn't badger, doesn't insult our intelligence with repetitions of the same stance from one work to the next, the same tone, offer up the same "revelations" again and again as too many so called "Meta-fictionists" have done with such one-note monotony. Katz, rather, trusts us to "get it" the first time.

There is much more Katz to get, more books and tales to read, much more to experience, and any readers who go on to the other works will discover rewards unique to each. All those comic and tragic effects, all the unexpected, only-from-Katz's-mind metaphors and images, the unearned delights and frustrations so true to life, the rumplings we find reflecting ourselves, dazzlingly arranged along structural armatures unique to the demands and goals of each individual work, all will be enhanced, all will have a deeper and truer way into us for our experience of having been opened by *The Exagggerations of Peter Prince.*

"You may not," said the woman of Peter Prince, before divorce had peeled them apart, "consider Siamese cats a responsibility, but I have to, because they're mine."

The refrigerator door gave in to Peter Prince with a light, magnetic tug. He reached in among the cold plastic packages and grabbed his Limburger. "Cats up your ass," he responded, moistening his lips. He peeled the foil from the cheese and loosed in the draughty palace air yellow waves of locker-room stench that made his woman's face-flesh wrinkle. Beneath the stone arch of the sitting-room entrance lay the carcasses of eleven cats, their necks broken. She kneeled among them, stroking the dead fur.

"These animals," she said. "Each of these animals was born on my lap, and I have a certain feeling for them, you know."

Peter Prince placed his Limburger on the sideboard so it would soften and be palatable after dinner-time, and he could eat it while his woman carried plates away on her freckled arms.

"I know, I know, I know. I know what your furry little brain is hinting. But I do absolutely nothing to cats, and never intend to. I don't like cats. I don't recognize cats' existence. I'm not sorry that cats are dead, and that death doesn't disturb me. I go in my direction and cats . . ." He paused and watched his toes moving at the tops of his soft goatskin shoes. "You really think I kill cats?"

She gathered several up in her arms and walked to the latticed window, dropping the stiff softies into the moat below. Peter Prince, his eyes were closed, could tell the splash of cats from any other sound. Or the sound of cats in the garbage disposal. Cats gathering up the blankets. Cats walking on pianos and typewriters. He hated his woman's involvement with cats. Wanted his own life, free of cats. Wanted to leave cats behind, so to speak.

"What does anyone around here think," he asked her. "Watching you drop cats out the window?"

She had just released the last one. "Now," she said, "I wish you'd get rid of that cheese."

"A good woman," said Peter Prince, "would forget about cats and learn to tolerate her husband's cheese."

She waved her arms in resignation and glided his way over the Glo-Coat. She was going to feed him dinner soon and he had to move. Cats, he thought, could be grounds for divorce; cats and ripening Limburger. He often wondered whether or not, when he was finally split from his woman, he would miss cats, and be able to forego Limburger, which he didn't like that much, however well it made his point. The truth is yet to come.

From the window Peter Prince stared out over the moat at heaps of wrecked cars that surrounded the dusty gardens of the palace in a widening ring: Tempests, Rivieras, Bonnevilles, Fairlanes, F 88's, Larks, Barracudas, to mention a rusting few he could see through the faint, enameled mist, and beyond those heaps that were high, but not yet higher than the walls of his woman's palace was the reassurance blinking in colored lights of *Tastee-Freeze* and *Dairee Treet* and *Dogs & Suds* and burgers at 19 cents. There were discount houses there in the glazed light. Peter Prince often wandered through, when he left the palace alone, the wild fluorescence of discount houses, the humming light of those new places, where he fingered the synthetic undies, the iridescent vases, the wrenches packed in polyethylene, shoes lined up like piano keys, and the lucent plastic fruit. Peter Prince had been in the army, had been wounded there in what might have been called a war, and peace to him was reassuring. Peace was somewhere out farther than he could see where a ring of state parks lay, recreation centers, where picnics happened, and the smell of charcoal starter and hickory treatment.

"My father," said his woman, as she put his french fries near his Pepsi glass, "stone by numbered stone brought this palace over and reconstructed here on this sight, in plain view, just as it stood in the old country. So we've got a little bit of everything now. We look forward toward the future but we brought along a little of the past of our . . ."

She told the same story every night, as cats moved about the table making sounds, as if she were saying grace, telling of the masons from the old country who came to reconstruct the marble arches and the balustrade, and those gardeners who tried the formal shrubberies, in vain. Her father, who had become rich late in life, had fulfilled his dream late, and had left his daughter to live in it, a place to keep her Peter Prince.

But Peter Prince was never sure that he fit in. He never felt his place was to dwell in his woman's luxurious inheritance, as charming as he found it. He didn't even have a feeling for cats, which caused guilt in him, and though he tried to think that he was somehow compatible to the situation he could only discover that he was secretly promising himself that after the divorce things would change, and they did.

Left on his own after his divorce Peter Prince bought cats, surprising himself and his friends. He gave up Limburger for muenster, and made his life on all counts more bland for a while. He would have remained alone all the time, but for certain necessities—the lack of quinine—the deliberate and sustained efforts by his friends to keep him occupied—the conferences his business required (he still held them, kept his business going despite the grief and confusion after the holocaust—if we can remember that far)—and despite his desire to travel, to see it, to learn it, everywhere—though he did, after a while, set out—traveled out, grew beards, learned new dialects, spent strange coins, wriggled through customs, shaved beards. In America sometimes the haze parted like gauze on a desert landscape and he could see distances, over the nap of sagebrush on the hills, the sand dunes, prickly pear, the Joshua trees, the yucca, and he would have liked a camel bazaar, carpets, men with braids of garlic around their necks, or even some habitable pueblos out of the land, the land itself flowering into people, instead of the encapsulated suburbs of the nightmare, like Tucson he saw, like Albuquerque, Denver, Phoenix, Reno, Boise, Laramie. He was disappointed. He spoke to the Mississippi and told that river with shoulders that in a time more in proportion—distances fuller between places, people tightened down—it could have separated nations, languages; it would have separated smaller animosities, and might have been crossed for wars. Wars. Although he'd fought in what might have been called a war once, and was wounded several times, he wasn't sure he disliked war and sometimes thought he could prefer it to a lazy and boring peace, but his conscience always capitulated. Peter Prince didn't know where he was, and most of the time it didn't matter, as long as he was trying to be helpful.

*

Enough! Katz, you're making this all up. It doesn't make a bit of sense. It's not a promising beginning. Why can't you follow the instructions? You can't write whatever you want: Peter Prince Peter Prince Peter Prince. Where's the story? How are you going to catch us up in it and write a novel so the reader won't be able to put it down, he's so involved. He'll put the book down right now and say, "Who cares?" without even a placemark. What will your friends say? They'll say, "Katz, cut it out, you're making it all up. You're fucking around with boredom in our heads." A reader wants to know what's going on. What's going on? Peter Prince, for instance, why write about Peter Prince? Every day of the summer more interesting people than he swim at Jones Beach, they eat hot dogs, the ball parks are full of them, they smear each other with newsprint in the subways, roll up their shirtsleeves and sit on the doorstoop, they lean from windows, they're honking at intersections on the cloverleafs, on the East Side Highway, they wait at the counters of the supermarket with their Kool-Aid and their instant rice. Boatloads cruise around the island and they meet each other, friendships depositing and eroding. It's difficult, Katz, to answer this question—Why Peter Prince?—when the wind itself is full of shapeless, hopeful folk blown about like empty plastic sacks, who could be born in a book. Born in a book at a profit to humanity.

Or if you must deal with Peter Prince, desert-head, at least let on that you know something about him: Where he was born and raised on chocolate bars and frozen prawns? Why did Peter Prince prefer Van Cortlandt Park to all the others with its granite cliffs and long wilderness? He preferred to watch the Bullets play their endless games with the Jesters. He sat on the concrete steps of the stands drinking an orange soda and watching the N.Y. Bullets go into extra innings with the score tied at 8-8. Thunder was threatening, and Peter Prince had the urge to buy a hot dog. This is the way a novel begins—sitting down. Come to your senses. Or start with Linda Lawrence, who was hired for this novel. Maybe she's the mother we're looking for, after all: The one who first let Peter Prince feed through heated rubber nipples.

*

Linda Lawrence shared a semi-private room with no one and she hoped that no one would come before she delivered. She was a veteran birth-giver but this time she was apprehensive, and since she was proud of her own bravery she preferred to be alone with her fears. The only person, beside the doctors and nurses, whom she could bear to see, was Philip Farrel, who came by with lilacs for her room, which the nurses removed after he left because the odor was too strong for the expectant mother. They gave her plastic irises in exchange.

"I'm really excited," said Philip Farrel, pacing the floor. "I don't know why, but this time I expect something special." He paced the floor. "I expect something different." He paced the floor.

"I've never been very nervous before either," she said, her voice quick and high pitched. She rubbed the sweat from her forehead with the back of his hand. He paced the floor. "I'm really nervous," she said, and the pain, coming now at three-minute intervals, caused her to bite her lower lip and squeeze Philip Farrel's wrist till he coughed. He paced the floor.

"Peter Prince is on his way." He paced the floor.

The pain folded back from her eyes. "Where is he going?"

"To Ethiopia, I think." He paced the floor.

"Why Ethiopia?"

"He says he wants to be helpful, and he thinks he can do that in Ethiopia." He paced the floor.

"Is he going to try to teach them?"

"I guess you'd call it that." He paced the floor.

"What will he teach them?"

"Methods." He paced the floor.

The pain came again to Linda Lawrence, and she pressed her teeth together.

"He's going to try to assist them, somehow." He paced the floor.

Her face wrinkled in agony, she grabbed his thigh with both her hands and squeezed till he coughed. He paced the floor.

*

She was happy enough with the room they had given her—a northern exposure done in decorator colors: plaster walls in warm eggshell; ceilings washable, two-tone peach and eggshell; the floors of linoleum, marbleized green and eggshell. The metal furniture was painted green except for one modern bleached wood chair that the minister sat in. The curtains: striped peach, green and eggshell. Her undersheet was white and the cover sheet of cotton: peach. In the mornings the sun reflected off the windows of the rooms nearby through the plastic irises, spotting the walls with lozenges of violet light. The old carts rattled in the hallway, carrying breakfasts. From the delivery rooms, which were down the hall, came the varied shrieks and calls and whistles and roars of women in childbirth, and the constant clatter of stainless instruments at the pauses, and the rare silences were filled with hissing sterilizers. Linda Lawrence thought she could make out sometimes from a distant nursery the sound of an infant, a human child, perhaps, she couldn't be sure. She couldn't tell what was being born, and as her body charged and discharged with pain she comforted herself in knowing that soon she would find out for herself, come what may.

"Spell birth," said the doctor, taking her blood pressure.

She did that correctly and he applied pressure to her shiny belly with his thin, curved fingers. "Now spell contraction," he said, staring at the plastic irises and nodding. It was his bedside manner, his way of setting a patient at ease, a spelling bee, and although Linda Lawrence could spell any word correctly at will she occasionally misspelled one for the doctor to make him look at her and wink the way he did, and pause to correct her. She thought the doctor quite handsome with his steamy eyes and she liked him to look her over.

"It should be," he said, "an easy birth."

"Will there be twins?" she asked.

"No," he said, and he squeezed her hand, and smiled, "but I could be wrong."

He put the stethoscope to her belly and listened, and then placed the earpieces in her ears, mingling earwaxes. "What do you hear?" he asked.

Linda Lawrence didn't want to say what she heard. It was like machinery, like office work, like the Golden Special leaving Chicago; it was tugboats and airliners putting down, pets at the dog-dish, a ski-lift on TV, an eight-story pack of filter tips, and the crash of penpoints on life insurance binders. How could she say that to the doctor? She smiled instead. "B A B Y," she correctly spelled.

The doctor licked a blue star and put it on her chart—a joke of his. Linda Lawrence spelled laughter.

"The nurse will call me when the pains pick up," he said.

She handed him his stethoscope.

Philip Farrel: It was his enemy or his friend and would cause the outcome to be either favorable or not; Time was, Time would. He rarely thought it over, and went on working, gathering, sorting and programing the pages of calculations that he offered in the offices of the vice presidents as his peculiar talent, the ability to keep it all straight, whatever it was, and to make predictions. With a few of the simple adjustments he knew how to make he could cut payrolls in half while increasing job opportunities elsewhere, if someone would only take to his plan, and he would ask for himself only a comfortable life, and for his family a little boat-basin on the lake, and water skis.

He waited to show his full stuff this time in the office of the President himself of the terrific concern. It was big time. He paced the floor. A final proof, this time, to the man on the top. Brass doorknobs on a walnut door separated him from the conference room where the conference was lasting forever, and each time the door opened and someone came out in a coughing fit or to ice the pitcher he thought it was his turn, but it never was. He sat down in the pocket of a leather chair of Finnish design and fingered the locks of his dispatch case, and looked with muted interest at the space and walls of the large room that held sculpture and paintings by the contemporaries—the President's private investment: A dirty peach De Kooning, with carmine and ochre, and bits of blue ripping in and out of space/ Some Rothko shimmering at its edges—magenta and grass green/ A black Pollock on paper, small, heavy/ A baby-blue Rauschenberg using the face of Mahatma Gandhi, a car door, some oil derricks and a series of curtain pulls/ A Lichtenstein torpedo launching—SWOOSH—with amber dots/ A Peter Dean monster in living color/ On part of one wall a film by Andy Warhol of a young fellow in drag doing the Frug was projected continually/ A Bruce Conner suitcase full of burnt plastic dolls and sheer webbing and melted jewels/ An orange canvas by Larry Poons spotted with tilted aqua lozenges/ A Wesselmann's woman at a stove with a pile of products beside her/ Four small rare oils of various deaths by Ian Müller/ On the ceiling a long green Sam Francis like a pine bough/ By Jim Dine framed, the manuscripts of his first poem, altered by porchlight/ At a desk on the far end of the room sat the President himself as a plaster figure by George Segal, his correspondence spilling over, his coffee cup nicked/ As if trying to rise for an interview a long, fur covered, rope-bound piece of Joseph Kurhajec, poking into a stainless steel cube/ Near Philip Farrel, made to swivel like a bingo cage, was a screened in box full of plastic astronauts, the apparatus set on spiraling legs built up out of wooden slats. It seemed to walk. By Sir Charles Ross, the President's San Francisco discovery/ And by young Robert Hudson a giddy sprawling painted construction in plastic and steel and fiberglass/ And the Jasper Johns, a painted brass mop in a bucket/ Oldenburg, lying in front of the big oak desk was a soft patent leather dictaphone one could sit on/ And the last to catch Philip Farrel's eye, on the far wall, next to the Irwin Fleminger ideal gum machine game was a pink woman flying through a coffee colored sky over a black beret, by Richard TumSuden, Thursday, Nov. 6.

*

"I see you have an interest in the arts," said the President, as he snuck up on Philip Farrel.

"Nothing in particular," said Philip Farrel as he worked up out of the chair and removed his gloves to shake hands with the President. "I see you have quite a lot of it," he commented. He was anxious to show his own business.

"It's my pride, my little pride," said the pudgy President, walking around in his collection and shaking his hand at each piece as if he were trying to get ink to flow in a fountain pen. "I make my own selections. A bit of my own peculiar tastes, I must admit. But it has a character." He wore the artist's uniform: corduroy pants and sneakers, a tweed jacket, a blue workshirt with a black bowtie. "But let me show you something special," he said. "It's my pride." He swung the hinged Barnett Newman from the wall to reveal a safe, which he opened to extract a large, bound sketch pad full of homo- and hetero-sexual pornography: cocks and tits and asses and cunts in special settings, delicately and clearly drawn like Audubon's prints—in fishermen's huts and fields of downed wheat and by the dusty windows, catching like distant thunder the delicate moods of monumental pleasure in gouache and tempera.

"I commissioned this to be done for me, and it's my pride." The President pronounced the name of the artist with a special, familiar emphasis, putting his hand on Philip Farrel's shoulder. "I mean this cost more than practically the whole collection. You're lucky to get a look at it." They went through the book again backward, stopping at a tempera of a young mother nursing her child and masturbating with an electric mixer fitted with rubber fingers while she leaned against a deerskin by an old Franklin stove. "I have a special interest in that company," said the President, pointing at the brand name of the mixer. "Don't be afraid to touch the pictures. They're permanently fixed."

Philip Farrel had come there with something else in mind. He knew that his chances were quickly thinning. It was his enemy or his friend and would cause the outcome to be either favorable or not: Time was, Time would.

The President put the book away and sat down to face Philip Farrel from his desk. Philip Farrel waited a moment to collect his confidence. How, after the President's book, could he open his dispatch case full of numbers and lay them out as if they were interesting?

"Well. What are you up to?" the President asked.

"I have a proposition," Philip Farrel said, his voice not quite so strong as he had planned it to be. "The efficiency . . . I mean I think I can save you some money, step up production, decrease payroll, curve it up, give the business a shot in the arm."

The President waved his head and he pulled out the large bottom drawer of his desk, where he kept his hooka, and he lit it, catching the smoke in his cheeks. The room filled with a smell like burning corn husks. The President sucked, held his breath, and offered the pipe end to Philip Farrel. "It's relaxing to take a poke after a conference. Chicago green, very nice. I always mix in a little hash to stretch it all out. This hooka. It's my pride." Philip Farrel swallowed the smoke and held it down and closed his eyes and immediately felt a smile thump into the back of his head and grow into his shoulders and hit his mouth with a tingling sponge.

"Like, uh, what's your bag?" asked the President.

Philip Farrel laughed very slowly. "I've got these numbers," he said. "In my dispatch, my dispatch case."

"Groovy," said the President. "Open." He raised his finger toward the worn brown leather case. It was always this way for Philip Farrel. He always drifted away, even when he wore his lead shoes. The course is never as straight as he would like it to be, and it's dangerous, for others sometimes. He forgets about it. He hasn't learned to swim.

He opened the little case and the computer sheets with numbers intact floated out like party favors. The numbers covered the Chamberlain, filled the lap of the Marisol, wrapped up the bronze Roszak, and piled as high as the lower lip of the Bontecou.

"They're nice," said the President.

"Yeah," said Philip Farrel.

"I mean I really, really dig them," said the President.

"Yeah," said Philip Farrel.

"Why?" asked the President.

"They're my . . . calculations," said Philip Farrel.

They smoked and they smoked. His enemy or his friend would cause the outcome to be either favorable or not: Time was, Time would.

"But what I really need," said the President smiling and closing the bottom drawer. Philip Farrel hadn't noticed before the emerald cuff-links on the President's workshirt. "What I really need is someone who'll handle this for me." He lifted a black fountain pen from its nest and one end of the long desk slowly fell away revealing the President's arsenal. "Will you handle this end of it?"

Philip Farrel took a rifle from the rack and sat back in his chairpocket. "Will you handle this for me?" the President repeated.

The same smile widened on Philip Farrel's face. The gunbarrel was black as a cave and the stock black as the President's car. "Will you handle this for me?"

Philip Farrel was lifted by the back of the neck till his hairs touched the ceiling. He looked out and saw Peter Prince running a course through the numbered corn, and through the telescopic sight he could see the inner folds of his ear.

Don't laugh. Don't call this frivolity. Here is where Peter Prince's end begins, and that's some serious trouble for all of us. Don't laugh at Peter Prince or his divorces from whatever he leaves, never back to the same spot in the same way, always after something new, exchanging histories, revising his biography, and never recognizing the repetitions. Don't laugh. Philip Farrel squeezed the trigger and that bullet dried its wings. That bullet. We'll get to know it. This is serious, even if Katz is making it up. Who'd say he was making it up?

I'd say he was.

I'd say he was.

I'd say he was.

*

It was transportation day and they wheeled Linda Lawrence from pain to pain through the corridors from contraction to contraction; over the cork tile floors, beneath the perforated acoustical ceiling, by painted plaster walls in dark pine and pale eggshell. Her mouth stretched open in pain like a rubber gasket, disguising the premonitions she had. She was anticipating something she couldn't name, because she knew that the birth in her was something more than the usual letting out of babies. She was thinking. Even while she was being wheeled into the delivery room, nurses and attendants rushing by, the anesthetist standing at the delivery table under the mellow jointed lights, her doctor entering the preparation room, even then she was thinking of Peter Prince, of him in Ethiopia, of how he had even been born, of how it could be now in Ethiopia, of how the birth had happened, of how Ethiopia would take to him, to Peter Prince who was so often overseas.

*

If Peter Prince were really in Ethiopia what action would he take and how would Ethiopia improve? Surrounded by dark, plumed men would he be too frightened to act if they stood in a circle about him, silent but for the click of their tongues against their palates, and the high plateau falling away from them in each direction, like a shield, studded with truncated hills, the air thin and blue, hooded vultures in the lankberry trees, and trees like candelabra, holding vultures, their gray and carmine heads flickering, and the small dark kites circling the umbrella crowned acacias. Phallic trophies. It seems he'd dreamed before about the Danakil who proved their virility by collecting phallic trophies and wearing them around their necks on grass chains. He was surrounded by tall black men, dark, plumed men holding their spears high on the hilt and leaning on camels. They bent forward from the hip, the bolts of coarse white cloth they dressed in hanging like draperies. Their hair grew in bushy caps from their heads, the way they wore it at war, to make them fierce. Bees had attacked Peter Prince on his way to Gondar. They had stung his knuckles as he drove his jeep through the Tigre province; they seeped under his cuffs and his lapel; they invaded his boots and pried at his lips and sneaked in through his ears, and he couldn't tell their noise from their sting, and his pelt was swollen and stretched, and his body rolled with great lounging throbs like a kettle drum.

It hadn't been easy for Peter Prince to leave his travels and come to Ethiopia, to lack comfort and the modern cleanliness, to rub his patience to the bone against the thankless needy, to leave Annette Anthony behind and just set out, as if he were a missionary, and he wasn't that, he was a man, that's all, and wanted to be at home in the world.

After the bees left him swollen and passed out in the dust the men lifted him and tied him in a sling to one of their camels and set off across the waste to where their village lay. The camels swayed from side to side rocking Peter Prince in his fever so he dreamed of a journey by sea, back to America, the harbor of New York, the glass skyline holding the ashy light of the sun's dropping into the smoke. The shadow of the Statue of Liberty passed over his face like a cold sponge, and the tugs sounded, and fireworks in the harbor as if it were the liberation. The Hudson, as they climbed it, fell away from the ship like a mesh stocking. The city itself let out a music, the monotone of tubas, like foghorns, and basses plucked at random, and Uncle Philip Farrel was relaxed there, one foot on Lincoln Village, his hand stroking the Pan Am Building. The Aunt Linda Lawrence, her elbows spread like compass legs, smiled at him over the cloisters. They were part of the threat, and another was the moorings, they couldn't stop because each dock filled with dark, noisy nets as the ship turned to enter, and Peter Prince looked up to the helmsman for help, who was filling his pipe, and it seemed that only Peter Prince and the ship itself were anxious to find moorings, and they kept riding toward where the river narrowed. The helmsman smiled at Peter Prince and bent down behind the window of the wheelhouse, leaving his pipe on the windowledge, and a thin stream of smoke rose along the glass. Peter Prince turned when he heard the voice of Uncle Philip Farrel.

"How long do you think it will take?"

"Some months yet," said Aunt Linda Lawrence. "It's impossible to give a close estimate, with all the work there is."

The captain rose again in the wheelhouse with a rifle in his hand, the barrel black, the stock blacker, and a telescopic sight through which he could see the inner folds of Peter Prince's ear.

In no time at all Peter Prince was awake, and lucky for him, because he had avoided those dangerous consequences, only a whistle and the "hey there" dimming into the stillness of his sleep. He could smell the soggy earth at his nostrils, and the sound of the heavy undergrowth, and he saw around the straw tick he was lying on some tiny roosters pecking among the sheaves of elephant grass the Danakil carried in to cover the damp floors of their *tukuls*. He was lying in a flickering, blue-gray light reflected from the vaulted ceiling. Through a space near the ceiling he could see slightly beyond the partition that separated him from the dark men. They must have been watching silent movies because they laughed occasionally in the flickering shadows. All around his bed, stacked nearly to the ceiling, were cages full of spotted rabbits gnawing on pulpy, red-veined leaves. It was feeding time for them. Dogs were howling in the village outside and beyond them the screaming of birds and the yapping of hyenas. They were near the jungle. Peter Prince was enough awake to feel the pain, as if he were strung along the shaft of a spear from his crotch to the top of his skull where the point was twisting to get out.

The laughter of a girl made him moan, "Noooo!" and he pressed his eyes closed till tears floated up onto the lids and down his temples. He thought of the worst they could have done to him, and tried to feel for the center of the pain. Where was it? "They didn't do that to me," he said aloud, startled at the pitch of his own voice, and he was afraid to move his hand down to his testicles to see if they had snipped them off. He was fond of them, and such a violent and meaningless act done by those very people for whom Peter Prince was trying to find the means to help would embitter Peter Prince to the point that one could predict that he would give up helping. He couldn't move his swollen arm. The pain for the moment seemed to have subsided and came back to him only when he shuddered in his fever, like Linda Lawrence in labor. He tried to budge his arm but had to let it rest on his abdomen. From the room beyond the partition came no noise—a silent film—and only the exciting moments punctuated by the little, high-pitched shouts of the warriors and some discussion in their peculiar dialect.

He tried to think about Addis Ababa. How long had he been away and how long would it be before Nicholas and Cindy, if they hadn't been sent off themselves on their assignments, would become alarmed and try to start a search for him? It would be months. It might already have been months. Who knows where that young energetic couple could be now building schools, developing irrigation systems, disseminating self-improvement programs?

A young girl touched his shoulder and he turned to see her dark eyes. She was olive skinned, an Arab girl, another captive. She rested her tray near his shoulder. It was feeding time for him. She squatted beside him and tried dipping the pieces of flat, sour bread into the spicy stew and touching it to Peter Prince's lips. He tried, but couldn't eat. The procedure seemed to her second nature as if she had been treating him for weeks; he could have been unconscious for who knows how long, lying there among the spotted rabbits night after night, movies in the room adjacent. He gestured painfully toward a cup that contained a sweet-smelling liquid, the tej, a honey wine, and she lifted that slowly to his lips, propping the back of his head with her free hand. The liquid warmth drove down into the cold spear of pain that was rising from his crotch. He liked the girl, and whispered a greeting, the only phrase he knew in Amharic. She answered him in English, and dried his brow. She was dressed in stained silks and wore a yellow kerchief on her head. Every service she performed for him she did in absolute silence, moving very slowly to avoid making noise, her face expressionless in the flickering light. She gathered the dishes back onto the tray and was about to leave, but Peter Prince wanted to speak with her some more.

"Why is this room full of rabbits?" he asked.

She stopped, and at first didn't seem to understand his question, but then she answered in a strange, chime-like accent, "To make you better. Spotted rabbits."

He tried to touch her, but his arm still wouldn't move. She knew his pain and came closer and kneeled, leaning her scarcely formed breasts on his forearm. She brushed his palm with her lips and smiled. He felt a dull, reassuring thud of passion. She had come to like him as if she cared for him. With the passion came another pain, rising to his skull.

"What have they done to me?" he asked.

The young person didn't answer but moved to leave again.

"I like you. You are a very nice young girl," said Peter Prince, trying to smile. "What is your name?"

The youth understood him, and smiled too. "I am not a young girl; I am a young boy. My name is Ahmad."

Peter Prince hadn't expected that. It was all tiring. He closed his eyes and started to sleep and just in time, because Linda Lawrence was there, in the delivery suite.

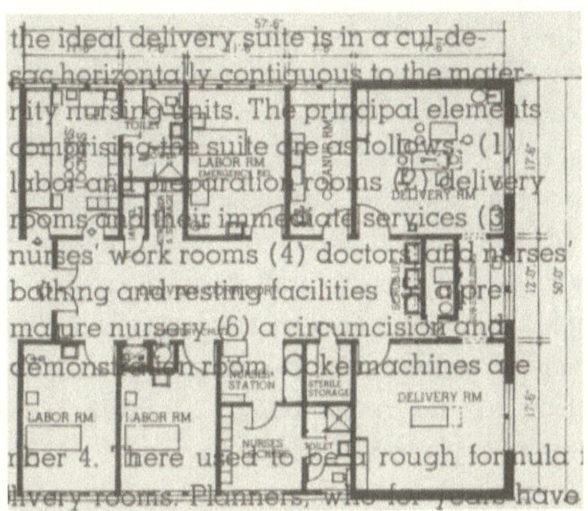

usually provided in number 4. There used to be a rough formula for
determining the number of labor and delivery rooms. Planners, who for
years have been using this rule of thumb, have recently been jolted to find
that it is not satisfactory. The reason is simple: High wartime birth rate.
Great scarcity of nurses, shortage of beds and bassinets. Length of stay
reduced. Increasing birth rate. Turnover much faster and the rate of
admissions doubles, triples. What's happening? At a nine-day stay with 75
percent occupancy the hospital can take care of 493 births a year—
including vacations—with 16 beds at 18.5 births per 1000 of population.
However, 1916 births a year would provide on the average 5.2 births a
day, alas. We all know that childbirth cannot be scheduled in the manner
of most operations, making for the facility-uncertainty principle. One
delivery room and two labor rooms would be normally sufficient. We
must plan, however, to equip the second labor room as a delivery room in
the event that two or more, or more mothers show up at close intervals.
We find in some plans two delivery rooms and seven labor rooms. The
reason for the excess in labor rooms is not apparent, and they wheel
Linda Lawrence in anyway, and she's having her pains, and she's going to
give birth, she's going to give birth: Birth:

The doctor prepared carefully and antiseptically for Linda Lawrence's delivery. He hated dull scissors and always carried in his bag five of them recently sharpened which he dumped into the large sterilizer in the preparation room. He used the hospital's forceps, and its clamps, but he hated dull scissors. He briefed himself privately, before each delivery, on Puerperal Fever. He'd never had a case and in his heart he knew he never wanted one. He visualized with rage chains of streptococci, clusters of staphylococci, and the individual bacilli releasing their poisons in the uterine tract, and he shuddered, and sterilized again, and looked for specks. He dreamed sometimes of nurses sneezing without facemasks and broadcasting over his patients the twenty-five strains of Group A beta *Hemolytic Streptococcus*. He remembered by heart the passage from Frederick C. Irving's popular book, *Safe Deliverance*.

"Should these streptococci reach the reproductive organs of women in labor or of those recently delivered, the broken mucous membrane and the placental site serve as breaches in the first line of defense. Unless a patient's power of resistance is adequate to overcome an enemy which has penetrated her fortifications, she will be overwhelmed by this rapidly multiplying and relentless foe."

He often thought about William Smellie also. He always had a fondness for the master of British midwifery: the man who with a single-minded conscience raised childbirth out of the middle ages. He had even made a trip once to the Smellie family tomb in the churchyard of St. Kentigern at Lanark. It was with the devotion and humility of Smellie that he liked to approach his work, a humility evident in at least one passage from Smellie's treatise the doctor could remember:

"As this was one of the first difficult cases in which my pupils were allowed to attend after I began to teach midwifery, I was really afraid, in time of operating, of being foiled and suffering reproach, for pretending to teach others, while incapable of delivering so strong and well-formed a subject without being obliged to bring the child by piecemeal, with instruments . . . Although when I lived in the country, I had been called to many such cases, yet I was never more fatigued. I was not able to raise my arms to my head for a day or two after this delivery; and one of the gentlemen who was present, being of delicate constitution, was so much afraid, that he resolved never to venture on the practice of midwifery."

This humility in the profession manifested as early as 1743. Linda Lawrence's doctor admitted to fears but had overcome them and had decided to go on anyway in the profession, such respect and admiration did he have for William Smellie.

Gloved hands raised, linen mask chained behind the ears, white smock impeccable, the doctor stepped from the preparation to the delivery room, where Linda Lawrence was giggling in pain.

*

The telephone rang on Philip Farrel's desk at home. Was he there to answer it? He was. Did he hurry to the phone? He was sitting by it. Was he wearing gloves? He answered the phone. Was he wearing gloves? "Is this Philip Farrel?" "Philip Farrel speaking." "Hurry down here right away. It's time." Was he wearing gloves? He threw on his briefs, his pants, his socks, his garters, his wrist strap, a white on white, his sport coat, his blue, belted overcoat, his overshoes, his Borsalino. Was he wearing gloves? He left immediately, and rather than wait for the elevator he took the stairs in threes. Was he wearing gloves? He had forgotten to wear a tie. Was he wearing gloves? He didn't return, however, but hurried away, tieless. Was he wearing gloves? He took a cab, and told the cabby to step on it, to Pier 43.

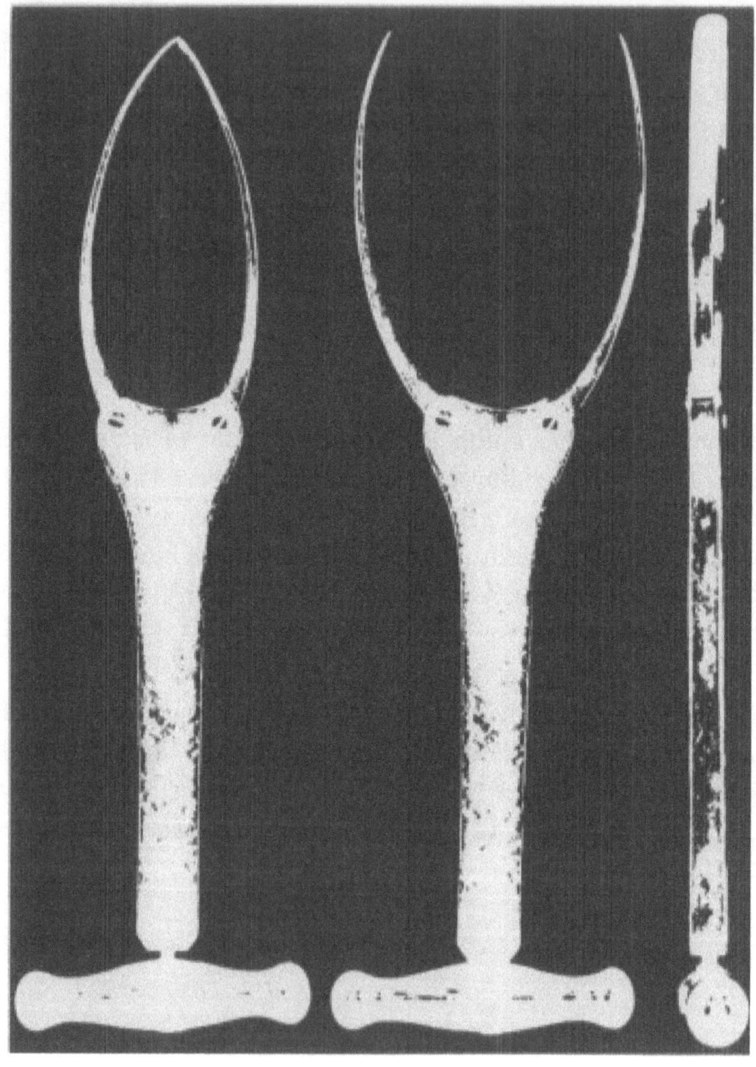

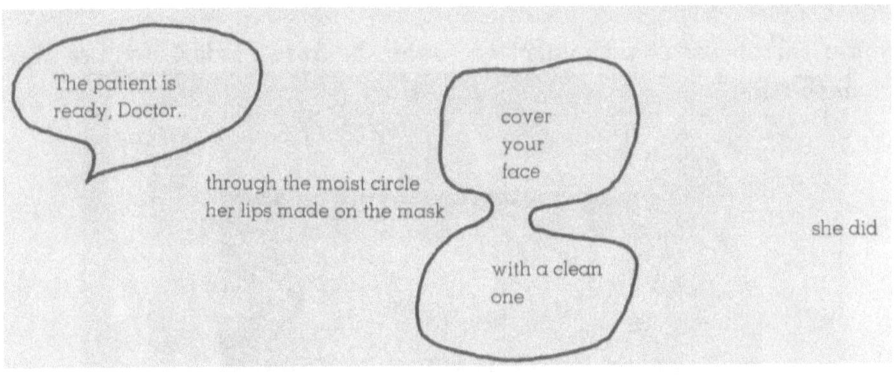
The patient is ready, Doctor.
through the moist circle
her lips made on the mask
cover
your
face
with a clean
one
she did

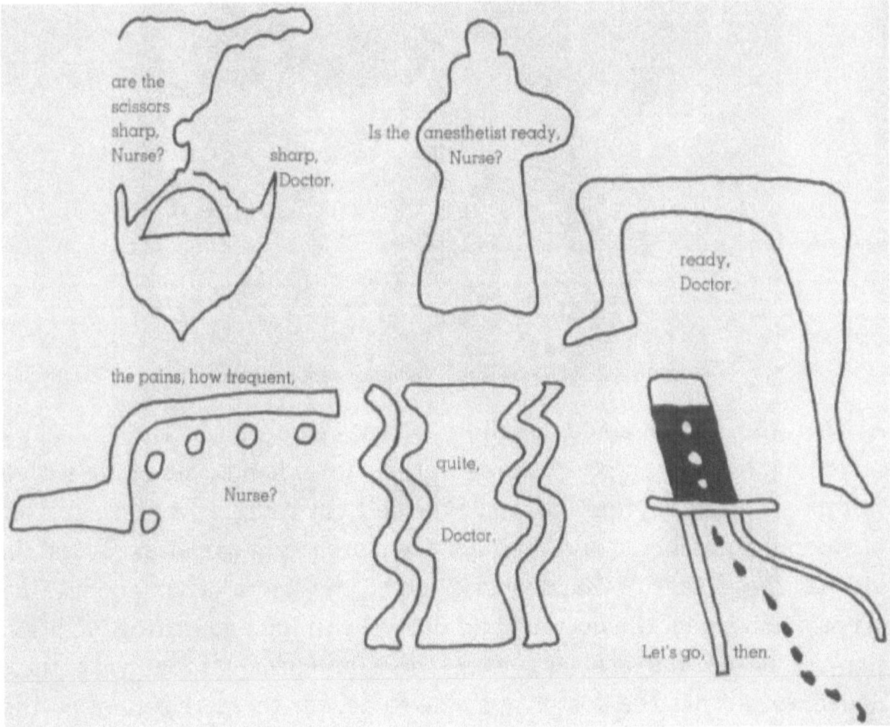

are the
scissors
sharp,
Nurse?
sharp,
Doctor.
Is the anesthetist ready,
Nurse?
ready,
Doctor.
the pains, how frequent,
Nurse?
quite,
Doctor.
Let's go, then.

*

Philip Farrel wasn't a moment too soon, because Linda Lawrence was giving birth.

*

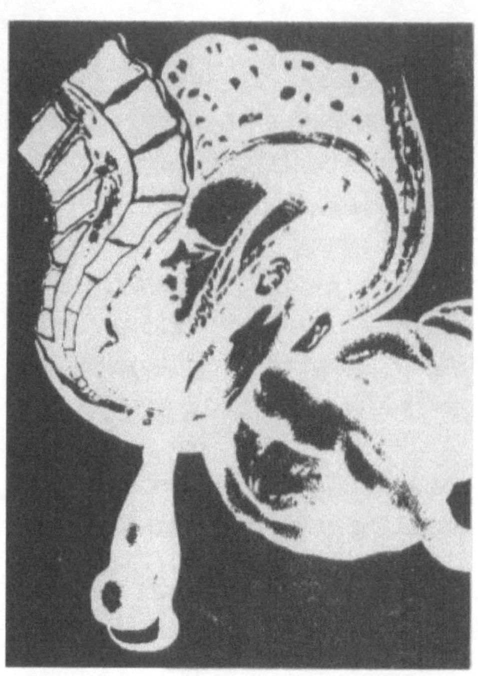

At first the doctor could handle it. They came out in threes, neatly marching, holding empty placards in their little hands, marching with a soft monotonous rhythm that made the delivery routine for him, a matter of snipping umbilicals, and even as they marched in nameless protest, in lots of three to fill the delivery room, the extra labor rooms, the preparation room, the doctors' and nurses' bathing and resting facilities, the premature nursery, and even the circumcision room with their murmurous ranks the doctor was able to deliver them, reassured by the steady, exhilarated breathing of Linda Lawrence in childbirth and her strong contractions, and his loss was minimum, a small percentage, a little heap of bodies by the anesthetist's table.

Philip Farrel got to the docks in time to hear the rich carbon monoxide growl of Harley Davidson, of the electro-glide 1200cc, with wing attachments.

"No. Oh no," said the doctor. He gathered up his scissors and dropped them into his smock-pocket. "This is out of the ordinary."

Blink, the wrench-lifter, was out of the ordinary on his white Harley described above, leading his group in a beige helmet, in rough-out beige jack-boots, in a beige motorcycle jacket with 43 zippers, a black kidney belt, chartreuse pegs (from a different era) with black pistol pockets, and following him close behind, two at a time, ejected with the rhythmical contractions of Linda Lawrence's parturition, were Dink the pot-merchant, Loop the breeze, Marvin, Martin, Marve and Marty, Simple Clyde and his fragrant princess, Bill, Bill, Bill, and others, like Tish, all on Triumph bikes.

Pain made Linda Lawrence hum, her tears reflecting the scialytic and germicidal light, but it was worth it, because the trolley car was next, old fashioned but remodeled, sparks dropping from its wires. Girls leaned out the windows and hung from the straps, and sang like warblers: Delicate Martha, Sprawl, the bent lutanist, Dingle, and Hairy in satin, Goosestepping Sylvia, and loads of others to think of names for, and hanging on behind, crouching to hide from the conductor, Swanny I, and Swanny II, the Swansons, big league prospects, and serious about it.

"Where are they all going?" asked the doctor, who'd let his facemask slip.

"To Pier Forty-three," said Melvin, as he sputtered past in his Saab GT, its sunroof down.

The pier was already stuffed with the new arrivals, the crowd squeezed out under the West Side Drive, among the vans and semis and stevedores eating lunch in the smoke.

To say the least the mother was delighted. She remembered a feature she had read in the *N.Y. Times*, Saturday, Oct. 10, 1964.

"Looking at their newly arrived baby is a source of infinite fascination for parents who have had ample time to speculate about its sex, possible appearance, and future potential during the nine months of pregnancy. Almost as fascinating to the onlooker is the proud delight parents show regarding their offspring, the thinly veiled sympathy with which they regard the wrinkled babes of their less fortunate fellows."

She had never thought those feelings could ever be hers again. But here she was. She liked a quiet baby, and the most unusual characteristic of the crowd on Pier 43 was its silence, even though it was a mixed bunch, and some of them were hungry already. Even the customs officials kept silent in the quiet of Linda Lawrence's bouncing baby mob. They were all waiting for Peter Prince. Philip Farrel was waiting for Peter Prince, to see if that day he would arrive, back from his journeying off. Philip Farrel's bent arms were a nest for the gun, for its barrel black as a cave, its stock black as the President's car. Was he waiting to use that gun on Peter Prince? Would he hold him in the crosshairs forever? What was Philip Farrel waiting for, and when would Peter Prince get home? These are the narrative questions and the reader can stumble through this book thinking them out. Suspense. Will Peter Prince be divorced in the end from a life he'd learned only to put up with, traveling around? He didn't mind it, though. He wanted to hang on, to make friends some more, get his pizza at the carry-out, even visit his woman when the floods withdrew their margins. Does Philip Farrel know what's in his gun? Does he really need to put that point across? Katz, Katz, Katz, tell us a story. You've really got yourself into it, with this drifting across the page. Figure something out, at least. What are you going to do for Peter Prince? Take up a collection? How are you going to help him, poor Peter Prince?

Fuck the 'Existence of God.' What does it mean to me when I can be incinerated with the whole rest of my race by men. Even if I accept it, for instance, and say He does lead me around on a leash. How could He possibly know what I need or even care about it when this is where He brought us so far. It's some kind of sport He's playing, the Stupid Asshole, and He's playing it with me. I mean, Job that poor fucker. Just because a two-bit devil puts Him on a little bit, Stupid Asshole has to take it out on his number one man. That's really tragic, when a guy you're supposed to respect is so gullible. And who's to think someone isn't conning him up there now, some space-freak leaking into his ear and telling him to dump on Peter Prince, and the rest of us, and all our demands? I mean why even think about it? Does it let me know where I am? If you cope, you cope, and that's it. What difference does it make what you're coping with? You do it, and if you get it done, there's no time to figure out what it was, the flood comes so fast, and it's over." Peter Prince was waving his arms and shouting in a whisper, because it was late. What he was saying mattered, though Eric Elliot, to whom he was speaking, turned his refracted gaze in another direction. Peter Prince could see his mother across the street and up the hill, leaning from her bedroom window and waving him home. "Sometimes I think the whole religion bit is a big cop-out for the adults. I mean they feel so guilty because they screwed it all up by not caring enough, and then they can say, 'Don't ask me. Pray.' They want us to lift our eyes, and slap our hands together, and dive, up there, but baby there ain't no water in that pool, just those stars, and that's cold. I'm not blaming them, I mean." He pointed at his mother who was gesturing wildly from her window. "They're grown-ups, the way we're kids and that's the way it is all around—impossible. But what I feel is that if something goes wrong it's my tough shit, and there's no one I can blame it on. I've got to build my own city, and lay it out with a lot of parks in it, and backlots, and riverfront."

A late bus passed along Ft. Washington Avenue, and taxicabs passed carrying dates, desperately necking. Across from the school steps on which they sat, a small park was settled in a pool of darkness, full of running noise, and whistling from the gang that inhabited it at night, harassing late dog-walkers and stomping the lovers.

"I believe this," said Eric Elliot, the friend with whom Peter Prince had been talking through most of the evening, a handsome, bony boy, who looked older than his sixteen years, his dark beard and pale blue eyes. Just two years later this unfortunate boy was to serve in Korea with the Forty-Third Division of the Eighth Army, 5th battalion, his squadron led by first lieutenant Philip Farrel, one of the few survivors of the infamous Fortune Cookie Ambush, where Eric Elliot was captured, tortured, then strangled in captivity by another crazed American PW who imagined Eric Elliot to be a spy. Perhaps he was a spy, or a turncoat, or something disreputable. Peter Prince never found out, because he didn't hang around the neighborhood for long. "I believe that the concept of a prime mover, an inception, a starting point, as if existence were a finite system, a line with a beginning and an end, is inadequate." Eric Elliot had been driving his own ideas along like a herd of cattle, not listening. "Every aspect of life that we come to understand is cyclical, everywhere, from empires to gardens. Even the universe is supposed to explode, expand into existence, and contract to explode again. I believe that the circle is a more true geometrical analog for life than is the straight line. On a circle there's no beginning, no end, no creation, no judgment. We come around, that's all. The circle is what's there—existence--no empty places—and we come into and pass out of existence along the continuum. One can't conceive of not-being. Even anti-matter is in its place outside our perception. Every time I probe the proposition that God created what is I can find no more meaning in it than simply that what is, is—without nicknames. That's an old dilemma—Who created God? Why should the assumption that he exists be any more valid than my assumption. In the beginning the Word. That conjecture demonstrates only that man sees himself larger than he is—because he can speak he describes a creation that he could imitate.

The word. We should know better than that now. What a reputation we give ourselves . . ."

In the park some girls were yelping and their noise sifted through Eric Elliot's exalted conversation, and Peter Prince felt a kind of exhilaration, as if he were floating on many substances, separating and fusing, sustaining him with an asserted confusion that was right, that was total, that was life.

"Peter Prince," his mother said, as she crossed the street, her pale blue bathrobe glowing in the yellow lamplight like the moon. "Isn't it about time you got home?" She was angry and disturbed. Peter Prince always felt guilty to see the weariness and desperation in his mother's face, but he couldn't be nice to her, he had to hold his own place, and know his strength. He wanted to learn, and not to be guided. He was beginning to know a desire in himself to take hold of the world, whatever there was, and to use what he constantly learned to make his actions more meaningful, more proportioned, and kind, and compatible, his example moving through experience like a ship's prow, leaving absurdity to foam in his wake. He wouldn't have minded being one of those exemplary people, like Mahatma Gandhi or Bertrand Russell or Henry Miller whose lives were coincident with their convictions. After some experience he wouldn't mind that at all, after he knew what his convictions were going to be.

"Didn't you see me waving at you?" His mother was close enough to him now to touch him, but she didn't, the skin on her hands like white powder in the lamp and moonlight.

"I was just sitting out here talking with Eric. That's more important to me than an hour or so of sleep."

"You should be home at this hour too, Eric. Listen to what's going on in the park. Your mother wouldn't want you to come home sliced up, or your clothes torn."

Eric Elliot lowered his eyes, and pulled in his profundity, and started away, leaving the young Peter Prince defenseless. His mother waited for him. "Go ahead," he said. "I'll come."

"You're not going to stay here by yourself any more. I'm not going to leave until you come."

"Don't you see, Mother, that I don't want to walk with you. You walk ahead, I'll follow."

Peter Prince could see that he had scorched his mother. She had withered like a prune, and when she turned to walk ahead, tears like shaved ice slid from his lower lids. He couldn't take it any more. He couldn't take living with her and hurting her any more.

Linda Lawrence sometimes remembers Peter Prince as a landscape, a treeless semi-desert clothed in the nap of sagebrush and outcroppings of lichened rock on his bare, shallow mountains. Cattle graze on his open range, and deer, and the sage hen, the doves, the chukka, the quail feed on buckberries and snowbrush. From time to time a mountain lion from an Eastern range crosses his slopes. The town, in the long valley near where he ends, is called Peter Prince, and down the valley into Peter Prince flows a serpentine river called Katz.

Linda Lawrence calls this story, SPUD HAZELEY'S MYSTERIOUS TRUNKS. At that time, living in Peter Prince, was a mysterious man by the name of Spud Hazeley, whose comings and goings aroused suspicion. He had a suspicious look

"What are you doing here?" said Hector Hastingford, nervously scanning ☜'s suitcases.

"Oh, baby," said ☜. "I just got so bugged with my scene at home, with my mother, and the constant supervising, that I had to split, and I thought I'd take you up on your offer for a few nights, if I could just camp here till I found a place. My own pad, or some new scene for myself. I'm just so strung out."

Hector Hastingford blushed. He didn't remember ☜, but he had a habit when he was drunk of inviting young boys to come see his loft and to stay with him. No one had ever appeared before, however, with suitcases. "Sure, baby, come in. Make yourself at home. Yeah. Groovy. You know, stay as long as you need to. Sure. I didn't know you had a bad scene. My impression was that you lived to him among the bearded inhabitants of Peter Prince. His face was always clean-shaven and his hands as soft as dove-bellies, as the hands of the barber, of the doctor, of the Indian agent, and in a town populated mostly by prospectors, miners, buckaroos, Chinese railroad workers and the like a man with soft hands made folks suspicious. Mostly there were the trunks. They arrived once every two months on the Southern Pacific, C.O.D., and he'd pay sometimes as much as $800 to release them. What was in them? Who was sending them? Why did he keep to himself so much? Nobody could answer these questions. Nobody ever saw Spud Hazeley alone, except Cyanide Pearl and one or two of her infamous group, but Cyanide Pearl never spoke, and was hardly ever spoken to.

The women of Peter Prince spent a lot of time over their mending, speculating about the contents of Spud Hazeley's mysterious trunks. Some of them imagined it was fineries, some that it was eastern frivolities, and some thought of coastal fripperies. The

alone. In fact, we were talking about how we liked the way you played the harmonica. It was, how shall I put it, funky."

☞ couldn't remember ever playing the harmonica for Hector Hastingford, and didn't remember ever mentioning that he played it. But it pleased him, anyway, the mention of his harmonica and he examined the loft. One third of the long space was separated from the rest by screens, where Hector Hastingford and his roommate, Little, slept. A blue light tinged with pale yellow smoke rose from behind the screen fuzzing the edges of their privacy. A long mirror covered most of one wall by the bar where Little, the dancer, practiced. The ceiling of the loft was too high to see, somewhere above the darkness.

"Look," said Hector Hastingford, and he pointed to the other end of the loft, which ended, ☞ imagined, at the soot-frosted windows. "There's a mattress over there in one of the corners. Just throw your stuff down there and flop. If you want some privacy I can let you have a screen." Hector Hastingford couldn't think of anything else to women were a pioneering lot of rugged ones and they knew little of the spices and scents that city women knew (and little, Linda Lawrence often said, of the foolishness that went along with it) and sometimes they would daydream together of baths scented with lavender, and seductive chiffons, and lace mantillas, although they knew nothing so fine was coming to them. They comforted themselves by saying that their hard work would be repaid,and that their children or their grandchildren would benefit from their hard life, their constant work, and would be able to enjoy the fine foreign imports, the manufactures,the rare stuff.

Sybil Jeffries, youngest of the mending group, daughter of Hugo Jeffries, foreman at the Empire Mine, and prize beauty of Peter Prince, was most curious of all to know what was in Spud Hazeley's mysterious trunks. She was a youngster, 22, and the dark brown eyes she inherited from her Piute mother were full of dreams and mischief. Her mother had disappeared when she was a child, do, although he knew that Little would be furious at the imposition.

The offer of privacy, more than anything else, relaxed ☞, though Hector Hastingford's manner seemed strange. He dragged his luggage into the darkness allotted him, and found the dusty mattress there, gnawed by mice, and faintly stinking of urine. He chose to use his own air mattress, which he put down under the window. With his fingernail he scraped some dirt off the window and looked at the street. Across from the loft two derelicts were leaning on each other and pissing on the wall, and in all the doorways men lay about, sleeping. Two well-dressed young men hurried by without looking at the bums who drifted from the doorways with their hands out, begging for nickels. A squad car pulled up, and a cop stepped out stroking his nightstick. He walked up and down, looking the men over, and then left. All this was happening under ☞'s gaze. Both pissing men turned, their cocks hanging from their flies, to smile at the cop, who was already gone. One of them sat down in the piss, covered his cock with his hand, and drowned, they said, in the River Katz, who has such a treacherous undertow. She had been left to care for her younger brothers and to bring them up herself, because her father was always North at the mine, but the hard work didn't spoil her beauty, which was even heightened by her restlessness.

"I wish I knew what was in those trunks." She looked through Claudia Swickle into the street. The trunks weren't what really mattered. Spud Hazeley had a mysterious attraction himself, scented as he was, and nicely dressed, like a San Francisco gentleman, and whenever she could she'd stare at him through her lace curtains, or between her gloved fingers, or through her sewing. He never noticed her.

"We all do," said the older Claudia Swickle. "Don't think you're special." She had a fondness for the girl and understood her restlessness. "But we have to accept what we have."

Sybil Jeffries looked at Claudia Swickle, and beyond her again, out the window of the sitting room, to the street of Peter Prince where the motionless dust was pink and

went to sleep. The other looked at him as if trying to speak, then waved his arm in disdain, pulled a bottle of Thunderbird from his pocket, drew on it, and walked away, moving his legs like stilts.

This was more like it, he thought, watching the street as if it were a ballet. He could watch it forever. As good as it was to discuss night after night the immense problems Eric Elliot knew about, it was better yet to change, to move, and to leave behind the waste of his old, confused attempts. He turned to find that Hector Hastingford had come up silently behind him to place some blankets and a screen by his mattress, and had silently returned to the warm light of the living end of the loft.

☞ felt a kind of delirium rising in his veins and he needed to giggle; he had made a move and had found the world friendly. He sat for a moment on his mattress in his own frothy joy, and looked across the darkness at the curling light of the other end of the loft. A typewriter was rapping intermittently and a faint hum that ☞ couldn't identify, like a vibratoless electronic note, filled luminous in the August evening night and she thought she saw moving there a carriage bearing Spud Hazeley and a steamer trunk to his mysterious cabin somewhere that smelled of cedar and bleach. She wanted to follow him, and she wished she had a plan. She wanted to know.

***

The men of Peter Prince were curious themselves, and when they got drunk they got angry because they didn't know what was in Spud Hazeley's mysterious trunks, and their wives talked so much about them.

This, therefore, is how Finch Whittle described his plan to Lingo Patcheguava, Kit Marshall and Jack Johnson.

"Nothing to it," he said. "And I don't know why we never thought of it before. It takes a long time for people to smell a skunk in the offing, but we ain't gonna let this go on no longer." He downed his whisky and swallowed a mouthful of beer. "We ain't gonna let Spud Hazeley's wool down over our eyes no more."

"You're right, Finch. We're fed up too. We have a right to know the silence. Hector Hastingford sometimes read out loud to himself while he wrote to maintain the rhythm of his style.

Those little sounds were so different from his mother's domestic noise. He had traveled. He could feel so much the texture of the air, and between himself and that life he had just left, distance thickened like a jelling liquid. It would be impossible to return.

Hector Hastingford sat on a piano stool, his face glowing red and gold, his portable Hermes Baby on a small, wilting card table, the pages of his manuscript scattered on the floor and his cot. He turned to ☜ who now watched him from the draped canvas door.

"Come in, baby, I'll just find the place to put a period."

Hector Hastingford's face was lit by a reflecting heater on the chair beside him.

"Come in. It's warmer in here," said the writer.

"How can you want more heat when it's hot as shit outside?"

Hector Hastingford raised one hand with its pinky extended. "I just like a lot of heat on me when I'm writing," he said. "It's like I'm what's in those trunks," agreed Kit Marshall, sniffing and blinking.

"It would be O.K.," said Jack Johnson, rolling his beer glass in his palms, "if it was just one trunk or two, but I've counted lots of them. Too many. And they cost him a pretty nickel, those trunks. I mean a man has a right to his private trunks, a few of them, but when it runs into . . . I mean all those trunks must mean something."

The bartender lit the kerosene lamps around the tavern and Finch Whittle's face began to glow with a shifting luminosity.

"What's your plan?" asked Lingo Patcheguava through taut lips. His eyes narrow.

Finch Whittle outlined for them his first alternative, and they smiled; he then explained the second alternative and they mumbled in apprehension and fear, but they concurred; and when he explained his third, most drastic alternative they leaned toward each other like the petals of a poppy closing in darkness, and they shut their eyes in resignation, and Jack Johnson wept.

Outside, on the River Katz, that cooking." He grinned and layed a period on the page with his heavy pinky. "I'm through." He unplugged the heater. "Don't just stand there, baby, you're one of the inmates now. Sit down." He rubbed his brow with his fingertips. "You're right, it is hot. I can never tell when I'm writing. I always get the chills." He shoved all the pages, some with only a few words on them, into a large breadbox. "You do look strung out," he said to ☞ without looking up.

"I feel better now."

"You'll feel even better when Little gets back. He's out scoring an ounce, and we can all be happy when he gets here. We'll mix in a little of this hash I have and beautiful. I don't like anything better than getting high."

"It never really affects me that much," said ☞. "I get a little buzz but I never really get that high."

"Oh, baby. You wait till Little gets back. When he scores it's always dynamite." He pushed the basket of papers under his cot, covered his typewriter and went to the mirror that hung over the rust-stained wash basin. "Do you think that I look creased?"

surfaced and sunk like a thread woven at random into the fabric of Peter Prince, a body, half eaten by fish, rose in the slow turbulence, and sank again.

***

"Where you going, Tom?" asked William Pool, as if he didn't know. He pulled his Model T up a few yards in front of where Tom was walking. Bill Pool was as proud of his Model T as Tom was of his walking. Tom walked everywhere, and was called, therefore, Walkin' Tom, and Bill Pool knew he would never agree to ride in the Model T.

"I'm walkin', Bill Pool, and you ain't gonna convince me to ride in that motorcar. I know what I got my feet for. If I'd needed wheels I'da been born with 'em."

"You're crazy, Tom," said Bill Pool.

"We can get you in to Peter Prince in four hours, at the most. If you walk it's going to take a couple of days, and then how much time you have to spend with Sybil Jeffries? Four, five hours? That's all before you gotta start walkin' back to the mine. You don't make no sense."

Walkin' Tom, who kept up a

"What?"

"Creased. Little told me I looked creased just before he left, that I should use face lotion. Do you think I look creased?"

"What?"

"Creased. Little told me I looked creased just before he left, that I should use face lotion. Do you think I look creased?"

The voice asking that question, thought ☞, was from another planet. The laughter he couldn't repress before turned to hiccups, and trying to hold them back made him tremble.

"I mean do you think I look like I'm getting old?"

☞ hiccuped.

The man examined himself closely, cheek, brow, and eyelid. "I hate that face," he said to the mirror, and then looked at ☞.

☞ hiccuped into his hand.

"Don't laugh at me," he said, lifting the back of his wrist to his brow. "I can think of nothing worse than getting old."

He seemed to have studied those lines. ☞ couldn't tell how old he was. He'd met Hector Hastingford always at parties, in the park, at good pace, was already past the Model T and William Pool had to drive slowly alongside him, the exhaust spitting and barking, making it difficult to hear what Walkin' Tom had to say. "I say this every time, and it seems like nobody listens to me. I prefer it this way. I like to walk. I like my feet on the ground 'cause they was made to stay right there. I like standin' up. I'm goin' to be buried standin' up, and you mark my words, these motorcars you're gettin' so crazy about, since everyone's in such a hurry; these motorcars are gonna ruin folks for walkin'. You see if I'm not right."

Walkin' Tom kept walkin' and William Pool gunned his Model T and disappeared into Peter Prince. Walkin' Tom took his own pace through Peter Prince, a pace that gave him time to smell the sagebrush, and to see Peter Prince carefully—Cat Creek, Wild Cat Canyon, Whisky Flat, Never-sweat Gulch, Big Squaw Canyon, Horsehead Gulch, Stinking Wells, Dead Camel Mountain, Dead Horse Wells, and Rattlesnake Springs were all parts of Peter Prince that he could see and that remained

hootenannies, always with the young people and he couldn't imagine him to be more than, say, twenty-six. Even that seemed too old. Time, he thought. The word flew into his mind like a winged bullet. There wouldn't be time for everything.

"Oh baby, you don't know," said Hector Hastingford. "Sometimes I get that feeling where I'm two hundred years old, like I'm really paying a price, as if I'm dead and walking around in my corpse. Did you ever get that feeling?"

☜ tried to say no but burst instead into hiccups and wouldn't raise his arms above his head to slow them down as his mother would have told him to do.

"I must really be fucked up, then," Hector Hastingford went on, while hiccups kept knifing through ☜'s chest. "You must really think that I'm fucked up."

☜ wished he had his harmonica or a dog to hold.

"I guess I need to shit," said Hector Hastingford. "I guess I'll go sit on the crapper." He retired to his bathroom stall while ☜'s hiccups subsided.

☜'s good humor had been

engraved on his memory. He never tired of seeing them. That's what his eyes were for—watching, watching as the places slowly turned into his sight and watching the contours change as he approached and letting the places slowly disappear through this peripheral vision as he passed. And he was never full of it, as much as he could look over the monotonous desert landscape he was never full of the nap of sagebrush on Peter Prince, and the outcroppings of lichened rock, and his bare, shallow mountains.

It was hot and dry, late August. Wavering spirals of dust rose out of the sagebrush and spun across the endless acres of Pumpernickel Valley, spewing tumbleweed. One of the heat ghosts caught Walkin' Tom's pack and nearly spun him around, but Walkin' Tom wouldn't spin. He kept on walkin', and he hummed constantly to himself a Lithuanian melody that the bullcook in his father's logging camp in Oregon used to sing. He had forgotten the words in Lithuanian but used words every once in a while that suited himself.

dissipated by Hector Hastingford's distress. He hated people to unload on him because it always ignited remorse in him, and guilt— irrational, as if he were somehow to blame for the share Hector Hastingford had in the miserable community of grief and frustration. That wrecked him. ☞ wanted to keep his concern for his own fate always in proportion, and remember how small he was in the world. That way he could act. That was the way one could leave the self behind that had been manufactured in his mother's adulation. Maturity, he felt, came as one began to understand his own trivial dimensions, and for a young man ☞ wasn't far off base.

That vibratoless hum he had noticed when he first entered the room stopped and then started again. There was a girl on the bed across the room from him that he hadn't noticed before—folded up, with her forehead on her knees. She had been making the noise. She didn't move, not even a ripple.

☞ had caught sight only of the light her hair held, like a submerged reflection: dark hair, thick as draperies, covering her

"Walkin' Tom, Walkin' Tom
Where you walkin', Walkin' Tom?
He doano, he doan care,
But he's dang sure he's walkin' there."
***

"What you got in those trunks anyway?" asked Cyanide Pearl on one of her visits with Spud Hazeley.

"In all the trunks?" He was evasive.

"Don't you know what's in all of them?"

"I haven't opened all of them. I only opened one."

"What was in it?"

"A lot of books."

"Books?"

"Is that strange?"

"I don't know," she said, slipping both hands into her loose copper bracelets.

It was evening and the wind was raising the dust, and blowing vague schemes of annihilation from doorstoop to doorstoop. Spud Hazeley gently took Cyanide Pearl to his bed, and spread her out on a mattress he had laid over four trunks. There he performed with her such brilliant sexual gymnastics, such variegated postures, such rump-rapping pleasure and prolongation that Linda Lawrence, when she tells this

face and hands. She sat in darkness, dressed in black leotards, on black sheets, against a wall painted black. What was she doing? She never looked out. The sound issuing from her was vibratoless, like an electronic tone, hardly human. He wanted to touch her—the Sleeping Beauty wakes up. Her stillness made him lustful.

"Who's the girl?" he asked at the bathroom door, but got no answer.

He wasn't sure he was really seeing her, the way she seemed to merge with the wall and bed-clothes. "Hey," he projected across the room. She didn't stir. He kicked across the floor toward her a book called Pertinent Facts, 1943. She didn't move.

"There's a girl here," he said again at the bathroom door, but still got no answer.

☞ had to make sure. He crossed the room to where she was. She was there. She didn't move. He stamped his foot. He could see the leotard stretch and loosen against her spine as she breathed. "I'm ☞," he said. Nothing. He pushed her. Still nothing. He rattled the bed, he whistled, he clapped his hands. "What is this?" he said. He pried story, gets that lonely, hunting look, that nervous shaking of her leg, and those milk of magnesia depths in her eyes of a woman who has never been satisfied. But there's no reason to describe that action here when it's going to appear anyway later on. It's sufficient to say that after the hours of viscous satisfaction and fractured breathing and exhausted tenderness she opened her eyes and said, "You haven't got no books in your trunks, Spud Hazeley."

"What's so unusual about books?" he asked, tonguing the sweat from the hollow of her throat.

"Nothing. Just that's not what you got in your trunks."

He rose from her and their flesh slipped back into place with a rubber slap.

"Spud Hazeley." She sat up too and threw her arm onto his back. "Why don't we just open all of the trunks right now." She lifted her chin and abandoned her waving arms. "All of them, just like that."

"No."

Cyanide Pearl pouted. "Shit. You don't care ever that I want to have some fun."

both her hands from her legs, spread her knees, and tilted her face back. She yielded easily, revealing an enigmatic smile, her eyes closed.

"I'm ☞," he said, as soon as he saw her shapely mouth. But what was this all about? As soon as he released pressure on her she folded again and disappeared into her hair. Was she some kind of catatonic plant? "I just want to talk to you," he whispered. "I want to ask you who you are." He got the urge to reach in and touch her breasts, but restrained himself. "Goddamit," he whispered into her hair, and backed off as some of it touched his lips in the breeze. "All I want to do is hear you say something."

"You've got a crazy chick out here," he said again at the bathroom door. "I mean she doesn't move, or talk, or anything. Did you know she was here?" Maybe Hector Hastingford stepped out. There was no noise in the bathroom. He guessed that he just had to hold on for a while, but it was strange stuff. He crossed again to the girl and pushed her over, and she sprang up like a weighted doll. The sound she

"I can't now."

"I waste my time here and lose money, and give you everything for free and come here all the time. Shit. You won't even let me in on your trunks."

Spud Hazeley had patience. "I know, Cyanide Pearl. It's not fair. But it's not time yet. It's not ready. Some day, yes. Now, no."

She stopped pouting, and smiled again. "I know you haven't got no books in your trunks."

He caught her few tears on his lips and then sucked her mouth into his, and they began again that action that was mentioned above, but not described; action that deserves description and will be described later in this book, or in some other book.

***

He figured to arrive at Sybil Jeffries' house when she was braiding her hair, and he wouldn't knock, and she'd see him through the mirror and ask, "Would you like to braid some, Walkin' Tom?"

He liked that. He held in his hand for a moment the heavy chain of started braid, silky, and then he would begin to work at it carefully with his tough, gritty hands. He

made never trembled. ☞ closed his eyes, and turned from her, and opened them to look around the room again. He felt dimensionless, as if he was going to spill to fill a container whose shape he'd never seen. The typewriter, envelopes torn open, the erasers, the carbon copies, the full breadbox: everyone finished with a way of life, and complained about it as he aged. That girl and her way of life, sitting there. What could it be like from day to day? And how would he get through it, ☞, who thought he had so much to do in the world, once he found out what. He lifted a carboned page from the floor that Hector Hastingford had dropped from his breadbox. There was a paragraph on it, and surprisingly enough, it contained his name: "Linda Lawrence sometimes remembers Peter Prince as a landscape, a treeless semi-desert clothed in the nap of sagebrush and outcroppings of lichened rock on his bare, shallow mountains. Cattle graze on his open range, and deer, and the sage hen, the doves, the chukka, the quail feed on buckberries and snowbrush. From time to time a mountain lion from liked that; a four-strand braid.

"It feels nice," she'd say. "I washed it in vinegar."

"I like the way it feels," he'd say, braiding carefully.

"It's so good when it feels good," she'd say.

"I like it to feel good," he'd say.

"Did you walk all the way from the mine to Peter Prince, Walkin' Tom?" she'd ask.

"Of course." He'd smile. "They won't get me to ride in one of them motorcars." He'd sometimes sing the bullcook's tune for her.

"You're a topnotch walker," she'd praise him, and that was worth everything; that could keep him going for as long as he needed.

"You goin' into Peter Prince, Tom?" said Daniel Cassidy, pulling up beside him in his Stanley Steamer. The car hissed softly.

"I'm goin' in," said Walkin' Tom.

"I'll give you a ride as far as the transfer post," said Daniel Cassidy. He was an energetic young mucker who had little patience with Walkin' Tom's old-fashioned habits.

"I say this every time and it seems like nobody listens to me. I prefer it this way. I like to walk. I like my feet on the ground 'cause

an Eastern range crosses his slopes. The town, in the long valley near where he ends, is called Peter Prince, and down the valley into Peter Prince flows a serpentine river called Katz."

The Katz river, and serpentine. In the Manhattan phone directory there were Katzes by the hundreds, and many of them with degrees—M.D.'s, L.L.D.'s, PhD.'s, chiropractors, stockbrokers, architects, Certified Public Accountants, research techs., construction men, plastics manufacturers, and ☜ had it flowing through him on a serpentine course. That was remarkable. He went to Hector Hastingford's mirror to examine himself. He didn't look bad. His face had a kind of square, rugged look that one could use in a Western, and when he contracted his brow-muscles he sometimes seemed worried.

"Whom, may I ask, are you?" Little entered with raised eyebrows, and leotards beneath his high-buttoned peacoat, and soft, laced shoes. "Surely you know it's more than rude to just walk in here with no one around like this." Little they was made to stay right there. I like standin' up. I'm goin' to be buried standin' up, and you mark my words, these motorcars you're gettin' so crazy about, since everyone's in such a hurry; these motorcars are gonna ruin folks for walkin'. You see if I'm not right."

Dan Cassidy hissed away in his Stanley Steamer. He hadn't made Walkin' Tom break his stride once on the way to Peter Prince.

Rodeo time was close and the weather was changing. Small clouds crossed the sky from the west and a sharp, tepid wind rattled the notices by the town hall. The sheepherders had made their last push into higher altitudes before turning their flocks back to the ranges, and the buckaroos were rounding up the last of the white-face calves and driving them back to the home ranch. That last warm wind was like the deep breath of an athlete before his last competition. The buckaroos could feel the change coming through their denim, as if the summer had turned a bend and the long range rides, branding, fixing the out-corrals, chuckwagons, bedrolls, long hot dusty days and chilly nights were

was talking from the doorway, his best profile to ☞, his eyebrows rising and dropping, his nostrils flared, his lips pursed. "Well? Tell me who you are." He tilted his head back and let his eyelids droop, revealing a faint application of mascara. He was blonde. "Speak up. You certainly don't expect me to stand around in my peacoat, waiting for you to say something. Speak. Out with it."

"I'm ☞," he said.

"Oh," said Little, shutting his lids. "Aren't you the playful one. I just don't feel like playing silly games with you, if you please. You're trespassing, you know. You can see that I'm too devastated to put up with much at this moment." His lips trembled, "So instead of being so cute and shy and trying to impress me with your," he shook his head and paused, "cunning, just say it. Say who you are." His lips trembled like a taut membrane.

"I said I'm ☞. I don't know what else I can say, except that I know who you are, Little, and that I'm a friend of Hector Hastingford. He told me about your dancing, and I've been looking forward to meeting you."

announcing their finish. It would be the rodeo. The town would be theirs after the summer alone: the distances shrinking, the sky shrinking, the stars disappearing. There would be a few wild, smoky nights.

Every year Sybil Jeffries wanted the wild, smoky nights to end her frustration and free her from the bondage of virtue; but temptation's presence was always surpassed by the pressure of fear that swelled to fill her skull; fear that there was really something to save herself for, to stay tight for, to hold back for; and the immeasurable weeping, the countless sad, lonely bedgoings that followed the wild, smoky nights, would fill a book or more to tell of Sybil Jeffries and her grief in Peter Prince.

"Sybil Jeffries, I would never have thought such an idea could enter the head of the daughter of Hugo Jeffries." She dropped her darning egg into a sock.

Sybil Jeffries shouldn't have confided in anyone, she realized, not even Claudia Swickle.

"It's not time yet. You're not ready. Some day, yes. Now, no."

"Claudia Swickle, you can't

Little accepted this simple flattery, and smiled, and shifted his hips, and let his eyes open and close very slowly. "I do wish you'd let me in on your real name, however." He let the words out like slowly escaping gas, at a pace that made ☞ uneasy. "I can understand your feelings, I mean about your reputation." He winked. "But it does get a little uncomfortable if I don't even know your real name, and you're a friend of Heck, and you come in here when there's nobody else around, except that one." He indicated with his hand and chin the girl who sat still folded in her hair on the bed.

"Who is she?" asked ☞.

"Who are you, is the question. I know who she is. Who are you?" "I said I was ☞."

Little stretched open his eyes in exasperation. "Peter Prince my dear fellow," and he pointed to the column adjacent, "you are a stubborn boy."

The use of "boy" angered ☞, and he was moved to assert himself. "I am ☞, and I can't see why you have to be so stubborn. Hector Hastingford has agreed to let me stay here on a mattress in understand how tight I am. You can't feel what I need, that I . . ." A knock on the door interrupted her plea. William Pool was there. He tipped his hat, and inserted two fingers under his collar to ventilate his neck.

"The message from my father?" Sybil Jeffries asked, crisply. She escorted him into the sitting room. Claudia Swickle dropped her darning egg into a sock.

"He can't be in for rodeo because they want to open a new drift before winter, right?"

"That's right," said William Pool.

"And my father suggests I stay away from the rodeo grounds on such nights as are coming up, and stay home at night, right?"

"That's right."

"And Walkin' Tom Cambry is on his way to see me. You passed him on the road, right?"

"That's right."

"Did you bother to come here to tell me that?"

"I drove here in my new Model T, Sybil Jeffries," and that last confession so embarrassed William Pool that he left before Claudia Swickle could drop her darning egg that corner." He pointed down the room. "I'm going to leave as soon as I arrange my own scene. I'm ☜."

The red rose in Little's face. "Oh," he said, hardly able to get words out. "Yes. Uh-huh." He walked over to the desk and slapped Hector Hastingford's typewriter. "He's agreed to that, has he? As if he wasn't already living with me and like he didn't have certain fundamental obligations to me at least. The bitch. He invites just any straight-arrow in here because he has a big cock. Do you have a big cock? The filthy cock-sucker." He finally took off his peacoat and layed an aluminum foil package down on the table. "I mean just to bring someone in here," he gestured at the typewriter, "who won't even let me in on his real name at all. You can get one thing straight here, sonny, you're not going to stay here at all unless I at least learn your real name." When Little turned to him ☜ could see tears in his eyes. "Where is Heck?"

☜ pointed to the bathroom door. Little walked over there and began to talk through it, glancing at ☜ over his shoulder. "Who is into another sock.

"Now that's just what you're going to do, Sybil Jeffries. You're going to see Tom Cambry. Not every girl has a man who'll walk all the way from the Empire Mine just to see her. You're luckier than almost any girl."

"Ooof. That antelope. The closest he gets to me is to hold my braid in his hand like a drill bit. It's been six years that my father hasn't come in for rodeo, and every year Walkin' Tom Cambry makes his way here to see me for a couple of hours. He gives me hay fever."

"Patience, Sybil Jeffries." Claudia Swickle dropped her darning egg into a sock.

"Patience. I've had patience. I need something else for a change." She was beginning to cry, and she grabbed her shawl, and left.

It was early evening and the wind that had blown all day left a slight chill in the air. Swallows knifed into the darkness of the hills silhouetted against the green and rose dusk. This rodeo night had to be her rodeo night for sure. She wouldn't hold any longer, she knew. No longer. She sat down on the riverbank by the third street

this young fellow, Hector? This refugee from his mother's menopause. Don't you let me have anything to say anymore about who comes into our household? I mean does his rudeness to me mean . . . Are you listening to me, Heck? Hector?" He rattled the door to find it open. "Hector Hastingford, you're not in there." He turned to ☞. "He's not in there."

"He went in there. I saw him."

"He's not in there. You look for yourself."

"I saw him go in there. He must have been here. He let me in to the apartment. He even brought me some blankets."

"I have the feeling, young man, that you just sneaked in here looking for adventure. You just happened along down the street."

"He even told me that you were out," said ☞. "That you were scoring some marijuana."

"So that's it. You're the fuzz, and so young now. The peach fuzz."

"Good God, now."

"A Jehovah's Witness."

"Stop. I'm ☞. I'm Hector Hastingford's friend. I was invited here."

"You're a sneak-thief, an

bridge, across which was that section of town where Cyanide Pearl and her group lived their nights. In the deepening dark over there the gaslamps pulsed like anemones. Sybil Jeffries sat in the cold twilight and listened to the wild piano notes and sour laughter. She began to weep, her tears falling like drops of oil into the River Katz. "Oh," she sighed. "If only something would happen to me. The River Katz floated the tears for a distance and then sucked them down in its undertow, where the carp nibbled at them and the catfish swallowed them whole.

***

The shadow of Limp Deeder, the blacksmith, fringed with yellow forgelight, darkened the room where the men were unloading the crates of guns. Besides Limp Deeder, Finch Whittle had taken into confidence Sailor Knotts, the Stutz brothers, Packhorse Harry, and a few other slash-faced, stone-muscled escapees from their own dark histories. The smell of graphite and powder thickened the air, and guns clattered from the crates like chains. The men, burdened with guns, walked with a

encyclopedia salesman, a plain-clothes fire inspector, a private eye, a dusty black Muslim, an art collector, a pervert, a cub reporter, a sensation seeker, a TV repairman, a dog fancier, a literary agent, an anthropological researcher. Don't put me on in your crude little way. You do shady dealings in my estimation. You don't belong here."

I couldn't tell what Little was thinking under that barrage through his variety of alternating smiles and grimaces. He had enough money for a couple of nights in one of the flophouses nearby. He'd do that instead. "Look, man." he said. "This is turning into too much for me. I'm just going to split, and that's all. I'll grab my wraps. This doesn't make any sense."

"You little weakling, you," said Little, sidling up to him and giving him a dry kiss on the cheek. "Of course you can stay. At least wait till Heck gets here. He'd love to meet you. I know that." He went to the mirror and looked at his eye, which was tearing. "Besides. I have this speck in my eye I'd like you to try to get out for me. It's causing me such excruciating pain." He heavy shuffle, as if chained.

"Finch Whittle," said the blacksmith. "Jack Johnson needs to talk to you."

The plump, bespectacled man looked up from the desk where he was working by candlelight. "Send him in."

"He wants to talk out here."

Finch Whittle turned back to his work. "Tell him to come in here. The light hurts my eyes."

"You guys," Limp Deeder said to the dark motion of men, "You guys loft your cuds into the spittoons tonight or you'll wipe the floor with your lips."

Jack Johnson approached the desk where Finch Whittle was writing in a large ledger with the date at the top of the page designated Rodeo Minus Two.

"What's wrong?" Finch Whittle didn't look up.

"Do you think we need all these guns, all this preparation?"

"Jack, you're pessimistic. You think we're going to use them. You're counting your chickens before the smoke is cleared. We agreed on this. This is just the third alternative we're preparing, that's all. A stitch in time is never too

held his hand out to ☞. "But what shall I call you in the meantime?"

"I can't pretend to be anyone but ☞."

"Oh, nonsense. Peter Prince is a figment. Heck invented it in his charming way. I'm going to have to call you Bruce in the meanwhile. You decided on Peter Prince because you saw it on the page, and liked it. Now, Bruce, come here. See if there's anything on the upper lid."

☞ breathed deeply and reluctantly went under the light with Little and lifted his eyelid. Little trembled. The eyewhite was covered with a mesh of fine veins under the lid and the corners of the eye were yellowed like old paper.

"Do you see it?" Little pressed his whole wiggling body against ☞'s. The sweat was locked in ☞'s pores. He backed away.

"I don't see anything there."

"Oh come here again and look, you hardly gave it a chance. Come."

"If it really bothers you, you should see a doctor. I really haven't the qualifications. I might hurt you."

"Oh come. Don't be coy."

"I don't want to."

many, remember." He looked up and took off his glasses. "This is just security."

"It still makes me nervous. Just to get in those trunks."

"Aim big, Daddy always said, and you're bound to hit the target. Daddy was no fool." He smiled. "Now is this all you came to talk about?"

"No." Jack Johnson laid a brass star down on Finch Whittle's desk.

"How'd you get that?"

"They gave it to me."

"Who? Dipper?"

"Yes, Marshal Dipper. He's expecting trouble. He says that he always deputizes a few extra around rodeo, but I think he knows something's up. I couldn't refuse."

Finch Whittle made a note in his ledger. "Don't worry about it. We're doing the marshal a favor anyway." He scanned the room with his outstretched arm. "He should be grateful. We're keeping all the bad ones busy. I wouldn't worry about this badge." He pinned it on Jack Johnson's vest. "You're going to be useful all around."

Jack Johnson wept. "Unless you choose the third alternative," he said.

"Really." Little sighed, and he sat down on the piano stool. "I was aware that Hecky had his other friends, and I tried not to let it bother me. But straight young men? Mister Bruce Thing. I suppose you're going to tease us."

"Don't worry about me. I intend to leave."

Little took a long draught of air, and smiled again, retreating. "Do you smell that? They used to have a perfume factory in this loft and every once in a while the smell seeps out of the wood. It sort of suits us, I always thought, Hecky and me." There seemed to be a tinge of perfume in the air, mingled with creosote. "Don't worry," Little went on, "tomorrow, tomorrow and tomorrow. You stay now. I'm really not such a bad one to know. You can even help me out."

"With what?"

"Tomorrow. I'll tell you what tomorrow. No need to rush now. Let's blow a little grass, and see what."

☜ sat down on the bed while that strange slender queer sat down at the typing table and ceremoniously began to roll joints. His mother, he thought, must have

"It's not a matter of choice. We agreed. We have to do what's necessary." The room was silent for a moment as if they had just submerged, and then the bolts began to click again as the men cleaned their guns, the barrels black as a cave, the stocks black as the President's car.

"Where you goin' Walkin' Tom?" Walkin' Tom was humming his tune, and hardly heard Nick Liberty pull up in his Stutz Bearcat. "I'll give you a lift into Peter Prince, if you want it. If that's where you're goin'."

Walkin' Tom just kept on walkin', not being impolite. He just hadn't heard Nick Liberty at all, he was so busy.

"You'll get there a lot faster if you ride, Walkin Tom."

Walkin' Tom saw out of the corner of his eye the yellow machine moving beside him. It wasn't natural. He didn't even want to look at it. It made stinking smoke."I say this every time,"and he looked straight ahead and kept on walking as if there was nothing at all beside him, "and it seems like nobody listens to me. I prefer it this way. I like to walk. I like my feet on

been knitting in front of the TV and feeling sorry for herself, tears dropping into the wool. Peter Prince would have liked to sleep and forget everything, that inscrutable and precious queer, and Hector Hastingford.

"You asked about that one, didn't you Bruce?" He pointed to the girl still humming on the bed. "Well, she," said Little, "is rehearsing."

"Just sitting there?"

"She's not just sitting, you see. She's fetal, she's static, stasis itself I mean." He handed ☜ a joint. "She's going to use it in a collaboration we're doing, you know, with some poets and a couple of painters, and dancers, a singer. At the Origen Church next Wednesday." Little looked at his watch. "She's got about eight minutes. She's going to sit that way, you see, through the whole performance. Tension." Little crossed his legs and settled to the floor. He lit up and drew in deeply, and signaled for ☜ to do the same. ☜ pulled the smoke down into his lungs, and he felt himself swallowing Little's dried saliva, the memory of a perfume factory in the

the ground 'cause they was made to stand right there. I like standin' up. I'm gonna be buried standin' up, and you mark my words, these motorcars you're getting so crazy about, since everyone's in such a hurry; these motorcars are gonna ruin folks for walkin'. You see if I'm not right."

The Bearcat buzzed away, throwing so much dust that Tom had to skirt the road wide to keep from choking. An hour later he passed that Stutz Bearcat again, Nick Liberty standing next to the car and swearing, and looking down the road for a lift.

"Maybe you got the right idea," he remarked as Tom passed by. Tom didn't stop. He didn't have time to, because he had planned to reach Frenchman's bridge in the next hour, and have his lunch there. Within fifteen minutes Nick Liberty was rolling by again in Pork-chop Wells's converted Model T van.

When he arrived he sat down on the boards of Frenchman's bridge and stared into the River Katz. It was muddier than he ever remembered it before. He spread a flowered handkerchief by the edge

loft air, the pages of manuscript, the girl's stasis and her noise, the bums' snoring outside in their own piss, all that burned down into his lungs, and his lungs felt combustible.

"It was such a groovy thing," said the girl, who had finished her stasis and was stretching near him by the bed now. "So groovy to have him come over and push me and move around and come on the way he did. It's so far out." She touched ☞'s cheek with her palm.

"Bruce, I want you to finally meet Sister. Sister, Bruce."

She took his hand that held the joint to her mouth and swallowed the smoke. "We have to put him in the thing," she said, holding the smoke down. "It was too much. I mean he has to do just what happened this evening. It's like a whole new dimension to my thing that we hadn't thought about. We have to use it."

☞ could see her now. She was a dark one, her complexion like an orange peel, marred by the corrosive New York air. "He should do it just like he did," she went on. "It would be the balance we need for all the other formal action—the and pulled from his back-pack a can of sardines, some crackers, and a shriveled boiled potato. He slowly ate, letting his eyelids drop slowly over his vision. He could hear some cattle lowing far away, and magpies chattering nearby over the flesh of a jackrabbit. The valley was waiting to feed. Large bubbles rose through the dense liquid of the River Katz, tinting the air yellow around him, and he sat in the midst of the digestion of Peter Prince breathing a slight gastric pungency that didn't bother him at all. What he did mind was the car exhaust and the dust.

Walkin' Tom knew that in only a few years the road wouldn't be fit to walk on in the traffic dust and exhaust, and then he would have to make his own track, like a cougar, through the brush, a more difficult journey, making Sybil Jeffries almost inaccessible. It made Walkin' Tom sad to think how Peter Prince, how the world was filling up with machines, as a miner's lungs fill with stonedust till he dies and the world was slowly divorcing itself from him, from Walkin' Tom, and he was beginning to feel his loneliness. The loneliness of

slide projections, the wall building. What a groove. His simple motion. He comes in carrying blankets." She kept describing it, and surprisingly enough ☞ was quite proud, despite himself, that whatever it was he had done it had been impressive to Sister, and perhaps useful. He had fallen in with strange people, extraordinary, talented people, and maybe he, starting with these small actions, was destined to do the extraordinary. Just being ☞, and following his shy impulses was perhaps the way to begin.

"Bruce, let's do it again," she said, out of her excitement. "Little didn't see it. You remember it?"

"Of course."

"No, no, no, no, no," said Little.

"We can wait till the performance. He'd destroy it if he rehearsed it. We need Bruce as close to what he was when he came in here, as youthful and sweet." He bared his gums at ☞. "We want all his . . . his Bruceness, the whole primitive thing, unsophisticated. Besides, I couldn't watch anything now. This grass has improved nothing but my headache. I'm going to sleep."

Walkin' Tom could fill a novel by itself.

***

As soon as Walkin' Tom got into Peter Prince his headache began. Dust packed his nostrils and mingled with the fumes that increased every year. As much as he had liked Sybil Jeffries, he disliked coming to town. But he could hardly see, each year it got worse, the backs of his eyelids chafing his eyes. Of all the attributes of the territory of Peter Prince he disliked Peter Prince most: the senseless activity, the filthy air, the commerce increasing, selfish people, and gambling. Even though his work in the mine wasn't the brightest job, filling his lungs underground with stonedust, he preferred that to the soft inactivity and frantic commotion in the town, and if it weren't for Sybil Jeffries he'd never come to Peter Prince.

She spotted him just as she was about to leave by the front door, Walkin' Tom, a block away, rubbing his eyes and heading her way. She didn't want to see him. She quickly bolted the door and pulled the curtains, and rushed out the back way. Seeing Spud Hazeley was on

"That's the best idea," said Hector Hastingford, who appeared again as if he'd never left. These people could merge with the darkness and disappear, reappear. He stared at ☜ as if he didn't know him.

"Oh," said Little, "that's Bruce, a friend of mine. He's going to stay here a few days with us, and he'll help me get that footlocker tomorrow. I think someone like himself would be useful, I mean less suspicious."

☜ stepped into the light so Hector Hastingford could see him better. He still wasn't recognized. "Little, you do manage to get the sweetest young folks down here."

"He's going to be in our thing," said Little. "He'll be Bruce with the blankets."

"He's so beautiful at it," said Sister. "I'd be willing to call the whole collaboration, the Bruce Event."

"I'm ☜," ☜ insisted.

Hector Hastingford looked astonished, and when he caught Little starting to giggle he threw his arms into the air, twitching his wrists, and laughed softly through her mind and she couldn't bear Walkin' Tom. The chickens made a commotion as she passed, and the back street was dusty. She knew the way to Spud Hazeley's cabin, had rehearsed the trip many times before, and when she finally stood in front of his door, her button-ups covered with dust, she felt as if she'd been there all along, as if she'd been waiting all her life to gather the courage to knock on Spud Hazeley's door. The door was ajar and she could see Spud Hazeley's mysterious trunks stacked around. She felt her heart swimming out through her bosom. Spud Hazeley was humming a new tune from back East, and his voice had a pleasant hoarseness. She held her breath, and with one hand tried to slow her heart in her bosom, while with the other she lightly knocked on the door.

***

tender convulsions. "Is that right? Oh sweetheart, how you manage to flatter me, unbeknownst. Peter Prince, indeed. I could tell you a flattering little joke but instead I'll let you read this." He reached under his bed and drew out his breadbox, from which he withdrew a handful of randomly assorted pages, slightly crumpled. He shoved these at ☜. "Here, and you know I rarely do this for anyone I've just met, so you can see how you've charmed me. Peter Prince, indeed."

And he retreated with the manuscript, at least for that night, he thought, to the corner of the loft that had been somehow assigned to him earlier. Amazing that anything at all got done, with the rate at which recognition dissipated. He sat down on his air mattress, lit a couple of candles from his pack, and began to read.

The sight of Sybil Jeffries at Spud Hazeley's door stopped Finch Whittle at the corner. He hadn't prepared for anything like this. To carry out the first alternative he had worn a suit—persuasion—to get Spud Hazeley's confidence, but he couldn't do it with that girl in there, and he never expected such innocence to get in his way. He couldn't walk in on her. He had to wait until she came out and that would endanger the timetable of both the first and second alternatives. He felt in his pocket for the cool silver of his timepiece and he drew it out, and when he looked at it in his trembling hand the crystal shattered and fragments dropped to the ground at his feet, lost in the dust. The watch-hands curled like burning leaves. It was 3:15 it seemed, and the

WHAT PETER PRINCE READ!

"What did you say you were here for?" the mayor asked, coming around his desk with a flyswatter.

"We want to save Peter Prince," said Philip Farrel, standing shoulder to shoulder with Linda Lawrence, she almost as tall as he, his dispatch case snug under his arm.

"Oh," said the mayor, as he nipped one that had landed on his inkwell. "What makes you think that Peter Prince needs saving?"

Neither of them answered but they stood there with their lips firmly set, like airplanes in rigid formation.

"The town seems to be getting along well enough, after all."

The two stood as if the stubborn strength of their presence was itself the response to any opposition to their project. He was wearing

"But I can't make love to you," said Sister, and she sat down as he was finishing the reading.

"Why did you cross over here, then?"

"I didn't want to stay there while they made love."

"Would they mind?"

"No, they wouldn't mind. I've watched them before, but I don't make a very enthusiastic voyeur."

Bruce listened to the high-pitched gasps coming from the other end of the loft, and the odd, shuddering homosexual giggle. He didn't know how he'd gotten into this weird column, anyway; but he'd never listened to any lovemaking before, and had made it only a few times himself so he figured he'd play along. There was nothing else he could do; it was his tough shit.

"You watched them?"

third alternative was to open up at 4:30, come what may. Inevitable. He had no signal to call them back, they were dispersed, ready, and armed. He kept looking at the watch in his hand. It was vibrating, strangely. It was an old watch, one he had bought in a pawn shop in San Francisco, and it had been a good watch, but now it rumbled, and seemed to be loosening up, as if some mechanical yeast in its workings had suddenly been activated.

Sybil Jeffries looked from trunk to trunk and could feel with her eyes the brass studs and bandings, the handles, the hinges, the elaborate locks; she could feel how tightly shut the trunks were, and how stuffed they were with contents. Cyanide Pearl was laughing. "Everyone wants to see what's in your trunks, Spud

a blue sharkskin suit that seemed to contain him like armor, and she a blue pinafore and starched white blouse. They looked in charge, not only of themselves, but of the hovering possibilities, like jugglers that have set so much in motion so fast that they seem to be standing still in the midst of the perilous balance of motion. The mayor, to say the least, was impressed. He chased a fly onto a brass doorknob that lay next to his old typewriter, and watched while the little creature rubbed its eyes and bent its wings with its hind legs. That must feel terrific, he thought, as he swatted it, and he turned to the rigid couple. "Just what do you think you'll do for Peter Prince?" The doorknob thumped onto the floor and rolled under the typing table.

"We'll plant trees."

"Trees?"

"I was curious about how they did it."

"Why can't you make love to me?"

"Because I wouldn't feel right," said Sister, and she leaned over to kiss him on the forehead. His mouth was dry and his arms trembled from the weight of his torso leaning on them. He wanted her whole dancer's body beneath him.

"Why?"

"Because I have a lover now. Not just a lover. I'm full of a man, you know. I couldn't make love. There'd be no room for you."

"Let me try, then."

"No, Brucey, you're very work. It wouldn't be fair to you."

Bruce shut his eyes. His bowels were thumping like a heart. He massaged with his fingers the nape of her neck. It was raining and the passing cars made a ripping sound on the

Hazeley."

"But Miss Jeffries," he looked at her and spoke politely, "why would you want to see what's in my trunks?"

Sybil Jeffries blushed. "I've been thinking about your trunks for a long time."

"If you want to know something, I don't know what's in all those trunks."

"Books," said Cyanide Pearl, winking at Sybil Jeffries. Sybil Jeffries was surprised to find her so amiable; softer, in a way, than many of her mending friends.

"I don't understand how you never could have opened them."

Spud Hazeley laughed, covering his mouth with his hand. "I never had the curiosity, I guess. I never needed to open them. I suppose I'm a little afraid to open them."

Sybil Jeffries was in love with Spud Hazeley.

"Apple trees."

"Here?" he said, as he bent over to pick up his fallen doorknob. "In the desert?"

"To save Peter Prince."

"And how do you expect to raise an orchard here?" He steamed the doorknob with his breath and polished it on his tie.

"Without water?"

"That's our problem, our specialty. We have to save Peter Prince." Linda Lawrence took one step forward and put one hand on the desk, letting her head droop a bit to express the emotion.

"If it weren't that you looked so respectable I'd think you were a couple of oddballs, or Easterners." He threw out a quick smile. "Where do you expect to get the labor? If you think you're going to work the Indians I'll tell you it's a big risk. They won't

Bowery. She moaned softly.

"I want to make love to you," Bruce said.

"Yes, yes," she cooed.

Bruce chewed on her neck muscle and tongued her ear. She hugged her knees immediately. "I can't."

"Go to your lover, then."

"I can't go at night. His wife is home. During the day his wife works as a nurse and he writes. I see him then. You can come with me tomorrow to meet him."

Bruce's breath came like river rapids, and he nuzzled in her neck again.

"I'll tell you what," she stood up in one effortless unwinding, "let's go watch them." Bruce released all his wind. He smiled weakly. "They'll love it," she said. He let himself be moved.

They crossed the loft together as if she were

"When do you expect to open them, then?"

Spud Hazeley looked at his watch. It was 4:22. "I guess I'll open them now," he said.

"The Sleeping Beauty," said Cyanide Pearl, and she looked happy. "The Sleeping Beauty wakes up."

It was time for the wild horse race, and nerves were drifting in the air. The horses shifted their rumps recklessly, and reared, threatening to go over backward, and pulled, and screamed through their nostrils. The wind had stopped suddenly and dust settled in the arena in little humps. The spectators inhaled and exhaled in unison, the space contracting and expanding. The women let their hats loose and the buckaroos tugged their horses to the starting line. Pale steam issued from the nostrils of the young girls in the stands.

show up for work, and you have to pay them as much as a white man." As he sat down he slapped his palm with his flyswatter. "That won't work."

Philip Farrel opened the door to the waiting room where his mob of children was waiting.

"Our family," said Linda Lawrence, "will do all the work."

"And there are more coming."

The mayor was charmed. It would be a delightful change for a while: the prospect of apples in Peter Prince. "As far as I'm concerned do what you please, and more power to you." Flyswatter to left front corner of desk.

"You didn't have to see me anyway. The Bureau of Land Management is more your meat." Flyswatter to windowledge behind him.

So Philip Farrel and Linda Lawrence set out

taking him shopping, or to the theater after dinner. He acquiesced by following a little behind her, and when they got to the room she took his arm. This was really a weird column to be in, but entertaining. The couple was on Little's black draped bed in the dark, and all Bruce could see was the luminous motion. Sister switched on the light. Little, wearing high leather boots was mounted on Hector Hastingford. Their bodies snapped like whips.

A couple of queer bastards, thought Bruce, too shy to say anything, since this wasn't his own column.

"Do you think that's interesting?" she asked. Bruce shrugged.

"I don't think much about it."

"Do you think it's disgusting?"

"No. It looks not so bad."

Silky Jeffries, Sybil's little brother, held on to the greased pole, three quarters of the way up, as if he could dent it with his bones to make footholds. He had to get to the top. He knew the wild horse race was ready to go, but he would miss it because he wanted those five dollars at the top of the pole, because with those dollars, and the money he had saved he could buy the silver Mexican bit he wanted and the tooled bridle. It had to be now, too, because Nellie Tucker, the tomboy, was waiting to follow him and she had almost made it on her last try. He closed his eyes before his final effort. He was up as far as anyone else had gone, but the last quarter of the pole was still thickly greased because no one had touched it yet. His chest thumped against the pole.

And the gun went to save Peter Prince with apple trees, and their family labored, as their family always did. They settled a quarter section of desert. They cleared the desert of sagebrush. They cleared the lichened rocks from the desert. They ploughed the desert. They dug fruitlessly for wells in the desert. They planted the fertile seeds of apple trees in the desert. They built a pump system and irrigation canals from the serpentine River Katz to irrigate the desert. In the spring they began to pump the water into the canals to start the apples growing, to save Peter Prince. The water flowed amply into the ditches and disappeared, hardly moistening the soil. It disappeared quickly down the hundreds of groundhog holes in Peter Prince, as through a sieve, and the water

"Maybe you have a little bit of ..." Bruce silenced her by finding her lips. "I'd rather fuck you," he said. Bruce never did. He never got a chance to do that.

The roommates were gone when they got up in the morning so Bruce and Sister went to breakfast together at a small candy store on Second Avenue. The woman who ran the little counter, a fleshy Jewish woman with a hairy mole near her mouth and a pulpy nose, sat next to them sipping coffee and complaining. "Gevolt. A little bit of yout', it goes a long way, you kids. You shouldn't know. My sister Ida. She takes every year a vacation in Florida. That refreshes her, at least; it's the fountain of yout' down there, you know, except for the element that goes there. The Galitziana. But it's a paradise, so who's to say."

off, the guns went off. It was 4:30 and the streets were filling, were filling with whistles and shouts. The competitors mounted and rode out of the rodeo grounds toward the death in Peter Prince. The spectators slowly followed. When Walkin' Tom heard the shooting and saw the eyes leveled at him through gunsights, he started to run, which he hated to do because it ruined the pace of his going. Silky Jeffries heard the starting commotion and regretted he was missing the race, and then he felt the pole vibrating like a longbow, and he looked down to see a man dressed in dark buckskins chopping at the base of his pole. His sister, when she heard the noise, went to the door of Spud Hazeley's cabin and was sucked out by a high wind that carried her up over quickly returned to the River Katz, where it always goes in Peter Prince.

WHAT PETER PRINCE READ!

"What's going on?" Philip Farrel slammed open the door of the little trailer that served as an office for Linda Lawrence. "What in hell is all this, out there?" His dispatch case slipped from his hand and snapped open on the floor. He was still slightly stoned.

"I'm just trying to do everything I can," said Linda Lawrence, never looking up from the maps she was studying.

"But this is ridiculous."

"We have to save Peter Prince."

She stood up and pullednaside the curtain to look at her children who were working on the railroad. They were setting ties, laying rail, pounding spikes. Lily

Gray, tired, bearded men kept passing in back of them through the store carrying large panes of glass to a glazier who worked in back.

"You youngniks," said the lady. "You should make of yourselves a something. Believe me, the years slip by like the BMT. And these days you don't recognize nothing no more. We don't even breathe the same air. It's terrible. Do you think I ever thought I'd live to see them take down the El? Now we got suntanned bums. It's like a boulevard."

Bruce looked over to see Sister picking the crumbs of a wheat muffin off her lips with her moist tongue. He liked her.

"You'll like my lover," she said, catching him looking. "He's got a strange sensitivity."

The lover's

Peter Prince to drop her into the undertow of the River Katz. Walkin' Tom jumped into the river off the third street bridge. The contents of Spud Hazeley's mysterious trunks were flowing into the air and turning like confetti in the celebrations. The air was full. Bullets crossed each other, having a ball. They whistled and laughed and chatted, and without greeting him at all, flew into Peter Prince while he twitched. Linda Lawrence tells that the River Katz jumped its bed, boiled, changed its course, sank 43 times before it was still.

the Moose, one of the oldest, with her red hair tied back under a babushka, was slapping creosote onto raw ties and tipping them up. Balub the pinsetter directed the laying of rails, since he was the one who had been on his own the longest, and carrying rail was Isor, Alan, Sildon, Martyn, Feeney, Tooth, Slugger, Maxwell, Swanny I, Lips, Wounder, and Frail Cindy's Whistle. They worked six-hour shifts, rested twelve, giving way to other crews of their brothers and sisters.

It always silenced Philip Farrel's protest to watch his children work, no matter what they were doing. It was a blessing.

"We have to save Peter Prince," said Linda Lawrence, wrapping her arms through his, "and this is the way we are going to do it."

"But Linda Lawrence,

apartment smelled of hot, airless sleep and oranges and incense, and her lover, a slender, bearded Negro, received them as if he expected Sister to come with a friend. It was a small, damp apartment, one room, the kitchen behind a partition, a roll-away bed still open and covered with streaked, wrinkled sheets. All the shades were drawn, and the air took on a yellow light like bouillon.

The Negro smiled at Bruce. "Who's the youth?" he asked.

"That's Bruce," she said.

"O yeah. Fine." He adjusted the top sheet of the bed. "Now if you came here for a freak show, baby I don't have the product." He turned on Bruce. "What do you need? Did you expect a freak spade?"

"Honey, please stop this hurt Negro act. You bore absolutely this railroad from Boston to Addis Ababa. It's going to take too long. I thought you were joking. Even after it's built at best it's going to be a long ride there and back."

"We are going to save Peter Prince."

"Do you think you'll ever get there to do it?"

"Look at the children."

As if suddenly the gears had shifted, their crowd of children was running and laying track at a rate that took them quickly out of sight. Philip Farrel got into the jeep to move the little trailer-office ahead. Marlene, Mildred and Mabel carried spike-buckets to the ten Larrys who drove them. It did relax Philip Farrel to see it so, and maybe Linda Lawrence was right. Maybe they were going to get there in time to save Peter Prince. The work, at any rate, was going well.

everybody."

"Oh, excuse me, Missy." He bowed to her. "You see I'm not a hurt Negro at all. I'm satisfied with the status quo as long as it stays quo for me. Like nobody hurts me and I don't hurt nobody. Like it's smooth, and I'm just riding." He closed his eyes. "Right, Missy?"

"You sure are acting strange."

"Alright, have the boy show me what he's written."

"I haven't written anything," Bruce said.

"Isn't this that racial reporter you said you were going to bring?"

"No, honey, this is just Bruce."

The lover smiled, and welcomed Bruce. "Here," he said, reaching over into the kitchen area for an orange. "Peel it." He threw it to Bruce.

Bruce sat down to eat the orange at the kitchen table while the

(By rights a novelist shouldn't try to do what I'm going to take the liberty to do in this column; that is, explain what's happening two columns over. Novels should contain their own logic, or at least an inevitability that the reader gets through his emotions if not through his reason; but since a miscalculation in the length of stories in these columns has left some free space over here, I'm going to overstep a little bit my province to let out a slight hint of what caused the third column to have its peculiar problem, and of why what's there is confusing, although it seems to be the happiest expedient at this point. You can choose either to read this aside with interest, or, as I would do in such a case, skip it

WHAT PETER PRINCE READ!

"Yeah," said the voice, breathing polyester and talking hoarsely above the communal lung. "The old megalopolis was burning, and there was no one around who saw it. Not a soul." There was no one to hear the voice either, as it spread out in the indirect lighting. It was a voice that lay, as it were, in the midst. It might have been his own. Peter Prince's own. If anyone else was around every precaution was taken. It was a voice, anyway, a monotone. "The smokeless white heat gathered the metropolis with its commerce, its organized society, that old community sense, skyscrapers and slums, brokerage houses and pushcarts, bridges, avenues, alleys, gathered the political maneuverings, the

lovers ignored him and began to make love. He was beginning to get the drift of the action in this column. It was like conversation, the way everyone did it in company, or like social drinking. He would like, he thought, a little more tenderness in it, and privacy. But he wasn't shocked at all, which surprised him. It was a way, he supposed, of sharing one's pleasure.

He opened the door to the refrigerator when he heard the mewing from within to allow the two cats trapped in there to get out, one a skinny Siamese, the other a gray tabby. Meanwhile the springs were singing and the windowshades rattling as they made love like Spud Hazeley and Cyanide Pearl. Peter Prince stood up when he finished his orange. Although he'd never seen a couple eat each other before, the whole and happily trust the author and expect to come to an understanding with him eventually.

Over there the problem is Bruce. What is he doing there? What right have Ito switch him in like that without preparation? Worst of all, what happened to Peter Prince? How can you just elbow him out of his own biography like that, when it's his novel after all, and he has the right to happen in it? I guess this tactic makes me, among characters, anyway, the most unpopular novelist going, shoving Bruce in like that where he doesn't belong, and can hardly fake the dialogue, and assing Peter Prince out like that, for no apparent reason, before the experience has even rounded out. Believe me, I worry about it, but what else can I do, just let Peter Prince die, or protest demonstrations, gathered the ethnic neighborhoods, the luxury apartments, gathered problems of divorce, addiction, delinquency, graft, taxation, pollution, ballot stuffing, neurosis, sanitation, the rising or falling cost of, gathered us in every variation, whispered, like whoops, gathering all, everything, and the variations thereof, as a flaming scythe would gather a magnesium garden: a sizzling moment, boom in the subway tunnels, and a flame like a bean sprout fingering the galaxy. And that's the end of it."

What really matters then is this: Across the stage of Radio City Music Hall the Rockettes kick in unison, and the house is full for the Christmas show. It's cold outside. The manger scene has expanded this time to include the first few situation was starting to bore him: his dark kinky head in her flaming pink meat, her pale cheeks swollen with the dark penetration of his cock. Bruce liked to participate, so it bored him, but not the cats who had found the lovers and were tumbling and rubbing with them, mewing like the personification of orgasm.

"I'm leaving," Bruce said.

"So long," Sister mumbled, her mouth full.

He felt himself released onto Third Avenue. It was fine to be alone again. He felt a gladness in himself and a kind of community joy. Although what he'd seen weren't the most comfortable things to observe, he had, through them, expanded the area of his tolerance, so that now even the derelicts who were starting to awake follow experience out of the range of my interest into some other novel? No. I have to do what I can, and believe me, it's not so easy these days with air pollution, traffic fatalities, population explosion, mind-zapping drugs, water pollution, job offers from industry, the FBI and CIA, the Cosa Nostra, catching up with everyone. It's not so easy under these conditions, believe me, to hang on to a character for a whole novel before he gets shuttled off into death or some other terminal experience, that craps him right out of the novel and into whatever else. If you want him around long enough so you can write him up, you have to devise methods to keep him hanging on, and that was the move I felt I had to make for Peter Prince, because it's no way to finish that boy

rows of the orchestra, roped off so the audience won't occlude the radiance of the stage, the apron, and the orchestra pit. A child lies under the colorful spots in the simulated straw, gazed upon by seven tiers of paying witnesses. It's a vast improvement, a fine hour. Providence and Grace enter stage right; stage left admits nothing at all dressed in an old hat and a motley bathrobe. Some blocks away a man in a navy-blue overcoat and gray scarf peddles his cooling chestnuts in front of The Museum of Modern Art.

"You're damned right I'm cold, I'm freezing my balls off," he says to Philip Farrel who buys a twenty-five cent bag. Philip Farrel is carrying a fire-ax, wearing his asbestos waders and coat, his head in a sloping fireman's helmet. The

in the doorways, and stand around feeling hungry, were subject to his smiling good will. He still had to help Little out, and that would be, he thought, pleasurable. Taxis passed, coloring the avenue, and intense, bearded young men, followed by serious girls in leotards stepped out of their walk-ups, their store-fronts, their lofts, to smell what Con Edison had put into the air that day. It wasn't going to rain. Bruce walked slowly through the charred sunlight following an old man who kept his pants up with a rope attached to the back suspender buttons, run under the shoulder flap of his old army shirt, and held out in front of himself like a leash. The baseball cap he wore with the brim in back had attached to it, to cover his face, huge plastic sunglasses with heart-shaped lenses. A short Negro off, in Grand Central Station. As you'll see if you read on, he's got a lot more to do in this novel and a great deal to learn, which you too can learn by following him, and although it might not have been artistically appropriate to shove him aside like that, and unload the fate on poor Bruce, I felt that my moral commitment to carry Peter Prince through his variety was stronger than any preconceived arty notions. I acted on this commitment and by this commitment I stand.

I can perhaps somewhat redeem myself to those of you who have developed a real concern for Bruce and his whereabouts by telling you his story, as it really ended, in his own column. You see, Bruce, during the Korean Police Activity, was in the same outfit as Eric Elliot, Peter

vendor blows his frosty breath into his cupped hands. "What are you standing around like this for, mister? You don't have to."

"I'm waiting here for Linda Lawrence. We're going to save . . ."

"For Linda Lawrence," the vendor interrupted. "You must be crazy."

"We're going to save Peter Prince."

"You are crazy. You don't wait here for that. You wait at the dock. That's where Linda Lawrence is. With all the rest of them." He stirred the few open chestnuts on his heater, their flesh green as seawater.

"Come on," said Philip Farrel. "What would they be doing down there?"

"Look," said the vendor. "I don't owe you no explanations, so don't hock me no charnick. I tell you a simple explanation just once, and that's enough."

woman in a dirty flower print, twisted on her body like bandages, stumbled up behind him, slapped him across the back of the head, and shouted, "You son of a bitch." The man halted, and slowly rotated, listing like a loaded freighter. He raised his free hand and opened his mouth, letting some sound stagger out.

"Gimmee a cigarette, you washboard," said the woman; her ruined face had the sheen of dubbed leather.

The man dug his free hand into his crotch and drew out a small, drawstring pouch tied to a beltloop. He pulled two large butts from the pouch and gave the woman one. She produced some matches and lit her and then his remnant. They leaned on each other and smoked. In little ways, Bruce thought, people could make life more

Prince's old friend, although he didn't survive, as Eric did, to be imprisoned after the infamous Fortune Cookie Ambush. This outfit was assigned to special shock corps duties in psychological warfare. Their job was to go out in squads of two on missions to plant powerful loudspeakers behind the enemy lines. The psychological warfare division of our U.S. Army had done exhaustive studies of Oriental superstitions and they figured they could scare the shit out of the enemy by blasting weird screams through these loudspeakers all night long; they wouldn't sleep, their resistance would be weakened, and they would chicken out. Since the operation was top secret, most American troops didn't know what was going on, and were scared shitless by the

What more do you want, I should hold your hand? They're waiting down there for what's his name."

"For Peter Prince?" He opened a chestnut. It was wormy.

"Yes, for what's his name. Now shoo, mister, and let me freeze out here without standing with no idiot dressed like you."

"Peter Prince is getting back," Philip Farrel mused, leaning his fire-ax on a hydrant. He squeezed another chestnut up to the top of his bag. Wormy also.

"Please, mister, go stand in the lobby and let me freeze here alone."

"Peter Prince, returning . . .

pleasant for one another. It was easier to see that down here, where people had nothing but one another. He could have wept for all the foolish struggle that went on for wealth, and his mother's frustrations without it, and he could have wept for his mother who was alone now, while he was learning how necessary love was in the world; all that was necessary was love and he couldn't give her any, at least not to her measure. Little. He had to get back and help him. It was an exoneration, that strong feeling of obligation he had to help Little.

"Put on a suit," Little told him.

"Why?"

"Because, baby, we're going uptown, and we wear our suits up there."

Bruce pulled out his wrinkled tweeds, a work-shirt, and his

screaming, and got little sleep while the psychological assaults went on. Bruce was in the know, however, and he slept pretty well, crying out every once in a while in his sleep, "You Gook Finks" or, "You Commie Bastards," or "Red Sons of Bitches." Unlike the skeptical Peter Prince, Bruce never for a moment questioned the quality of his country's actions, and even when he was awake, out of his fervor and his frustration he would scream out, "Finky Bastard Commie Pinkoes," or "Red Gook Yellow Chickens." In fact, this was the way he met his untimely end.

Eric Elliot didn't like to go out on missions with Bruce because he knew that Bruce was likely to stand up at any time and scream his invective at the enemy and since missions always took them

These unfinished pages, among other things, are what Peter Prince read, and he found them dimly consoling, though he didn't understand all the attention that was being paid to him.

mashed wool tie, and started to put them on.

"It's so hot, sweety, you'll look like a sweat freak in that weight. Superfluous. Haven't you got lighter, lighter uh . . ."

"It's my only suit."

"This heat. You'll die in it."

"Here," he said, pulling some light cotton pants and a silk jacket from Hector Hastingford's closet. "And use this, it's mine." He threw him a yellow ascot. The clothes fit, though the cuffs were a little higher than he'd been used to, and the jacket of a little finer stuff.

"You know it's just that uptown people," Little explained, "look at you as if they know what you look like. I mean the way your father knows what you look like. Mine was a cook."

"Mine's dead."

"Better that way. I

behind enemy lines, this could prove dangerous, but he had to go with him from time to time, and when he did, the only solution he knew to Bruce's instability was to keep him busy enough, holding nails in his teeth, so he couldn't shout.

It was late afternoon, raining, and it had taken them longer, through mud and through undergrowth, than they had anticipated to reach their objective. Eric Elliot had the speakers strapped to his back, and Bruce carried the tools and a reel of wire strapped to him that unwound as he went. They had already layed the first speaker and were starting the second when it happened. Bruce, as he was tightening a connection with his pliers, accidentally crunched his finger. Eric Elliot, alert for mishaps,

haven't seen mine for eight years. The last time he beat me up with an iron ladle for being a fairy. It's always best if one of you dies first, decay, before you come to that." He fluffed up Bruce's ascot and kissed him on the cheek. "It gets so dreary sometimes. But I think you do look improved."

On the IRT uptown Bruce watched Little flirt with everyone with his curved eyelashes, waving them at two young sailors who snarled threateningly and blushed, at two neat children beneath the massive arms of a Brooklyn mother, at the conductor who ignored him, at a salesman who pretended indifference, but whose adam's apple kept bobbing up above his tie-knot to look, and a young couple in immaculate sneakers, at a scholarly priest, whose waxy complexion made him, with the smile that immediately slapped his palm over Bruce's mouth. Eric relaxed, having averted that disaster, but immediately Bruce did it again, and jerked upright, spitting out nails, so he could suck his finger and scream, "Dirty Pinko Commie Cocksucker Red Bastards."

"Blam, Blam, Blam," responded the enemy in the woods, killing Bruce through the eye, the liver, and the hand. Eric Elliot crawled all the way back to headquarters on his belly.

Whether you like it or not, that was the real end of Bruce in his own column. Those of you who came to this book to learn about Bruce, and that's all, can put the thing down here, close it, and go out for a hot fudge sundae; but those others who need to know all about Peter Prince, can read

trembled across his purple lips, look like a lit devotional candle. Bruce could feel the thickness of his thighs stretching the crease in his borrowed pants.

They reached Grand Central Station, whose golden light had been in Bruce's imagination through his life, angelic dominion; the golden light that seemed to contain the travelers in a rich, various orderly system of going; the balcony of huge, healthy, illuminated Kodak ads, and refreshing Schlitz and Coca Cola. And the redcaps with their gliding carts, passing the baggage through the gateways, rivers of folks climbing and descending the ramps, and beautiful girls. He always saw the most beautiful girls in the radiance of Grand Central Station: pale fine redheads in loose chiffon, the way you see

themselves some more,
at will.)

them in ads for
menstrual inserts, their
lips sanguine, their eyes
misty, long hair drifting
loosely in the radiance:
perfect. He felt winged,
more charged for flying
from that golden light,
than he ever did at
fluorescent LaGuardia,
or vacant Idlewild.
Trains really left the
city, issuing from the
tunnels of the railroad
complex like a birth.

As they waited on
line at the baggage
window, Little waved
his eyebrows around the
station, as if looking for
someone. A boy sitting
on a pile of luggage
waved at him, and Little
waved back, opening
and shutting his hand
like a European.

Something about the
air in this column was
beginning to worry
Bruce. It was changing,
not the smell of it, but
the feel of it, and an
inexplicable discomfort
in Hector Hastingford's
clothes, as if they were

tightening into his skin, and a sound he heard, a new one whose directtion he couldn't determine, as of a multitude whistling in the distance. There were a lot of things Bruce knew nothing about, and a lot of places he'd never been, and it was weird to him that he'd gotten involved in a column like this. All the people were strangers to him, including himself, and that noise was coming from somewhere.

Little chimed in, "Listen, just ask for the footlocker for Hazeley."

"Where are you going?"

"Just ask for it?"

"Why not you? Are you leaving?"

"I'll be behind you, sweetie."

Holy shit, thought Bruce, something was happening that he didn't understand. The train announcements came out so garbled he couldn't understand them, and that whistling was getting louder. Death, he thought, not knowing how the word got into his head, as if he'd seen it. Hector Hastingford at the mirror. Mirrors shattering.

"What do you want?" the clerk asked.

"A footlocker for Hazeley," he responded automatically.

The shutter of the Kodak advertisement dropped like a guillotine.

"Do you have the ticket?"

He turned to Little, but didn't see him anymore. Something (was it in his head?) was happening in this column that he hadn't been prepared for.

"My friend here . . . no . . . I don't have a ticket."

"Wait a minute," the clerk said. For the first time Bruce noticed that the clerk wasn't wearing clothes, as far as he could tell. Kuhhrrrist. If this was some kind of surrealist novel he was involved in he didn't want any part of it. It was fucking rude to shove someone like this into the middle of a column, without an introduction. Absurd.

"This is it," said the clerk, and he dropped the footlocker on the counter. The locks popped open. Spud Hazeley was stenciled across the lid. "Now just identify the contents."

"I don't know what's in it. How can I know what's in it? I just got here."

The air around him was stuffed with whistling. The clerk rotated the trunk so he could examine the contents. It was full, full of Oaxaca Gold, of little white packages, of sterilized syringes, of sugar cubes. It was full.

"Not mine," said Bruce, "I'm not that Hazeley. I'm not." And the two men who grabbed Bruce by the arms pulled a wallet out of the pocket of his borrowed jacket that identified him incontrovertibly as Spud Hazeley.

"I'm not the one," was Bruce's shout, muffled in the golden Grand Central air by the whistling bullets, and the laughing bullets, and the chatting bullets.

"Did you ever hear this one . . ."

"Force, force to the utmost . . ."

"A hell of a way to make a living . . ."

"Let no guilty man escape . . ."

"The Chinese must go . . ."

"They hired the money, didn't they . . ."

The bullets seemed to know the way.

By now I'm sure you want to know what's really happening, where it's really at, what's actually going on and where. I'm going to tell you, and believe me you're not going to find it nearly so pleasant as even some of the more seedy environments I've described so far. First of all, where am I? This is an air-conditioned library study, done in decorator colors—plaster walls in warm eggshell; ceilings washable, two-tone peach and eggshell; the floors of linoleum, marbleized green and eggshell. There's a cork bulletin board above my table, with the regulations tacked up there: (1) No food should be left in this study. (2) A tackboard panel is supplied over your desk. Please use it. Please do not nail, tape or otherwise attach objects to the walls or door. (3) A supply of typing stands is available. If you need a typing stand, please apply to the Director's Office. (4) Damage to any furniture or equipment and necessary repairs or replacements should be reported immediately to the Director's Office. (5) Please keep your study in neat order. An ash tray and a receptacle for trash have been provided for each study room. I think even the Director has been in here checking up, and no one, yet, has complained about this book, and that's my biggest source of encouragement. As you may be able to tell from the way this book looks, the light in here is fluorescent, and you can believe I'm troubled by that, because I know that the best books so far have been written by natural light, or long ago maybe by candle, oil or kerosene, and recently, incandescent; but fluorescent? You never hear of any. It's such a new thing for me that I'm a little nervous about it, the experimental quality. You never know, having no previous models to follow, how it's going to turn out, like I'm always pushing out in my craft toward the new boundaries visible under this new light.

Also significant is the air conditioner, which provides the even temperature and texture of the stuff my skin is immersed in while I write, that I pull into my lungs. You might say that air conditioning isn't novel at all, that these days all books are climate controlled for your comfort and convenience, and that a book produced without air conditioning would be stifling, to say the least; but a peculiar characteristic of this air conditioner produces a unique situation, as far as I can tell, among modern literary works. This air conditioner plinks. This air conditioner plinks like a music-box plinks. This air conditioner plinks like a music-box plinking random notes. I arrive in my plinking library study, sit down in a straight-back wooden chair, and fall asleep with my forehead on my forearm to the random plinking of my air conditioner. I sleep in it, sleep through it, dreamless in that continual surprise, that anti-melody, that effervescence. And I wake up in fifteen minutes, or a half hour—who knows how long?—with my brain tissue softly twinkling like the night sky shuffled into unfamiliar constellations. Like great chords those random notes soak up the space in my study and send me rolling over through this hazardous narrative, or better yet, turn me like a spitted calf cooking in the random laps of sound, and this strange phenomenon, as you have probably already guessed, has a lot to do with this book. If anyone knows any books, published or not, produced under similar conditions I'd appreciate your contacting me at home, or through my agent, Lurton Blassingame, Sixty east 42nd St., New York, N.Y. 10017.

Meanwhile I want you to imagine the difficulties involved under these conditions, holding the various threads of this narrative together, the subplots, the counterplots. In this environment any surprise is possible, and as much as I try to avoid chaos, chaos too often waits for me at the end of a story line, squatting there, wiping his lips on his wrist. Despite these gloomy predictions I'm going to try to demonstrate that I'm a novelist in good faith. At this point I'm going to attempt to tie in one of the ends that was left quite loose some pages back. I'm doing it because I know you need some sense of continuity, and so do I, and getting this done now will save my having to tuck in this strand with all the others at the final denouement.

You must remember Peter Prince and his plight in the stifling heat (a reassuring plink) of Ethiopia. Let us return to him there, as he was, prostrate. The question raised, though never stated, was: Had Peter Prince been castrated? The answer is, quite frankly, no. No, he was not. What happened to him bears some disclosing, and wrapping up, nonetheless. Actually they had done quite the opposite to Peter Prince. They had performed on him rituals, and with their various medicines worked to increase the size of his penis, and make it more responsive and alert. Actually, seeing Peter Prince undressed, and admiring the whiteness of his skin, they took it on themselves to cultivate his virility, which they pitied, because they thought his penis small by their standards, hardly a phallic trophy, like one of a small boy. They stretched it with splints and rubbed it with the pitch from the Zegba, a kind of highland juniper with medicative powers, and they wrapped it in warm *injera*, their spicy bread.

As his condition improved Peter Prince felt he wanted them to stop the treatment, but his servant and companion, Ahmad, whom he had learned to trust, admonished him, explaining that he was really getting preferential treatment, and he told him his own sad story, and of the cruelty of men. A few years back, when he was only nine years old, he was traveling with a band of thieves and cutthroats that roamed the desert from Aswan to Wadi Halfa, at the Sudanese border. He worked as their camel boy, collecting the feces and urine, and keeping the chief's white camel combed. Near Wadi Halfa the band was attacked by a large force of British customs police and the fight that ensued made Ahmad weep to describe. The camels were all impounded and the members of the band scattered and fled into the desert. Ahmad, himself, was wounded and rather than surrender to the British customs officials he ran off and hid in the rushes by the banks of-the Nile, where he survived on reed shoots and raw frogs' legs until his wounds healed.

He was discovered there one day by an old woman who took pity on him and brought him home, and treated him for a while as if he was her own son, but she already had three grown sons who were greedy and cruel and who schemed, against their mother's weeping, to sell the boy into slavery, which they did at a meager profit. They sold him to the traders that brought slaves into Saudi Arabia, who decided he would do well as a eunuch. Ahmad's descriptions of the months he spent drugged, of the bamboo devices sunk into his crotch to develop, after he was castrated, his desirability, are too terrible to recount in our modern age, to a civilized audience. Luckily he survived, and before he could be sold he was stolen, surprisingly, by the Danakil, who had harems, but weren't known for keeping slaves. Despite his maimed sexuality he had a certain vivacity that made him a favorite. He didn't seem to resent his life in slavery. It was easy enough for him, and pleasant. Peter Prince tried to make him understand freedom, and its desirability, and Ahmad sometimes would admit that he longed for freedom, though he didn't seem to understand what it was. Peter Prince would sometimes get feverish and mad, calling Freedom by name, and moaning a peculiar song about it. At those times Ahmad, out of love, would tell Peter Prince how much he too wanted to be free, and Peter Prince would calm down. But Ahmad also advised Peter Prince not to complain about the treatment he was getting, because things could go much worse for him, and Peter Prince followed this advice.

The treatments did work, making of Peter Prince's medium-sized member a large, nobby showpiece, somewhat disclored, but impressive; and his endurance improved too, which was tested on various young near-virgins. One of the sons of the chief, a fleshy young man, who looked more like a Shankalla than a Danakil, took a liking to Peter Prince, and would spend time with him, improving the English he had studied in Addis Ababa, and bringing him girls. Peter Prince enjoyed most of this: his new sexual prowess, his confidence in Ahmad, his friendship with Prester, the king's son, but always like a song at the back of his mind was the idea of escape, freedom. He would mention it to Prester, but Prester would ignore him, because he was holding onto Peter Prince.

"Ahmad," he said one day, when from a fit of depression he rose to a decision. "If I don't get out of this place I'm going to lose my head." Ahmad was wiping Peter Prince's fingers after he ate, and gathering the soiled earthenware.

"Yes," said Ahmad.

"I need freedom."

"I'm sorry for that," said Ahmad.

"Why do you say that?"

"It makes you so unhappy that you should want it so much, whatever this freedom is. So far I've watched you and I think that this freedom must be a nervous disorder, when you have everything and want it just the same. I am satisfied. I don't need that stupidity. As I live I live, and in life it's important to be happy. Look how unhappy you are."

"Ahmad, I have to be free to go where I please."

"You can go where you please here, if you can get there alive. You mean you want to be able to go where you've been."

"It's more a state of mind," Peter Prince tried again to get it across. "Being able to think what you please. Free."

"Are you such a slave that you can't think what you please now? I think what I please, it's easy."

"Don't say 'slave' to me." He walked around the room very quickly; just a few rabbits were left in the cages, which meant he was almost cured. The room was very hot (plink), and the coarse cloth he wore scratched him. "I mean," he said, "free to say what you please, up to a point."

"Say it," said Ahmad as he wiped some bread in the left-over sauce. "Who could understand you?"

"And do what you please."

Ahmad put the sauce-soaked bread into Peter Prince's mouth, a gesture left over from when Peter Prince was a complete invalid. He performed his duties gracefully, like a young wife. "Do what you please," he mumbled. "You have crazy ideas. How do you ever know what it pleases you to do? It would make you a slave. You'd do the same thing all the time. It would be boredom. It's better to leave what you do up to a lot of other people. At least you're in for some surprises."

"That's not true."

"Look at the way you weep," said Ahmad, noticing Peter Prince's moist cheeks. "You're like a new girl in the harem. What good is this freedom that you should cry over it. It makes you so unhappy."

"Oh Ahmad, you have to live in freedom for a while to understand it. You haven't lived in it."

"I've lived enough," said Ahmad. "And I know you now, and I don't envy you."

Peter Prince paced the floor and sucked in his breath till his new penis tickled. "You have to live it, breathe it, eat it, sing it, love it. Freedom. You have to learn to live it."

"And after you do all that, and waste your time, you're miserable without it, aren't you? You call that freedom?"

"Yes."

"Beh." Ahmad shrugged. "I'm glad it's your troubles." He took a pot off the flames and poured Peter Prince a cup of black Abyssinian coffee. "Tell me. If you were in America, how would you have freedom? What would be different?"

Peter Prince's eyes glazed over, and he grinned. "If I were back . . . I would just . . . I would . . . I'd be free . . . you know."

"How? What would you have?"

Peter Prince looked at his fingernails. He had let them grow, and they were longer than they'd ever been. He hid them in his palms. "I'd have a new car. I'd have an apartment." He took the first bitter sip of coffee. "I'd go on trips with my girl. Maybe I'd go back to school. I'd eat lots of steak and french fries. I'd go drinking with my friends, and we'd go surfing, skiing." Peter Prince closed his eyes to see this life flickering like color TV at the backs of his eyelids. He missed so much what he thought he never could miss: simple American things: Freedom.

"That sounds more like American wealth than freedom," Ahmad said. "What if you are poor?"

"Freedom is wealth, Ahmad," said Peter Prince, surprising even himself with cheap wisdom.

"But what if you're poor? If you're poor in America, what then? Freedom sounds expensive."

Peter Prince smiled, and reached his cup out for more coffee. It was futile, he thought. It was an impossible job. Ahmad was too simple to understand the possibilities outside his own experience. But he was likable in his naivete. Peter Prince offered him the rest of the coffee.

"Ahmad," whispered Peter Prince, "can I trust you?"

"You are my master."

"Stop! I don't want you to say that any more. I'm nobody's master." He put his hand on the young eunuch's soft left shoulder. "I mean, can I trust you as a man?"

Ahmad smiled.

"I know you can be trusted." He took Ahmad's hand in both of his. "I'm going to escape. I have to be free."

"Ahhhhhh," Ahmad moaned, sinking to his haunches. "Yes."

"You can come if you want to."

"What for?"

"We can be free. You can make your own way. You'll get to know what freedom is."

"You told me what it is."

"Well?"

"It makes you go out to kill yourself."

"That's right. That's how much it's worth to me, you see. Will you come?"

Ahmad laughed. "Of course not."

Peter Prince sighed. "Will you help me, then?" he asked, after a silence.

"You are my master."

With the help of Ahmad Peter Prince managed his escape in the next week while they were visiting Aksum with Prester, looking at ruins and steles, and discussing the early development of Christianity in Ethiopia. Prester promised in the following week to take Peter Prince to Lalibala to see the famous monolithic churches, hewn from the raw granite, and as much as he was attracted by the prospect of that excursion it didn't budge him from his intention to escape, which he did, to his host's dismay, running into the nearby wilderness where he wandered free for forty-three days and nights, and was finally captured, with an enormous appetite, by a band of Galla, another fierce, illiterate tribe, and he became a favorite of theirs, held by them for a long time, and participating in their strange marriage customs.

*

This is what happens. I want to put THE END and I have to put TO BE CONTINUED. I never know. I figured tying it up would be easy. I keep my study neat, I pick up the crumbs, I stack my books, and Peter Prince gets involved again, and he just won't be wrapped up. Also, when I set out in this direction, look what happens in another direction. There's Linda Lawrence sweating and weeping. Writing this book is like trying to hug a plastic cleaning sack (beware of that plastic cleaning sack) stuffed with Jello. Philip Farrel is running around hunting for the thermometer.

"I wish you'd stop your damned crying," he said. "It's hard enough."

"Peter Prince, Peter Prince," she moaned.

"I'm getting tired of this. He'll be alright."

"We have to get to him," she said.

"I have to get to work," he said. "Rectal or oral?" he asked, standing with the thermometer poised above vaseline and alcohol.

"Rectal," she said.

"Oral," he insisted.

"It's such a shame," she said, before he stopped her mouth. "I never would have predicted this move. He made such a good beginning." The thermometer silenced her, and Philip Farrel went to call the vice president he was heading out to visit. Even he thought it was true about Peter Prince. No one ever expected the following:

Supreme my holdings; greater yet
My need, thoughtless I go out.

*

Out of pity or boredom or despair, the cause was irrelevant, but the act itself counted, a way, for Peter Prince, into new modes of living when he set up house with Bebo to become the father, after her husband left her, of an Oriental orphan they had adopted, those new modes including selfless emotion and tenderness. Peter Prince felt a special tenderness for that child, though he had no special love for Bebo and at times resented the worst of her whining and hissing presence, but with a feeling for the child he knew must resemble fatherhood so much did a vague guilt swell in him sometimes like a cloud dissipating at its margins. In New York Peter Prince sometimes felt that all there was to separate his smoldering insides from the charred, sooty air was a pericarp of cold fire called his flesh and that reflected in car windows or in the polished marble and glass façades of the new buildings in New York he could see through chips in his integument the waste within himself, himself layed waste and penetrated by the wasted air, and though he didn't expect any more from himself than what others seemed to offer the world that self-consumption he contained frightened him. He needed to connect somewhere and make his disappearance known. To change and to change was the way. Despite these moribund self-evaluations Peter Prince seemed always happy enough. He never acted bored or desperate and was rarely self-pitying; moments of depression from time to time assailed him but he always found enough of what was left of life to be cheerful. He knew, however, that there wasn't much left, that there should be somewhere more available of life that he could get at, more loamy possibilities. A feeling of uneasy equilibrium, that one has in a house that has been robbed, came on him often in supermarkets and airline terminals and automobile showrooms and appliance stores, in front of TV, when he walked past the shopless facades of new office buildings that reflected dimly his charred going. It was all attractive stuff, not to touch; and his senses buzzed in it; but he couldn't help thinking it wasn't good enough, that someone, something had made a huge, incalculably stupid investment, and that

Peter Prince, whose substance had been pirated to that end, was suffering from the receipt of ever diminishing returns. He moved against the flow, and had to keep moving, a flow that backed up against his desire and will, and he moved into it like a rescuer holding his victim above the flood, and those shoddy places: the shopping centers, airline terminals, showrooms, were not places he actually visited, but they most effortlessly swung down at him in the flood, coaxing him, softly battering his intentions. He consumed himself in this countering and he felt wasted, and that was why he chose Bebo, as if he could add substance to himself from the outside, something he could steer in his own direction, at least. Bebo and the child. He could learn something from that.

They moved the contents of their two small Lower East Side apartments out into the smoke and swamp of Queens. Their rented truck, a yellow and black mule, with gaskets blowing, stripped its differential on the Triboro Bridge, and Peter Prince, a load of alien household furnishings—frying pans slamming into the vanity, picture frames, a new freezer-frig combo—had to be towed off the bridge and he had to load each possession into another truck. He hated possessions, but the problems seemed necessary to him, the way to start off, as bad as possible, so one could appreciate the good times afterward and learn whatever the situation could yield him. He had invested his and Bebo's savings in a small co-op apartment, brand new, on the fourteenth floor (in a building that had no thirteenth) of one of the ten 143 family dwellings in the new Ma-Jo development (the name a synthesis of Marion and Joan, the first names of the wives of the two principal investors in the project). The options offered them were astounding. Rather than dull composition flooring they could choose a floor of wood veneer if they agreed to cover the kitchen floor at their own expense. For a minimum fee they could buy the burglar kit—alarm, pick-proof locks, window seals, and a one-way door mirror. They could choose to pay for air conditioning, which was built in to the heating system, or trade it for the price of plumbing fixtures. At a little extra expense they got continental light fixtures, brass hardware, slide-o-matic drapery pulls, the better Roll E-Z wardrobe doors, the Jingo Jalousies, extra Glo-Coat coats, deluxe cupboards, lux-o-matic drain covers, silky saddle toilet seats, all of which would have had to be removed if they chose inferior products. Peter Prince bought it all, feeling with this gesture the prosperity he knew he was entitled to as a citizen, a prosperity that the newly rich must feel when they first contribute to charity. He wanted Bebo, and himself, and their little Oriental charge to start out well.

"I'm so excited," said Bebo, as Peter Prince loaded with books came through the door, her soft tweed coat over his head.

"Grab some of this stuff," he grunted. She blithely swung the coat off his head and danced around the room. "It's so beautiful having a place. We're going to be happy." She wrapped her small shoulders in the coat and stroked one of the climatizers. "Winters and summers and springs and falls," she sang. "We'll have our own little weather here and we never have to be uncomfortable. I could chirp." She kissed Peter Prince when he straightened up from discharging his load.

"Chirp," he said.

He went back down the elevator, down the long hallway to the truck. The lobby was lined with divans and bureaus and sideboards waiting for the elevator. All the older folks stood by the windows down the hallway watching their children move in and conversing in Yiddish, in Puerto Rican, in Polish, obviously happy that their children could move out of the slums, and here it was so clean, they all agreed.

"There's what I call a real spirit here," said a huge woman in a black overcoat carrying a fry-pan and a plastic sack full of hair-curlers. By the mailboxes greetings and instructions from the managerial committee of the co-op were posted, each announcement ending with the slogan of the place: COOPERATION MEANS POWER.

A snappily dressed fourteen-year-old retarded son of one of the incoming tenants cooperated by holding the door open for the carriers, his shoes spit polished, pigskin gloves, felt collar on his topcoat. He laughed continuously and offered sprays of incoherent weather information and sympathy.

Peter Prince entered again with a load of records. "Wazzlo dhe sish Wockaroll?" The spittle glistened on the boy's lapel.

Upstairs Bebo was really chirping. She was small and pretty and her elation at having Peter Prince to carry her household in made her tingle with happiness. It made Peter Prince feel happily strong to see her. She was unpacking towels and blankets, pressing them to her cheeks as she carried them to the new linen closet.

"Don't go down yet," she said, after Peter Prince put down his records. "Rest just a minute." He folded his trembling arms in front of himself. She wiped the sweat from his face with a large, orange towel. "I want you to feel like a king." She formed a turban around his head with the towel. "Come to the window."

From their living-room window they could see the distant smoke of the city, and close by the construction of the new shopping center, their own, and the parking lot, crowded already. The other houses of the project were being stuffed with families, their possessions swallowed by those buildings. Bebo took his hand.

"I didn't think I'd like this at all, I mean moving in with all these squares, but it's really kind of exciting. Everyone seems so alive, as if things are better. I don't even think I'll mind being clean." Bebo giggled. "I guess I'm about ready for the bourgeois scene." She turned a little latch and rolled back for the first time the Roll E-Z to the terrace. The air was a little sweeter here and they both breathed it and smiled. Jetliners came down in the distance over the low suburban homes, trailing exhaust like stretched shadows, and dropping into the black dust. They were hit suddenly from below with a crackling spasm of John Philip Sousa, drums rattling, brass bellowing out of tune. In the empty part of the supermarket parking lot a marching band from the local high school was practicing. The band was all Negro because the neighborhood before the Ma-Jo development had been all Negro. The development was going to change that. The band had purple uniforms and the white plumes of their caps bobbed on their troubled sound.

"They can't make that ofay music," Bebo said after they stepped back in and closed the Roll E-Z. "My ofay king." She kissed him.

"I need to get this done. Then I can appreciate everything." His arms, freed from the weight of packages, felt as if they were going to float away from his body. He caught them in Bebo's armpits and squeezed her.

"Peter Prince," she said. "You're doing so much for me. I don't understand why."

Peter Prince closed his eyes because he felt tears coming to them. He rested his lips on the hot, pale curve of her neck, and the trembling in his arms floated inward till his heart rattled like an idling motor, and he squeezed her with recovered strength. "I don't understand why you're so good to me," she said. Neither did Peter Prince understand, but he felt this tenderness, a great necessity, moving into himself, and populating him where he lay waste. Thwang-Nuc, the child, was asleep in her own room. It was for that child.

The experimental use of napalm for psychological warfare by American advisers in her native province only half-maimed the child for whose sake Peter Prince really decided to "set up house"; one side of her was roasted and slightly paralyzed, her fingers gone, her body thick with scar tissue like callus. Because her cheek was destroyed and her mouth partly seared shut she had difficulty speaking her native Oriental dialect, and she could manage only a little whistling, like small sirens, out of the side of her mouth that could open, which she took to be the American language. She was bright enough, could write some of her own language, and was learning American, though she was hardly five. Her name, Thwang-Nuc, they had changed to Teresa; she was Catholic. Peter Prince didn't pity her, he loved her. When he watched her unscorched profile he saw how beautiful she might have been, and indeed was, a smallness of feature, a fine, narrow nose that had remained miraculously unscarred. She was changing, with some difficulty, from being naturally left-handed (the left side of her being the one destroyed) to using her right side, which would frustrate her sometimes when she was trying to draw, or balance blocks, difficult manual play, and she would swing the left side of her body around and beat on whatever she was doing with her stump, that was usually hidden in knitwear, knocking blocks across the room and smearing paint. Breakdowns like this would destroy the frail Bebo, making her tremble and cry, and Peter Prince had to comfort both of them, holding Teresa on his lap, and reassuring Bebo across the room that she was as good a mother as she could expect to be. Teresa had bad dreams and often kept Bebo and Peter Prince awake with a low, gurgling scream that she uttered in her sleep. That was Thwang-Nuc.

The spastic youth downstairs jumped up and down when he saw Peter Prince again. He shouted and pointed and hissed. Everyone stared at Peter Prince: the old folks, the young men with their arms full, the delivery boys. "It's a crazy bunch moving in here," said the huge woman in her black overcoat, staring at the top of Peter Prince's head. "There's gonna be an investigation."

The boy drooled through his fingers that covered his mouth. "Waffo tha... waffo tha . . ." he asked, touching the forehead of Peter Prince. Peter Prince saw the broken image in the polished doorframe of the orange turban still resting on his head.

"Whatta you, a maharaja or sumpin?" said a man in coveralls who passed, holding up his end of a long, sagging couch.

*

"Deep one two three, Now one two three, Breathe one two three, Yes one two three." The gatherings of the Golden Mackerel began with breathing exercises, and all the trim, athletic men and women, dressed in dinner jackets and cocktail gowns winked at each other over their expanding and contracting chests, and so easily did the breathing come to them that they could manage to smile. This was where Peter Prince worked to support his home. The folks quoted their collective lung capacity at forty-three bushels or more, so great that the waiters, Peter Prince among them, had to hold the windows and doors during the exercises, to keep them from slamming. A few minutes of this ritual and the evening got going in a convivial atmosphere. The club accepted for membership aging young adults, full adults, and junior senior citizens, all of whom had wealth in common and a desire to keep fit. Each of them had his pet exertion like scuba and sky diving, rock climbing, yachting: sports the better advantaged Americans liked to invest in, sports that could keep them in tiptop condition well into their junior-senior citizenships. Each of them was proud of his condition and of his ability to maintain it though he smoked and drank. As Fellup Firrel once put it, describing the Golden Mackerel over closed TV to a Boy Scout jamboree, "We are a group of people young in energy who get together because of what we like to do, not because of what we think. *Activity* is our byword; *Do It* our only imperative." The Boy Scouts cheered and applauded, and the M.C., a smiling redhead, walked into the scene, applauding, "Yes sir, scouters," he said. "That's it. That's where the scouting spirit takes you, and that's why we know that Americans everywhere are the big daddies of the world." Peter Prince learned that what Fellup Firrel said was true. Though once in a while the conversation came round to philosophy or politics, and different persuasions were voiced, and even some hostility rising from the elaborately spiced game and the organs of exotic beasts, that hostility would subside again because in the American Way the members of the Golden Mackerel kept their sporting natures. The hostility was rare because the breathing exercise was a cohesive ritual for their brother and sisterhood, like the passing of a peace pipe, or a fraternity handshake, or camp songs; the mingling of their exhalations represented the bond uniting them. Often when members met on the street or at parties they would "take a quick breather," as they put it. It was a kind of trust.

"Yes, I was saying about cats, they're my raison d'être. Not so boring when I can train cats. Spelunking bores me." Fowler Phelps watched Linda Lawrence nip her Nile Valley legumes. He ignored Peter Prince the waiter who wanted him to order. "The substance of life with cats . . ." Peter Prince got his attention. "Creamed chipped Kudu," he ordered authoritatively. "And a sable-fern salad, if the ferns got here this morning. They clog my sniffer when they're wilted." Linda Lawrence made Peter Prince wait. "Cats. Cats," she murmured. "You'll find it delightful," he said. "A bit of the wild." "Skewered lark," Linda Lawrence finally ordered, expecting it would come with a paté.

Peter Prince had the jargon and timing of his new profession. "Koo in five and a lark skew." Old Wang, the ageless Chinese broiler man, stared at Peter Prince and tested his knife-edges on his wrist. "Listen," said Coombs, an older waiter, just before he hoisted a tray and jolted the OUT door with his rear. "It's just like oysters, a little saltier, but they wash it out first." Peter Prince served the rolls, butter in a silver dish, and their favorite relishes.

"Old Wang wants to heave that knife at you," whispered Coombs, when Peter Prince got back. "He's touchy about casseroles, and don't cross him on a rarebit." It was dangerous, a conspiracy against waiters in the kitchen. There was the Kudu casserole cooling on the counter, and it wasn't Peter Prince's fault. He smiled at Old Wang whose expression didn't change. "Could you reheat the Kudu?" Wang hissed and grunted and seemed to throw a knife with his left hand, which Peter Prince ducked. The knife was in Wang's right. "You order the jelled salads too quick," said Flo, the salad lady. Peter Prince could, nonetheless, transform kitchen chaos into elegant service. He served the simmering Kudu, and gracefully slipped the skewers from the larks. Back at the bussing station he watched their faces for hints of satisfaction.

"Waiter," Linda Lawrence called without turning around. Peter Prince moistened one end of his towel just in case.

"Do you remember me?"

" I do, ma'am."

"Do you notice anything?"

In panic Peter Prince scanned the table. "The rolls," he exclaimed. "I didn't bring . . ."

"Not the rolls." She still wouldn't look at him. "But my paté."

"Your paté?"

"With my lark . . . paté. Always paté."

"Don't alienate the lad," said Fowler Phelps. "It's never guaranteed paté, my dear. Would that something were that certain, but never so. The lad will run off and do your paté, if that's what you need. Run off lad." Peter Prince ran off. Hearing himself called lad, that cheered him up. With his Bebo and his Thwang-Nuc and his Ma-Jo apartment Peter Prince didn't think of himself as a lad any more.

"My lad," said Fowler Phelps, after Peter Prince had placed the pate. "You mustn't let your pitfall be timidity. If you want something it's up and face it. Without that I'd have gotten nowhere training cats. That's so." Linda Lawrence darkly lipped her pate.

"Your achievements are remarkable, sir."

"Right." Fowler Phelps half rose from his seat and pulled Peter Prince closer by his red lapel. "Now be good and take this back to the kitchen and have them heat it over. I've been talking so much that it's cooled and chilly creamed casseroles aren't worth eating. Gummy on the palate."

There is no terror, Peter Prince knew, like the fear of broiler chefs. Old Wang stood by the broiler eating his rice with chopsticks. Peter Prince dumped the chilly casserole at the dishwasher and ordered a fresh one. "That's from your own pocket," said Milly Malt, the checker, who saw everything in the kitchen.

"Fine now, fine. Fine." Fowler Phelps grinned over the freshly bubbling Kudu. "You're a fine lad and deserve special treatment. Some day at my private quarters you'll watch me work out with cats."

Even Linda Lawrence was smiling now that she had finished her pate.

Thus Peter Prince became the darling of the Golden Mackerel. Of all the waiters Peter Prince was the favorite. No doubt of it. He was the youngest and had potential. They could call him "lad." They liked him so much that they would ask him to hang around after meals to meet their wives and daughters, and listen to sports lectures and travel tips. The people bored him, but he hung around anyway, though it made other waiters jealous and alienated him from the kitchen crew. He'd hang around, perhaps just to have something secret from the life that had developed for him in Queens, and from Bebo, who was jealous, more than anything, of his evenings at the Golden Mackerel.

*

"Sometimes," she said. "Sometimes you look so disgusted with me. Sometimes you look at me as if I'm despicable, despicable, as if you'd rather be with anyone else but me. As if I'm deformed."

"Fold this shirt," he said. He collected his black socks, his black shoes, his black suspenders, his black cummerbund, his black garters, his polished buttons, his cuff-links, his starched red jacket.

"I'm so miserable," she said, folding the shirt.

"Oh baby, please don't start this again. It wears me out."

"Peter Prince, I'm miserable. I'm miserable." She handed him the folded shirt and stretched out on the couch, pushing her face into the corduroy. In the other room Teresa's blocks were tumbling.

"Do you love me?" she asked, sitting up and holding a cushion on her head. "Do you think that you can love me?"

"That's a question you promised you'd never ask me."

"Do you think . . ."

"No. No. Shut up."

"Then why do you live with me?"

"Bebo, Bebo, please. That's a question I promised I'd never ask myself. I decided to live with you. That's all. I'm here."

Bebo hid her eyes. She was crying. Peter Prince pretended to look for grease spots on his black bowtie, but her sobs felt in him like fists pummeling his chest from within. He wanted to smash her. He'd better not care, he thought, and he left her to clean himself up in the bathroom. He hissed into the mirror at his helpless face. How did he get here? He couldn't give a shit for Bebo and yet he let himself be caught with her in this pressure cooker they called a home. The bathroom smelled faintly of ammonia all the time. He got at least that out of it, a clean bathroom. His shaving brush wasn't in the mug. Bebo often hid it. She knew how much he liked to shave, that it was one of his last intimacies with himself, the hot lather and straight razor, and she wanted a part even of that. It was like a comic routine. She bought him an electric razor, but he wouldn't use it; she got him all the varieties of explosive canned lather, but he couldn't stand them, like grease guns. She was desperate and lonely, he knew, and tried to enter his emotions everywhere, but how could Peter Prince spend so much help on her when the struggle was to keep himself from disappearing. He gave her so little, he had so little left, she was jealous of his shaving brush.

She had moved to the kitchen where she was listening to rock and roll music and pouting. "My shaving brush," he said. She didn't move. He looked in the cupboard, in the cookie jar, among the pots. It wasn't there.

"My shaving brush," he said softly, but firmly. It was a tender issue between them.

She slowly unbuttoned her blouse to reveal the badger bristles between her breasts. When he reached for the brush she kissed him on his elbow-crease. He touched her cheek with the brush.

"I'd like you," she said. "I want you to fuck me right now."

"In twenty minutes I go to work. You know that." He touched her breast with his brushless hand. "And Teresa is up."

"I know all that," she said, and she sucked on her lower lip. "I know all that but I still want to." She was looking at the ground with her hands in her apron pockets, like a stubborn child.

When Peter Prince lathered his face he could hear Bebo press against the bathroom door. "Peter Prince," she asked. "Would you still stay with me if I didn't have Thwang-Nuc? If she were dead?" He turned the faucet on full force so he couldn't hear her and shaved slowly, pulling the lather down with the long blade. He didn't want to have to leave her. He didn't want it to finish badly.

Bebo had turned the rock and roll up and was dancing by herself in the living room as Teresa watched, happily shaking and jerking in imitation. The Beatles: "I Should Have Known Better," "I Want To Hold Your Hand," "All My Loving." "Why don't you," Bebo paused, and Peter Prince winced because it was one of those evenings when Bebo pummeled him with impossible demands. "You never take me with you to the Golden Mackerel. Couldn't you take me with you just one night?"

"Bebo, I work there. It's a private club. I can't just take you there."

"But you stay afterward for the parties."

"They aren't parties. Those people would bore you to death. They stink. They're the worst people you've ever met."

"Then why do you stay there late?"

"If they ask me to stay I can't very well say no. They feel like they're giving me a real privilege."

"I just want to be with people for a change. I want to have someone to talk to instead of floating here fourteen stories up."

"Bebo. Please."

She stared at Peter Prince. "You have some shaving cream on your ear."

Their little girl stared at the argument from the couch with her one good wide beautiful dark eye, her stump raised, as was her habit, to cover the mutilated half of her face. When they looked at her the child began to whistle and grunt, trying to speak American. Bebo took her back to her room and closed her up with her toys, where she was silent.

"She looks like she understands all this stupidity," said Peter Prince.

"I just need to get away from this."

"Bebo, buddy, coming down to that place won't do you any good. Besides, what about Teresa?"

"We'd get a baby-sitter. That's easy."

"We can't get a baby-sitter for her." It was hard for Peter Prince to talk about these domestic things; he threw his words twenty feet out in front of himself and watched them act. "You know the way she screams. We can't ask a baby-sitter to handle that. It isn't even fair to Thwang-Nuc."

"Fair to Thwang-Nuc. To her. To hell with her. Be fair to me for a change." Her face turned white, and she lifted her fists to her breasts.

"Bebo," said Peter Prince. "Be patient."

"I can't be patient. I'm miserable."

The wind shifted, and carried to their home from the airport the noise of rocket-assist take-offs that rattled the Jingo Jalousies and Roll E-Z doors. Bebo's misery nauseated him. He could hardly feel compassion for her tears, her fists beating softly on her breasts. An external, perfunctory pity, was all he'd admit, because he was doing what he could for someone he didn't love, and he couldn't tie himself up. He had to live the life of Peter Prince who was making his own lonely sacrifices. The woman tried to thicken his guilt, which guilt he bore because he loved the child.

"Sometimes I wish that we had gotten a good one," Bebo said.

"A good what?"

"I mean Teresa."

"Bebo. What an evil thing to say. You're crazy now."

"I don't mean what you think," she whispered. "I mean it could have been so much easier if we hadn't had so much pity. We could have picked one without scars, one that was perfectly all right."

"Teresa is perfectly all right. I can't believe you're talking to me this way. Don't talk any more." He pulled his shoes out from in back of the mattress. "Here. Polish these."

She held the shoes in her hand as she hunted for polish. "I mean I wish I didn't have to pity her so much. Sometimes I think I pity her so much I don't have time to love her." She smeared the shoes with black wax.

"Don't say any more." Peter Prince covered his ears. "You're despicable." He went back to the fluorescents by his shaving mirror. His face looked like an apple skin, spotted.

"You see what I said in the first place?" She leaned around the corner. "That's the way you feel about me. Why don't you ever try to understand a fucking thing that I say, damn it damn it damn it. All you ever listen to is yourself."

"Christ," he shouted, and watched the color shift on his face. "What do you think I'm doing here? Why do you think I came to live in this screwy collective mortuary? Because I don't understand you? I took this whole fucking thing on myself." He splashed water onto his burning lips and cheeks. "And I don't want to hear you cry anymore."

"Peter Prince," she screamed, out of sight. "Will you let me come with you tonight?"

"No!"

"Shit," she blasted, on all her tweeters and woofers. He heard his shoes hit the shatterproof.

On the F train Peter Prince relaxed. He needed the anonymity. The subway was his place, it seemed, more than the Ma-Jo development or the Golden Mackerel. He felt at both those places only tentatively welcome; impossible as it was to keep Bebo and a small family happy, so much did waiting tables seem impermanent, a new sport he was learning; but the subway: the stench of passageways, greasy walls, men in the muddy light of change-booths, dealing tokens and sliding coins into pools. It was like a shrine, less likely to change than the city's surface. The subways would be overlooked because they were unprofitable, unnoticeable, a persistent sickness the city had grown used to, and the filthy quaintness wouldn't disappear for a while. It was reassuring, that rhythm of the express. Out of the chaos of his life in the Ma-Jo development, or the frantic worry at the Golden Mackerel of pleasing customers he would walk down into the subway, and from the subway he would emerge into a calmed world, the silence of the dining room at the Golden Mackerel before opening or back to his apartment, when it was quiet, Bebo almost asleep, the radio softly humming. It worked for him the way church must work for some people: He always entered out of the total disorder of his life, and left it to find peace in his life, as if something really happened in there to calm down the world.

Despicable. Despicable. Despicable. That word was caught in the rhythm of the subway car. It had issued from Bebo as if it grew onto her tongue out of her bloodstream. Poor Bebo. Despicable ran in her brain with a steady rhythm like the subway. Had he caused her pain? Could he prevent it? He had entered their relationship with only a limited commitment, to provide, and why did she test him then? Why the tasks, when he wasn't trying to win anything of hers? Miss Subways for that month stole his eyes, a pale and smiling Negress.

"How is it, baby? Man we haven't heard of you for so long, like you've been hiding." Hanging from the handgrip above Peter Prince was a thin man with a spotty beard and long, ash-blonde hair.

"It's been fine," said Peter Prince, before he remembered who the man was. "I mean I've been hassling, but it's been O.K."

"Wow, what a drag. I mean such sadness in Queens, I mean trivial sadness." The man sat down beside him and put on his sunglasses. Peter Prince remembered him, a friend from The Snug, his old hangout, a painter. "How's Bebo? Like things are different without you two around. The groovy people all disappear, I mean it."

"Everything's cool," Peter Prince lied. "I've got a job now."

"Such tragic stories, all my friends lay such tragedies on me. Doing what?"

"I'm waiting tables."

"What a drag."

"I don't mind it."

"Yeah. I guess you always dug those funny scenes, but it's a drag you have to do it. Have you been working?"

Peter Prince read the headlines of the sheet a man across the car was reading: WIFE GRINDS KIDS, FEEDS HUSBAND. He wanted to find out more about that, he couldn't let it go by : the meat-grinder, the kids, the meal with both of them smacking grease from their lips, the ketchup.

"Are you working?" asked his friend again.

"I said I've been waiting tables."

"I don't mean that, baby. I mean working, you know. Writing. You said you were doing a journal thing last time I saw you."

"Yeah. I'm still working on that," Peter Prince lied again. It was that lie he left on the Lower East Side, and it was uncomfortable now to feel it catch him up again. His label, socially, when he lived there, was as a writer, but he never wrote. He'd sit down at a ledger he'd bought on Canal Street to use as a journal, but could only embarrass himself with the banality of what he thought. He'd carry it under his arm, the pages full of shopping lists written slantwise, newspaper cutups hanging out on paper clips. He'd get stoned with his friends and sit down later to write about it, or would try to write while he was stoned, enjoying the making of letters and the slow encouragement of ink marking paper. He rarely finished a word, and when he did he was too exhausted to start a second. That ridiculous inertia, that stupor he was in, made it right to leave with Bebo, and to rearrange his life. He would write some day, he had to, but that day had to come.

"It's a groove if you can keep working, like in Queens. I mean you have to keep working to stay alive anywhere, but in Queens. I can't believe what I see every time I go out there, those housing developments, like tombs. And people in madras, what poverty. It's the death of the eyes." They sat there for a moment, thinking it over. "The death of the eyes." Peter Prince enveloped that phrase and closed his eyes, opening them when the man spoke again. He had a gaunt profile, with small, curled ears, and loose skin that was impossible to shave. "Look. I'd really dig it if sometime you'd make it with Bebo up to my loft. You could read some of your journal to me. And I want you to see my new work. You remember what I was doing? Well everything is changing, like I've exploded. I mean I'm building out of the canvas, and things move, I mean the imagery is the same but it's come alive, as if what I've been looking at all this time is finally talking to me. You have to see it. I mean come any time, and we'll blow some grass and sit around."

"That sounds beautiful," said Peter Prince. "I'd really dig that."

"Yeah, I mean you have to relax some time. You must really be working, you looked so wiped out." Peter Prince didn't feel tired, but he could tell that worry was digging out its permanent design. It was becoming a father's face, a waiter's face. His bearded friend was right, it was time to visit the scene again.

"Listen," said the painter, rising, "I split at Fifth Avenue. Could you lay five on me till I see you? I'm really hassling now, but I expect a job next week designing some toys."

"Sure, baby, here." He pulled a bill out of his wallet.

"Crazy, you're beautiful, thank you. I'll have it back for you when you come to see me. Be sure to make it, please. Don't cop out." He went out the door at the Fifth Avenue station.

Five dollars. It was so easy to touch him for five dollars. Tired Peter

Prince was becoming simple and soft. His family made him tired, his job made him compliant. He didn't even remember where the painter lived. He'd have to hunt for him at The Snug. The five dollars was a down payment on his return to his friends. He'd have to strengthen Peter Prince.

On the way out of the station he bought the sheet that had the story of the meat-grinder murder, and he read it over coffee. It was disappointing. The woman was a giddy fool who was drunk, not hungry when she did it. On the story page was a photo of the husband crying over a pile of what was supposed to be ground child. It was an obvious montage. The husband was quoted. "I didn't know what I was eating. It tasted a little strange but it could have been anything so I asked her if it was horsemeat and she began to laugh and cry like she was crazy." There was no picture of the woman. That night at the Golden Mackerel business was stiff, with much special service: fish to bone, kabob to flame.

*

Peter Prince got home before midnight to find the apartment softly sleeping, a test pattern on their new TV screen, the kitchen lit by the refrigerator light, its door left open, the room filled with the odor of his Limburger. He peeked into the dark bedroom to hear Bebo breathe. She slept well. He would have some Limburger on Triscuits before he turned in. These were the moments he liked in their Queens apartment, this silence when he came home and the wind was blowing toward the airport. In the adjacent apartments he could hear sometimes a heavy-footed creature go from bed to the bathroom. He could hear lightswitches, the toilet flushing, the bed creaking. He sometimes thought about the places he could take Teresa, dress her up and take her to museums and gardens when she was old enough, and teach her about the city, his girl. He wanted her to be something more, something forgiving, lavish . . .

Teresa had begun to cry, small gasping whimpers at first that slowly could grow into her furious fits of screaming. Peter Prince wished she'd get over that, he hated her screaming. If she wasn't calmed down she could go on all night, shrieking.

One night they had let the child scream, hoping she would be cured by knowing she couldn't get attention that way, but it didn't work, and the next day the child, worn out, slept most of the time, and every time she opened her eyes to see Bebo or Peter Prince she would scream at them. The poor child had bad dreams and wasn't able to speak.

Bebo was best at calming her, but she wasn't awake yet, the pillow over her ear. He approached the bed intending to awaken her and then saw the other man in bed with her. It was a Negro, her husband in bed with her again. The inundating notes of Teresa's fright drenched his anger. She lay there with her head under the pillow and he with an arm across her back. It was perfect, homey, the way they breathed together and didn't move. The room was damp, the air conditioner off. Peter Prince quietly switched it on and turned it as cold as it would go. Teresa's screams ran through his skull like a tape recording, another time, away. He waited in the room until he could feel the cold rising, and then he stepped out and closed the door.

He took the child from her bed and let her scream into his ear, while he whispered into hers her Oriental name. Her breath from fear smelled bitter like passion, and her body contracted in spasms like the reflex in a dead limb. He slowly calmed her, trying to hold her still, her forehead cracking against his till her fury subsided into sobs that she pulled from her throat like chains. She fell back to sleep in his arms, drooling on the back of his neck, and he put her down in her padded bed. A light rain had begun outside and the windows were smeared with moisture, blurring the lights from the highways in the distance. He watched the child and tried to listen for noises from the other room. He heard none. The child was sleeping now, a moist spot spreading slowly by her head. Peter Prince stayed to watch her sleep. He knew he should make some dramatic gesture, enter the other room and declare himself free of the mess of Bebo and her confused loyalties, her inability to understand the worth of Peter Prince, her desire for too much, for everything; but the child would be destroyed, that poor, neurotic victim. He felt for her an immeasurable guilt, a pressure in him that made any rational adjustment for him seem trivial. This act, he thought, looking at the maimed child, deserved retribution; this prideless act should be avenged. And Peter Prince let that vengeance be taken out on himself. His fault. It was his fault that Bebo destroyed the loving in herself. It was his fault the child's screaming, his fault the pain, his fault the earthless fourteenth-floor apartment, his fault the jet booms slamming the windows, his fault the mattress, his fault destruction, his fault Bebo's accepting her husband back again, who would degrade her again by leaving. His fault, and he deserved the pain.

Somewhere in the house a couple started arguing, screaming, and throwing things at each other, their running not shaking the house, but audible everywhere like an echo. "Keep all your goddam . . ." "You don't have enough . . ." "You asshole . . ." The whole house had been moving around earlier in the sounds of his argumentwith Bebo, like part of the atmosphere. Every sound made was heard somewhere: Teresa's screams, Bebo and her husband, Peter Prince's late arrivals. The noise released of memories, self-delusion, despair, like a sound track without a film, matching, overlapping, dispersing through the project, and Thwang-Nuc's screams mingled with it all. For all this Thwang-Nuc had been sacrificed to napalm, for these shoddy apartments, for this desperate communal note, for noise of complaints in housing projects sifting through the apartments like dust through rubble.

A door slammed that could have been the door to his apartment. Bebo was alone now, he could see, her head on the other pillow, still asleep. He turned on the light. She smiled abjectly, automatically. "It's icy in here," she said. She was naked, her bathrobe over a chair, a towel in which she wrapped her hair after she showered fallen by the side of the bed. "It's so chilly," she hummed again out of her sleep. He didn't feel the cold. It was just right. He pulled the covers off her chilly body. "Oooooooh," she muttered, showing her teeth in a sleepy smile. His cock was stiff and huge, as if he'd packed all his frustration into it. He undressed. She opened her eyes for a moment and smiled when she saw the cock. "That's nice," she said. "Warm . . ." He caught her mouth with his and pushed easily at her cunt, which opened with a hot explosion, like gas rising through the mud. He wanted to wound her, to split her in two from inside, but she covered his face with kisses and tongued his ear repeating, "I love you, I love you, I love you," in a gentle, confusing patter. Her breath was bitter like Teresa's frightened smell. He clawed her but couldn't hurt her, and she bit at him, matching the fury of his anger with the fury of her lust. She screamed, they screamed together, and felt those screams dropping from apartment to apartment below them, and they came together, her teeth in his shoulder, his hands tearing at her ass.

He rolled over with the pillow under his shoulderblades and took a long breath through his nose. She reached over to finger his cock, which was still erect. "You're so strong," she said.

He closed his eyes. He wished it could be as good as it was, as it seemed.

"As strong as he is?" he asked, not wanting to say it, the words muscling out.

"Who is?"

"Your husband."

She leaned over and tongued his ribs. "I can't even remember what it was like."

Leave it at that, he thought. "He was here," he said.

"What? Who was here?"

"Your husband was here."

"When? When did you see him?"

"You goddam bitch, don't fuck with my head. I saw him here in bed. Where I am right now."

"You're crazy. He wasn't here. I was here all night."

"I saw him, Bebo. I came in here and he was lying here."

"You're crazy to see such things. No such . . . For all I know that idiot is back in Vietnam. He re-enlisted. You know. Peter Prince, you made it up."

"You're lying." He sat up, afraid to look at her. Afraid he would destroy her if he looked into her face.

Her voice became suddenly sweet, playing a moment with the safety of coyness. "And what if he was here? What difference would that make, Peter Prince? He's still my husband, and you're not. He has a right to me that you don't even want."

"Bebo, I'm going to beat the shit out of you." He lifted her head by her long hair and slapped her face. "He was here."

"He wasn't."

"You just admitted it."

"You're crazy. I can't help it. Let go of my hair. That man is thousands of miles away. I was just lying here awake till you came because I wanted to apologize. I've been shitty, Peter Prince."

"You trivial cunt. Sleeping. You didn't even hear Teresa scream. Did you?"

"Teresa didn't scream."

"I suppose I hallucinated that too?" He jerked her head around till her mouth was twisted open in pain.

"Peter Prince, please."

He let go of her. "If this happens once more I'm going to kill you," he said, or he didn't say. He didn't want to remember.

*

But he did remember, and the memory embarrassed him, his outburst of stupidity. After that night Bebo met him regularly at the gatherings of the Golden Mackerel, waiting for him, dressed in spangled clothes, in the employees' lounge. They left Teresa with a baby-sitter, whom they could retain only by paying her double wages after the first night when she realized her duties were to keep calm a terrified child. Peter Prince actually enjoyed Bebo's company at the Golden Mackerel. To his surprise she really enjoyed the people, and knew how to act with them. She'd been brought up in wealth, disowned when she married a Negro, but her own social set had been very much like the Golden Mackerel set, and she could socialize at will, show interest in conversations, and rise discreetly on her toes in enthusiasm when the men described their sporting occupations.

She wore glittering make-up on her eyelids and hair, and never complained to Peter Prince about her clothes, though he could see they caused her some embarrassment in the presence of Linda Lawrence, for example, who was always fashionable, and she would come home sometimes at night and throw her outmoded duds across the bedroom, causing Peter Prince to feel he provided inadequately for her. He needed to provide for her. It was satisfying.

"Poor Peter Prince," she said, when he started bringing new clothes home for her, "You're doing so much for me. I don't understand why."

Peter Prince couldn't come to terms in himself with that stupid jealousy he had felt to see Bebo's husband in bed with her again. He had no right to it, and he knew it was hypocritical. He had come to this new life choosing to bear little of the emotional burden of Bebo, to remain detached from her and to protect the child from too much pain. But his involvement was more than he'd counted on. He had come to dole himself out carefully, and to expect nothing. He had no right, even, to Bebo's loyalty. He wanted to be to her as a tugboat to its barges, pulling the weight, indifferent to the cargo, but that evening he had felt betrayed, though he knew he had no right to feel so, betrayed in some residual memory of family loyalties, because it was a household he had established himself that was violated. He'd been stupid, furious, blinded. He'd threatened to kill her. He had never known that violence in himself before, rising in him like sewage. He disgusted himself. He never wanted to be alone with her again. He wanted to prevent that anger from recurring. It was himself he despised and though he still felt a certain tenderness when they were with the child, and though he was comfortable with her at the Golden Mackerel, all his free time he would spend alone, haunting his old, downtown hangouts, and talking with old friends. He told her he was writing and needed the solitude. This was another turn he hadn't expected, thinking he could never turn back after the change to Queens, that his old life in those corners of indolence was over, and that he would never return. But he returned, and it was comforting, and he pitied himself.

It was a lavish pity in the subways, on the shadowy streets. Sometimes, out of self-pity, he'd spend the night with Milly Malt, the checker at the Golden Mackerel, when her boy friend was out of town. There were no complications with her. She liked Peter Prince in bed. She was taller than he and her sharp voice caused him some discomfort, her face was full of cosmetic scars. She wasn't pretty, but it was uncomplicated.

"I like it this way," said Peter Prince, fingering the fringe on the embroidered cover of her victorian love seat.

"It's strange," she said. "You're just like the last one Old Wang didn't like. Young, energetic, popular with the members."

"What happened to him?"

"He was blinded."

"How?"

"I don't know. He just didn't show up for work, and I was told he was blinded. Then they hired you." She kissed him. "You look scared."

"That scares the shit out of me. Old Wang has death in his eyes when he looks at me."

Milly Malt laughed. "A broiler chef with death in his eyes. Ha Ha. That's rich."

*

One night he searched out his painter friend at the Snug and spilled the whole complaint, cleansing and sickening himself at once. He tried to tell the truth about himself, climbing slowly the rises of self-deception, and dropping in cascading phrases into confession: Bebo, the child, his strange guilt, her lack of gratitude, his lack of concern.

"Oh baby," said the painter, "like that's the whole exploitation scene, that American chick. Like split, and leave it there. It's not your scene," the painter commiserated. "Look, baby, like there's no reason at all for what you told me, for what you just told me. Chicks will do that. They'll try to run your head. My wife played that bit with my work."

Peter Prince kept his eyes off the painter as he spoke and looked about the loft at the obsessive imagery of his work that lay around in disorder. The persistent image was a gun, or more frequently a bullet, done in a variety of manners, sometimes crowds of them with faces, conversing bullets, smiling, coughing, crying, singing. Two wrinkled bullets doing the Watusi. Bullets with wings and enigmatic smiles, bullets polishing their nails, bullets yawning and peeking from their gunbarrels like groundhogs, bullets in bed, bullets, raining from the clouds, bullets in buses, on ferries, on motorcycles, bullets smoking pot, sniffing cocaine, cooking shmeck, bullets playing basketball, delivering sermons, giving guided tours, ice skating, bullets abstracted, gray and blue, riding through stripes of silver and gold paint, like Byzantine icons, motionless. Paranoia. And in the latest work they were beginning to fly off the canvas on springs, to hang down from the ceiling out of foreshortened gunbarrels, bullets on vibrating ribbons, some of them huge, with smiles and wings. The titles were, in some cases, painted right onto the canvas, titles like: *The World Must Be Made Safe for Democracy; There Are No Atheists in the Fox Holes; Force, Force to the Utmost; Pick Out the Biggest One and Fire; I Shall Return; Let No Guilty Man Escape; The Sun Will Go Down on a Million Men in Arms; You Furnish the Pictures and I'll Furnish the War; My Spear Knows No Brother*. One of the compositions called, *The Chinese Must Go*, was just a gun, neatly polished, like a trophy, with a bullet lying just outside its barrel, set on a long, white stand with a tape recorder hidden in it that constantly repeated this message,

"Knock, knock."

"Who's there?"

Silence.

"Knock, knock."

"Who's there?"

Silence.

"I know I should leave, baby," Peter Prince said. "But I'd feel like such a shit to do it."

"The chick doesn't even care. I mean she lays out there with that other cat, with her husband. Believe me, baby, once a chick has had black eyes there's nothing a white man can do. That chick will have him back, and have him back. She doesn't care about you, baby. You're colonized."

Peter Prince knew that the painter's estimation wasn't true. That vindictiveness wasn't Bebo's attitude, because she was pitiful, helpless in her way. She wanted to be able to love Peter Prince, if Peter Prince would let her, and to leave her old husband alone, if only Peter Prince could have it that way, but he couldn't, he had to stay loose. "I've invested all this bread in the place; I mean I own that apartment, you know. And the kid. If you could see that kid. I was never sentimental before, but that kid tears out your heart. She's maimed and neurotic at four years old, and Bebo can't handle it alone, and with her husband it was worse. It's a sweet kid too, and there's something about its being Oriental. This might sound stupid, but I feel guilty about her. Like I'm American and it's all my fault. I never said that before. You know she screams in her sleep, sometimes all night."

"What a drag."

"I don't really mind the screaming. I'm used to it. Like I deserve it. Bebo sleeps through."

"Not the screaming, I mean being American is a drag and getting into the hang-up you're in. I think the worst thing in this world is to be born white Anglo-Saxon Protestant American. With all this guilt. To live in this horror show."

"I can't believe that. I don't like to believe that."

"Right. You don't like to believe it. Right. I believe it, though. I believe we've fucked up the whole world. I believe we're feeding our faces on the whole starving world. I believe that our interests on every continent do nothing but keep the Orientals, the Indians, the Arabs, the South Americans on every continent starving. I believe that. We support the few wealthy up on top with our aid, and turn our backs, not us, but a few of our fattest oil assholes, and murderous munitions producers. We use the oil interests, the natural resources, and fix the industries to our own profit, and nothing goes to the people. They eat the scabs off their arms. We sell them Coca Cola. And we exploit our own poor, foolish population.

We dry out their brains. Even forget the spades, look at the helpless suburbs." As he talked he cut pictures out of old, glossy magazines and arranged them on the table in front of himself, never looking at Peter Prince, and Peter Prince couldn't look at the painter. "I know I sound like an extreme idiot, but I really try to understand it. I try, and I can't. Look at me. I come from a wealthy family, really wealthy. My father is like the biggest packaging engineer in the country. He's the boss of those tabs that keep bread bags closed, of that little strap that holds milk cartons together, of the machine that seals strings of lollipops and gum in cellophane, all that evil, efficient shit. But how can I use any of that money? It's death. It's the death of the world, of the heart. It's the death of the hands. Death of the eyes. Death of the mouth. I mean New York City. It's the best America has to offer, at least in culture and taste, and what are they building? They're putting up this glass and steel nightmare, nothing that a person can look at and want to live in. It's the greed, the money of America, the gluttonous few that deal out grief for everyone. Everyone here is ashamed to look everyone else in the face. Death. And the West Coast, holy shit; we call the spread of that disease down the coast a sign of energy. That's not energy, that's inertia, every house down that coast built to the same pattern. Not enough energy to change an idea, eight hundred miles of the same boredom they build for themselves and call it prosperity. Ha. Energy makes variety and pleasure, not monotony. I haven't even begun to wail about smog, water pollution, food adulteration, obsolescence, plastic idiocy. Baby, I believe it, that we're naively making it impossible for human beings to live, and that we're going to ruin the world if we can. You feel guilty and want to help that little Oriental victim, but what about the rest we're destroying, and will destroy for pride and saving our ugly face?"

"Stop talking."

The painter was suddenly silent, and he looked at Peter Prince, and took all the pictures he'd clipped and arranged and tossed them into the air, and they fell like confetti: faces and car parts and fashions and bottles. "Stop talking? I say the truth, baby. I say it like it is. America is shitting on the world. We're all murderers."

"No," said Peter Prince. "I just can't listen to that kind of frantic wailing any more. It's not the truth. It's as hurtful as what it puts down."

"What is the truth?"

"Wow," said Peter Prince. "I mean all I'm trying to come to terms with is that somehow I'm in the world. I'm Peter Prince, and I'm in motion. That's all I can do. I think I can tell what's not the truth; what is? What is? Just keep ducking."

"Yeah, I see that. Like I could be a Communist but that's bullshit. That's not truth. Politics is all the same bag from any side. But I know we screwed up. We're doing it to the world. I care how the world looks. I pity anyone who sees what's happening, and you, and that poor kid. That's a big thing you decided to do. You're a big man, Peter Prince."

"Sometimes I want to scream like you do," said Peter Prince, looking around again at the bullets and guns. The painter took out a little medicine jar full of marijuana and began to roll joints. "But it's futile to scream. No one hears you. I can't do anything but a kind of silent penance, and there's no time to complain."

The painter put on a record by Jim Kweskin's Jug Band and they smoked in silence, coming to rest. Peter Prince could feel that she was there, Teresa, coming to him as a grown woman. She was whole, and beautiful, and she moved silently, with Oriental grace.

*

The kitchen crew was yapping and the waiters elbowed for position at the pick-up counter. It was a rush night. The pantry women cursed the waiters under their breath as they backed through the door and hurried into the silent dining room. Old Wang was unruffled, and seemed to work more efficiently as he got busier; he never looked up except, Peter Prince thought, to fix him in a yellow stare; it seemed to relax Old Wang, releasing the threat through his eyes. It was an especially busy night for Peter Prince because he was carrying his usual heavy station and a half of

Coombs's station, who was having his piles operated on. It was almost too much for him to keep in his head. Bebo was there, besides, showing up in her spangles in the doorway of the employees' lounge to see if Peter Prince was finished. She was restless and made the crew more nervous.

With Bebo's visits work at the Golden Mackerel began to change for Peter Prince. The resentment the rest of the crew felt for his socializing with the members crystallized when Bebo joined him. She looked like a Golden Mackerel, thin, Anglo-Saxon, and she spoke with their nasal note. Because she was unaccustomed and uncomfortable around their coarseness Bebo could treat Peter Prince's colleagues only with the cold indifference and casual condescension she had learned as a child to use with other people's servants. They resented her, Wang hated her, and this feeling was reflected in their treatment of Peter Prince. He no longer got favors from the pantry girls; if anything, in fact, they would try to put his orders up a little bit off his timing. Peter Prince, however, had become so efficient, able to coordinate in his head so many orders at once, that the slight stubbornness in the kitchen didn't ruin his service; but he had to be, at all times, on top of his memory and in control. Only Wang rattled him, sharpening blades, glaring at Bebo when she appeared, the threat dimming his eyes, daring Peter Prince to make a mistake.

"Listen. Come by this evening after work," said Falkup Firrell who was making great demands that evening. "I want to show you my cats."

Peter Prince rushed past without pausing or smiling. He was swamped. He had to bone a partridge at a table on the other station, and do a crepe service. He was also behind on salads and relishes for his last table. He had to order a mixed game broil and a braised zebra tenderloin medium for he didn't remember whom. He felt chills inside himself, a pressure in his backbone that pushed cold sweat out his forehead. The members showed no sympathy, but were nervous, unfed, complaining. Charlie, his station captain, was nervous too, but he trusted Peter Prince to handle it in the end, to pull it through. Peter Prince didn't trust himself. He had stored up in his head an arrangement of his tables' orders in the order they had to be served, but he knew there were too many, that they were piled precariously and a slight disturbance would topple them beyond reconstruction. He could lose it all, all the orders, the timing, and be paralyzed.

"Pick up one bitty bird and two elk strips," he shouted at Wang as he hastily grabbed his salads, a relish tray, two roll baskets, and called for the crêpe set-up. He avoided Wang's eyes that stared at him and pushed the crepe cart out in front of himself as he carried his stacked tray in his right hand. "You look like you're in trouble," said the checker, Milly Malt. He winked at her bravely.

He got there, served the elk strips, neatly boned the partridge, rolled the crepes in an elegant blue flame of brandy and Cointreau, served some relishes, rolls all around, iced some water glasses, and breathed.

Fallow Falcon tugged on his jacket, "We're getting hungry," he said, looking at his watch. "Can you take our order, old buddy." Peter Prince stood there while they ordered, letting the words register, dodging the dirty glances he was getting from a table of Coombs's regulars across the way. He took some relishes over to pacify Coombs's regulars, who didn't like him, and with his back to Charlie the Captain touched the cold sweat from his brow with his towel, a dining room sin.

All the waiters were lined up at the broiler and Peter Prince had to hold. Bebo was watching from the door of the employees' lounge, and he could see Wang glance at her quickly, furious.

"When will you be through?" she hollered.

"It's busy. Go back in. Quick." He waved her back.

"It's so late. I'm getting bored."

"Bebo, leave me alone. I have enough trouble now. Stop pestering."

He was the last at the broiler pick-up and swept his two orders onto his tray without looking at them. "Hurry up, please," said Bebo, as he accelerated out the door. He arrived just in time at his tray stand, because the customers were turning to look for the maitre d'. He set the zebra tenderloin in front of Felton Firko, and uncapped Linda Lawrence's dish saying, "A little tardy, but delicious just the same." Not till he returned with the roll tray did he notice her face, frozen in displeasure, her hand playing with the comb in her upswept hair. He wanted to ask her why she wasn't eating, to tell her he didn't have time for her to not eat, please. There was something wrong.

She pushed aside the roll tray he offered her. "You do recognize me, don't you?" Linda Lawrence wasn't looking at Peter Prince, but at the plate in front of herself, and he too looked down to see not the mixed broil she had ordered, but the face of Old Wang grinning through a tender portion of broiled sea bass in paprika, with a nest of spinach and bacon. No. He had carried it out without checking, Bebo rapping in his ear, his haste cutting him down. "Aaaaiiii," he despaired. The grin on his face threatened to rip into his cheeks.

"You do know who I am now?" she asked.

Peter Prince looked at Fallen Feller, "I'm quite satisfied myself," he said. He was chewing.

"Young man. Don't you notice anything?" Peter Prince straightened up with his roll tray. "Well, is anything strange?" Her lips were drawn thin like bloody knife-edges.

He wanted to ask her if she would just once eat the sea bass and not send him back, but her stare demanded of him a professional response.

"I'm very sorry. I'll take it back to get your order. It's a terrible mistake."

"Who am I?" she insisted, touching the top of his wrist with her painted fingernail.

"You are the mixed broil, madame," he said, and her lips relaxed into flesh and she let him go.

What Peter Prince should have done was to take the dish through the door, into the street, down to Third Avenue, to leave it on the doorstoop by a snoring wino. He should have said, "Forget it, to hell, I'm fed up." He should have put the dish down at Linda Lawrence's place with the fish still on it and told her to eat it, the trivial cunt, anyway. He should never have taken the extra half station. He should never have taken a job at the Golden Mackerel. He should never have moved out to Queens with Bebo. As he slowly walked out to face Old Wang, hefting the sea bass, he knew everything he should never have done, and would never do again, a pale lightning in his head like a distant storm, the calm now; he was calm, and he thought of Thwang-Nuc in her padded bed sad. He backed through the IN door into the stare of Old Wang like two thousand candlepower of blackness. He put the dish up on the counter. "Sea bass . . . my order was a mixed game broil." He leaned against a wooden upright and closed his eyes.

Old Wang smiled and waved his head on its stem like a swamp-flower and before Peter Prince could see his hands move, his knives were in the air. They revolved once in the yellow light and thudded into the pillar he leaned on and caught him by his excess jacket and pinned him there, the last knife into his crotch-cloth.

"Your mixed broil," said Wang, setting it on the counter, as the whole kitchen crew watched. What could Peter Prince do now? He wasn't in an easy predicament, immobilized and facing a hostile kitchen crew. He couldn't shout for Charlie the Captain and he couldn't move too violently, afraid to rip his waiter's costume. Linda Lawrence, he knew, was devising pain for him while she waited in her hunger. Flo the salad lady, and Betty from the dessert pantry came up to look at him close.

"Look at him," Flo said.

Peter Prince could feel on his face the rancid breath of Betty from the dessert pantry. "He has green eyes; I've never seen that before."

Through his green eyes Peter Prince in desperation watched the mixed broil cooling on the counter. He was losing.

"Please," he asked the two women, "get me loose from here."

"What are you talking about?" Betty asked.

"I need to serve that mixed broil, badly."

"O that. Go ahead. Serve it," said Flo, and she turned to Betty. "You have to admit that there is something cute about him." They hustled back to their station when Charlie the Captain came IN through the OUT door. His face was swollen and discolored. He stopped in front of Peter Prince with his mouth open and seemed to be shouting, though Peter Prince heard nothing. He leaned forward from the hips waving his tongue.

"Please get me loose, I'll serve the mixed broil. I just need someone to get me loose."

Charlie the Captain slapped his own forehead.

"Loose."

Charlie the Captain closed his eyes, and clenched his fists, and gave up.

He picked up the mixed broil himself. "Just pull these knives out," Peter Prince said.

"I'll serve it myself."

"You're through here. That's it." said Charlie the Captain. He carried the mixed broil OUT to the dining room through the IN door.

"I told you," said Milly Malt, the checker, as she came around the pillar. "I told you trouble comes. Now you've really had it." She had the grin of a raven, beautiful, and he saw in her face his own destruction feeding on him and rising from the dust.

"Can't you get me loose from here?"

"I'm sorry, love, I can't do anything for you. It's your hang-up."

"Just loosen the knives so I can pull away."

"You're babbling. What knives? Don't be dumb. You broke down but that's never fatal. You'll recuperate, eventually." She returned to her station. What knives? He looked for them, but he couldn't see them either, but they held him, and he couldn't move. Milly Malt's cash register rang and rang and rang. He couldn't move and nothing was holding him. Nothing. He was afraid to go crazy, sweaty, licking the salt from his lips. Milly Malt's cash register rang and rang and rang. Bebo came by in spangles.

"Peter Prince, will you please finish up. I can't stand waiting any more."

The kitchen had suddenly closed and they were cleaning up, ignoring Peter Prince. He felt his weight bearing on the knifeblades, as if he were on a meat hook. The sweat from his forehead dripped into his eyes, burning them, making him cry, and he could see Bebo only faintly through his mist of tears.

"Come on," Bebo urged. "Let's get out of here." She was impatient to leave the damp kitchen because her hair, which she had teased earlier, was getting unruly.

"Can't you help me, Bebo, out of this predicament?"

"What predicament? You're so damned moody."

"Just help," he said. He felt pitiful, and confused, and embarrassed.

"Oh fuck it, Peter Prince, I'm going to go. I'll see you when you get ready to come out." She left him alone, and he stood there waiting to learn how to move again. They had mopped up around him, put everything away, and left him there in the antiseptic blue light they turned on at closing. He was alone, and he had stopped sweating. He stayed there, afraid, and counted to 52,943; then he decided to try to move an arm. It moved. A leg. It moved. His torso. It pulled away from the pillar. The reason he hadn't been able to move, he realized, was because he hadn't tried to move. It was simple as that.

By the time he had washed and changed almost everyone was gone from the Golden Mackerel gathering, and Bebo had already left, he was told. No one knew, for sure, where she had gone, but there were rumors of going to see cats. It was a kind of relief to Peter Prince that he didn't have to cope with Bebo right away, he felt light, as if he had more power than he needed, like a tugboat with its barges released. He had been through a failure, a defeat, he had not been able to face up to a challenge and it made him feel glorious. On his way back to the subway he dumped his black shoes, his black suspenders, his black cummerbund, his black garters, his polished buttons, (he kept the cuff-links), his starched red jacket into a trash basket. The last time he could remember feeling this good was when he didn't make his high school baseball team. To hell with it, he shouted, I'll go on relief.

The cleanliness of the Ma-Jo development struck him for the first time when he arrived that evening. It was pleasant. He walked beside the dim reflection of himself in the long window of the hallway and he saw through it the freshly painted wall. The reflection made him giddy outside the building, walking beside his own ghost, a transparency of himself beside him through which he could see the new decorations—one corner of the hallway, separated from the rest by a velvet rope, was a model sitting room, use prohibited to the tenants: a wavy mirror in a gilt frame, a few plastic, plushy straightback chairs around an imitation marble table top on a roughly gilt corrugated pinewood stand. A Canaletto reproduced: gondolas on the grand canal coming from the Rialto. He saw all this through his own reflection, and he liked it, the cheap emulation of foreign elegance. It filled him with a kind of gaiety and he kept repeating to himself, "I'm alive, after all."

"Wazah luh borboon kff it," the young, demented son of a tenant greeted him as he came through the entrance. The teen-agers were up late that night, with their portable radios on their ears.

He called Bebo's name as he entered the apartment but got no answer, though a light was on in the living room. He could see through her half-open door that Thwang-Nuc was asleep, the light from the window reflected on her face a soft peaceful sheen. Bebo wasn't home, and he didn't see the baby-sitter; but under a light on the living-room couch a Negro man was reading. It was Bebo's husband. Peter Prince leaned on the entryway. The man saw him, and stood up, and backed around the side of the couch, and placed his left hand on the backrest. He was half in light. "I dismissed your baby-sitter when I got here. I'm waiting for Bebo." He took six steps to the wall and stood facing it, in darkness.

Peter Prince took four steps into the room and folded his arms across his chest, right over left. "I don't know where she is." He pivoted, took three steps, and pivoted again.

The man turned, took five steps toward Peter Prince, stood still and silent for three minutes, then lifted his left arm to point a finger at Peter Prince. He remained silent. Peter Prince moved around the upraised arm and backed away from the man. When the chairseat rubbed the backs of his legs he sat down. "Sit down," he said.

The man took eight steps diagonally across the room to a wooden rocker, decided he didn't want to sit in it, moved sideways five steps to the couch, and sat there, removing a book from under himself.

Peter Prince looked at him. It was the first time he had ever been able to examine Bebo's husband close up. He was surprised. He had expected someone thicker than himself, not this slender man, but a finger-snapping stud, something sweaty and sensational, not this fine-boned blackness, pink lipped, his voice tired and thin.

"You think I'm an ignorant, irresponsible black bastard for leaving Bebo and the kid, but you make allowances for me because I'm a nigger." He let his right arm slide from the armrest and moved his left hand to his chin, touching it with three fingers.

"I never thought about that," said Peter Prince, he leaned forward from the waist, and placed his hands palm to palm in diving position.

"People tell you you're noble to take over this mess, and you probably expect from me some of the same recognition, the community opinion, since I'm called the cop-out in this case, but I won't . . ."

"I don't expect anything." Peter Prince extended, palm up, his empty hand, and raised it toward the ceiling.

"I won't because you're a white man."

In three distinct motions Peter Prince rose, took nine steps to the window, and pressed his palms to the glass. The Negro rose too, arrived at the window in four steps, and put his right hand up to the glass, his left rested on the climatizer. They saw the lights snapping off all over the Ma-Jo development. They saw some cars on the highway. They saw planes leaving the city and arriving.

"You see I'm clean, because your guilt is so immense, white man, it washes the sin out of my desertion, and you're trapped in that guilt, and your guilt lasts forever."

"I don't think . . ."

"I'm talking now, baby. It's your hour for silence. You see you know the weight of our flesh, and you're carrying it, tons of nigger-meat, and that makes us light. We move quick. Because that little yellow child, and you know it, could be my little sister that you hold on a pitch fork in the flames of the cross. You did that, over and over, and that's why you should be grateful that I copped out at all."

Peter Prince turned from the window, took four steps to the couch, and leaned his belly on the backrest. The Negro moved two steps over at the window to where Peter Prince had been. They both pivoted to face each other.

"So don't expect this nigger to thank you." Left thumb to belt buckle, back of right hand to cover right kidney.

"I don't expect anybody to thank me." Right knee raised, left index finger inside shoe to scratch instep.

Right black index finger across pink lips. "Shhh. Keep your cool. I mean I understand why you'd want to move your complexion in on a darkie girl, to get all that passion." Black moves six steps toward couch, and leans on armrest.

Two white hands compress the air between themselves and a soft clap escapes. "Bebo isn't a, you know she's not a . . ." White stops talking without being interrupted. Black smiles, and scratches kinky hair with fingertips pinker than the backs of his hand.

"She isn't a nigger. Your powers of observation are a credit to your race. A credit to your race. To your race's credit. I enjoy saying that. But there's one thing you don't understand, or maybe aren't aware of; you see, the injection I gave her doesn't wear off, master. If I were you I would never let another nigger in my house."

White takes twenty-two steps to the refrigerator, and black takes eight to the rocking chair. Nineteen steps bring white back to the sideboard with two bottles of beer and two glasses. Black rocks. White pours one bottle into the glass on the right, the other bottle into the glass on the left. White takes two steps with the glass on the right and hands it to black. Six more white steps to the couch and white sits down.

"Why do you attack me?"

"What a display of corpuscles when you can call the truth an attack."

"I came to live here because I was fond of Thwang-Nuc."

"Simple as that."

"Simple as that."

"And I should polish your shoes for that simplicity."

"Why can't we talk to each other?"

"We are talking to each other."

"I mean as people. As people."

"We are talking as people. I'm black, you're white. That's people."

"I'm Peter Prince."

"I'm Coleman King."

"I want you to know me. Me."

"You're getting to know me, boy."

"But I know nothing."

"Bebo will get here, and she'll speak first either to you or to me. She'll look first either at you or at me. She'll want to ball either with you or with me. Black or White. The North Pole, The South Pole."

"Nothing."

At the laughter that followed Coleman King's last words Peter Prince rose and took five steps back to the window. It was nothing, and that was right. Venom over nothing, jealous over nothing, slogans to protest nothing, Ma-Jo erected on nothing, the jetliners rising out of nothing in the terminals—LaGuardia nothing, Idlewild nothing—lifting their cargo of white bodies, no one, going nowhere. The power defended, the power envied, the power over nothing, which was the world, and what was really there was the brink, always the edge on the words, the beings in confrontation, their edges honed, so many crowds rubbing along the razor's edge, generations in and out of nothing, of empty crowding, of the noise-mass rising. He looked at Coleman King who was rocking in the chair, and staring at nothing. He sat down on the couch silent with Coleman King, and Peter Prince stared at nothing.

He sat there all night sleeping like a bird with open eyes and was awakened in the morning by the colored marching band practicing Sousa in the parking lot. The other man was already gone, and Bebo hadn't yet come home. He went to the child's bedroom to look at her for a moment among the blankets. He loved to see her sleeping. She was silent, she hadn't screamed all night, poor, wounded child. Her face still held that strange sheen he had noticed the evening before. Her burnt side was exposed, the scar tissue shiny and stiff like wrinkled ceramic. Something was different. He could hardly see her breathing. He stared at her blanket to see it move just a little in the blue shadows. The breathing was faint, if at all. He touched her hand that was cold, the joints stiff. Her face was covered by a fine, plastic membrane. Nothing. She didn't breathe at all. Peter Prince turned away to the window where her room faced the repeated forms of the rest of the Ma-Jo development. "No," he said, and tried to tear the membrane from her face. It stuck to his hands like oil. It was a plastic cleaning bag (I told you to look out for that plastic cleaning bag). It tried to smother his arms. Nothing was there. She had been dead. Right. That was it. Nothing had come in a plastic sack and had roosted on her face.

*

"Ninety-four point three," said Philip Farrel.

"Both rectal and oral?" Linda Lawrence asked, sitting up with the sheet drawn to her chin.

"Both."

"Well," she chirped. "I guess it's alright. I guess everything's O.K. then."

"How can you say O.K., alright, can't you see what's going on?"

"It's normal, for me ninety-four point three is normal." She swung her feet down to sink them into the lavender fur of her slippers.

"Not that. I mean Peter Prince and the child, look what's happened there. How can you call everything O.K. with that going on?"

"Of course it's O.K.," she insisted, dropping a black slip over her head. "You're so gullible. If you look at things long enough and hard enough they're O.K. Just go back and read that section over, sentence by sentence. There are some nice sentences in it. What more do you want? Some nice style, some neat scenes. It's emotionally packed, but it's well written just the same. Read it some more. What do you have to worry about?" She put out for herself her sequined yellow sheath and delicate narrow blue-gray Italian suede shoes.

"I'm worried about Peter Prince. A few moments ago you were worried about Peter Prince yourself. How do you turn off so quickly?"

She did a small rotation on her vanity bench, holding poised in front of her face her eyebrush flecked with pale blue mascara. "It's not that I turned off, it's just that I know now."

"What do you mean, you know? What do you know?"

"I know that things will be alright because Peter Prince is leaving the country."

"When? How do you know this? When is he leaving the country?"

"In the next scene, you imbecile. He's leaving in the next scene. Don't you remember? It was written long before this last one. In fact it's been around to publishing houses, literary journals, Guggenheim foundations, long before Bebo was even thought of. It's archaic. In a sense you don't even have to worry about what's been happening so far, because as far as I can tell the story begins in the next scene. Of course if you're sick of the whole thing you can just walk out through Gottlieb's Exit on the next page, don't worry. You're free. As for Peter Prince, he's shipping out." Her last touch was the sparkle she sprayed in her hair, and she walked out through the door in a sputtering of sequins.

Philip Farrel waited till she left, and then turned around to gaze back through the pages he'd come. "Can't anybody do anything? Doesn't anybody have some control?" he shouted down the mute, irretractable corridors of sequence.

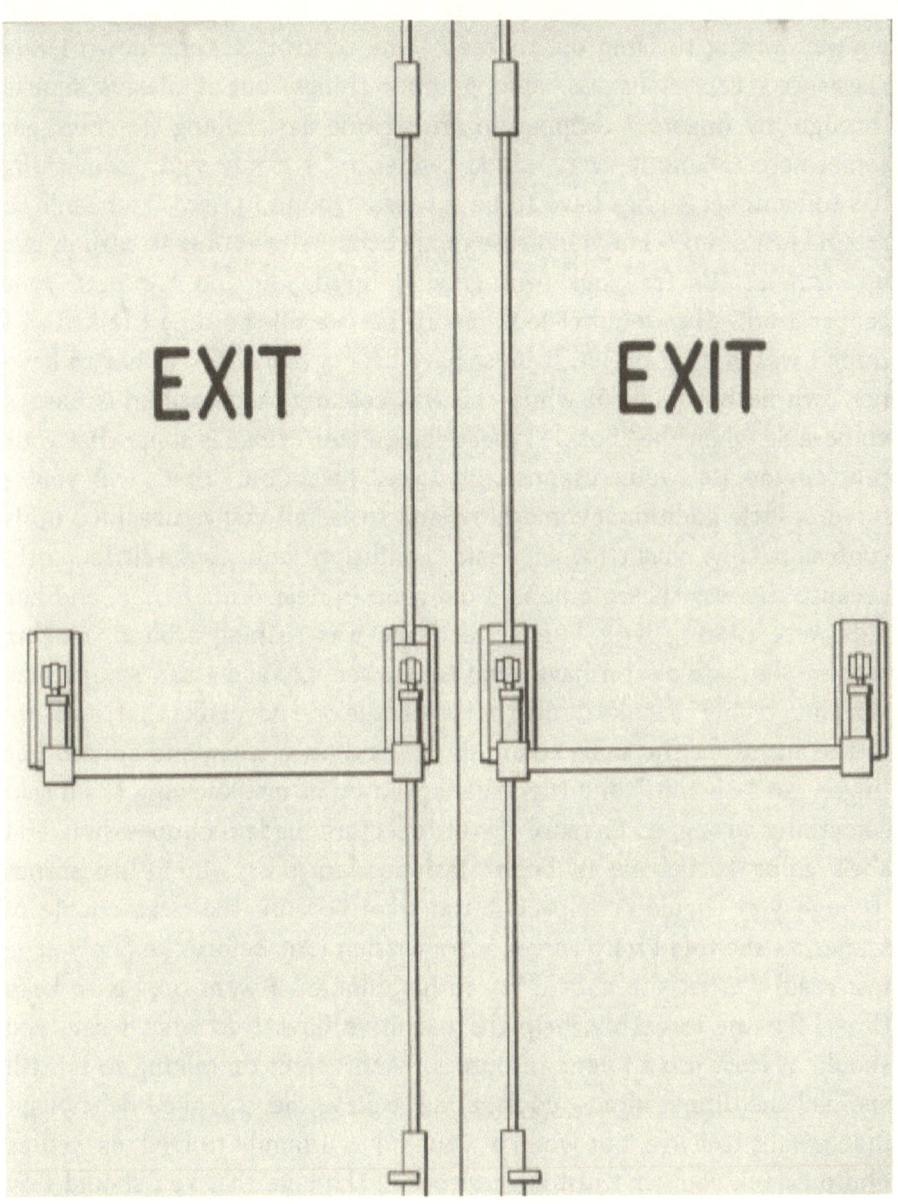

EXIT
EXIT

I've tried to reassure Philip Farrel that I've been holding up my end anyway, trying to hang on, to keep some control, to tone down Linda Lawrence's capriciousness, among other things, but it always squirts through my fingers. I dropped in on her one day, hoping we could get somewhere talking it over. "Linda Lawrence," I firmly said, "something has to be done. Things have to be squared around in here. You can't go around just doing what you please in my book. Who's going to read it, put up with it? It's for your own good. I hired you and I expect your cooperation." She wouldn't look me in the face all the time I talked so I think I was getting to her. It must have been a real shock to her to have her own author walk in while she was cooking. A character is always vulnerable when she cooks. "I mean look, Peter Prince is somewhat your problem too. He's your responsibility here," I went on. "That's why you're hired, a little additional something, and so far all you've dreamed up is confusion." She blushed when I said "confusion" and cried a little, partly because she was slicing onions. I did drop in near dinner-time, and her kids were roaring with hunger, and she was rushing around, making sauces. She didn't even have time to answer me, and I can sympathize with her, trying to make dinner in the middle of a novel like that, and talk to the author at the same time. All she said once when she burned her finger was "Oh shit!" and then she looked up at me, knowing she'd said something wrong, so I'm sure my little lecture made its impression, and she's going to behave in better fashion, less bossy, in future scenes (though you shouldn't expect it too soon because the next couple of scenes, as she told Philip Farrel, were written long before the one you've just read). "What you should try to help doing," I went on, "is to keep things flowing smoothly, help the narrative flow. I do what I can, you should at least use all your resources." And I went on talking to her till she had the dinner almost cooked and, believe me, it looked delicious; I didn't want to leave, but when a woman has a family to feed, as well as Philip Farrel, you can't just suggest out of the blue that you should stay for dinner, especially when you've been hanging around uninvited in a kind of official capacity.

I was really hungry, but not just a hamburger hunger, so I figured to hell with it, and I came back here to my study. I realized that there was some truth in what Linda Lawrence said to Philip Farrel, that in a sense the story is just about to begin, with Peter Prince heading overseas. Those of you who are already worn out by this book, I don't blame you. You can turn back a page and go out through Gottlieb's Exit. Goodbye. Believe me, if I didn't have these responsibilities I'd take off with you. Meanwhile I was so fired up over my lecture to Linda Lawrence that I came back here and made this into the neatest study you've ever seen: everything is in stacks and piles and bunches, books on the shelves, labels on everything, notices tacked up, cards in cubbyholes, and then, because as an artist I believe that you should always oppose society a little bit I tacked the following notice from the *Humboldt Star* and *Battle Mountain Scout* on the window of my door, in clear violation of rule #2:

$825

REWARD

for information leading to the discovery
of the whereabouts of
DELBERT HOWARD

He was a fine man, an Indian who represented the Piutes at the intertribal council, and served as president of that council, and now he's missing, disappeared, feared dead, and I should like to help in what little way I can.

This book continues as follows:

*

It was ready on time, the dinner was, whatever that time was, and the dinner was there on the table and he still wasn't home, whenever he was supposed to be home—on time—he wasn't home on time. And she had to consider the children: Martin and Joseph, Wanda, Timothy the Hammer, Clyde, Margie-in-cottons, Tucker, Toby, Bemmy (the year of the flood),

Kipper, Tuck, Marsha or Joyce or Wendy, Flinch, Spurt (with her withered arm), Candy and Rudolph, Jane I, II, and III, the Michaels, Philomel and Carloman, Wimpy, Toulouse (after the city rather than the painter), Tancred, Bert the lapdog, Ari, Beverly, Four Anthonys, Mitchell, Lotty's direct approach, Corfu (a windy day but the water calm), Ozark, Gregory and Leo, a pair of Archies, Jonathan, John, Tickle, and not to forget little Bobby. The table was almost set. She placed a porcelain boat of cold green sauce between the boiled calf-heads. The children would soon get cross and restless and begin to whimper. She stepped back to look at her table set so invitingly, the calf-heads a steaming centerpiece, and the little brown potatoes around. O slippery love. Once her husband had come home on time for dinner and they had a happy table, the children dividing among them tongue, lips, jowls, ears, cheeks, nose, leaving the eyes for little Bobby and the brains for Mom and Dad. The children sat politely at their places and waited now, with hardly a noise from them. That wouldn't last forever.

At twenty-seven she felt mashed; not by her children, each of whom shared equally her abundant love, nor by her husband who, as his desiring of her dwindled, would offer her only more and more brittle praise, love saved for his mistresses: He had his own weight to carry; but by the fraying of her own dreams: The Linda Lawrence that she could have been unraveled into the Linda Lawrence she was. A gnat was grunting in her sauce boat and she picked it out with a pewter spoon and glared at its smothered wings. The particulars of her life had turned as banal as the details of a French novel, one of those books about a woman disintegrating in her delusions. She wanted her husband to come home. She wanted Philip Farrel to come home.

Home. Through the gate, down the garden walk, his raincoat billowing in the river breeze, 43 dreams bore him up in the elevator. He thought of his friend, Peter Prince, who by now had passed Gibraltar and was standing aft to watch the dolphins playing in the wake. Was Corky Cluny on his arm? Did she love him? Would he, after everything, stand up to her? The question is: How strong is Peter Prince? Next to him stood a Greek seaman traveling tourist class, back to work for Onassis; a handsome man of forty-five, thick-shouldered, his long gray hair pasted to his skull in thick locks. He stood in the center of the deck and stared out back of the ship, as if he could still see Gibraltar.

"This is the most exciting thing that has ever happened to me," Corky Cluny said, squeezing the forearm of Peter Prince. Peter Prince lifted his arm from the deck-rail and shook loose of Corky Cluny's tiny grip. He couldn't listen to the banal particulars of her still-born emotions in the presence of Nikos, who had lived, precisely because he had suffered, and she not yet; but Nikos had lived.

"Do you find that Greek fellow more interesting than me?" Corky Cluny asked, and turned to face Nikos, who hadn't moved. "You've spent more time avoiding me during the day so you can find time for him than you spend at night in bed with me. I may as well disappear. You treat my feelings as if . . . You were never like this before we set out. Only since you met him." She hurled her white fist at Nikos who turned to them now.

"Very calm today," Nikos said, and smiled.

"I shouldn't let you even come near me," Corky Cluny whispered at Peter Prince. "You don't care about me." She let her fist drop and faced the sea again. A gust of wind blew her red hair away from her face to reveal her one crumpled ear. Peter Prince smiled to see the anger breaking so like waves inside her. She spoke through her teeth: "I should let you find someone else to sleep with."

"That would be interesting," replied Peter Prince.

"Sssssssssss," she hissed at him, narrowing her eyes and folding her hands together in front of her face. She lowered that doubled fist into his chest. "Sssssleep with him." She thrust her chin toward Nikos who was now squatting on his haunches and studying the young couple. She slipped her knuckles down his chest to his belt and pushed till he had to grab the rail for balance. Peter Prince turned uncomfortably to watch her escape down the deck. She swung her hips disjointedly in a parody of sexiness. Peter Prince wanted to laugh loudly enough for her to hear, or to shout after her some crumbling invective.

"Peter has his trouble with the women." He felt Nikos' hand squeezing his shoulder, and he turned to shake it off.

"No trouble." He tried to smile.

They looked out toward Europe in silence. Behind them a plump, young Yugoslav woman had come on deck with her little child and he was playing at the bulkheads.

"That girl," Nikos said, "Corky, she is very good. She means a lot to you."

"Not so much," Peter Prince said.

Nikos turned to look at the Yugoslav woman who leaned now on a rail and stared out toward Africa. She was humming.

"I should like to find out about that one," he said. "She has an ass like a Greek woman. Did you ever think about her?"

Peter Prince was always suspicious when Nikos talked to him about women that he was trying to catch him being American and foolish.

"I haven't noticed her," said Peter Prince.

"Oh! You haven't noticed her. You Americans are eunuchs. You don't know what the appetite is we Greeks have for the ass. That's why the women like us so much. A girl like your Corky with all that pretty you find in her hair and eyes only. It's the sweetness of the buttocks I look for. You've got no substance. You see what happens when you get Corky Cluny started the Greek way."

"Nikos. You talk like one . . ." He looked at Nikos, and shook his head. It was frustrating to feel more mature than the man whose manhood you wanted to emulate. Peter Prince moved along the rail to the stern where he could watch the Mediterranean churned out behind the ship. That sea was so still one felt suspended looking out any distance over it, like the gulls, dipping and balancing, in the turbulence behind the ship, waiting for garbage.

"I don't understand, Peter Prince," said Nikos, following immediately, "you tell me your Corky means 'not so much,' and you leave as soon as I talk about her. What is 'not so much'?"

"Will you please leave it alone. Leave it alone," Peter Prince yapped.

Nikos laughed. "You are very young." And they both stared out to sea.

"Now do you see it?" Nikos suddenly leaned over the rail.

"What?" asked Peter Prince, and he turned around, the Yugoslav woman and the child were gone. A few stewards smoked cigarettes by the door to the galley.

"Out there," Nikos said, "the Costa Brava."

Peter Prince gazed toward Europe but could see nothing but the emerald and blue and gluttonously beautiful sea.

"It's very beautiful," said Nikos. "The most beautiful coast on the whole Mediterranean, I think, but for my islands."

"You think Greece is more beautiful?"

"Ohey!" said Nikos, "there is nothing like my Greece." He shrugged and smiled and laid an arm on Peter Prince's shoulder. "Do you know what I like more than anything?" he asked. "I like little babies."

Peter Prince laughed. "What makes you say something like that?"

"I am going back to Greece, to Lemnos, to see my little baby."

"I didn't know you had a wife."

"Yes."

"How long have you been away?"

"Almost two years now. I made the baby before I left, and now I'm going to go back to hold it in my arms." Nikos' maturity was an eternal boyishness.

"And then what?" Peter Prince asked.

"Of course," Nikos said, "for Onassis I'll have to go away again. But first I'll make another baby."

"You're crazy," Peter Prince said.

"Hah!" said Nikos, and raised his arms.

Peter Prince glanced out again toward Europe. "I see it," he suddenly shouted, surprised by the Costa Brava, the pastel cliffs, pale blue and green and yellow, cleaving the sea from the sky.

"By our seas," Nikos said.

Peter Prince looked to Spain and wanted to cry and he looked at Nikos and wanted to embrace him as if he too were coming home.

"Did you ever miss your wife?" he asked.

Nikos laughed. "It would be no good coming home, would it, if I hadn't missed her?"

"But do you think you'll want to get away again?"

"When you marry Corky Cluny," Nikos didn't answer the question, "you'll start to make babies. That's when you begin to care about everything."

"I don't think I'll marry my Corky Cluny," Peter Prince replied.

"There are many Corky Cluny's," Nikos said. "One of them you'll marry."

"And your wife?"

"There are as many women like my wife as there are islands in my country, but there is one difference." Peter Prince liked about Nikos that he could speak without changing his expression, so different from the Italians, no inscrutability, but an absolute confidence.

"That difference is what?" asked Peter Prince.

"The difference is obvious." Nikos blinked slowly and placed both his hands on Peter Prince's shoulders. "The difference is my baby, whose soft hair I'm going to touch, whom I shall take in my arms and rock because babies like to be kept in constant motion. You should hear the way I can sing to babies."

"But any other woman could give you a baby."

"Not this baby," Nikos said.

"You've never seen him."

"But I know him."

Peter Prince wanted to giggle. "Would you say then, Nikos, that there are many Corky Cluny's but that only she would give me the child that she would give me?"

"You can't decide that at all until it's time."

"When is the time?"

"The time is when the child is in the womb; then you know if you are pregnant or not."

"I don't intend to become pregnant, Nikos."

"I've known many confident people who are surprised."

"You don't think I have a choice?"

"You don't know anything," Nikos said softly. "Look out there," he pointed toward the shore, "it's gone." When Peter Prince looked this time he saw that the coast had faded back into Europe and there was only sea and sky. "We tease ourselves to think we can choose anything. Do you expect to know when to choose?"

"Is this one of the songs you sing to the babies?" Peter Prince smiled.

"I'm singing to one," Nikos responded, and left Peter Prince to look for someone with a cigarette.

Peter Prince hoped to find Corky Cluny on the foredeck. It was almost time for lunch. A Greek couldn't understand the relationship between an American man and woman: the reciprocity. How the relationship faltered when one of them had nothing to give, and there were moments when one or both of them could give everything. Commitments were temporary, to allow each his own privateness, each one himself to be transcendent, when he felt his own heart inside him to have grown apart in its largeness from any association possible with others: That was America, he thought, incommunicable: The huge, individual hearts in counterpoint, at every moment creating a tradition of themselves: And when they met, two people free of each other in petty mundanities, each of them in truth egotistical, and they coincided for a moment in hugeness, and they transcended that moment together, expanding with the infinite present to obliterate time, and to live, at once, forever. That's what Peter Prince thought as he passed the engine room, the old diesels of the *Saturnia* chewing distance, and his sigh, as he moved to the forward deck, flowed out from him in expanding rings to the last dense circle of his horizon that included then the route to the Asias, Africa, and Europe in its sweep.

He spotted Corky Cluny at the rail, vomiting over the side. "I think I'm seasick," she said, lifting her green-hued face above the rail, and looking at him sideways, tears blearing her eyes, her lips fouled with bits of food.

Peter Prince moved closer to her by the rail so his arm felt the beat of her slight body. "Are you all right?" he asked.

"I'm seasick," she said, and began again to vomit over the rail.

"Will you be able to come to dinner?" he asked, and he covered with his arm the skin exposed where her skirt and sweater separated as she leaned. She didn't answer him. "Will you be able to talk to me? I need to talk to you now."

"I'm sick," she straightened up, "look at me." A convulsion climbed her torso and she leaned over the rail again, vomiting dryly.

Peter Prince leaned over beside her. "Strange that it should happen now on the calmest part of the voyage. The ship could be standing still. You weren't sick before at all. Why do you think . . ."

"Stop talking. Take me down to the doctor." The loudspeaker announced the lunch.

Peter Prince left Corky Cluny in the doctor's office and went to lunch. Of the German couple that sat with them at the table only the girl had arrived, a skinny, wry-faced aryan, with bloodshot eyes and lips tobacco-stained.

"I hate him so much," she whispered, "and you think I love him, but I hate him."

She leaned over her plate to stare at Peter Prince who looked up at her from his pasta. "You should eat your pasta before the waiter takes it away," he said.

The girl stuffed down a few mouthfuls.

"And drink some wine."

The girl did.

"I hate him. You think I didn't pay for him all the time we were in Canada. For two years I worked and he sat around like a swine. He'll know the worst of it. I paid for his ship to go over too, and we traveled everywhere on my money and he ate like a pig: hamburgers and french fried potatoes and lobster tails and hot dogs; while I worked till I'm so skinny as you see me and now when I'm upstairs he's downstairs or when I'm downstairs he's up, always the same thing, with a girl. Now he won't come to dinner because he's with a girl, the pig."

During her tirade her boy friend sat down to his pasta and ignored her as he noiselessly sucked the spaghetti into his narrow, hairless face, the strand-ends slapping his lips. While the girl went on talking he looked from time to time at Peter Prince and drew his reddened lips back from his teeth.

"When we get home it won't be so easy for him. I'll tell his family and they won't leave him alone. Every day how he ignores me for these other women. He doesn't eat like a German boy, but like a pig."

"Oh be quiet you noise-maker."

"You see," she said, without turning to the boy, "how he talks to me. As if I meant nothing to him. You would be surprised if I listed the things he has done to me, and I have done everything for him. Everything." She reached across the table and took Peter Prince's wrist. He pulled away quickly, rattling his plates. He wished she understood that when he ignored her it meant he didn't care to hear any more. He wished his Corky Cluny was there to take his attention from the Germans. He despised them. They had been hating each other since the first day, and that hate, he felt, had infected the voyage for him, had turned him against his Corky Cluny, had made her sick, and if it hadn't been for conversation with Nikos would have ruined the voyage entirely.

The boy was talking now, taking over the polemic from his girl friend, ". . . as if she's the perfect 'fräulein,' the perfect little German girl. These stories she tells. Look at her. She's got a wart beside her nose that bleeds whenever I touch it. She is ugly. She tells you these stories. I could tell about her some stories: the wasp . . .

"Would you please hate each other quietly. There has already been enough of your hating." The two were silent for a moment, and then began again their spite. Peter Prince left without finishing his dinner and breathed on deck his first damp lungful of the sirocco. No one else was on deck, and he could see on the bridge some officers stirring, and watching him. He sat down in a deck chair and watched two jetstreams curve northward, the fuselages catching the sun. He meditated on war, how terrible it would be this time: The sound of it. He wasn't ready for a war. The compounding of misery. That German girl was so unhappy, and yet he couldn't take her German unhappiness seriously because she expressed it with such abject bitterness, and forced it on strangers. True to form the Germans were. But it was just the depth of her misery that made her shove it against anyone who listened. The jetstreams thinned and bent in the twisted currents of the stratosphere. He couldn't hear the planes, their noise orbiting out there. How did he sound with Corky Cluny? Did he make her so unhappy, and did they together seem as petty in their spite as the two Germans? And Corky Cluny; he had forgotten her completely.

He realized that he was more concerned than he had pretended to be, because after a long search that took him to her cabin, through the deck chairs of all three classes of the ship, back to the infirmary, up again to the dining room, into the gymnasium and chapel, he found that he was sweating, dreadful and cold. He found her finally in his own bunk with Nikos seated on a stool beside her, and Nikos was saying nothing, but watching her sleep.

"I have made this damp towel for her head," Nikos said, "she has a fever. She came to the dining room to look for you after you were gone and I could see that she was sick."

Nikos rose from the stool and motioned for Peter Prince to sit down and felt Corky Cluny's brow. She wasn't very hot. Peter Prince liked to look at Corky Cluny when she slept, to watch the peaceful heaving of her belly. She was pretty then, her expression free. Nikos stood by the sink washing, suds caught in his hairy wrists.

"I didn't know where you were," Nikos said, "and someone had to do something for her. I'm going to go now to find something to eat." Peter Prince closed the door after Nikos went out, and as soon as Corky Cluny heard him on the stairway she sat up on the edge of the bed with her hands folded between her knees.

"They told me I might be pregnant. I'm glad your son-of-a-bitch, that friend of yours has left. I would have castrated him if he laid another hand on me; the way he pretended to own me because he found me sick. And I was thinking he was queer for you. He's queer for anything that will melt under his palms; he wanted to give me a sponge bath and to show me what they do in Greece. He assured me I'd like it, on my stomach, with my knees drawn up, or on my hands and knees, and that there'd be no danger 'that way.' He stopped when I told him that under his influence you'd been trying to get into my asshole for two months and that I wasn't learning that trick. He didn't expect vulgarity from me, and it set him back; but I think he was just about to whip out all his love potions when you came in."

"Stop. What's gotten into you?" Peter Prince sat down on a stool by the bed.

"Your fucking child."

"Stop it. Speak reasonably. I want to know what that doctor said."

"He said, '*Buon giorno*,' and after he took my temperature he asked me to lie down on the table. Men like me in that position. Then he gave me a rectal examination. You see how attractive it all is."

"That's pretty damn unorthodox."

"Peter Prince, you know that men always look at me as if I'm standing on my head. Corky Cluny's Caressable Cunt. She cleans it, keeps it sound and well trained, and now that it's seeded . . ."

"Cool it and tell me what he said."

"I told you. He said that I was with child, belted, incinta. There's nothing wrong with me."

"Is he sure?"

"What difference could it make to you? I'm the one. It can't mean a thing to you. The suggestion of it is pretty nice, though; brings a lump to your throat. I mean that all our fucking comes to at least something more than conversation. You don't have to worry."

"Of course I have to worry. Of course it makes a difference to me."

"Don't begin to brag, Peter Prince, too soon. It shouldn't make any difference to you in any way. You can't be responsible."

"What do you mean by that?"

"I mean just what it seems."

"Will you try to tell me that I'm not responsible for . . . That I'm not the . . ."

". . . not the father?"

"That's possible," she said.

"I think you've invented this whole thing."

"That's possible too." She leaned back against his pillow and filled her lungs. "I feel better," she said. "More like I'd like to." She smiled at Peter Prince, showing her little tongue between her teeth. "Why don't you fuck me?"

"How can you do this to me?" Peter Prince pleaded. "Will you please tell me where I stand. You behave like an old whore."

"The old whore has already said," said Corky Cluny, faintly smiling, "and you heard me." She pulled the pillow from under her head and covered her belly with it. "Right now you stand on the ground," she giggled, "excuse me."

"You're not being very fair to me. If I were pregnant . . ." Peter Prince took a deep breath, and lowered his head, and put his hand to his cheek, and blew out slowly, finishing with the syllable "suck."

"Well then," Corky Cluny wiggled under his sheet, "will you bring me some supper when you go up? A bit of antipasto. I'd like to be served supper in your bunk, especially after you've fucked me three hours."

"Why do you avoid talking to me about what happened with the doctor? You're impossible. Isn't something going to be done. Can't something happen?"

". . . to see her belly rise," Corky Cluny sang.

"Could you have an abortion?" asked Peter Prince, weakly gesturing, with eyes closed, toward her face.

"I don't want to talk about that."

Peter Prince could say nothing else, so he undressed. Corky Cluny was undressed before him and lay on the bed with her arms spread and raised, her legs bent at the knees and spread, and she waited for him to settle as a boat into its trailer. He stuck his tongue into her crumpled ear and she switched on.

"This is what I like," she moaned, "oh do I like this."

Peter Prince was indifferent to the fucking, though he did it well, and kept Corky Cluny in motion, causing her to sweat and fart and sing. He wanted to please her now and didn't care about coming. He wanted to know about the child, whose it was, how it came about. He had her legs on his shoulders and paused at the bottom of his downthrust to think about Linda Lawrence and Philip Farrel and how they had come through so much trouble, with so much to hold them back.

"Oh, my Peter Prince. You are so good to me. I think you make me want to sleep."

Time had slipped by him. "Fine," he said. "Then you sleep and I'll bring down some food for you, and then we can talk more reasonably." Peter Prince was satisfied for his part.

"Anything . . ." Corky Cluny wearily responded.

At dinner he sat down with Nikos and two other Greeks to avoid listening again to the German couple.

"You say you don't like Germans," Nikos said, "but I like them. I like them better than these Italians."

"How can you like them?"

"You can trust them, Peter Prince, more than you can trust these Italians here." Nikos looked around the room. "These people will never do what they say."

"You can trust them to be cruel," Peter Prince said.

"That, at least, is something," said Nikos. "Listen. When the Italians occupied my village they threatened every day to kill us if we did something against them, but then they would get us in prison and beat us up, that's all. Even when we had killed one of them. Then they'd set us free, nothing else."

"Is that bad?" Peter Prince asked. "They showed at least some sense of humanity."

"It's not honorable," Nikos shrugged. "I'll tell you a story now of the German occupation, and you can tell the difference. After the Italians had fouled things up the Germans sent into our village a Lieutenant Schmidt, a very severe man who never smiled, and didn't seem to like Greeks. A blonde fellow, very pale. The village people were very much afraid. There was trouble, you see, in my village, with the partisans who kept killing the Germans. One day this lieutenant, who was always complaining, by the way, about the dirty people in my town, proclaimed that for every German soldier that died one hundred men in my village would die. There were only a few more than four hundred men in my village and the surroundings so that made very few Germans we could kill."

Nikos stopped talking for a moment to eat some sherbet. Peter Prince arranged salami, olives, chicken slices and asparagus on a plate he would bring to Corky Cluny and the thought about the child that she was going to have, all that happening inside her, and he remembered Nikos' mentioning earlier about a man's knowing when he was pregnant. He searched for that feeling within himself. He wanted to know about the child. He looked at Nikos, and would have liked to ask him if he really had made a pass at Corky Cluny.

"That's very nice," said Nikos, pointing at his plate for Corky Cluny. "That's for your girl. Here. Give her these cookies too and say they're from Nikos." He laid two sugar wafers on top of the salami.

"What happened then," Peter Prince asked, though he was only barely interested, "in your village with the German lieutenant?"

"He killed all the men in the town, because the partisans, who were used to the threats of the Italians, one night blew up one of the German barracks."

"So he had all the men killed?"

"Every one."

"And you call that good?"

"At least he kept his word. He was tougher than these Italians who are so soft. You know they couldn't conquer us at first and had to call in the Germans to help them, a little country like Greece."

"But they killed everyone?" Peter Prince was trying to understand Nikos, to figure out how this could be the same man who had earlier talked about his child.

"How did you escape being killed?"

"I ran into the hills and stayed with the partisans."

"You ran away?"

"I was very frightened."

"And every man in your village was killed?"

"Almost four hundred. A few more ran away."

Peter Prince wondered what Corky Cluny would say about this. "How can you have any praise at all for the Germans after that? Just because you weren't killed you say that they're good?"

"If I had been killed I wouldn't be able to say anything at all about them. But you have to admit that the way they do things is good, that they are a good, strong people. The way they are now after that war when they were destroyed. They are a strong people and there's no doubt about that."

"Beasts are strong, Nikos. What you say is impossible. We need a little humanity. Strength is nothing at all. That was so much killing, senseless murder."

"I wouldn't call it murder. They told us what they were going to do, and they did it. They kept their word."

Peter Prince looked across the room to his own table where the German couple was still eating. The young man was shoving chunks of wine-soaked bread into his mouth while the girl beat him on the back of his hand with her fork. Nikos was an enigma. His carriage and his confidence gave Peter Prince a respect for him that no display of stupidity could discourage. Peter Prince always liked these weather-eaten men who had somewhat suffered. He liked Nikos' sobriety. He spotted the young Yugoslav woman at the other end of the dining room feeding her child and murmuring to it. He smiled and looked again at Nikos. "Don't you care that all the men in your village were killed?" he murmured incongruously through his smile.

"My father was one of them," Nikos said, his eyes moistening, "an old man. I loved every man in my village. Peter Prince, you haven't lived enough trouble. At least with the Germans you know where you stand. There is no fooling or evading; no sloppy actions. What they tell you they mean. You should think about that."

"I think your ideas are distorted."

"Ah . . ." said Nikos, and dismissed Peter Prince with a gesture.

Peter Prince took the full plate to his cabin where Corky Cluny still lay in his bunk, and the young Spanish stonemason too had come in and was snoring loudly in his bunk. Corky Cluny giggled when Peter Prince sat down.

"He didn't even notice me when he came in. I would have let him fuck me if he had answered when I said 'psssssst,' but he didn't even notice me." She thought it very funny and shrank beneath the blankets in giggles.

"How do you feel?" he asked.

"You know how, Peter Prince. Don't play papa-dear. You did me well, but not enough. I want some more of you."

Peter Prince avoided her outstretched hand. "I brought you some food." He handed her the plate and she sat on the edge of the bed. Peter Prince lay down behind her and bent his legs to form a backrest for her.

"Do pregnant women always get like you?"

"How is that?"

"Sexier."

She shoved a sugar wafer in his mouth. "Those are from Nikos," he said.

"Then I'd better take it back," she said, and leaned over to suck the sweetness from his lips. "So you've decided that I wasn't lying?"

"I haven't," he said, "I've decided not to care."

"Good," she said. "There are two of us." She filled her mouth with sour carrot. "Do you like Nikos or me better?"

"Nikos doesn't get pregnant."

"I don't mind, Peter Prince," she said, and turned to him, her fingers on her lips.

"What don't you mind?"

"If you make love to him, as long as you have enough for me too." He beat his knee against her back, and she pivoted to bite him on the thigh.

As she ate he thought about Nikos and the Germans. Nikos and his baby. "Tell me," he said. "Tell me at least something you know about the baby. Why do you want to make me think it's not mine?"

"I don't want to make you think anything."

"Then why are you so evasive?"

She leaned over and rubbed her head in his stomach. "Because I don't want to think about it. Because I want to have fun. Because I don't want to think about it at all."

They lay for a long time with her head on his belly, listening to the young Spaniard snoring on the bunk across from them. Peter Prince tried to picture Nikos' island—the clear Aegean around the blue rocks of its hills. How would Peter Prince have acted given Nikos' predicament during the war? Was Nikos a coward? Did he run away because he was afraid to face the death his father and his friends were forced to face? Would death be so hard for Peter Prince, his wanderings, his horizons, his careful disattachments all scattered by the bullet? Was Nikos a coward? These were questions even Philip Farrel couldn't answer, didn't want to answer, because he wasn't a judge. He wanted to let live.

He opened the door and shouted the name of Linda Lawrence down the hall, and then hurried to the dining room. The table was set with a steaming meal. He was late. He wondered where the time went. He looked to the kitchen where his Linda Lawrence worked and saw her coming through the door with a sauce boat in her hand, weeping.

"What?" he asked.

"They're dead," she cried, and fell to her knees and buried her head in his groin.

"Who?" he asked, but he didn't need to ask because he looked right then to the table and saw a file of them tipped over: Wimple, Mickey the turnip, Jack six, seven and eight, Martha, and including his favorite Bertha; all of them in that line, their heads dropped to their soup bowls, their blue lips stretched back from their teeth, some of their arms stiff across the table or above their heads.

"You made us wait too long," cried Linda Lawrence.

Philip Farrel collapsed beside her. He loved his children, and he hated to see them die.

*

There are thirty pages of transition here which I have decided not to write, during which time Peter Prince does a quickie tour of Italy, visiting some sequestered spots like Gubbio, Alberobello, and Città Vecchia, and even does a short term stint in the Peace Corps, and he splits for Morocco where in Tangier he smokes kif with Ira Cohen, and to Beirut, and he stops in Iraklion, a brief excursion into the Minoan ruins, and he visits Israel, and he talks with David Dalton about his trip to Afghanistan, and he visits the Baleares where in Mallorca he buys a pony-fur coat that costs him too much so he has to go home or sell it at a profit, which he does, and he returns to mainland Spain to spend too little time in Madrid where the Prado bores him, not because it is boring, but because he is bored, and he visits Scandinavia, happy in Copenhagen, depressed in Stockholm, amazed in Oslo. He takes a boat to Finland and doesn't talk to anyone all the time he is there, but he visits Lappland where he gets a tan to the surprise of all the tourists he meets from the Riviera, and he heads back down to Yugoslavia where he goes to Dubrovnik and is charmed, and he goes through Macedonia into Greece where he is treated with great hospitality which embarrasses him because he can't repay it; and he goes to Istanbul, which he decides he should visit later, at length. He has various reactions to all these places, a group of impressions, a batch of moods, which were to be described in the thirty pages I decided not to write, all of which could add up to sensitivity galore, but you'll have to take my word for it.

As for Philip Farrel and Linda Lawrence, most of you understand by now that they aren't per se characters in this book, but hired hands, like mercenary muses, working under pseudonyms, whose real names I can't divulge, but who have agreed to work at a low salary that I can afford, and a small percentage of the take, if any. They show up

whenever they're needed, sometimes causing a little ruckus, but usually on the job, as you will see in the following passages:

*

Linda Lawrence leaned on her ax and looked up to the crown of the tree through narrowed eyes. The weight of the branches was mostly downwind; she would have to start her cut high and angle slightly the back-cut. She gazed then down the line from her tree-trunk to the red flag tied to the stake she was to drive into the ground with her felled tree. She felt tired already, though she was anxious to begin before dinner-time, her children's return. Her temptation was to swing blindly and let it roar down through the underbrush anywhere, as long as it was felled; that was the point, after all, and the business of becoming expert, all the baroque of action, excess, expertise, that was impractical to learn and useless to practice; yet she wasted her strength in the learning, wherever she was, of esoteric skills. She scratched her back against the coarse bark of the tree, and the heavy wool of her checkered shirt stuck, leaving some red and black threads in the pitch. She wondered when Philip Farrel was going to get there; he had such a habit of keeping her waiting. She sank her double-edged ax into a tree stump and stepped up to her tree again, examining it at eye level. It would take three of her, she thought as she tried to embrace it, with arms spread, to encircle the tree. That was satisfying. It would be also satisfying, if nothing else, to drive that red-flagged stake into the duff, with the tree's immense momentum at the felling. The fire danger was high. A tiny shrew raised puffs of dust in the duff, skittered around Philip Farrel's boots, and found his hole again.

"I'm glad you're still here." Philip Farrel puffed on his curved pipe. He wore a blue denim jacket over a heavy red sweater, and thick suede pants.

"You always keep me waiting," she said.

"Do you have time to finish that story?"

"I want to get this over with first." She pointed at her tree.

"You always want to get something over with. Haven't you done it enough times?"

"Have you ever seen it before?" Linda Lawrence asked, and rubbed her thumb over the edge of her exposed ax-blade.

Philip Farrel pulled a newspaper from his jacket pocket, spread it at the roots of her tree, and sat down. The pipe smoke rose around his face. "There's plenty of time. I'll wait till you finish the story."

Linda Lawrence flipped her horn-handled hunting knife with practiced accuracy, end over end at Philip Farrel. "You're so damned complacent," she said. Complacency was Peter Prince's pose, confronting the turbulent and destructive course his life had begun to take as a result of his journey. Pregnancy. He had lost his Nancy Nottingham, sometimes grinning with his child inside of her, off guard, that stupid pregnant grin and softened look. He was slowly losing her company to that child within her as she melted slowly inward. He was through with posing and could take no more of her, her bedtime whimpering and grainy passion, when at every moment she depended more on him and made it more impossible for him to move.

Don't worry. I decided to scrap this scene long before I talked to any editors about the book. From what I could see it just didn't have it. I would not want to belittle the job Linda Lawrence and Philip Farrel do here. They live up to their reputations, so I'm hanging on to their little bit while X-ing out most of the rest. Any scene that takes so long to do so little deserves a drubbing. There was a time, actually, when I thought the effect here was impeccably apocalyptic, the little psychological inversion that takes place, the revelation of Peter Prince and his first experiences in Europe with Europeans, some prickly insights into Americanism and the attitudes of certain Europeans toward that stuff—I can't remember now what I had in mind, but it was important to me at the time. Now it makes me yawn. Peter Prince's sexuality taken to task by a batch of Danes, tough on him as it is on anyone brought up with the cowboy movie mentality. At the time I knew I was telling the truth but forget it. Let's X it out and come what will.

To Move. He couldn't pose any longer, to pretend to accept his paternity, to offer her his assurance, as if his dreams were coincident with her parturition. He would explode.

Explosion was in his mind as this scene unwraps in Verona between trains and they sit at the cafe by the station waiting for the Brenner Express to take them to Munich and the Oktoberfest. Peter Prince is playing his B flat Höhner and Nancy Nottingham turns to him to say,

"I wonder why all these policemen are walking around. I never saw so many of them all at once."

Peter Prince, blowing on his Höhner, looked around indifferently at the *carabinieri*, still in the summer whites, mingling independently with the crowd, and the khaki-clothed army men who marched about in groups of three, the middle one carrying a carbine. "Mostly *carabinieri*," he said.

"I can see that," she said. "But why are they all here now?"

Peter Prince stared into Nancy Nottingham's empty eyes. "We just read about it this morning. If you can only keep something in your head. They're probably here because of the bomb the Tyrolers set off in the baggage room yesterday. I told you about it. If you'd only listen to me sometimes. It killed a baggage clerk."

"That's terrible," she said.

"It happens," he replied.

"Do you think we should still sit here?" she asked, crossing her arms over her belly and leaning forward.

"For Christ sake," said Peter Prince, thumping his Höhner in his palm. "Forget it. Cool it. I can't keep traveling with you any more, if you're going to jump at every little thing. Just hang onto your fucking cool."

Nancy Nottingham began to cry.

By this time Peter Prince was fed up, ready to quit, explode. He turned from her to look back at the children playing among the tables around their parents waiting for trains, and caught too the four people at the table behind them, staring.

"Stop crying, Nancy Nottingham," he said. "Those people are watching us."

"So, what?" she said, but dried her eyes.

He was ashamed sometimes to be with her, she was so touchy with his child if he could be sure it was his child. He put his hands to his temples and stared beyond her, to the bus canopy where the drivers and toll-takers in gray uniforms were gesturing.

"I've stopped crying," said Nancy Nottingham, and Peter Prince looked at her face again where the pout remained and then back to the table of people staring.

This Danish fellow whom I have eliminated over there was totally amazing— a stupendous Danish sculptor by the name of Sorensen whom I met while I was living in Verona. He came there every year to cast his bronzes at the Brustelin foundry (a place about which eight novels should be written). I notice that at the time I made the following entree in my journal about him:

> *Sorensen—like the perfect American—Drives fast because he likes the strength of the car. His freshness unposed. When he tells about a book he's read it's as if he had experienced it. Perhaps because I'm a writer I feel ponderous around him, like a grandfather. Jane with a perfect sweetness, like Pat—she makes Jon sweet. His sculpture sacrifices its strength to a sweetness—a desire to please children—almost as in Heerup—as if he's afraid to look with aging eyes at the world. It's funny that around him I feel that I'm always catching my breath I want to keep up with him like an old man trying to match enthusiasm with a youth.*

One of his constant games was baiting Americans, though he did it more skillfully than is represented in this scene I have eliminated. I wrote that dullness just to introduce these Danes, and included even an irrelevant Bolognese who leaves as soon as his train arrives. He is an Italian sculptor named Quinto (because he was the fifth child) Ghermandi, whose beautiful wife, one evening in Bologna, prepared for Sorensen and me a palate-smothering pasticcio alla bolognese, and we sat around drinking a rare, exciting wine from the vineyards of his father-in-law, of which only 500 liters a year were produced, 200 of which Quinto took, 100 of which the father-in-law kept, and the last 200 of which they gave to Giorgio Morandi, whom I have always admired. In return for that memorable evening I thought it fitting to include Quinto in this scene. Goodbye scene.

Only one was still interested, a blonde man frowning with his brow lowered to nearly hide his eyelids. There was another blonde man, somewhat older, and a blonde woman holding a little blonde girl on her knee. The fourth was a dark man, an Italian, speaking constantly and smiling. As Peter Prince watched the one who had been staring stood up and stepped his way.

"He's coming over," said Peter Prince. Nancy Nottingham's pout disappeared.

He was about thirty, tall, his back slightly bent so his stained suede jacket fell loosely from where the round of his shoulders pressed against the soft leather. He leaned on an empty chair and smiled at Nancy Nottingham.

"Have you been fucking that woman?"

Peter Prince looked at the man's friends who were all staring now as if the fellow had been sent over on a dare.

"That's a dull way to introduce yourself," said Peter Prince, not knowing what to say.

"We've been listening when you talked to her," said the blonde fellow, gesturing towards his companions with his chin.

Nancy Nottingham pushed Peter Prince's foot under the table. "Why don't you stand up and push him away?" she mumbled close-lipped, and looked up at the man, who smiled. She closed her eyes and turned from him, releasing through her lips a high-pitched note and puff of air. "You're so damned complacent, Peter Prince." She leaned her cheek in her hand.

Peter Prince himself rose and offered his hand to the Northerner. "I'm Peter Prince," he said, "and this is Nancy Nottingham."

"Nilsen," the other said, and he took Peter Prince's seat so he could face Nancy Nottingham. She grimaced and turned away from him.

"Please send that man away," she said. "I can't stand him. Why should I put up with him? He insulted me, Peter Prince." Nilsen laughed. "I like him," said Peter Prince, grateful for his boredom relieved. "You don't like me," said Nilsen, "because you still haven't answered my question. Do you fuck her or don't you? I asked you simply that." "Yes. He fucks me," Nancy Nottingham turned on him. "We didn't ask you to sit down here. He fucks me, and I fuck him. And now I'm pregnant, and that's more than you asked for. So go away and tell your friends. You make me sick."

"That's unusual," said Nilsen, "for Americans. You learn something new about Americans every time. You are American?"

Peter Prince nodded. He always was annoyed by how quickly he was identified as an American.

"Then you won't like me," said Nilsen, "because worst of all I am a Communist." His features knotted. "Americans don't like Communists. My friends are all Communists too over there, even the baby. It's my baby, you know, and I'm almost sure of the older girl too. And that woman, I fucked her, I tell you, and it was marvelous, very good. It could have been just a Danish baby, because we're both Danish, but it turned out to be a Communist baby, and we're very happy with it, sometimes. You're going to have just a Capitalist baby, wait and see."

Nancy Nottingham reached for Peter Prince's hand under the table. "Can't you get rid of him? Do we have to listen to his jabber?"

"Rid of him?" said Peter Prince. "I like him," and he reached across to lay his hand on Nilsen's forearm. "She wants to get rid of you. What do you think of that?" "I suppose," he said, and winked at her, "she just doesn't like Communists." "You're no Communist," Nancy Nottingham covered her breast with her folded arms, "you're just a rude fool." "You see how she talks to Communists," Nilsen shrugged, "just like an American."

"Be civil, Nancy Nottingham," said Peter Prince. "You ask me to be civil?" "Be civil," he said. "I mean just relax. We make a bad enough impression."

"Meaning who makes?"

"Americans," Peter Prince whispered. "For Christ sake. You have no pride." "Shhhh." Peter Prince stiffened his back against the plastic strands of his chair.

"Why don't you ask your friends to come over here?" he said to Nilsen. "No," he said, and winked again. "Your friend would be very unhappy with so many Communists, and a Communist baby is a bad influence on a pregnant American girl."

"Don't be silly. We'll come and join you."

"I don't want to do that," said Nancy Nottingham.

Peter Prince rose after Nilsen and without waiting for Nancy Nottingham to follow or object he stepped through a crowd of fifteen American children playing, bouncing balls, shouting at Italian waiters in ruptured army jargon, and crossed to the table of Danes.

The other Danish man was older, his face battered into a permanent, smile-like grimace, his gray, broken teeth bare and dark as solder. Nilsen's woman was a shy, skinny, waif-like woman. She held one child in her lap and rocked the other in its carriage. They looked on Peter Prince with cordial mistrust and he sat down without hesitating because he wanted to inspire confidence in them. The Italian, a short, ound-faced Bolognese, well fed, smiled immediately at Peter Prince and shook his hand

"*E simpatico*," he said to his Danish friends.

"What sort of a man are you?" asked the older Dane.

"He's an American," said Nilsen, "and he wants to see what Communists are like."

It always disturbed Peter Prince that the Europeans he met, and liked, with whom he wanted to be intimate, would treat him, whatever his approach, as if he had been catalog bought, an American, and not Peter Prince, who he was. He didn't want it to matter that he was American. He wanted to be Peter Prince, and to be understood as honest, and interesting, and willing to accept whatever was strange they told of themselves. He wanted to be generous, but they wouldn't let him. He wanted even to be humble and deferent, but they forced him to seem foolish.

"We might corrupt your mind," said the older Dane. "Who allows you to listen to Communist talk? Who? They watch you all the time in America, to be sure you don't learn anything."

"They let us do what they please," said Peter Prince, trying to restrain his anger, a little tired of being misunderstood by Europeans. Peter Prince didn't want to hide behind an adopted identity as so many of his expatriate friends did.

"Don't speak to me like that. You don't do what they please. You think you do what you please. And the FBI and the CIA does what it pleases whether you like it or not."

"You people always exaggerate what rumors you hear," said Peter Prince, drawing his fist across his head

"Of course it's exaggerating," said the Bolognese, spreading both hands and shaking his head. "My friends exaggerate. They talk this way about Italy."

"It's exaggeration, right," said Peter Prince. "America is huge and various, and there are many options."

"The only option we see," said Nilsen, "is the shit of your policy here and in Africa and in Asia."

Peter Prince gripped the arms of his chair and leaned forward, extending his elbows like wings. "America is the most generous world power that has ever existed," he shouted.

"Generous in taking," said the older Dane.

"All of you are alike, and don't want to understand . . ." Peter Prince turned at the touch of Nancy Nottingham's hand on his shoulder.

What those police Nancy Nottingham is bugged by are all about and what actually happened is totally more interesting, in fact, than the story makes it out, and maybe I'll write it up some day. Why not? It's about me, and Sorensen, and his friend Willi (pronounced Weelee) and how on April 1, 1963, after the terrorist bombing of the Verona Railroad Station in which one poor baggage clerk died we were tailed from the foundry to the Caffe Fillipini and all over Verona—finally hauled in to the Questura for our suspicious looks. We were badly dressed, blondish, and they interrogated us for hours, thinking we were Tyrolers, suspicious men of vicious intent, and how we just ate all that up and felt super-mysterious, like Tom Sawyer.

"Are you enjoying your friends?" she asked.

"Will you please leave us alone and stop your talking." He looked up at her. She had closed her eyes. "Of course I'm enjoying them," he said. "Now sit down, you, and I want to introduce you to them. These are very nice people." He started a smile for her, his last words sweetening.

"I don't want to sit down now. Our train is leaving soon. We should go to get ready if we don't want to miss it."

"Sit down and don't be such a foolish woman and talk for a while."

She bent to whisper in Peter Prince's ear, "I don't like all those police watching you here. They have a circle of watchers around this table. I was watching them when I was alone, and I'm sure the don't trust these people, especially these people. Who are they? They make me nervous. They probably set that bomb."

"Sit down, don't be foolish," Peter Prince insisted, as he eased her into a seat next to the baby carriage, and looked at the police around them all staring into Peter Prince's eyes. He turned quickly to Nancy Nottingham who registered her uneasiness by closing her eyes again, and then turned to regard one by one he people he was with.

"You try to talk about a police state in America," said Peter Prince slowly, his voice trembling like a muscle in tone. "Look at these policemen around us here, all over. What do you suppose they are doing?" He hoped to find something registered in their expressions that could warn or reassure him.

"They think we bombed the station yesterday," Nilsen laughed. "Jorgen looks very suspicious here, with his blonde hair, and his evil face." Nilsen leaned over to whisper, "I personally think the Americans did it."

"Peter Prince. We shouldn't sit here with these people. They just want to make us into fools."

"Signorina," said the Italian, "my friend speaks sometimes too quickly, and he is always joking. He likes you."

"Of course we like you," said Nilsen. "Your friend here fucks you, and that is wonderful, and so we like you because he likes you. Americans are likeable."

"We have to catch our train," said Nancy Nottingham, pulling on Peter Prince's forearm.

"A few minutes," he said.

"What train is that?" asked Nilsen.

"To München," umlauted Nancy Nottingham, disdainfully, "to the Oktoberfest, and I doubt that we'll want to come back to Italy."

"What do you want to go to Germany for?" The Danish woman broke her silence. "You are crazy to want to go to that country."

"What have you seen of Italy?" asked the Bolognese.

"The Americans all like Germany, where there are no Communists," said Nilsen. "They waste their time up there and drown in the beer that makes them piss like a lake, and they like to link arms with them and sway back and forth singing '*ein, zwei, züffer*' to a tuba-band. The whole place smells like piss. You don't want to go up there."

"Peter Prince, let's go. It's almost time."

"Be quiet," Peter Prince said. He was sick of hearing her whine at his shoulder. "Maybe we won't go at all now. Maybe we'll stay, just for a change. Stay, and to hell with our plans." The promises he had made to himself before he came: to have freedom of motion, no schedule, to be able to change at will his plans. And now Nancy Nottingham was pregnant with insecurity and nervous anticipation. "Maybe we'll stay here tonight. Maybe tomorrow night too. Maybe we'll stay for a week."

"You should stay," said the Italian, as he took Nancy Nottingham's wrist in his hand. "You haven't seen Verona yet. San Zeno. There is no more beautiful city this size in all Italy. You are lucky to be here. If you stay you can see the Mantegna, and the Pisanello. After the war I used to take tourists from Venezia to Vicenza and Verona, and they'd learn how beautiful it was. The Americans," he said enthusiastically, "liked especially that this is the city of Romeo and Juliet. You can see everything. The house of Cappello; and Juliet's tomb."

Nancy Nottingham began to cry again.

"Will you stop your goddam crying. I'm sick of you."

"Be good to her," said Nilsen, "you fucked her, remember. Those are your tears she's crying."

"Peter Prince. Please take me away from these people. Nothing good will happen here." The *carabinieri*, tightly watching the rest of the station, were gathered at the tables of the caffe casually looking over the customers, in particular taking in Peter Prince, the Danes, and the Bolognese. Peter Prince made up his mind.

"We're staying."

"Marvelous," said Nilsen. "You'll come around with us."

"Then let's get out of here. I'm sick of this place already," said Peter Prince, his arms crooked like wings at his side. He was about to rise.

"Peter, our tickets, what do you want to do this for and ruin our going. We have to go. We can't afford it."

"Don't worry, signorina," said the Bolognese, "the tickets will be good tomorrow anyway, and even the next day."

"Peter Prince," she cried, and her eyes shut.

But Peter Prince had already risen, and with him the Danes. Peter Prince placed both his hands on Nancy Nottingham's shoulders and urged her to rise. She did. The man from Bologna explained that he couldn't come, was waiting for a train to take him back to Bologna, another beautiful city. As they walked to the car Peter Prince thought about America, Philip Farrel, Linda Lawrence, at work and play.

This was such a great idea when I got it that I leaped out of my seat and zipped around my study like a house on fire. "That's it," I shouted. "You've got it. A genius touch." I kissed my knuckles, my shoulders, my desk. I had a lot of glee and in my eyes was sparkle. Three times, with the O.K. of Philip Farrel and Linda Lawrence, I would repeat this paragraph, and each time I'd make a little shift in the state of Peter Prince. I thumped on my chest. Alas. Here I am X-ing it out like a lady tweezing gray hairs. Mutability. If I had an instant I could call my own I'd lean on something and ponder that.

The knife spun slowly in the air catching light, arrived at Philip Farrel, creaked and dove in. Linda Lawrence looked up through narrowed eyes at the ravens in the trees' lowest branches, and wooded mountains beyond the ravens, and the big, tough cumulus climbing the sky beyond the wooded mountains. Philip Farrel cupped his hands over his chest where the knife had punched its hole. "I'll begin again," said Linda Lawrence as she took a whetstone from her pocket, moistened it with spit, and sharpened her ax.

"Where are we?" asked Peter Prince as they left Nilsen's Peugeot parked on a narrow street of warped beige walls lit by white lights swinging between the buildings in a gentle wind.

"We are going to a restaurant," said Jorgen.

"We've already eaten," Nancy Nottingham told Peter Prince.

"Just sit down with us," said Nilsen, "we want to have some tripe and talk a little and drink some wine. Verona wines are the best in Italy."

They entered a small, tunnel-like trattoria with a large, noisy fan at one end lifting the wine-stained tablecloth. Working men leaned about the tables in back in their blue coveralls, their berets resting on top of their heads, the dust from their stone-work or carpentry settled on their collars. Nancy Nottingham swept the crumbs from in front of her, pouted, and faced the yellow, moisture-spotted wall. The little blonde girl climbed onto her lap and she automatically supported it with an arm, didn't look at it, still faced the wall. The Danish woman reprimanded the child for being a nuisance, and apologized to Nancy Nottingham who smiled and shook her head to indicate it was fine for the child to sit on her lap. Nancy Nottingham asked if the woman could speak English and was

I absolutely back off at the idea of eliminating this little scene where the sounds of Nilsen (who is Sorensen) are most like himself, and he is infinitely lovable. I'll not X it out. And don't let the tripe scare you off—it is delicious in soup or sauce, and there are countless wonderful places to eat in and around Verona, including the Dodici Apostoli, which was immortalized in the Pisan Cantos by Ezra Pound. Restaurants beyond your most efficient dreams, O townships of America. This scene shall remain therefore unscathed, and you who dismiss it for its faults may your bowels be scourged by barbed wire in endless coils.

delighted to find that she could and the two women passed much of the time of tripe and wine conversing.

"We should drink tonight until we get sick," said Nilsen.

"Why do you want to get sick?"

"I thought you Americans like to drink." Nilsen filled Peter Prince's tumbler. "I had an American friend; his name was Billy and he was crazy. His father was a colonel and he was a Communist, and he would bring me whisky because it was so cheap for him when I was in Paris. It was mad. We would drink the whisky like we are drinking this wine now."

"It makes no sense to get sick," said Peter Prince, and he drew in some wine and held it in his mouth.

"No one said there was sense in it at all. What good is sense? It's better to be drunk out of your head, and if we were more often drunk maybe we wouldn't tie ourselves to these children we have. Sense. You are crazy for sense. Maybe . . ."

"Nilsen, not so loud," said the Danish woman.

"The women," Nilsen bellowed, "they have your children and they begin to run your life and shove you around. O you," he said to his woman, "why do you talk to me like that?"

"Because you are too loud, my man," she said gently.

"See what I mean?" he said to Peter Prince, "You can't trust them to be nice to you." Nancy Nottingham was smiling because she had obviously made a friend, and she looked to Peter Prince as if she had let down her burden: her grin, and her heavy lids.

"There seems to be a nice . . ." said Nancy Nottingham, and she paused to hunt for the word, ". . . atmosphere here."

"You do talk too loud," said Jorgen leaning across the table to Nilsen.

"You too are like my wife, Jorgen. My Christ. One divorce, and I get married again, and now I have a wife and a friend too to haunt me." He stood up and began shouting down the restaurant in Danish and the Italians stopped their card games, stopped their arguments, and turned to look at him. They began to applaud Nilsen who delivered whatever he was saying with great spirit.

"Nilsen," said the woman, "you're being a fool."

"How do you know what a fool is?" asked Nilsen, raising his arm across the chest as if he were going to strike her with the back of his hand. "Why don't you bring us some tripe," he shouted down the hall in English. "*La trippa.*" He slapped the table.

The waiter, shouting as he hurried down the room, put the steaming bowls of tripe soup down in front of them.

"Haiaiiee," Nilsen grunted, staring like a Viking at the waiter, "it's about time," and he dipped the soup and slippery tripe into his mouth.

Nancy Nottingham was laughing.

"Why are you laughing," Peter Prince asked.

"Because he's so funny," she said. "He's completely funny. He's making it all up."

"He's making what up?"

"He's not as bad as he plays at it. He's just fooling you, and he's making up all these opinions. He's really very nice."

Peter Prince felt suddenly helpless, and didn't know that he saw any more what he looked at. He looked at Nilsen's woman who was talking again with Nancy Nottingham, and then to Nilsen who was drowning with his large hook almost in his soup bowl. He looked at Jorgen, who ate slowly and carefully. He felt brittle suddenly, of such fragile consistency that he believed his life could fracture silently.

"Why are you people all here in Verona?" he asked Jorgen, to begin again; but before Jorgen could answer Nilsen was speaking.

"Have you ever been drunk when you were all alone, really alone, I mean nowhere near home? That's a feeling you should get, and if you do it you should do it in Venice where it is so beautiful you can become a pig," he sucked a tripe-strip through his lips. "It's the best thing you can do. After I was divorced I did it the first time, and believe me I don't feel bad about it at all because it cleans you out." The soup dripped to the tablecloth from the bottom of his spoon. "You begin to drink, and at first you don't think you are going to drink very much because you feel very strong. And you feel you are doing what you should be doing. Then you begin to get into it, and you get going, and wind up." Nilsen gestured roundly with his hands and paused in his speaking to eat. "Then you are very sad before you drink enough, and then you drink a lot, and you walk around and are angry. And you begin to get into it, like a pig, and as you are further into it you are more happy, until you are very happy, and you go around talking to people in Piazza San Marco, people sitting there in caffes and with pigeons getting their pictures taken, and you speak to them like a stupid pig, and they all love you, and you try to touch them, and you step into a gondola on the Grand Canal, tied to a mooring, and it rocks up and down and then you get sick. You hate yourself, like a pig, and you want to hide for nine days, and you go to the public garden and lie down and with your vomit up comes Giovanni Bellini, Giorgione, and the whole lagoon, and the Doges' Palace with its pink stone, and St. Mark's Church is in your stomach swimming around. And you want to shit. And you lie in it all and moan, and children stop to look at you, and people walk far around you because you stink like a pig. You want water. You want to drink water, and nothing else, and never take another drink again."

"And after that you want to do it again?"

"You like it. It cleans you out."

"You still want to get sick again. You can't tell me you were enjoying what you were doing there."

"You are no American," said Nilsen, looking into his soup bowl.

"Because I don't like to get sick you say I'm no American?"

You will notice how this scene vaguely foreshadowed the apocalyptic bathroom scene near the book's conclusion. Goodbye structure. Goodbye well-made-book.

"Because I like you I say you are no American. I don't like Americans. And my friends here are getting me tired."

That last remark nauseated Peter Prince, and he rose from the table.

"Where are you going now?" asked Nancy Nottingham.

"I don't know," said Peter Prince.

"I've just begun to have a good time," she said.

"I'm going to the john," he said.

He went to the john, passing the tables of the other tripe-eaters dressed still in their soiled work clothes. At a small marble-topped counter at the back, where the wine was poured, he tried to communicate his need to the young girl who worked there. "*Dové il gabinetto*," he said, as clearly as I could, but she refused to understand him, thinking his accent was Danish. The girl's smile was as friendly as any Peter Prince had ever seen and he liked her. She looked about in real distress for someone who could help her. She couldn't understand him. Peter Prince liked her dark eyes and pale northern skin held in the invented lyre of her long dark hair.

"*Ecco il cameriere*," she said.

The waiter discerned Peter Prince's need immediately, held up his thumb and index finger, and pointed to a corridor in back of the counter. Peter Prince crossed behind the girl who didn't glance at him again but coyly bent her head to let her hair fall over the wine bottles. The toilet was a sty, a moist, chilling breeze circulating the piss smell, some soggy newspaper on the floor. The latrine was a squat type, with foot spaces with steel handles for balance that gathered moisture like a sweating woman. Peter Prince locked the door. The wall behind the john was very thin and he thought he could hear someone moving there, perhaps a woman's bathroom. He had to rest a moment and think clearly about himself, and Nancy Nottingham, who was destroying himself. She was unpredictable and contrary. He needed to take hold and present himself for what he was, whatever that was, whatever the outcome. No trivial masks. He wanted to be an American, and strong, amicable.

He rose from his squat and let loose the handles at the impatient knocking of someone waiting by the door. He turned and pissed, the piss streaming on the cold porcelain and making him tremble. His stream loosened bits of dirt and washed them through the drainhole.

From the back of the room, standing near the girl with the wine bottles, Peter Prince could see Nancy Nottingham laughing, and Nilsen the Dane entertaining her with elaborate gestures. The sound of their voices reached the back of the room wordless, in muffled explosions, like distant fireworks. Peter Prince closed his eyes and leaned for a moment on the counter, and listened to the girl who

spoke softly as she poured flasks of wine and received orders. Four men watched him from a table near the counter and conjectured that he was drunk and wondered if he was German.

Peter Prince started back to his people. The hilarity spilling from the table made him weary. He regretted that he had started out with these people at all, his mistakes compounding. With a sigh he couldn't hold back he sat down in the noise of his friends. Nancy Nottingham had shifted seats to be closer to Nilsen and Peter Prince found himself next to the Danish woman who was burdened with her children. Nilsen had hardly noticed Peter Prince's return. He felt slowly growing at the back of his eyes a blinding desperation that obscured understanding. He didn't want to lose himself, but he didn't understand either how he had so quickly changed, suddenly slipped. He noticed a remarkable sweetness in the slightly twisted expression of the Danish woman. Her pale blue eyes. Her features, asymmetrical along the slightly curved axis of her face, bent permanently like a tree in the sea-wind, betrayed the pressure of living with a fellow like Nilsen, and at the same time revealed a permanent satisfaction, the massive joy and containment that adjusting to him gave her. The baby slept in the carriage beside her and the older girl sat in her slender lap, her wide, deep blue eyes open, a thumb between her lips. When Peter Prince looked at the child she smiled around her thumb, her cheeks fattening.

"Why do you people live in Verona," Peter Prince asked the woman.

"We don't live here always," the woman smiled, offering English in a handsome, vowelly, Danish accent. "We come here only some months the of the year to use the Brustelin foundry. Nilsen is a sculptor."

Peter Prince looked at Nilsen again, who was leaning across the table and speaking softly now to Jorgen and Nancy Nottingham, and then he looked at the woman again. She was nice, and he felt at ease. The fact that Nilsen was an artist comforted Peter Prince and explained, it seemed, a great deal of what had troubled him about the evening: the police, the exhibitionism of Nilsen, his irrational political outbursts. Peter Prince liked artists. He thought of himself as one, since he knew that eventually, soon, he would begin to write; he had to; he would buy a notebook and begin to.

"And why are you two here?" the Danish girl sweetly asked. Her voice comforted Peter Prince.

"We're just traveling," he said.

"Traveling," she responded. "I like very much to travel."

"You must travel enough with Nilsen."

"The children," she said, "make it very difficult. Nilsen often goes places

Here, I guess, is a good place to pick up a discussion I dismissed hastily earlier: fluorescence. In my case fluorescence is a luminescence emission that is caused by the flow of energy into the emitting body (the flow of energy distinguishes it from phosphorescence, under which you just can't write. This energy here is a sixty cycle alternating current flowing through a glass tube coated with powdered phosphor and small amounts of mercury.), this emission ceasing abruptly when the exciting energy is shut off. The decay of luminescence in my lamps is temperature independent over a considerable range of temperature, and (God willing) follows an exponential decay law:

$I = I. \, exp \, (-t/\int\int)$

to be expected for spontaneous transitions of electrons from an excited state of an atom to the ground state when the atom has a transition probability per unit time I/∫ ∫ In this equation I is the luminescence at a time t, and I. is the intensity when t=0. I mean if that's not quick I don't know what is, milliseconds, no more, and the light is out, in the blink of an eye, and who's to know? ME. I know it. And don't think it doesn't twist this book. The result is that stroboscopic effect, a very disturbing factor, which causes similar disturbances in my book. The light here, you see, isn't just on all the time, but it's switching on and off at a rate of sixty times per second because those electrodes in that fluorescent tube are constantly alternating their charges with this alternating current, and the fluorescent light with that quick-die technique I just described goes on at that rate. I'm not calling the light vindictive, or even frivolous. The light does what it's used to doing and leaves the rest to me, but don't think this book isn't influenced by the fact that sixty times each second it gets dark in here, making over the period of years it takes to write a book, no matter how small each instant, an appreciable amount of darkness. This condition of intermittent darkness explains then some of the empty avenues in this book, gaps like highway right-of-ways through the timber, like missing teeth, transitions that are unreadable because you can't see them, all more easily explained now under the heading of Stroboscopic Blind-Spots. I do suggest that you finish this book, if you haven't already started it that way, under fluorescent light, preferably in phase with the light in the lamps of this book. That way you miss the barest minimum, or am I wrong? For further technical information write to this library.

without me, because I can't leave the children."

"I know," said Peter Prince, looking at the children and admiring how well they were tended. "It must be very difficult."

Her smile at him, for a moment, suddenly made me see himself in a pale golden evening light, the well tended lawn, a charcoal burner, and Peter Prince in his starched chef's uniform warning the ring of children around his cooking to stay back from the fire that spit sparks. That was a possibility he'd like to write about.

"Now let's get out of here and do something else." Nilsen raised his hand to indicate that he wanted to pay.

"I'll pay that bill," Peter Prince weakly insisted from his dissipating golden light.

Nilsen reached across and pulled Peter Prince's arm down to the table. "You won't pay that bill," he said, "you Americans care only to show off your money." Nilsen flourished a 10,000 lire note which the waiter plucked from his hand and rushed back to the girl at the counter.

"Now what shall we do?" Nilsen asked, "Maybe we should just see Verona. We'll show you Verona, very slowly." He looked at Peter Prince. "It's a very interesting city, except it should be very difficult to find a whore here, and Jorgen says it's very expensive. Not like Milano, that is, where you find them on every corner and you can have them for three thousand lire. But here maybe it costs too much." He winked at Nancy Nottingham, "We'll look at the house of Romeo and Juliet then."

They left the restaurant and walked the few blocks to Piazza Bra and the center of Verona. The Roman arena, built of red brick and tufa block, was lit softly by spotlights and the people, at the end of their *passeggiata*, were strolling slowly about the broad esplanade in the dim golden light. At the restaurant, Le Tre Coronne, waiter were flaming crêpes for American tourists, Americans smiling at the blue, disappearing flames. The caffe tables were full of people lingering. In the park across the street Peter Prince could see children playing by the illuminated fountain, and he suddenly liked them, children, more than anything he knew. His child in Nancy Nottingham. The American families eating and sitting about were packed with children, and some American families, children circling like pigeons about the adults, were strolling among the Italians. The police watched Peter Prince from the edges of the park, and he turned to see behind the pillars of the promenade more of them, dressed in white.

"Let's walk this way," said Nilsen, leading them into a narrow, brightly lit street that was closed to car traffic.

A glance behind him assured Peter Prince that the police were still following.

He caught up with Nancy Nottingham who was following directly behind Nilsen the Dane.

"The police are still following us," he said.

"So what?" she responded, looking into the window of an elegant china shop. "So they follow us?"

"What if they mistake us for someone else then. They could make it very uncomfortable for us."

"I couldn't care less at this point. I'm having fun and meeting some real people for practically the first time. I was nervous before, but let's not worry about it now." In two long strides she drew ahead of Peter Prince and caught up with Nilsen who began immediately to speak to her and show her things along the way. Peter Prince wasn't afraid of the police, nor did he think any trouble would come of their following him, but something about what was happening annoyed him. He was playing such a minor part, and his control over Nancy Nottingham was slipping, her stubborn turning from him. He thought of the two, of Philip Farrel, Linda Lawrence. Would he ever go back to see them? Their huge involvements. Why did he always come to think of them? The knife spun slowly in the air catching light, arrived at Philip Farrel, creaked, and dove in. Linda Lawrence looked up through narrowed eyes at the ravens in the trees' lowest branches, and the wooded mountains beyond the ravens, and the big, tough cumulus climbing the sky beyond the wooded mountains. Philip Farrel cupped his hands over his chest where the knife had punched its hole. "I'll begin again," said Linda Lawrence, as she took a whetstone from her pocket, moistened it with spit, and sharpened her ax.

"Where are we?" asked Nancy Nottingham.

"This is called Via Mazzini, said Nilsen the Dane, "and soon we'll come to Piazza Erbe, and then to Piazza Dante, both very beautiful; there are no more beautiful in Italy for their size. You can become sick here with beauty: beautiful piazzas, beautiful buildings, beautiful paintings, art in the toilets, everywhere. It makes you sick, and the people are too sweet. They're not dangerous here like in France where the people hate you, and don't want to see you. Here the people love you, and they're not tough, and after three months I want to get out of here. I can't stand it."

They tried to walk fast along the narrow, elegant, and brightly lit street but it was too full of people strolling, showing off their fine soft shoes, and some of them still in pale summer suits and some changed to autumn fabric, the ladies turning and smiling, with singing talk and laughter, their hair teased and piled on their heads holding light, in the smell of coffee shops and they passed slowly, letting their flesh press the cloth they wore and tempting strangers. Peter Prince followed behind Nancy Nottingham who was abreast of Nilsen, and Peter Prince was followed close behind by Jorgen, with the Danish woman, her carriage and her child, far behind. They passed the elegantly decorated

Some of these paragraphs in here I'm reluctant to eliminate because of Mark Seiden. He liked them. Something about them. I can't remember what. Some of his other ideas about this passage were remarkable though I never understood them. Nonetheless I'm grateful for them. Thank you, Mark, and I'm sorry.

windows of notion shops, china shops, haberdashers, leather shops, shoe stores, candy stores.

Peter Prince tried to keep up with Nilsen and Nancy Nottingham but they managed to keep some strollers always between. He wanted to hear what Nilsen was saying to her, he as talking so much, and he didn't care at all to hear Jorgen who was throwing comments at him from behind, and trying to catch up with him. Where Via Mazzini narrows just before it opens out into Piazza Erbe Peter Prince got lost, his friends out of sight, in the people rubbing together to pass, the faces gathering light from the movie theater there, red, green, and white lights, and Nancy Nottingham ahead somewhere with Nilsen the Dane, and behind him, he didn't know where, the voice of Jorgen trying to catch him still; only the noise there of everyone talking, no motor cars, and the slow, patient motion of the crowd through the bottleneck. He'd been in crowds this thick before, at baseball games, one-cent sales, subway rush hours, but never without machinery before, or escalators, or motorized carts, and never with people going in so many directions and separately talking. He wondered where the police were, and how they kept track of him in the push. He wanted to see the policemen. For a moment he backed into the lobby of the movie theater and looked at the notices for three Westerns, *Samson meets Maciste*, Antonioni's *Eclipse*, and Charlie Chaplin in *The Great Dictator*. The last made him smile and he stepped out refreshed into the intoxicating mumbling. He could see none of his friends and could hear only the bewildering conviviality of Italians parting from one another.

He drifted out into Piazza Erbe and at first didn't see his friends, but small cars turning and a *filobus* packed with passengers, turning.

"Peter Prince," heard, and looked about. "There he is. Peter Prince." He could see that the police had followed after all and were waiting about in front of shops and under the gray umbrellas of the open market, conversing, in their various poses.

"Peter Prince," Nilsen's Danish accent reached him from the edge of the market place. He saw them. They had all passed him somehow, even the wife with her child and carriage, and were standing now at the edge of the market where they bought watermelon from a vendor who had her slices layed out on a long block of ice. They all held the pink meat away from their clothes and bent forward, letting it drip onto the seed-strewn pavement, holding their heads forward, their bodies curved, and baring their teeth to bite.

"It's wonderful," said Nancy Nottingham. "I've never tasted such watermelon." A stream of pink juice circled her protruding chin. "Try some." She wiped her chin wit the back of her wrist. Peter Prince looked at them all and felt strange in their company, as if they'd suddenly slipped away from him completely, all of them, including Nancy

Nottingham. She pulled a piece of melon from the ice and offered it to him, smiling. "Aren't you going to have any?"

Peter Prince took the melon slice and held it a moment in his hand, and Nancy Nottingham smiled as if she'd won a small victory, and turned her attention back to Nilsen the Dane. What were these pressures? Peter Prince filled his mouth with the sweetness of melon, and spit the seeds into the gutter. That was all. She would feed on him no longer. What pity could he have on her, pregnant or not, if she showed him no loyalty, nothing, and with any Dane she met in the railroad station would take up, offering him such strict attention to his words that she had never shown to Peter Prince. She never listened to him. A woman should follow a man about, he thought, and let him feel important, whatever he was. How could Peter Prince ever get where he was going harnessed to her leaden chariot?

"What's good about Italy is what you can see here in the day," said Nilsen the Dane, "the fruit, and the food in general, what you eat. Everyone here likes to eat." He indicated, with his extended hand, the whole market place, and made Nancy Nottingham regard, one at a time, the closed food-stalls, their umbrellas folded, the counters wrapped in gray canvas. "At these stalls you can buy for very little as good food as you can get anywhere in Europe: blood oranges, spinach, artichokes, they peel little swallows for you, mushrooms, anything you like."

Peter Prince moved closer to Nilsen's woman who stood watching from a small distance. "Do you like this?" he asked her.

"Nilsen is always like this," she said, bitterness repeating in her voice. "When there's a new hen in the barnyard he can't resist pecking her into shape."

"You're hard on Nilsen," said Jorgen.

"I'm not hard on him. I have his children."

"If you didn't have is children what would you do?" asked Peter Prince.

"I don't know," she said. She looked for a moment into Peter Prince's eyes and seemed to register with her own who Peter Prince was. That was the woman he needed, a woman like that. "It's not even a question at all," she said, "Nilsen needs me now."

"But if he hurts you?"

"Any way I turn I can't avoid being hurt."

Peter Prince looked at Nancy Nottingham who had begun to follow Nilsen through the empty market. He felt suddenly sad for her, carrying his child and still wanting to show him she was free, though still so dependent on him. What a brave woman was the woman of Nilsen to follow the man about as she did and tolerate his unwieldy ego. But Nancy Nottingham. Could she ever make so strong a commitment to imperfection in her man as did this Danish woman? Could she be tolerant enough? He slowly stepped out

NOTA BENE
"What?"
"The . . . something."
"What? What?"
"The excellent description."
"Oh toosh."

Sorensen's wife deserves all the mention she can get. She's a peach. I made the following entry in my journal after visiting all of them in Paris:

> *Janna emerges as the most lovely in the room, her face reflects her moods so strongly there's an honesty makes her lovely—Despite Bramsen's splendid stately wife, though pregnant, alert—and Willi's lovely unwed mother, heavy in the legs. A gentleness in Janna, complete lack of selfishness one finds in her face. She reminds me always of Jingle; but Jon reminds Jingle of me.*

Bramsen, unfortunately, never gets into this novel, though he is a real friend, and a wonderful, surly, kind, drunken, gentlemanly genius Danish lithographer who lives in Paris. Love to him just the same.

Nike, the name for Janna in the book, is the name of a young Danish girl I met at the Biennale in Venice. She was young and bright. I walked back to her hotel with her and met her father who said, "What kind of a man are you?" as he shook my hand. He looked like a wardrobe pederast, and he turned out to be a ceramist, and Sorensen's first teacher. "I taught him," he said, "everything he knows."

with Jorgen and the woman and her children to follow the two who had headed for the alley that led to Piazza Dante and he saw Nancy Nottingham's flowered yellow shift suddenly extinguished by the lamplit brick of the tower on the corner when she moved out of sight. Nausea rose in him like a mercury column.

"He's not so very bad . . . Nilsen," Jorgen said. "He only makes a lot of noise. He likes to make Nike unhappy."

Peter Prince didn't want to follow any longer. Nancy Nottingham was trying to make him unhappy and he wouldn't have that. He wouldn't have her annoying him and stunting his intentions. What were his intentions? He scaled with his eyes the lovely Verona tower, the narrow alternating rows of brick and tufa, past the one-armed clock, to the white, octagonal belfry. That was what he wanted. Something like that. To absorb in himself the delicate structure of humanity's heritage and to act from there. That's why Peter Prince had come to Europe, and not to follow Nancy Nottingham around with her random Danes. He swallowed, and turned, and looked at the Danish girl.

"I'm sick of following them," he said. "We'll sit down at a caffe and I'll buy you a drink. We can wait for them to find us." He spoke strongly.

The Danish woman smiled at him, and agreed, and they walked to the Caffe Fillipini, Jorgen following, and sat down in the low chairs of plastic rope facing the market-place fountain. The sound of water dropping settled on them like sleep.

"What did Jorgen say your name was?" he asked the Danish woman.

"Nike," she said.

"Nike?"

"Like the Winged Victory of Samothrace," she said. "My father was inspired by my birth. He was Nilsen's teacher once. He's a ceramist."

"I'd say that was really an inspired name," said Peter Prince.

"I don't know if I disappointed my father or not," she said. "We live in Paris now, anyway, like my namesake."

"In Paris you live," he repeated, charmed by the thought.

"We have a house here," she said.

This is more like it, thought Peter Prince, settling back to sip his Campari Soda, to sit in the sound of an Italian fountain sipping bitter drinks and amicably conversing with expatriate Danes who have houses in Paris.

"What do you do?" Jorgen asked him.

Peter Prince decided that he liked even Jorgen, that mutilated face held such kindness in the eyes. "I don't know," he said sympathetically. "I hope to write."

"Every American I meet hopes to write," laughed Jorgen. "What have you written."

"I really hope to write." Peter Prince wouldn't be intimidated.

"Everyone comes to Europe to be another Ernest Hemingway."

"There's Peter Prince," Nancy Nottingham shouted in her nasal falsetto as she and the Dane emerged from a narrow passageway that connected Piazza Dante with Piazza Erbe. She came and stood over him at the table and he felt a weight in his throat again. "You simply have to get up and see Piazza Dante. It's indescribable." She tugged on his shirtsleeve.

"I prefer to stay here." He didn't look at her.

"Don't spoil everything now," she whispered in his ear.

"I'm not spoiling everything," he shouted, spraying her face as he turned. She backed away.

Nilsen sat down by Nike and looked at Peter Prince. "You are very lucky to fuck a girl like that," he said. "Look at the bones I have to fuck."

"If you want to fuck her," said Peter Prince, "take her."

"Peter Prince," Nancy Nottingham snarled, "what are you saying?"

Peter Prince turned to Nike, who had turned to watch Nilsen, who had turned to look at the fountain and say a few words to Jorgen who had turned to listen.

Nancy Nottingham tried to make Peter Prince listen. "I'm really glad we stopped here," she said, "really glad. This is one of the prettiest towns."

Peter Prince didn't listen to her. "Do you live right here in Verona now?" he perfunctorily asked of Nike. She moved her head as if she hadn't heard and he repeated his question, hearing Nancy Nottingham speaking into the back of his own neck.

"I don't know what Nilsen wants to do now," said Nike, as if in response to Peter Prince's question. She smiled politely.

Nancy Nottingham punched Peter Prince to make him listen. "No I don't want to see that damned piazza," he said, turning on her. "I'm sick of piazzas." He meant, of course, that he didn't want Nancy Nottingham to tell him what was worth seeing. Nancy Nottingham punched him again. "Didn't you hear me?"

"What did you ask me?" Nancy Nottingham didn't answer him, but waved him away to follow Nilsen again.

"We'll walk back now," said Nilsen. "Come on." He stepped out.

The last warm gulp of Peter Prince's Campari Soda burned his throat as he stood to leave the table with the rest. He followed. Via Mazzini was empty now but for a few late strollers and some people drinking coffee at the bars. He walked silently beside Nancy Nottingham as Nilsen and Nike walked ahead, Nilsen carrying the little girl in his arms. Jorgen spoke infrequently in Danish and moved with rapid, hare-like motion from side to side of the street looking in windows.

Nancy Nottingham whispered, "This is really a beautiful street. Really elegant. And the shops have such windows. It's like a little Fifth Avenue. I'm really glad, Peter Prince, and sorry I'm so timid. I'm glad you made us stop here. You don't really get to know much about Italy from just the tourist stops."

"You're a very interesting girl," said Peter Prince, though he knew she was saying just what he wanted her to, and he had no reason to be cruel, but couldn't control himself, "and I'm glad you appreciate what you see."

She stared at him a moment, raising her fist to her throat. "Peter Prince," she moaned, "why can't we get along any more?"

"We're getting," he said, "we're getting along."

"Why can't you listen to me when I say something?"

"I listen to you, Nancy Nottingham. Tell me what you said again."

She opened her hand at her throat and stroked her neck. "I said I like Verona," she weakly repeated.

"You show refinement of taste," Peter Prince told her, and his eyes knocked shut. He wasn't saying what he wanted to say. He touched her moistening cheek. "Why are you crying?"

"Because you can be so hard on me when I've done nothing to deserve it, and so unfair."

"O slippery love."

Beyond Piazza Bra they passed through the last city gate, decorated with a stone tablet inscribed with Romeo's lament at his exile from Verona, in English, and translated into Italian. Nilsen stopped to let Peter Prince catch up with him. The young girl was sleeping on his back, her saliva dripping to his collar from her lip.

"You see that one across the street," said Nilsen, turning his shoulder toward a thin woman in a tight silk polka-dotted dress, carrying an umbrella, walking slowly down the other side of the avenue beyond the city gate. "She's a prostitute."

"I wouldn't have known," said Peter Prince.

"Do you like her?"

"I can't see her very well," said Peter Prince, not looking.

"We'll cross over to her then."

"We don't need to."

Nilsen was already starting across the street. "Come on. It's good." Peter Prince hesitated, but started himself when Nancy Nottingham did. has a very good ass," Nilsen explained. "Jorgen can tell you she is very good, wonderful. Especially good at sucking cocks. You ask her for Francese." He turned to his wife. "How do they call it?"

"They call it 'alla Francese,' " she said.

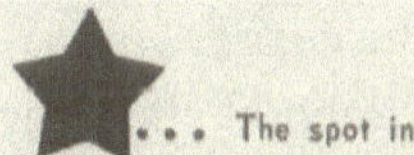 ... The spot in Nevada where Delbert Howard's body was found is indicated by the star. The location is 14 miles southwest of Reno close to the main byway of U.S. 395 in Washoe County.

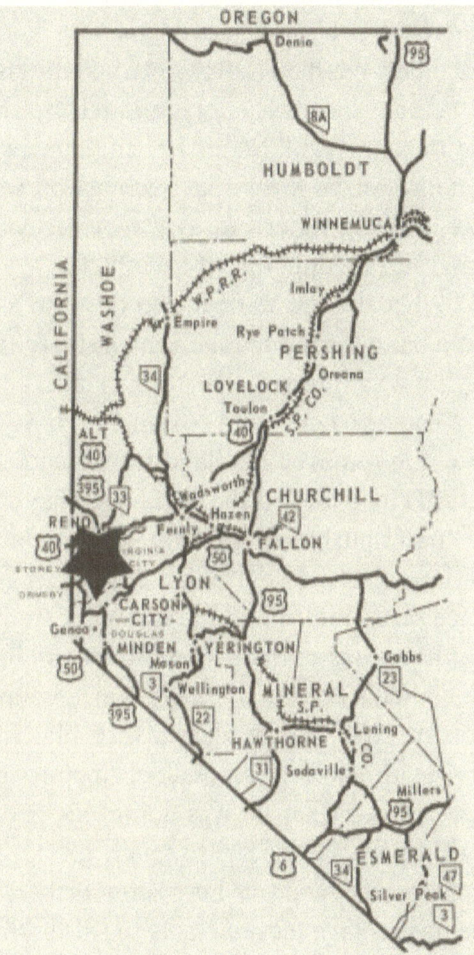

"Ask for Francese," he said, "very good."

"I don't want to go with that prostitute. I don't need her."

"You need her tonight," Nilsen smiled, "tonight you gave me your American girl." He removed one arm from the support of his little girl and placed his hand on Nancy Nottingham's hip.

Peter Prince was angry, and felt he should do something, should fight the Dane, or yank Nancy Nottingham away from him and he would have done it, but he knew that such action would make him seem foolish and categorically American as a movie cowboy, and he wanted to be more generous. He didn't want a conflict.

"What do you want me to do?" he asked Nancy Nottingham, putting out a hand for her to take, which she refused to notice.

"Do what pleases you, Peter Prince."

"You ask her," said Nilsen, "or if you're shy I'll have Jorgen ask for you." He removed his hand from Nancy Nottingham's hip to lightly urge Peter Prince toward the woman as they stepped up on the curb.

"Don't push me," said Peter Prince, as he watched the hand slide back to Nancy Nottingham's hip. "If I go, I'll go." He knew the trembling of his voice made him sound foolish, adolescent, but how could he act when his manhood was offended, and it was undiplomatic to respond. Trivialities. He couldn't act for the little burdens, those pressures on his skin, those women, that woman always with him who worked him into tiny angers that made motion impossible. Nobody understood that he wanted to be alive, to see what he was doing, his gestures meaningful, his action laid out properly, in the right sequence.

"Are you afraid of her, Peter Prince?" asked Nancy Nottingham. She seemed to have moved closer to Nilsen the Dane.

"I'm not afraid," he said, and pounded his thigh with his fist. He turned, and at that moment the woman who had been walking in front of them at a distance turned too and pointed at Peter Prince with the point of her scarlet umbrella, and with her eyes and lips gestured him nearer.

"*Per dieci ci vado,*" she said, meaning ten thousand lire, and with the umbrella hanging from her wrist she spread all her fingers to make sure he understood her price. Peter Prince looked about at the police in the various doorways, took the whore's elbow in his hand, and then stepped out.

The knife spun slowly in the air catching light, arrived at Philip Farrel, creaked, and dove in. Linda Lawrence looked up through narrowed eyes at the ravens in the trees' lowest branches, and the wooded mountains beyond the ravens, and the big, tough cumulus climbing the sky beyond the wooded mountains. Philip Farrel cupped his

Alright. Here's the end of my purge, and I feel better for it. Yippee. I feel lighter. It's a loss, but it's also a gain. Wahoo. I've done something for all of you, made it a little shorter through this book; and now I'd be grateful if you'd do something for me: Read Carefully. What follows is Serious Creative Writing!

hands over his chest where the knife had punched its hole. "I'll begin again," said Linda Lawrence, as she took a whetstone from her pocket, moistened it with spit, and sharpened her ax.

"*Allora, dove siamo?*" asked Peter Prince's whore, meaning that she wanted to know what he'd like from her catalog; whether he wanted her to suck his cock, to rub his cock between her breasts, to fuck him with his cock in her cunt, or for just a little extra lire, because it was painful for her, to make use of her asshole, causing friction and deep satisfaction. An overwhelming pang of lust suddenly assailed him, and not having decided what of that she offered he would prefer he began to move toward her, reaching out to touch her neck with both his hands. She took him expertly by the wrists and led him to a little sink in a corner of the room. As he handled her breasts and her backbone she unbuckled him and zipped his pants down, and soaped up his cock and balls with cold water. She straightened up.

"*Prima mi paghi,*" she said, rubbing her thumb across her fingers to show him she wanted money.

"Money, you want, you swindling bitch, and you call yourself a good whore. You expect me to pay before I've tasted the product? Do you call that reasonable? Good business? And you expect to take me like a foreigner. You expect I'll fall for that swindle?"

She didn't understand a word, and stood there with her hand out patiently breathing, her eyes half shut.

"You think you can take unfair advantage cause I'm American. You think we're all millionaires and can just spend as if nothing were bothering us. You, you are all the same, that's what. And you won't admit that you're exploiting our good nature and that's all . . ." Peter Prince went on.

"*Prima mi paghi,*" she reiterated, shrugging off his tirade and keeping her hand out till he was through.

Peter Prince paid her.

On the following day they sat again at the caffe by the station waiting for the Brenner Express to take them to the Oktoberfest, one day late, taking a chance on hotel rooms, hoping there will be something available, never sure, expecting the worst. Those were anxieties they shared. Otherwise Nancy Nottingham tried to ignore poor Peter Prince. She was peeved. She wanted him to know it. He spoke humbly, apologetically.

"Nancy Nottingham, you haven't said a word to me, and don't even answer my questions. How can we go on traveling together if there isn't a word between us?"

"What do I have to say to you any more?"

"Don't play the wronged woman. You brought that on yourself. You just remember the way you acted, playing the promiscuous one with that Dane. I should have told him some more about you."

"Promiscuous woman! We didn't do a thing."

"That's why you're upset then?"

"Peter Prince, I can't even talk to you. Nilsen was harmless. You should have seen that for yourself, man of the world that you are."

Peter Prince puffed through his closed lips, pulled out his B flat Höhner and began to play on it. The children of the servicemen who were waiting for their train, 43 or 46 or 75 of them, stopped their games to watch Peter Prince. The station had calmed down from the day before, a little less sky visible through the clouds, the sunlight sweeping like the train of a gown across Verona. There was something female about the day, that Peter Prince could recognize, and it made him feel uneasy and a little cold. The vibrato of his Höhner-blowing trembled. Police seemed a little looser, less of them, less military, but a greater proportion of them, Peter Prince noticed, staring right at him. He looked down to the 14 children gathered by his chair, and with a heart bruised by admonishments he played for them *Three Blind Mice*, without embellishments, and some of them sang.

Nancy Nottingham looked at him tearfully, and started to say something, but covered her mouth with her hand. Peter Prince removed his Höhner.

"What?" he asked.

"I don't know," she said.

"What did you want to say?"

Nancy Nottingham sighed like rattling cellophane. "I think you can be so nice sometimes."

Peter Prince smiled and lifted the Höhner again to his lips to play for Nancy Nottingham a slow "Greensleeves," her favorite.

"You know," she said, slowly beginning to talk, and relax, and things were getting better. "What we did last night?"

By raising his eyebrows over the tune Peter Prince indicated that he wanted her to tell him.

"Well all we did was go to see Nilsen's sculpture while you were with the whore."

Peter Prince's smile squeaked.

"He took us all to the foundry," she leisurely recounted. "It's not far from here, and showed me all his stuff. He's really good. I mean good enough to make me feel lucky that I've met him. His sculpture is full of form, and kind of sexual, I mean organic, like exploding, I don't know what . . ."

Peter Prince stopped playing when the noise, like human coughs erupting from the station, turned him from Nancy Nottingham. Men were running, and uniformed men following them. The police turned momentarily from Peter Prince to see the fracas but turned back to him immediately and watched him more carefully, because they were assigned. The shooting strolled across the broad street in front of the station, hoarse speaking of automatic rifles, and whom was who shooting? Peter Prince handed his Höhner to Nancy Nottingham who took it in mid-sentence.

". . . don't, Peter Prince. Don't leave here." She tried to hand him back his Höhner. "Don't put me here alone."

He rose and walked into the crowd, past the policemen who followed him in procession. This was the moment, he thought, to see what he could do. Before him was that chaos he couldn't remember anticipating, but knew now that he had hoped for it, to reassemble into orderly and reasonable action Europe's old fracturing, its disputed borders, and the slaughtering of folks. Peter Prince was in line to do something, would reconcile with his new, his sense of *living-for*, of *growth*, of *restless as America*, the old disparates, the bordering hatreds.

Had the gunfire stopped? He no longer heard gunshots, nor could he see where they had come from, guns all holstered or slung; just the wheeze of the *filobuses* coming to port under the canopy where the drivers argued. Had he heard them at all? Had that coughing and thumping he had heard been shooting at all; the soldiers and *carabinieri* he saw so calmly pacing about. He was sweating. And then he listened, and heard Nancy Nottingham's voice, he thought, calling him to turn around, and he did. Then he saw what it is, for it whistled at him, "hey there," first to attract his attention, as a boy from a block away with his thumb and forefinger to his lips, the sound falling, and then rushing at the end upward, dragging with it all the air from his atmosphere, through the tough, mountainous cumulus, beyond them, climbing the sky, "hey there," that bullet, as if he'd seen it before, coming slow from the muzzle cavernous, waving its arms and smiling at him as if that really was what he'd been waiting for, coming like a friend indeed, shedding color and light, "hey there," and Nancy Nottingham said, "Oh no," when that bullet thumped, and went in.

"Now," said Philip Farrel, "you've done it." He wiped the blade of Linda Lawrence's knife on his denim sleeve.

"Done what?" asked Linda Lawrence, taking the knife from his hand.

"Something absolutely senseless."

"Do you call Peter Prince's death senseless? His one attempt at purposeful action, senseless?"

"Senseless." Philip Farrel rose, took a brush from his jacket pocket, and cleaned the debris from the cuffs of his pants. He folded his newspapers and restored them to his jacket pocket. His hands were wet.

When Philip Farrel moved, Linda Lawrence went back to her tree and stroked the place where she was to begin her cut, and with her hand on the place she turned to look at the stick with the red flag. It was there. She would drive it down.

"Senseless, you say." She turned indifferently to Philip Farrel because she was ready to begin. "I have to admit it was a senseless death; poor Peter Prince. No sooner did he start his begin but we stopped it." She was concentrating on the first blow.

"You didn't even give him a chance to start the writing he did."

"Did he start to write? That's interesting." She looked at Philip Farrel for a moment, and then back to her first cut. "Of course I knew all along it was on his mind to begin."

"He began to do it soon after he left Verona, and to do it well, so you see what you ended?"

"You don't say," she grunted as she laid the first ax blow into the trunk of the tree.

"I'll tell you the first anecdote he put down if you'll listen. It was quite good," said Philip Farrel. "Will you listen?"

"Of course," she said, and the first neat wedge of her tree slipped out and fell to the duff, white and moist. Then another fell, and they fell regularly.

"This was the way he wrote it: " said Philip Farrel.

: Philip Farrel stood on the tar- and slime-covered rocks at the riverbank

watching the man with the moustache cast for eels. The whitecaps of the choppy water were tinted pink in the late sun that was flattening on the Palisades across the river, and there was an autumn chill in the air. Philip Farrel had been watching since early afternoon when the man arrived, with only a short break to turn his back and piss on the rocks. He hadn't yet seen the man catch an eel though he saw him persistently cast and draw in his line and cast again, replacing his bait occasionally, working with metronomic regularity that could make one think he was professional; nor did he ever pause to sink the crab-traps that lay on the rocks by his side.

The man with the black moustache hadn't yet turned once to recognize his audience, and the only sound he made was a monodic hum as he drew in his line, and a grunt as he cast out. Philip Farrel wanted to hear him speak, was resigned to, because he stubbornly squandered his time to stand there watching. The red lighthouse under the bridge was already darkened as the Palisades shadows thrust into Manhattan, and Philip Farrel noticed the slender file of bridge lights lit along the ramp. Had they been just turned on or lit all along? As he lowered his head back to see the fisherman he noticed the golden lights on the long arches lit also. When had that happened? How had he missed them?

The fisherman now was collecting his gear in a large canvas pack and smiling at Philip Farrel as he worked. He folded the traps into his pack and removed the reel from the rod. Philip Farrel took two steps toward him and then waited. The fisherman slipped the packstraps over his shoulders and straightened up, and with his creel under his arm stepped across the rocks toward Philip Farrel.

"A cold wind," he said.

Philip Farrel hadn't felt the wind. "How can you fish like that all afternoon," he asked.

"1 wanted to ask how you could watch me fish all afternoon."

Philip Farrel smiled.

The moustached fisherman put down his creel and squatted on his haunches. Philip Farrel imitated him.

"My name is Armando Amante." The fisherman offered his tar-streaked hand which Philip Farrel took. He revealed his own name.

"Do you come here every day like this to fish?"

"*And you to watch a fisherman?*" *Armando Amante lifted the cover of his creel. "I can't understand that you don't get bored or annoyed with catching nothing." "And you?" the fisherman asked.*

A muscular tug drew four barges up the river toward Albany, and behind them the evening. Philip Farrel became suddenly restless and wanted to get back to the city.

"You didn't sink the crab-traps once," he said, and stood up again.

"It's bad weather for crabs," said Armando Amante.

"And for eels?"

Armando Amante pointed into his creel and Philip Farrel saw that it was full nearly to the top with eels catching on their scaleless, silver sides the diminishing light, luminously moving. How had Philip Farrel missed it? When did Armando Amante catch them? Had he been watching closely enough? Had the eels come off at some time with the bait? How does one tell eels from bait? When?

"The river level seems to be rising," Armando Amante commented carelessly as he started away.

"You said? . . ." Philip Farrel shouted after him.

". . . seems to be rising."

*

"I haven't finished with it," said Peter Prince, "but I think it will be something like that, this book. A book in which separate worlds grow simultaneously." Peter Prince lifted the beer stein to his mouth and left a moustache of thinning foam on his upper lip. It was good beer, though the atmosphere was brutal, the Hofbrauhaus with its shallow leaden-yellow vaults, and dirty shadows on the walls, a Bavarian band of tubas and horns filling the piss-stained air with tarnished sound. A bony, black-haired girl from Nurnberg ran about the room with a strobe light and Hasselblad, photographing yokels.

Marsha Meltzin leaned against Peter Prince and listened to him because she admired him, and because she was a little frightened by, though she thought them picturesque, the Müncheners arguing across the table beside them.

"That's very good," said Marsha Meltzin, pointing to a page of his journal.

"Just that little story seems very, how shall I put it? . . . mysterious. I mean there seem to be some symbols in it, and everything. I'll bet you're going to be very good. What do you mean by those fish?"

Peter Prince looked again at the page as the Hasselblad strobed and snapped him. A huge waitress, with five steins in one hand and three in another, tried to see what was written on his page, and Peter Prince said, "I don't think I can really say. I don't know. I mean sometimes . . . Perhaps it means that sometimes it's so hard to tell what has really happened. It's impossible to know. That's why I want to develop multiple possibilities simultaneously. One is an Olympic world of almost omnipotent gods, and another, over which they exert arbitrary control, is the real world: ours." Peter Prince held his stein up for . . .

*

"That's enough," said Linda Lawrence as she neatly laid her ax in to rest where she was going to begin her back-cut, "I see right through that story. Could you ever tell a story that wasn't about yourself?"

"My dear Linda Lawrence, do you think that story was really about me?"

"It was about Philip Farrel."

"A name he chose."

"That's your name he chose, and that's why you wanted to tell that story."

"You misunderstand me."

"I don't misunderstand you. You're vain and irresponsible and lazy and imperceptive and that story demonstrates it, how you stand by the river and wait, as if you expect to learn without doing."

"If you had a mind to use, my lady," he drew the newspaper from his jacket pocket and slapped it against his palm, "you might be able to see the holes in your understanding."

"I know," she said, running her hand through the even V of her first cut. "I know who you . . ." But she stopped, and turned from Philip Farrel to the woods because of the noise she heard. It was a chiming sound dispersed through the woods as if a flock of bells were coming. It was their children. Philip Farrel moved up to stand beside Linda Lawrence and watch them come singing, their toys chattering, and waving flashlights in the dim, to the whole perimeter of the clearing, their white shirts like the spots of fawns at evening. And Philip Farrel called as they came, "Clipper, Timmy the Beetle, Brown Beth, Mark, Thomas, Chunky-it . . ." their names, and Linda Lawrence: "Sylvan in the Stands, Flake, (from younger days), Ari, Ben-Engle."

They had promised the children a picnic. The skies cleared, in the darkness a campfire, roasting meat and pots of broth, the steam rising to the huge trees leaning over them from the high darkness, and into the darkness their voices, rising; in chorus, rising.

*

Well I'm sorry for the delay after all my promises, but blame it on Sukenick. He said, "Just wait here for me, Katz, and I'll put you in my novel."

So I waited.

"That's why I haven't got Peter Prince from Italy to Egypt yet. I'm waiting just where he told me for Sukenick to put me in his novel, here on the street corner with the busted lamp. It can take some patience, because if he ever shows up at all he's usually late. And it's probably some little insignificant thing he's going to have me do, a little trip to Long Island, or a conversation with one of those characters of his who always wears tinted contact lenses. Even for the best friendship it's not worth neglecting Peter Prince, especially when he needs to go on a trip. Quality writing is measured by its transitions. But I promised, and I'll have to wait it out, that's all, and I beg for patience from anyone who is still around. In the meantime, as one of the feature presentations of this novel, I am proud to be able to present a paragraph by Peter Schjeldahl who has, among other things, been remarkable. The following paragraph is by PETER SCHJELDAHL:

*

Authorless, gleaming, Peter Prince felt fortunate so suddenly to have been removed, by some means (never mind), to the eleventh century where the noonday sun seemed somehow brighter and agreeably dry-hot, and removed too from Verona now all balefully transmogrified to Roman ruins; and Peter Prince exchanged his promontory on the grassy plain the better to view the construction of Venice. The early rash of dreadful watery disasters seemed over now, the surviving workmen having grown in cunning, and already a few brave blocks of houses, shops and hostelries stood out all charmingly enyarded by the lapping, lucid blue. And here and there, more to the point, a dusky pier grayly increasingly fingered the harbor, workers groaning it toward completion lest the nascent city be embarrassed with a stunted look in the crow's eyes of the first vessel that would chance upon it. And not the least of anxious seaward glances was our Peter's. Lovely as he found both site and industry, something in or on him yearned outward toward the hustle and the bustles of Cairo, Queen of the Sea. And how could he avoid some slightest articular tremor sensing about him the vastly assembled incipient citizens of Venice — bankers, firemen, stevedores, housewives, Jews and all — all fiercely attending the first crash of modernity, the throwing open of urban pantries, gates and doors? For how far, after all, Peter Prince reflected, could these creatures, as yet unrefined in docilities proper to metropolis be at remove from recent stage of savagery — Dark Ages, how opaque?! Even now our Peter felt perchance unfriendly gazes polishing his surfaces: these including wescot, pearly buttons, leather patches, pompadour, spats, acne, Western buckle, silken hanky, Screen Gem shades and vynal ring; comment c'était malàpropos!

* * * * * *

Wow. Isn't that amazing? Not only does this paragraph turn out to be about Peter Prince, but it almost gets the job done, and in a manner far more breathtaking than the author's own small capabilities. In fact, the whole problem with this troublous novel is that it probably found the wrong author in the first place: Me. I fart around here waiting for Sukenick, trying to get into his works, instead of paying attention to Peter Prince. It's a great literary loss that Peter Schjeldahl didn't write the paragraph that would get Peter Prince to Cairo; it could have saved some time for everyone, and would be delicious. Maybe Ted Berrigan will do it. He always does something for everyone, and he's always getting into everyone's works. I have a suspicion he has already written part of this novel, but I won't tell you which part. It could be the very next paragraph.

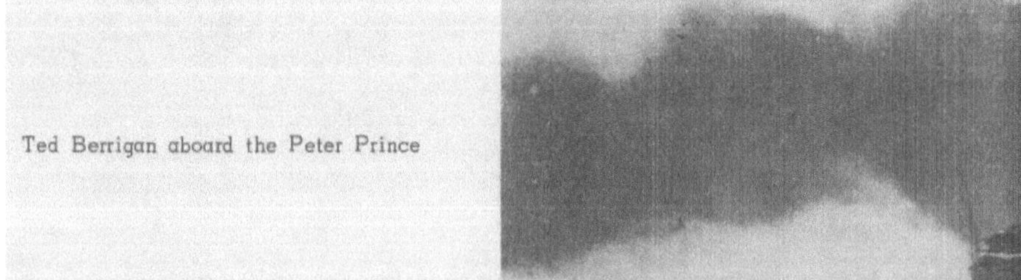

Ted Berrigan aboard the Peter Prince

puh-puh-puh-puh-puh-puh-puh-puh-puh-puh-puhr-puhricks-pricks & cunts & cocks : pussy pussy pussy pussy pussy pussss pusssssssssss : buhIllaaaaatt : fffffluullllll : take me : vomit take me : boirllll : Blah : Oh cancer sprout in my lungs : splennnnn : lunch dinner breakfast : fatty foods : grosssss grossseries : faaaaat : lip it out the lipsplurge lips : palm the bastard : poooooor basssssturd : pity me : don't pity me no : iced : I'm paralysed : Poor Peter Prince : lost peter lost prince : Heezafind find trash of a man in these mountains of evasions lost : bowwwwwwwwwww wwowwwwww : from me to him and him to me over months that passed not a word has passed : pissed away it's been pissed away : slopy farts sweaty slaps earruns and nosesnots and gobbled come : what's up when its all down on poor peter the prince whoever the fuck : what's that : what chance does it have : all my flapping all my spluttering tons : there it comes : hi : the little brain-meat surfaces : nibbles an oxygen : folds over itself : sinks : like a slug : hermaphrodite : here there : it's throbbing : the troooth the arroquent fact : hermesaphrodite : I'm outupin foritnow

How can I ever finish this book when it's always beginning? Come on. Peter Prince, he's got no history. He's pieced apart. I never know where to catch up with him. His past erases itself like a disappearing wake. I'd like to launch him once and for all beyond belief with a costly bottle of vintage bubbles to show the extravagance of my care, how I love his evasive divisive hide. Out there he's anchored maybe just out of sight like a Russian trawler. And I go nutty insomniac, my cheeks in my palms like a worried mother, my elbows pressed to the formica, my coffee going chilly. What's the use these days to even try to make a character, for all that you can add him up to? I ought to grab hold of myself and finish this novel without characters: just vacancies in the environment, that's good enough. That's the truth. The demands the little feebles make these days: show compassion, don't make it too hard on them, little crises, don't make the acts too heroic, just modern predicaments, send them to psychiatrists, dress them nice, find them girls and undress the little twats for them. If any character of mine ever goes to a psychiatrist he does it on his own time, at his own expense, those mind-bleachers, those commiserating pirates. But Peter Prince. But Peter Prince. Just a little bottle of table wine would be enough for the launching, *vino nero*, *yin ordinaire*, and he'd be on his way once and for all through some long coherent narrative excursion that's worth the price of admission. He likes the simple stuff, can polish off a good liter of wine with a meal, and then seal the feast with a slug of *grappa*: that stiff burn of raw booze always sets him on his feet, gnashing his teeth. He pushes away from the table after the meal, stands up, pulls his napkin from his belt, and wipes the big moustache that curves into his mouth like a pushbroom. "Deeeeelishus," he says, and slaps his gut in satisfaction. One tail of his workshirt flops out in front. "Absolutely mmmmmmmmmmmm." He stretches and you can see his extremities heat up with satisfaction. "I feel terrific." He yawns. "A good meal is better than a good . . ." Then he spots me. He leans toward me over the table. "There you are. So. Well. There you are." He lets out a creepy little muttering giggle. "I've got you pegged, you know. I've got you just about doped out.- His body sways back and forth on his stiff arms.

"I know what you're about."

Don't think that doesn't hit me right in the nerves. fffffffuuuhhhhhhhh. I dip into my glass of yogurt with a serving spoon. I didn't plan on the materialization of Peter Prince just at this moment. And with this kind of what shall I call it? balls? arrogance? it can't do me a bit of good. I've got an idea of all the things that he must know about me by now: a certain dullness, emptyheadedness, that he should resent by now. I'm not really the most intelligent author, with my head busting apart the way it does, and it can't hold with one idea long enough to work it out. He could also indite me for my laziness, this inertia, this white, weighty vacancy where the world should be. I'm like some anchored sea animal who would starve to death if the words didn't drift into its maw, and even when I know how to say it, it's a lot of trouble to bother. But worst of all, for me, for the author of a character like Peter Prince, I can't remember a thing. It all slips away. Where others have a memory I have a soapy fist, there it goes. And what happens to Peter Prince? He becomes something else from one page to the next, his eyes blue, brown, gray, green, his brow thick, furrowed, clear, twitching—whatever happens to suit the page I'm looking at. And when he says, "I've got you doped out. I know what you're about," that's what he means, hitting me right in the folds of my guilt.

From his vest pocket he draws a long cigar and he sits down. "You." He points the cigar at me. "You've got something lacking." I stare at his forehead, to avoid his eyes. "You lack something. You are going to fail." He slips the cigar from its cellophane wrapper and rolls it under his nose between his thumb and forefinger. My own character. My own brother, I could say. He licks the cigar from tip to tip and watches me. Such complacency. "Why don't you say something about me? What do you know about me?" he asks. "In this whole damned book there's not one passage of honest description. You don't know a damned thing about me. When have you shown it? You get in here and talk about yourself all the time. Sure you have to save yourself, but what about me? Oblivion . . ." He becomes silent and stretches out his palm toward me. "Admit it. There's not one passage in the whole damned book of honest description."

"Peter Prince," I finally say something into the gap. "That would be like . . ."

"Admit it."

"Like trying to write a whole . . ."

"Admit it."

That's enough. I shut up when my own characters start to get rude to me. As far as I know people are really starving in India, Pakistan, Brazil, Egypt, Yemen, Guatemala. Villages are burning in Vietnam. The prisons of the world are stuffed with the innocent. And I sit here wasting my hours with Peter Prince, this ill-conceived shadow. Children are burning, I think. I have never measured the terror in the world. An old woman watches the snow from her enclosed porch. Where can I begin?

"You can begin . . ." he pauses, his cheeks cave in, and he sucks a match-flame into the tip of his cigar ". . . begin with a description of me. A good one. Honest. Direct. Take a good look for a change."

He deserves the dirty look I give him. How out of place is his behavior in this novel, making demands. "It would be like trying to write a whole different novel," I try, fruitlessly, to explain in a nice way.

"You're going to fail."

"Peter Prince. I don't even want this kind of action for you, this overeating, all this wine and food, greasiness and gluttony. Who wanted you to show up here?"

"Definitely something you lack."

I want to do something to destroy his grin.

"Just begin to describe me. Direct, simple. Begin a damned description, or else . . ."

Presumptuous. I slam the table with the nearest book by Saul Bellow. Talk like that to me in my own novel. That's real gall. "Or else what, goddam it."

He puffs and he puffs. "Or else I'll leave."

I squeeze my temples and moan.

"It can't be that hard for a writer. Just look and describe me."

"You're fat now, Peter Prince, and greasy around the lips, and gluttonous. You look like a selfish imbecile."

"Is that the way you'd describe me?"

"It's certainly not the way I want you to appear in this book."

At this point he gives me an enigmatic grin, revealing some wrinkles that have set in the corners of his eyes since the beginning of this book. He was a kid when we started, with a big shock of hair and a steady gaze, full of uncertainty, but a real candidate, if you can remember the way he managed time after time to keep his friends out of fights. "Well then fake what you please," he says. "It's better than nothing, and that's what we've got here. Adjust what you really see to your . . . your Overall Conception, for all I care. At least it's a little something."

The tone of that last remark makes me feel that Peter Prince isn't just toying with me. There is some desperation in it, but what can I do for him and still remain true to myself? "Peter Prince," I try to reason. "I'm the novelist here, and I know a little bit more about this business than you do. Listen to me. DESCRIPTION lives only when it's appropriate to the ACTION that embodies it." I blink, dust off my sleeves, and go on, "DESCRIPTION, you might say, is the MEDIUM, the BACKGROUND, the AMBIENCE, in or before which the ACTION takes its COURSE. But the ACTION has to GeNeRaTe the NECESSITY for the DESCRIPTION."

"Yes. O.K. Describe me anyway." He puffs some more, impatiently. "Or else . . ."

"Or else you'll disappear, right?" I try to bend the book by Saul Bellow.

"That's right."

I hum a little classical music and rap on the table with my yogurt spoon. I always figure when the pressure's on, relax; if you don't fight, it passes over just the same, and the worst it leaves is a reconstruction job. Take it easy: smell the smells, listen to what's hissing, pick your nose: cool it.

The empty dishes fade away, and so does the tablecloth: the chair I am sitting on softens and slowly disappears. I have to stand up in a dark space. Peter Prince is permeated by the deep, flowing atmospheres and is tugged away in gauzy sections.

"WAIT," I shout (too late, he's disappearing) and I hastily, though reluctantly begin the description he demanded. I try to breathe it out in the dark space where I stand. OK.

Let us assume that Peter Prince is a medium-short man, 5'8" give or take a half inch. He could be fat, and I guess he is fat. Sandy hair which is usually messed up, bushy, disheveled eyebrows. His ears don't stick out. I have mentioned his moustache but not his beard. He has big, puffy cheeks; we might even say that he's all over somewhat tubby.

"What's that?"

What I mean is that he tends somewhat to be hefty a bit, though he's active enough to be in fair condition. He has thick strong shoulders and a big chest but that strength doesn't carry into his frail hands and skinny wrists. He has a soft grip. Perhaps that's why he stutters, that confusion of frail extremities wielded with too much power. That stutter is a weakening, a slight but evident slowing up of his otherwise forceful speech, accompanied by a little moan, like that of a suffering woman. When he is getting into serious matters people mistake it for a reflective pause, but not so. I've decided to leave that stutter out of this novel because it's tough enough for Peter Prince to get along without tripping over his speech. I will mention, however, his right calf, because it itches like hell, and he has scratched little scabs in it, and he doesn't know why it itches.

In this description the feature I feel most obliged to tell of, even in one as tentative as this, is his eyes: They're strange ones, blue granite opacities. Impenetrable. Even when aimed at you they seem to be gazing elsewhere. The Northwest Indian poet spoke of the eyes of the men of the Lewis & Clark expedition as being so blue as the hard sky when even the eagle fears his wings. That's what Peter Prince's eyes are like, eyes as blue as obsidian is black. He's after something, somewhere else, you feel, and sets his eyes therefore on the nothing around you, or within you, always on nothing, just as I stare like a fool at this empty page, every face an empty page which he would imprint, gazing as I gaze into the mute indifference.

"This book, I think, is a step backward." One editor has already seen a piece of these exaggerations and decided that, using up part of a Saturday afternoon, and scanning over a late Sunday breakfast, while he dropped toast crumbs into his soft-boiled eggs, and two women tried to talk to him. Don't think I disagree with him. You know as well as I do that I don't see where I'm going. It might as well be backward. I'm just trying these empty spaces with luminous motion, and things. Things, things, things: How a novel can fill with them like a barrel with sponges. They rise like pieces from a sunken ship and lie noiseless on the tide. How beautiful they all are: a faded blue-flannel smoking jacket, the chipped frame of a dark seascape, brass fire-tongs on the terra-cotta hearth, some knotty pine shelves full of books: the poems of Carl Sandburg, half an encyclopedia set, *The Egyptian, Das Kapital, Symonds Tree Identification Book,* some novels by Upton Sinclair—all faded clothbounds. The easy chair has a flower-print dust-cover, a rack for ten pipes is set on an end-table nearby, with only three pipes in it, and a dog-eared *Reader's Digest* leaning on it. In one corner a mandolin rests on its bowl on top of a baby-grand with its keyboard locked. I sit here in the air conditioning and am suddenly surrounded, and I can recognize the place, smoke a pipe there, build a fire, and best of all a dog can walk in there, sniffing and wiggling, a big brown one with a sloppy mouth, and put its head in my lap. That's the best of all. I've never had a dog, and I've always needed one, wide, hairy, tough-ribbed, a dog that will stick his nose in the snow. Peter Prince hasn't a dog either, because he's always in motion, splitting the scene, after something new, and there's no room in his economy for stuff like dogs, that makes experience weigh. He's always skimming. He never leaves a wake.

Peter Prince in motion. I sit still and try to get the book launched. My sedentary commitment. Where would Peter Prince be without that? The more I sit on my ass the better he moves. I hear it's that way all over: oppositions, actions, reactions—the forward motion, the canceled thrust; matter and its anti-. Ha. Love and hate they say in me is intermixed. And I say, and listen to me, I say that no one knows what's going to happen next. So.

So he's gone. Lying out there somewhere like a Russian trawler, while I go crazy in my sleep, drink coffee in one place or another, face in my hands, elbows on formica. In the old days those guys did pretty well appealing to the muses, but it never works for me. I dip into that Pierian spring and get a fistful of mud or gravel. I try. Every day I leave this little room and walk out into the library stacks where books sit like little managers, and I walk around slapping light switches and reading titles, and mumble, "Calliope, honey, come here and give me a hand. Clio, let's straighten things out down here. Any one of you beauties: Euterpe, Erato, Terpsichore, Polymnia, Melpomene, Thalia, Urania even. Any one of you give a little look at what I'm doing, I can't seem to get it right by myself. Give me the way. Calliope, baby, I've got the need for you—lay some of that honey on my tongue. Not a chance. I might as well be in orbit. My brain aches like a dose of blue-balls, and my tongue is throbbing. Those chicks have built themselves a fall-out shelter on Mt. Olympus, and they're not peeking out. The fluorescents buzz, the page-light blinks, librarians, like hospital attendants, pass holding the little cards and whispering call numbers to themselves. I settle for a sip of chilled, chlorinated water from the cooler, and return to my box where there's no hint of Peter Prince. Five months without a word, and you see for yourself what kind of appearance he makes. There's some defect in my manufacture. Nothing gets started, nothing happens. I gather repetitious trivia, and step backward, and backward: into the word

"Shhhhhhhhhh." (The word is that Peter Prince is in Egypt, ready to go down the Nile for a glimpse of Nubia, before it goes under) "Don't wake him up."

"I've got to get him up. You know that. That's why we're here. Peter Prince has got to get going." (I got the word from these two, Linda Lawrence and Philip Farrel, who are the closest I ever get to a real operating muse, being my field representatives.)

They stand beside the bed where Peter Prince sleeps back to back with

Sarah Spurgeon. The hero of this novel is smiling in his sleep, his lips fluttering, and it is Sarah Spurgeon who snores, licking her lips. Linda Lawrence and Philip Farrel stand there silently for a while and watch the couple sleep, she with her knees to her chest, he with the small of his back arched around the curve of hers.

"It fits so nice, I almost hate to waken them," says Philip Farrel.

"Shhhhh," admonishes Linda Lawrence.

"You know I have to wake him up. I mean it doesn't make any difference to me or anything, but . . ." and he points off the page to where I am sitting. "I just have no choice." This embarrasses me no end, because I sit here picking wax out of my ear with a paper clip, and expect to hear Linda Lawrence say at any moment, "Nothing bigger than your elbow, sweetie."

Philip Farrel is dressed as usual in his neat business suit, his dispatch case wedged into his armpit. He lays the case on the nightstand, and lifts the coverlet slightly. "Peter Prince . . ." he begins, but Linda Lawrence tugs him gently away.

"Let me do it," she says.

Philip Farrel is impatient with the whole business. "I promise you I'll wake him, but gently," she says.

"I am being gentle."

"I know," says Linda Lawrence. "But I'm a woman."

"It's not me." Philip Farrel points my way again. Linda Lawrence winks at me, as if we have some secret understanding. Truthfully, I am just waiting to see what happens, because I know how impossible it is to get things to work when you push. I nod ambiguously.

"O.K. with me." Philip Farrel shrugs, and he leaves the scene. He has, after all, a lot to do while this novel is going on. He goes to get interviewed, he fixes up proposals, he prepares his data sheets, he clinches deals, he charts the progress.

Linda Lawrence tosses her long brown hair from her cheeks and places a hand softly on Peter Prince's shoulder. "Prepare to go on a journey," she says.

Peter Prince twitched, and rolled over, and Sarah Spurgeon sucked in a long, high-pitched whine as she straightened her back. Linda Lawrence leaned over and let her hair fall in a narrow tunnel through which she looked at Peter Prince.

"You're going to go on a journey."

"A journey," mumbled my protagonist, passing his hand over his wavy black hair.

"Please wake up," she urged him by rocking the mattress on its springs.

He twisted, and moaned a little, on the brink of rising. I thrilled to see this happening, and did a joyous fade-out, and so did Linda Lawrence fade out, but she in a different direction.

Peter Prince sat up, rubbed his eyes, and tried to focus on something in the grainy dimness. "What did you say? Hey. Who's that here, anyway? Who's here?" His voice was still hoarse with sleep. He went barefoot to the balcony door and quickly raised the shutter that covered it. "I know you're in here. I heard you." The orange glow of Cairo before sunrise cast his shadow, rust-hued and amorphous, across the room. He saw no one. Sarah Spurgeon was still asleep on the bed. No one else. He slid the closet door back: his one suit, Sarah Spurgeon's eighteen dresses. "I'll find you. I saw you in here, damn it," he said into the microphone that was hidden in the lamp fixture. He had never felt this before, this state of siege. It felt weird. The hotel room was bugged, he didn't know why, a microphone in the closet, in the vase of plastic flowers, in the bathroom. It was impossible to make love in this spying, especially to Sarah Spurgeon, who was against it anyway. He looked at the lump of her beneath the sheet, breathing. Why didn't she wake up? Was it worth it? She was paying his way, but exacting her toll.

He shook the mattress where she was lying until she opened her eyes. "Listen. There was someone in here watching just a moment ago. Spying on us. I heard him."

"Ohhh," she shut her eyes. "Awful." She hugged her bedsheets in a wrinkled bunch and shoved her head under the pillow.

It made no difference anyway. Peter Prince left her to step out on the balcony. It made no difference that she slept. So what? He couldn't speak to her. They were together like two animals of the same species, getting what comfort they could out of that recognition. Not a word of understanding had passed between them since they met in Florence and she took him up on his dare. The wind was strong and full of dust. It was difficult to breathe in Cairo; sometimes it hurt, as if your lungs were turning to stone. He lit a cigarette. Below a detachment of street-sweepers was marching by in a ragged line with their crude twig brooms on their shoulders. The streets were always noisy. The sweepers seemed to scream at each other in Arabic. Peter Prince flicked the half-smoked cigarette over the side and one of the men below picked it up without looking up and put it in a leather pouch on his belt. Peter Prince closed his eyes.

He didn't want to see this Cairo. It could have been Chicago the way it looked from there, its broad avenues lined with expensive American cars, and the Nile Hilton, and the Semiramis, and the New Shepheard's hotels. It was boring and evil. It wasn't its own place anymore. What he wanted was his trip down the Nile to begin then, immediately. He wanted that break into the past. THE PAST—back there. He wanted to see Nubia, to have it tattooed on his memory, before the High Dam put it under. Abu Simbel—all those places. He couldn't remember the names of all the places that would be inundated, the timeless Nubian villages strung along the Nile from Aswan, into the Sudan, that beautiful race of Nubians evacuated. It was tacit genocide. They would be moved into faceless modern developments along the new lake's perimeter, their centuries snuffed out. Starve the damned Egyptians, thought Peter Prince, looking out through the dust, rather than kill Nubia: The centuries snap like a plexiglass dowel. Nubia would drown in its white robes, in its flooded heritage; all for the unfeedable masses of Egypt who would fill the streets of Cairo faster than food could be provided for them. Luxor, Memphis. Those names: Nefertiti, Ramses, Cheops. They were great stone dreams. Not like the Italian names whose history was imaginable, but names that have known 6000 years of recording the Nile's flood. The Nile was and

Egyptian names were timeless, history a Greek invention: The Nile like the chain of a great watch, that watch in Europe, running down.

These were the vile thoughts of Peter Prince. He opened his eyes as a clanking yellow bus rounded the corner near his balcony and continued down the street, backfiring. He heard it stop a few blocks away, its brakes squealing, its doors rattling open, probably discharging workers into one of the hotels. The life they led looked hard.

"Ah Egypt," Peter Prince sighed, as he slid over to make room for Sarah Spurgeon who had put on a net bathrobe and come out to join him on the balcony.

"Tell me what you're thinking."

Peter Prince looked at her and smiled perfunctorily. She moved closer to him on the railing. "I always want to know what you're thinking. You always look like you're thinking something that I'd really like to know about. What was it?"

"What?"

"What you were thinking."

"When?"

"Just now when you were thinking, just before I came out; you were thinking something."

"I wasn't thinking anything much."

"Oh stop. I know you were. You think all the time, I can see it. And you'll never tell me anything about it. You said 'ah Egypt,' just when I got here, I heard you, so you must have been thinking something about Egypt."

Peter Prince moved his hand across her breast and she backed off. She was boring. He couldn't say anything to her if he couldn't even touch her. "I was wondering," he turned away from her to face the street, "what someone was doing in here, sneaking around in the room before I got up. I heard him,-and I think I saw him, and then he was gone."

"That's dreadful." She touched his hand with her cold, flat palm. "It's a silly bore to have someone snooping around, for them and for us, as if they could learn anything about anything from what we do. We're innocent as little, little . . ." She put her two palms together in a prayer gesture.

"Little eunuchs," Peter Prince said.

"Yes," she giggled, "whoops, me too. We certainly should put a complaint in about all this at the desk. What's that?" Another bus, this one screaming and whining, turned the corner. "Oh that's an awful contraption. Imagine having to ride in that every day. I don't see why people have to put up with it. They should go on strike and get a better bus." Working out that idea made her quite proud of herself and she smiled at Peter Prince as if expecting him to acknowledge her sound thought. "But it wouldn't do any good, would it, to call?"

"What?"

"To call the desk and complain about snoopers."

"They'd think I was crazy. I can't really prove there was anyone in here. I mean I know there was someone in here, but they don't have to believe me."

"I believe you. They could at least wait until we're gone from the premises before they start hunting for their microfilm or secret weapons, whatever they think we have. I always thought snoopers and spies had at least a certain discretion."

"You got that from the movies."

She stared at him for a moment with that empty look on her long, oval face, her small lips drawn in an inverted pucker. He didn't want to know her. He didn't care about her. She could remain this stranger to him forever. Even the lovemaking that might eventually be possible was a waste of time to worry over. He was, anyway, her pick-up; in public her gigolo, in private her roommate. "I would love it so much if you would just tell me what you were thinking."

"I told you."

"You said what you were wondering, not what you were thinking, with that 'ah Egypt' you let out. You never really tell me anything, about what you really think. You've got those deep thoughts. I can see them when you sometimes look at me and it's as if I'm not there, but you never talk about them with me. I would love to hear sometimes what you really have to say, but it's so trying the way you clam up. Men always do that. They always hide. We women are so open and giving and caring and free with ourselves. We throw ourselves open. But you men never anything. Nothing."

"I'll write poems to you," said Peter Prince.

"Will you?" she started to fan herself with the lace collar of her bathrobe. "I hope it doesn't get too hot. Do you think we can get breakfast now?" A manic smile suddenly appeared on her face as if a spring had been released. She took both his hands. "Let's start drinking now. I have to do my shopping today."

"Shopping?"

"I have to buy some things, you know, little things just so I can remember I've been here."

"Ohhh. We were going to leave this hole today."

"Yes." She put her finger to her lips and looked at him as if from under a veil. "But there's tomorrow and the rest of the days. There's so much I have to get done, and the man at the boats was so sweet. No. Today I'm going to buy myself some of those pointed Egyptian slippers and a something for Franco, you heard me yourself. I promised him a tarboosh. You know he expects it."

"I'm going to go out of my mind if I don't get out of here today, Sarah Spurgeon."

"Sooooo hot," she moaned, and slipped back into the room. "Why don't you call down and have them send up our breakfast, and have them put on a bottle of that sweet, licorishy stuff. If I don't eat now, Peter Prince, I'm sure I won't be able to eat when it gets so hot."

Peter Prince followed her in, biting off his hangnails.

"And I want to get one of those bathroby things, you know. I like to have all that stuff around when I'm home again, just to wear, you know, on some nutty occasions."

"I didn't want to stay here another day." He was hardly audible. What could Peter Prince do? His way had never been bought for him like this before. It was embarrassing to push his demands. His will was embalmed in her cash. It was an impossible position he was in, and he hated himself for it, though he knew he had brought it on himself. But he hated most, from all the depths of his Peter Prince, all her dull spoiled impertinence, the way she stared at him through that rude, tranquilized calm produced by the pills she took, that gave her eyes a soft distracted focus as if she looked at him through frosted glass.

"I still would like to know what you were thinking," she insisted. "You're thinking some terrible things about me, I can tell. I can see it."

"Sssshhhhhh. Don't be ridiculous."

"Look how you lie to me. You're almost blushing. I know you hate me because I don't let you make love to me. Men always hate me when I spend money on them. There are some things I know that you don't have to tell me, because I see them right through you. Men aren't opaque in everything."

"No, no. Please, no." He put his hand in the small of her back and drew her stiff, reluctant body toward him. "You're inventing this all. It's not like this." He kissed her on her sprayed, starchy, thick honey hair. "I'm really grateful for this. I could never have got here without you. I'm really grateful. Of course I want to make love to you, you know why? Because . . . because that's the way I can thank you for all this. That's the most beautiful, the only . . ."

"You lie. You never say anything to me. If you were grateful you'd talk to me about interesting things, but you never do. Those beautiful dark brown eyes you have that never look at me, but always you're gazing off somewhere. You never see me."

The sun suddenly appeared thick and red between the buildings, and the wallpaper's pink and white stripes took the hue of raw pork. Peter Prince felt his throat narrowing as they stared at each other.

"Another day." He looked down.

Her mouth snapped on that smile again. "Let's see, the pointed Egyptian sandals, the red tarboosh for Franco, and of course a little something for Peter Prince. I'll have to make a list." She lifted the phone from the hook and handed it to Peter Prince. "Breakfast," she said, "and a bottle of that licorishy stuff."

Peter Prince took the phone. It was not yet seven, and there was no response from the desk, but he placed the order anyway on top of the buzzing. Then he dropped the shutter to the balcony and the room was gray as an oyster. He lay down beside her on the bed. She was muttering about shops and bargains and he tried to turn her off inside his skull but she went on and on like advertising and as he lay there on the bleary verge of sleep a mild despair simmered under his eyelids. He snored lightly, keeping himself awake, and found his cock suddenly stiffened like the handle of a rubber stamp. Indifferent words issued from her mouth. He sighed, and her head tilted to look at him. As soon as she saw his erection the pitch and pace of her talking increased, articulating prices and places of interest. He shifted one of her hands to his cock and tried to move his head to kiss her.

"No," she turned away, "I can't. Not with that microphone on." She tightened her fist, as if she didn't know her hand was around his cock, and squeezed the lust out of him. "I'm sorry. It's just not good this way."

"What way?"

She didn't answer, but curled up on her side again, with her back to Peter Prince. "I wish they'd bring that breakfast."

He took the phone again, and this time got someone at the desk, a squealing, servile voice, with whom he placed the order. He fell asleep after that. An hour later Sarah Spurgeon was thumping on his shoulder. She was dressed now in starched white bermudas and sneakers, no socks, a starched blue blouse. "They still haven't sent up that breakfast," she said. "Get up, Peter Prince."

The light through the slits in the shutters hit Peter Prince in the eyes. He stood up, a little sick.

"I called the desk once while you were asleep and they said it would be right up. That was thirty minutes ago. Egyptians aren't used to listening to women. Call them, Peter Prince. I'll pass out if I don't get something to eat right away, and have a little drink." She pouted and sat down on the bed. She was going to cry. Peter Prince got on the phone immediately and began to threaten the man at the desk. It had been two hours. His lady was starving. In years of travel he had never known such service. It was a disgrace. He could see as his voice got louder and his threats more eloquent Sarah Spurgeon's unhappy expression change to a smile; she began to giggle. "And if you don't get that food up here within ten minutes," he said, "I shall come down there and see that you are dealt with severely." He hung up. Sarah Spurgeon kissed him on both cheeks and went on for a while giggling and telling him how marvelous he was. Peter Prince felt sick, having shouted for her miserable sake at some poor, underpaid, underfed morning clerk. He went to the balcony again and lifted the shutter to feel the full blast of the sun. He deserved that unbelievable heat. Sarah Spurgeon was sitting on the bed again. Twenty minutes passed. No breakfast.

"Peter Prince, can't you do anything? Do something."

He looked at the telephone. "Give them ten more minutes."

"You'll have to go down there. You have to do something, Peter Prince. I'll faint. I'm going to pass out right here, just like that."

Peter Prince had no gripe against anyone. He wasn't the person to scream at a poor hotel clerk, get him fired. He would rather murder Sarah Spurgeon for her pitiful billfold, and solve the problem that way.

"Peter Prince, please."

"Stop putting on this terrible act."

She threw herself on the bed, face down, and began to sob, trembling all over.

Peter Prince stepped up to the vase of plastic flowers and parted them to expose the poorly concealed microphone. "Damn it," he shouted full into the mike. "I'm going to the tourist bureau and advertise how lousy the service is in this damned hotel. I'll put an ad in the Paris *Times* and *Tribune*, goddam it. You're getting me sick over this. Don't tell me to calm down now." He kept shouting, slowly fading back from the microphone.

Within eight minutes the breakfast arrived, a bottle of zebeeb, compliments of the house. As her stomach filled Sarah Spurgeon mellowed. Peter Prince found the sweet anise liquor to be good at breakfast, and he drank enough to feel a nice buzz, though not as much as Sarah Spurgeon who drank enough to get silly.

"Oh, so hot. It's going to be hot." She reached over and grabbed Peter Prince's shoulder. "And I need to do all this shopping. And . . . Oh fuck . . . What time is it?"

Peter Prince lifted her wristwatch to her face. "Oh, ten thirty," she giggled. "I don't know how I got worried. I lose track. You see Franco said he'd call at five thirty this evening to wish me a good trip, so I have to be back here. You see I'd thought it was dinner. You know, I had to get permission from Franco to take you with me. The dear Italian. He said he'd be so lonely without me. Italians are so romantic, Peter Prince. They're real romantics, and that's what makes them so lovable."

Ohhhhhh, Peter Prince thought. Who is this chick? And what has this ridiculous babble got to do with me? Her hand still held to his shoulder and he wanted to move it, but didn't feel he should, so peculiarly bought did he feel, as if it wasn't his own meat.

"Oh fuck," she said. "I do have to get going, and that's certain. Get a hold on myself. You're not going to come with me at all, shopping? You look completely disgusted, sweet little Peter Prince. I'm sorry. I'll bet you're sorry you ever decided to even come to Egypt with me. I must try your patience. I know. You let me spend all this money on you. You think. . . I can see it right there in your cheeks. I'm frivolous, and trivial, and a silly woman. If you knew what I've been through to end up this way."

He couldn't tell if the wideness of her eyes and that stretched grin was hysteria or happiness. She was twanging like a strung bow. He reached out perfunctorily to touch her hair and comfort her.

"Don't worry," she said, pulling back. "You'll get your trip down the Nile."

Peter Prince stood there for a while, trying to see her face, but she kept turning away from him. He gave up. He grabbed his bathrobe and went into the shower room and turned the water on himself, letting it fall in sputtering, foul-smelling draughts. No. He wouldn't work on it any more. It wasn't worth it. He'd ignore her, and let her go her way, whatever she wanted to do, even if she would leave him stranded. He'd been worse off. He didn't want to see any more of this Cairo. It made him uneasy with its broad avenues and its rows of cars. He didn't want this third-rate modern scene. He wanted his city packed with spices, with Syrian pears, quinces, pomegranates, fine silks, purple dyes, a city of camels and stained glass, of sable and lynx, a city of men who could make chains for fleas and could train lions to walk at your heel like a dog through the bazaar. He wanted a city out of time, not even old Cairo, that seemed to apologize for itself. He couldn't do it unless he set right out and got a feel for the river, dipped back toward what was stone. Not in Nasser's Cairo, but in Egypt.

"What are you going to do all day?" He could see her shape blurred through the shower curtain.

"I'm going to stay here under the shower till we're ready to get on the boat."

"Lucky boy. I do hate this shopping business, but it's an obligation, you know that." She stood there quiet for a moment, and then in a most back-scratching voice, a voice that always got its way, so thin it was, and taut, she said, "Peter Prince, will you do me just a little favor since you'll be here. I'd be ever so grateful to you. Try to listen for the phone at five thirty when Franco calls. I'm really not sure I'll be back, and I'd hate for nobody to be here. Just accept the charges, and take the message. It would be a dear thing for you to do and would ease my conscience while I shop."

"Try to get back yourself, will you. I'm sure Franco doesn't want to talk to me."

"Of course I'll try to get back. Dear Franco. But you'll be here just in case, won't you, just to ease my mind over this."

"I'll try," he said.

"Promise me, Peter Prince. You're so sweet."

He looked out from the shower. She had put on bright red lipstick and powdered her face, and looked like a Japanese puppet. "I promise," he said, taking the easiest way to get rid of her.

"You sweet Peter Prince." She placed the mark of her lips on his shoulder, and left him through every door.

"Ahhhhhhhhhh," said Peter Prince when she was gone. He would really take a shower now, wash off the whole filthy morning, that lipstick on his shoulder, flood away the whole commitment he had made, the debt he was in for this trip up the Nile. He was giving her his what? His presence? His time? They were both going crazy under it. That trip up the Nile could erase from him the stain of time. He needed to come to a new understanding, some new understanding of what was here for men, what was available, what he could use, what he could do again. He had never done anything, as if he'd never had time, always too busy discovering what came at him as he lived. He wanted to go down there into Egypt and come back armed and useful. It would be impossible with that woman creaking around in his head. He turned to face the dwindling shower stream and turned up the cold water. The shower-head sputtered and dripped. He turned the water off and then on again. Two short spurts of searing water hit his neck, and then nothing. Off and on again. Nothing. He slapped the nozzle with his right and then left palm. Nothing. He beat on the shower stall where he thought the pipes went down. The shower-head hissed. Nothing. He turned . . .

*

I guess Peter Prince is busy enough for a while so we can leave him alone puttering with his shower. For a while there things are in good narrative order, and I'd rather hunt around and gather up some other events that need telling before this book reaches its delicious and unsuspected climax. You can rest assured that nothing needs to be told about the next few hours of Peter Prince's day. Nothing. He gives up on the shower and goes out into Cairo in a lousy mood, where it's hot enough, and dusty enough anyway to drive anyone crazy, and he doesn't see anything worth repeating, though he does try a cup of warm goat's milk charged with cinnamon, which he can't stomach. So let's forget him, and work a little while with Philip Farrel, who is not waiting in the outer office any longer, you know, but is in on a committee meeting proper of an aforementioned terrific concern, and he's being talked to by one of the board members, a principal stockholder, and a man of influence in that community, with a daughter at a leading eastern university, and a son in Naval O.C.S. A white man, a liberal, with his middle finger missing. A man whose wife runs many charities.

"We understand that the man we're interested in is an acquaintance of yours, if not a friend, at least close to you, that he'll probably see you before almost anyone as soon as he steps off the boat. That you sometimes correspond with him, and that more than to anyone else he'll probably listen to you." The man had a square, gray face; he was aging in good condition, with a little muff of fat at the nape of his neck. When he talked he tucked in his upper lip for a tough, head coach effect, and tapped on his notepad with his ballpoint. "You've got a certain influence over him that we could perhaps say no one else has." He paused, and drew back his lips in a smile.

Philip Farrel was playing it cagey. He didn't, of course, have much of an idea yet of what they were talking about, but he didn't want them to be aware of how little he understood what was actually going on, so to make them think his gambit was to be evasive by playing dumb, he tried to play dumb, and they regarded him warily and with respect, as if they knew that his maneuver was to get as much out of them as possible before he revealed anything they wanted to know, so they understood his silence as a tactic they admired, most of them having been trained at the poker bench, and he, in turn, was successful in not revealing his bewilderment, successful in clouding the fact that easier and in fact more possible than trying to speak and explain was this pose of knowing taciturnity he had assumed, this silence. He kept silent. Maybe eventually he would speak and let them know something. It was his enemy or his friend and would cause the outcome to be either favorable or not: Time was, Time would. He rarely thought it over, but hung on, waiting to be asked to open his dispatch case, which was all he really cared about. Their problems were their own problems. He would fit in only if he could do it and still maintain his shape, he had resolved. He slid his palm over the surface of his case and admired the conference room.

It was beautiful and modern, the wall panels of a rubbed walnut veneer, and hung on every other panel was a portrait of an executive either retired or passed on. The conference table was of modern design, wider at the middle than at either end, made of a lustrous black wood, and surrounded by firm though comfortable leather-covered chairs, some of which swiveled, though not the one Philip Farrel sat on. Hidden behind the panels, most of which swung on hinges, or slid on rollers, were sinks, bathroom facilities, a bar, a TV and stereo, some small computers, a variety of electronic equipment to record and put on video tape everything that went on in the room. Lenses were pointed at everyone in the room. The whole room was lit with a diffused natural light, the source of which was not apparent. In case of an all-out attack the room was designed to lower like an elevator through the basement into a lead-walled chamber where business could go on as usual. In front of the President, who sat at the head of the table, was a panel that slid back to reveal the console that operated from one position all the devices in the room. But for Philip Farrel, who wore a suit, everyone in the room was in his shirtsleeves. It was without a doubt a working conference, with papers scattered over the center of the table, and the President, a pencil-chewer, in a blue workshirt, with his sleeves rolled up, his tie undone, his cuff-links in the ash-tray beside him: the whole group a work-force, brain-trust.

"You can talk to him, can't you? We're not wasting our time, are we?" asked a nervous one in a striped button-down. His face was thin and oily and he blinked a lot and rubbed the creases by his nose. "I mean you have the access we need, don't you? We're not wasting our time with you, are we?" An almost inaudible buzz sounded at his place and the man looked immediately to the President who silenced him with a quick show of teeth. He spoke to Philip Farrel himself.

"What we want you to do is just simply a matter of exerting a little of your influence; it will hardly even embarrass you, if at all. You will just ask him . . ."

"I'll ask whom?" Philip Farrel decided finally it was time to sound a small note. The members of the board smiled. They admired the resonance of his voice and its self-assurance reassured them.

"Ahhhhhh," they said as a group, suddenly realizing what had caused the block in communication.

"Ohhhhh," said the President, straightening up in his seat and pouring some water for himself. "You didn't know we were discussing Peter Prince? Come now."

"I never came here to talk about Peter Prince."

The members of the board all straightened up and sipped on their water tinted green from the minty ice.

"The reason I'm here is to show you how I can be useful to your operation. I render a service, you see, I mean a kind of control, computerized, that is unique."

"But we've already decided the use you can be put to, you see. That's why we asked you to come in here," said a man on his right.

"That's not why I'm here." Philip Farrel nervously clicked open the snaps of his case, and closed them again.

"Don't get nervous. Don't get nervous," said the President. "You're too sensitive. You have to understand our viewpoint before you stab us with your integrity. We're businessmen. This is business, and not unsuccessful. Hard, ruthless business for profit. We're involved in that, every one of us here. It's our life work, and though it might sound ludicrous to you, we believe in it. So when we call you in here it's to satisfy a necessity we have, not to see what you have to offer. I'll put it this way: We have a job that needs doing and you're the man we feel can do it. We're not wasting our time, Philip Farrel."

What could Philip Farrel do but let his pride suffer a little. He thought of the dinner table with the various mouths he had to feed on little or no income. Linda Lawrence was there preparing the evening meal for that whole tortuous mile of feeding youth. Could he give himself up to this grinning aggregation of self-aggrandizers? Could he compromise his project, which in itself was already a compromise, fouled with a profit motive. It would betray Linda Lawrence, giving up like that, and his bad example would haunt the children. They "believe" in it the President had said, with their phosphorous smiles, their thin, workless arms, their faces eroded by drink. Involved. Involved in what? The President was waiting in his phony calm to get back to the inner office, the art collection, his hooka. Philip Farrel could remember all that. What was he ready to give up for any of this?

"What precisely . . ." asked the youngest member of the board, a well-groomed, blue-eyed bachelor, with dark hair, and a large, ruby graduation ring loose on his bony finger. He lifted his shoulders up around his neck like birds' wings when he spoke. ". . . is your relationship with this Peter Prince?"

Philip Farrel smiled and shook his head as if he were showing forbearance to a youngster. "You wouldn't believe me if I said it. It's not what you would expect a relationship to be."

"Philip Farrel, we already understand something about it, you know," the President smiled too with forbearance. "We've invited you to this conference not because we don't know something about you. We just want to hear it from your own voice."

"Wow. O.K. I'll say it, but this is too much. This is the first time I've said it, and the last time, I hope." For some reason it embarrassed Philip Farrel to talk about it. Even the eyes of the portraits around the room seemed to widen in anticipation. The whole room hummed with electronics. "We're both . . . uh . . . it's hard to say this so it sounds reasonable. Well, we're both characters, so to speak, in the same novel; it's . . . uh . . . an unfinished book by an author whose name I won't mention; it's irrelevant to this meeting."

"Well that's nothing we didn't already know, is it? We wouldn't have asked you here if we hadn't already known that, would we?" asked the man to his right.

"Yes, Philip Farrel, answer the question. Just what relationship do you have to this, how could you say it in technical terms? This . . . protagonist. If you can call him that," asked the President.

"What do you mean?"

The President showed his impatience by folding his hands together into a big fist. "It's clear what I mean. You know what I mean. What do you say to him? How do you influence him in the plot? What dialogue do you have with him? Is there ever a confrontation scene, where you tell each other where it's at, or you rescue him, or hold some kind of discussion with him?"

"That never happens."

"Come now."

"I don't talk to him. It isn't that kind of novel."

"What do you mean, 'not that kind of a novel'? What kind of a novel is there? It's a novel, isn't it?"

Philip Farrel sighed. "Yes. Right. But it's not what you think. I mean I don't understand it even that well myself all the time. I'm just there, that's all."

"You're trying to tell me that you spend a whole novel with Peter Prince and you don't get a line of dialogue, not one little joke to tell him, in the margin?"

"I don't talk to him at all. Don't ask me why? I'm supposed to be on the lookout for him, but I don't talk to him. I mean I drop a few words into the text while he's sleeping sometimes, but he never hears them."

"Philip Farrel," said the President, as he unfolded his hands and stretched his arms in front of himself on the table and rested his chin on a blotter. "We know better than that."

"Better than what?"

"We know that by the end of the book you speak to him at least once, perhaps more than once, and a conversation that has no little influence on him."

"Nonsense. The book is almost over. I understand my function in it and it's not to talk to Peter Prince. I know what I do by now. I wasn't hired as a talker to Peter Prince." Philip Farrel smoothed his sideburns. He could tell that things weren't going as he'd expected them to. He wasn't sure, flipping quickly back through the pages, that they ever did. Maybe he was wrong.

"You'll see," said the President.

"How can you say you know this?" It wasn't only Philip Farrel who was surprised and made uneasy by this presumptuous prediction. It stirred me up a little bit. I have nothing like a conversation in mind at all for these two, nothing like that. It sent a chill up my backbone to think that someone could be looking on like that at what I'm doing, a constant surveillance. Nothing makes me shake as much as spying. Even I wasn't sure. Maybe he did know something I didn't know, something my characters were going to do. Don't think it doesn't scare me.

"To make it easy, let's say we figured it out, a little extrapolation, a probability. It just figures that you're going to talk to him eventually. The possibilities are limited, and that's a most likely one. It's a matter of knowing what's there and predicting what's going to come."

"Then you're not sure of it?"

"Oh, we're sure of it."

"I doubt it," said Philip Farrel weakly, his voice nearly crumbled.

"You see," said the President, and as if the suddenly sharp tone of his voice were a signal all the members of the board leaned forward like the tentacles of an anchored sea animal closing on the edibles that have drifted in. "What we're interested in . . . what we care about, is what the subject of your conversation with him is going to be, when it finally comes about. We'd like to address ourselves to that possibility."

Philip Farrel, shaking like a membrane, lifted his dispatch case again to the table. "I came here, gentlemen, to talk about what is in this case." Though his resolution seemed strong, his voice disappeared into a series of scarcely audible hoarse little peeps.

The President ignored what Philip Farrel said. "We're not sure under what circumstances you'll have this conversation, whether when he's coming off the boat, or when . . ."

"Look," Philip Farrel pulled together some of his voice. "Maybe we're just wasting our time. I didn't come to worry here about whether or not I'm going to talk to Peter Prince when he returns in this novel. This here," he thumbed the latch-buttons on his dispatch case again, "is what I care about, actually, in real life, and what I want to discuss with you. This is My Work. My Work." He started to lift the cover of the case, but at a signal from the President two of the board members reached across to hold it shut.

"Mister Farrel," the President's voice was firm as a taped telephone announcement, and he rolled down his cuffs and slipped on the emerald cuff-links that he wore at the opening of this novel. "We want to cooperate with you, but we have a certain agenda, and it pleases us to follow it. No doubt we find some interest in your real life projects, and would like eventually to discuss them with you, but our business requires that certain matters be taken care of first, certain matters that we consider more important, and one of them is your conversations with Peter Prince. Perhaps we can get around to your other matters, but we have to ask your patience and that we first attend to the issues as we see them. After all, we pay the salary, if there is to be one forthcoming, and I'm sure that you haven't come to us with anything to give away for free." Philip Farrel became aware of a muted plinking sound in the room (the electronics were going), distant, as if in another dimension, a sound with nothing human in it, as if a music-box were being plucked at random. "If you like you can leave now," said the President. "Or you can stay."

Curiosity was perhaps Philip Farrel's tragic flaw; it was the word that struck him first, at least, when the alternatives were put to him. I'm curious, he thought, and that rationalization took precedence over his conscience, because he knew he should leave, and avoid whatever temptation could come, for these were ruthless men who would not hesitate to ask him to betray his trust, his Linda Lawrence, his author (me).

"Alright. I'll stay. But don't expect too much."

"All we want, don't we?" said the man who rubbed the creases by his oily nose. "Is for you to get him to mention our product, isn't that it? To say something about it, right?"

"I don't think I get it," said Philip Farrel. I didn't understand either, but it became all too clear to me, and disgustingly so, as the President spoke.

"It doesn't amount to anything much. We just thought that at that moment, you know, at the climax of the novel, when the truth of something is finally revealed to Peter Prince, you know, all novels have that moment when everything comes together, and a revelation is at hand. Well we thought that at that moment if Peter Prince could mention our product, just say its name, and maybe recite a little testimonial poem, a few of its qualities, you know—it would be a really significant moment for our product."

"I can't believe what you just said."

"Sure, that's what we want, that's sockeroo." An older member clapped his hands and grinned.

"Just think how beautiful it would be," said the youngest member, obviously a creative force in the terrific concern. "If at that moment of seeing again his native land, and all his friends expecting him, he's full of that triumphant wisdom you get from years abroad, and he sees his lovely Dolores again for the first time in many years waiting for him in tearful anxiety, and he embraces her, and leans back to search in her eyes and holds her by the shoulders and says, 'Dolores, in the blue box, etc. etc. etc.' Think what that could mean for our product just to get him to say it at that very moment."

"For what product?"

"Oh we have lots of products, said the President. "We would decide when the time comes which needs the boost the most."

"You mean you want to turn the novel into a kind of TV commercial or something. You want the whole thing to add up to a big sell gag. That's what you want."

"Nothing of the sort, Philip Farrel. You exaggerate. We just want that moment, that one moment when the reader's attention is high. We'll slip it in then. That's all there is to it."

Believe me, this made me sick. I wanted to puke. I wasn't really afraid for my work but I was afflicted with that nausea one gets when he is confronted with the shoddy desires of men, their paltry material aims. I didn't even want to look on any more, or listen, I wanted to get out of there. Philip Farrel looked the President in his face and said, "Do you mean that you believe I would sacrifice the aims of this book, a work to which an author has devoted years of his life, do you think I'd sacrifice this to your shoddy desires and paltry material aims?"

"You exaggerate, sir, the worth of Peter Prince," said the President. "It's not much that we're asking you."

"Everything." I was fainting with nausea. I hung on just long enough to see Philip Farrel get up and make to leave. He grabbed the dispatch case and slapped it under his arm and the force made it slip and fall to the ground, where it popped open. Everyone (myself included) was surprised, even Philip Farrel, because within were not the reams of calculations, statistics, number facts, that we've all come to expect from Philip Farrel, but there was that gun, that original gun, that opening gun, its barrel black as a cave, its stock as black as the President's car. That was enough for me. Back to Cairo for me. Back to the hotel room for me, where Peter Prince was finally returning, weary, bored, resentful of the fact that there wasn't even a message for him at the desk from Sarah Spurgeon, and that he felt a ridiculous obligation to hang around, not that he could plan to go anywhere else, and receive her phone call. The room was infernal. The shower still didn't work. It was ludicrous, this situation he was in, with this woman, this deadly, competitive, cuntless product of New York fashion magazines. She was so striking and slender, and seeing her first in the American Library in Florence had produced in Peter Prince a peculiar nostalgia, after his time abroad, a vague ache for the girl he'd never had but always saw on the covers of *Vogue, Harper's Bazaar*, in lingerie ads, that clean, cadaverous look, that hard-edge, castrating indifference. She was waiting to read the copy of *The New Yorker* that he held on his lap, and pretended to thumb through as he watched her. She looked like a model, the way she posed herself, influenced by the Italian elegance of gesture, but trapped in the jagged, uncomfortable postures of American fashion models, thigh and hip at right angles, neck thrust out, while she maintained toward Peter Prince that inscrutable profile or three-quarter face of patented mystery and desirability.

She approached him as he closed the magazine, and to his surprise was friendly when he tried one of the nervous jokes he sometimes used to pick up women. It turned out that she didn't care much for reading *The New Yorker*, but really preferred to go with him to that marvelous little restaurant he knew off the Piazza del Carmine, where they served a delicious *bistecca alla fiorentina*, and bottled a dry apple wine to drink with your *zuccotto* at dessert. She was fine to look at as she smiled and chirped and lipped her cut-glass jewelry. And she was rich besides. She paid for the meal, and when Peter Prince mentioned in passing his distant desire to get to see Abu Simbel before it was inundated by the dam she thought it was neat, and three days later offered to go with him and pay his way.

The whole business was weird. They left from Naples in a first-class stateroom, overnight in the same bed, not fucking, touching now and then the retractable warmth of her body. They arrived midday in Alexandria and the city was roasting while they pulled in, waiting in the air-conditioned bar and sipping Ricard until it was time for their train to leave. They had already run out of conversation, and he felt as if they were acting out a bad American movie; she was one of those women like Bette Davis, Gene Tierney, Deborah Kerr, he couldn't remember which; those keen, schizoid rich women in American movies, whose good hearts get hurt by young scoundrels they are always towing into port.

He was stuck with her. He had no money, would be stranded without her in Egypt, a place where he felt nowhere. He stripped to his shorts and started to smoke cigarettes. The tobacco wasn't bad, rolled in brown papers. Through the room the smoke spread slowly, settling into thin layers like wafers. The air wasn't moving. The sun lay ruminating in the sky. So strong was the light on the buildings outside his windows that they seemed to disintegrate. What was happening to him? How did he get himself into this mess of boredom?

When the telephone rang Peter Prince let it go for a while before he picked it up, and then got only the voice of the desk clerk asking him what he wanted. After a moment it went off again and he lifted the receiver to find himself eavesdropping on a conversation in French. The third try and he was connected with the call. It was Italy, alright, Franco Guicciardini, so he accepted the charges and apologized for Sarah Spurgeon, who wasn't there. It didn't matter to Franco. He had a speech prepared in English of which he seemed to understand little himself and recited almost incomprehensibly into the phone, translating little obvious bits into Italian. All the tenderest confessions of loneliness and love poured from the receiver into Peter Prince's softening ear. It made him giddy to hear the words "*amore*" and "*ti amo*" lofted to him over the Mediterranean. He responded with appropriately soft grunts as he took down all the messages.

After the conversation Peter Prince sat gently stunned on the bed. The heat had broken. He pulled the blanket down and lay back on the sheets that were cool. He was relaxed with the phone call taken care of, and weariness swept over him in easy tingling waves. He should have, he guessed, a certain pity for Sarah Spurgeon who too was on this difficult earth, after all, and had to submit her stunted needs to the kind of passion Franco had for sale, and the kind of companionship Peter Prince stingily offered. Outside the room Cairo began its evening hum like an alien planet. Poor Sarah Spurgeon, no self-assurance, no charm, just a batch of undefined needs, of frustrations grafted to her like limbs, with which she had to reach the world. It was Cairo. Peter Prince was there, falling asleep, dreaming of his return to America, passing under the shadow of the Statue of Liberty. How could he carry home this burden of knowledge? The centuries he'd accumulated, the admission that he'd done no good? There was nothing excellent he could do except adapt to where he was, and that wasn't always possible. He could solve no one's problems. Everyone existed on the earth, and had his way of being there, and causing a brief disturbance. Could he take home the message that the best

Peter Prince could do was to leave things alone? Was that as useful as he could get? He mumbled as he fell asleep about wanting to help and being helpless, and he dreamed then of the party there would be on his return. It would be somewhere, in a big room with mirrors and lights and all the friends he'd abandoned would be there to teach him the dances that they had learned while he was overseas. He had missed a lot. Even the language had changed so that he didn't understand many of the new expressions and couldn't make himself quite understood. The girls were cleaner than he'd remembered them. He dreamed of the party and the chubby girls in short dresses, and when he woke up he was in good humor. It was dark. He stepped onto the balcony to feel the thick, cool night air. It made the lights of the city gently pulse as if they were submerged. He would like to take this light with him back to New York, and such air with this clear density.

The shops had been closed for nearly two hours and there was still no word from Sarah Spurgeon. Relaxing as her absence was, he felt anxious, his distaste for her mixed with guilt. He had a responsibility to her for her generosity alone. He dressed and went to the lobby where he found no message had been left. It would be one of her tricks to disappear, go sign up in another hotel, take off for Afghanistan, just to make him worry. It was 10:43, late, but not time to panic. He didn't care about her. Anything could have happened to her. He crossed the street to a caffe called Americabar. It was like an Italian bar with a few tables near the window and a machine for making steam infusions of coffee. He sat down at a table near the window from which he could see the door to the hotel and ordered iced coffee and some toast.

"Excuse me," a man in a blue blazer, wearing an ascot leaned over the table. His thinning hair was combed in black ridges back from his brow, he held his hands behind his back. "Excuse me, but you're American, aren't you?"

Peter Prince glanced up quickly. "Yes, I am," he said, and turned back to his vigil. He didn't want to miss her.

"May I join you?"

"Suit yourself." Peter Prince didn't look up.

The man sat down and placed his order. Peter Prince looked down when the order came and noticed a blue tattoo on the man's wrist. They sat in silence for a while with Peter Prince still gazing out the window. The man began softly to speak, "I've been away from Americans for so long that it does feel good to sit and chat with one for a change. I spend so much of my time with Egyptians or alone, and you know as long as one is in a foreign country, it makes no difference how long, there are still some things he can't understand about them, and some things he can't communicate with them, no matter how well he speaks the language. There are basic things. It's not just a language, it's a cultural thing. I don't know how long you've been away, but haven't you noticed it to be true?"

Peter Prince nodded at the question. Since the man had sat down with him three women and eight men had entered the hotel, some of them Arabs.

"I detected that you were a writer immediately. You are one, aren't you?" Peter Prince nodded again. "I took you for a writer right away by the way you stare off like that and don't look at anything. It's like you're listening to some inner truth, some inner voice that only you and no one else understands. It's a wonderful thing to be able to do that, just be yourself, staring off like that. If I could do it I'd just do it all the time and not bother to talk with anybody. I'd just stare off at nothing with that wonderful distracted indifference on my face, I'd stare off and I'd think things up. I'd think everything up."

Peter Prince finally turned from the window to look at the source of this insipid voice. The man sipped warm milk and dipped with his index and middle finger from a dish of melted chocolate. His face had a network of fine veins near the surface of the skin that gave him a permanent flush. When he smiled he showed a lot of gum and two teeth capped with gold. He looked like an English teacher at an exclusive prep school. "First I came over with a CARE mission, but then decided to stay on my own. Maybe it's a mistake, but rather than go back, because, you know once you get used to the pace here it's impossible to face it at home, the way it's rush rush rush. So I decided to stay, and now I tutor, and teach English, and do some odd editing for the consulate. There's always a demand for a little something I can do. I get along that way, just get along." He leaned toward Peter Prince and his ascot slipped out of his frayed button-down. "Just what are you writing now, anyway?" He tucked the ascot back in.

Peter Prince smiled inscrutably. It was nice to be taken for a writer. He wished he had a notebook with him.

"Oh I know you must not want to talk about it. Authors never do, and I don't blame them. After all they wouldn't have to write it if they could tell about it."

"As a matter of fact," said Peter Prince, with a kind of magnanimity, "you could say that I'm into a novel now."

"Oh, is that nice," said the man. "How far along in it are you, would you say?"

"Quite a way through it."

"Splendid," said the man, and he sucked his index, and his middle finger. "I should really like to see it some time, to read a bit of it, if you intend to remain in Cairo for a while I should love it. You know it's been my feeling for a long time that the novel is a dead form already, an issue of the past. Our century and mentality hasn't the patience for it, what with the film and TV and tape recorders and transistors and who knows what else. It's almost dead. I can't really see that there'll be an audience for long, don't you think? It's too boring. I assume this isn't a conventional novel you're into, you don't look the type. Or is it one of those novels of confession? But I hope it isn't one of those modern mishmashes; you know, since the conventional novel has broken down it seems that anything, just anything goes these days. All sorts of self-indulgence. It's such a distressing situation. Throw anything together, cut things up, shuffle pages, write on those drugs they take. Of course I shouldn't talk, since I'm not an artist myself in the strict sense of the word; that is, I don't write or paint or anything but I have a feeling, and it's just a feeling, like a remote sense so far, that something else is happening. It's like a calling, but you must know what that is, being an artist. That it's more necessary than ever before these days to shape one's life into a work of art; that's the vision I sometimes have. One can devote all one's energy and resources to making a beautiful life. Making a life that's perfect, that has proportion, unity. Don't you think it's so?"

Peter Prince felt hypnotized. "That's possible, possible," he mumbled.

"That's the sense in which I'm . . ."

Suddenly Peter Prince realized that he'd been looking at the man instead of at the hotel door, and Sarah Spurgeon might have gone through while he was learning these special theories. The man talking was bright red from them.

"I have to go," said Peter Prince.

"Oh what a pity," said the man, and he fumbled around in his pocket. "Let me at least leave you my address and get yours; I should like to converse some more over this. It's an engaging topic, don't you think?"

The man scribbled his address quickly on the back of an old receipt he had in his wallet, smearing it with the chocolate sauce left near his fingernails. He handed that to Peter Prince, who pushed the hand aside, but noticed the tattoo on his wrist was the design of a blue artichoke, with the letters G X N beneath its stem. "It's no use, I'm sorry, but I'm leaving tomorrow, and I don't think I'll be back in Cairo." Peter Prince left in a hurry. He had been off his vigil enough for her to have come and left again. He felt a small throb of guilt from being rude to a stranger. He was a lonely man, a sad bore, weak in the mind. He could at least have taken the address to be civil. That would have helped.

He walked into the hotel thinking about the blue artichoke on the wrist and the G X N. What did it mean? He would have liked to ask a few questions about that. Sarah Spurgeon still hadn't got back, not a hint of her. It was almost midnight. Anything could have happened to her. It angered him to think that she could cause this anxiety in him. He really cared very little what happened to her. The idea of white slavery crossed his mind and cracked him up. She would be a big disappointment on the market, or maybe not. Perhaps she needed the crack of a whip, that sting of cruelty to turn her on. He sat for a while in the lobby, reading *Der Spiegel*, and other German magazines, and then he went up to bed and slept well. She wasn't there in the morning, but there was water in the shower, and he enjoyed that. He spent the whole day waiting for her in an anxious stupor. By evening he was nearly crazy. He took her luggage out of the closet and went through it all, finding nothing. He emptied the overnight case and felt around in the lining. There were some bills there, under the lining, stitched in. A thieving sweat pressed through his temples and forehead and nose and he took out his Swiss army knife with its seven blades and made a neat cut just above the bulge where the money was. He pulled out the bills, nine of them, it was money alright. He felt like yipping. Three hundred and forty-three dollars, enough for everything alone, for him to get on his way without Sarah Spurgeon's deadly company. What would he do about her? He might as well have murdered her and got away with it.

In the morning he decided to report her missing and leave. He sneaked his bag past the desk clerk and went down to the river pier and booked deck passage on an old steamer. There was a small wind on the river and it swelled the graceful sails of the *feluccas* like spinnakers, and Peter Prince felt bellied out like that with the possibilities of going. The boat would leave later that evening. He left his bag in the cabin of the boat and payed a boy a few piasters to watch it, promising him more on his return.

The officials at the consulate were shocked. "For three days she's been missing," said a minor one dressed in a hand-tailored Italian, double-breasted suit. He pulled a load of forms out of a filing cabinet. "You could have come here sooner. Why didn't you come here sooner?"

Peter Prince could feel himself blush as he was about to tell his half-truths. The air conditioning in the room was exaggerated, and he was freezing. "I figured she was probably alright. She's always disappearing like this. She's likely to do that. She just takes off and disappears for even a week or two at a time. It's not unusual. That's why I didn't worry." Peter Prince could see suspicion like a twitch cross the man's face. He paced back and forth in front of the desk and then mumbled an excuse and left the room. Peter Prince felt a danger in staying. They wouldn't be nice to him. There was a portrait on the wall in back of the desk of the President of the United States wearing a tarboosh, and a glassed-in bookcase full of leather-bound volumes. It was too late. The official came back with another man. This one was big and gray and heavy, with a face that never looked clean-shaven. He offered Peter Prince one of his hands to shake, but didn't say his name.

He sat down and leaned his chin on his hairy knuckles. His voice was peculiarly high-pitched. "You say . . . that she just went shopping three mornings ago . . . that would be the morning of August third. And you haven't seen her since then?"

"As I said to the other one, it doesn't mean anything. She's always disappearing. She has her own mind about . . ."

"My good man, I can see that you don't realize that you're in Egypt, in the Middle East, and not back in Western Civilization, where you can expect the probable to happen. You don't realize how serious this could be." The Lost Person forms shook in the heavy man's hands, and the thinner man buttoned and unbuttoned his double-breasted jacket. "She could be locked up now where we would never find her. She could be on her way to Saudi Arabia to be sold. Who knows? White slavery, we keep it quiet as much as we can, but it goes on. It goes on. When it comes right down to it they don't really like Americans here, and to tell you the truth we don't like them. She could be buried. Is she Jewish?"

"I don't think so."

"About a month ago some young girl named Levine disappeared into Old Cairo just like that, and we still haven't found a trace of her. They don't like them. We can't even have them working in the consulate. Why didn't you get here sooner, man? It might be too late."

"As I said to you and to that one, she just often takes off. She might arrive back at any moment."

"But this is Egypt."

"She leaves without warning."

"Have you been to the Cairo police?"

"No."

"Good. It's always better to begin with us. We know how to get the cooperation, what cooperation we can get. And we know the proper channels. This isn't the first time this has happened to us. These Egyptians are an awful bunch of bureaucrats. If they started now to search for her she'd be an old woman before they got a clue." The man arranged the forms in front of himself and pulled a wax-paper bag from his inside jacket pocket. It was full of a sticky Egyptian candy that looked like balls of toast dipped in honey. He offered some to Peter Prince and to his cohort, both of whom refused. He set the mess down next to the forms and pulled pieces off as he worked, using his tongue as a washcloth to wipe the stickiness off his fingers. The thinner man sat down and leaned on the desk, scrutinizing Peter Prince.

"Now. Will you answer some questions for us about this lost person in question. How old was she?"

"Between twenty-three and twenty-five."

"Don't you know for sure?" the slender one probed.

"No."

"What did she look like?"

Peter Prince paused and reflected and tried to get together a picture of her. Nothing. He couldn't remember what she looked like. He closed his eyes and saw a procession of skinny models posing for *Vogue* magazine. Awkward gestures, threatening smiles. He looked my way, his face an abject plea for help, but I was determined that he would learn his lesson. He was on his own. "She was very thin," he offered weakly, "and . . ." Nothing followed for a long moment.

"And what?" The heavy man was getting impatient, down to his last piece of candy.

"And . . ." Peter Prince shrugged.

"For God sakes, man, don't you know what she looks like? Haven't you been living with her? You must remember what she looked like. Something. Her eyes? What color were her eyes?" His pen hovered over the proper square for eye color.

Peter Prince couldn't even remember the color of her eyes, not even if they were light or dark. Green flashed into his mind with an ad he remembered from *The New Yorker*. "They were blue," he said.

"That's better, what else?"

He closed his eyes. He opened his eyes. He walked around the room. "She was thin," he repeated.

"MY good fellow, you've said that. Doesn't she have anything else to distinguish her? You must give us something to go on."

Peter Prince could think of nothing. She had disappeared for him. He stared at the befezzed picture of the President behind the desk, and the eagle on the seal looking to the right, out over his right claw, that held the lightning and not the olive branch. She looked something like that, but he couldn't say it. The thin man kept whispering in the ear of the heavy interrogator. Peter Prince was strange to them.

The thin man rose to his full height and came around to where Peter Prince was sitting. "Can't you say just a few more things about her? This doesn't look very good, you know."

"What was she wearing?"

"Sneakers," Peter Prince said.

"And . . . ?"

He could remember noting her clothes, but not what she was wearing. He might have fashioned a Madison Avenue pastiche of clothes and posed looks, that would have satisfied the two bureaucrats and set him free, but he had no inclination to do even that.

"Well," said the thinner man. "This is strange indeed."

"He must be upset," said the heavier one. "Look." He placed a page, with carbons for triplicate in Peter Prince's hand. "We'll step out for a while and you write down here whatever you remember of her. How she looks. Characteristic marks. Everything. Write it down. Use the typewriter, if you like. It's electric."

The men left. How the distrust was growing in the room. Peter Prince could feel that. He wasn't a person they would ask any more questions. They would use their strategies from now on. He put the paper down on top of the typewriter, and stared at it. Nothing. They were right, the typewriter was electric. He switched it on and listened to it hum. That was it. Fuck it. Let them find her. He didn't know or care about it at all. He found the other door that was open and sprinted out for the river pier. The deck was already full of brown-skinned, half-blind *fellahim* with their dogs, goats, rusty implements, sacks of manure, squawking chickens. He sat down near the rail, facing out of the city, and waited for departure, and he slowly forgot about Sarah Spurgeon as he listened to the bleating, the clucking, the whining, and the thick, live guttural talk.

"That junk," said Linda Lawrence. "Shut off that Peter Prince nonsense. You can't get a decent show any more on the TV. Turn it off." Linda Lawrence covered her eyes with her knitting.

"I'll try a different channel." Philip Farrel with some difficulty rose from his easy chair and moved to flip the dials. Most of the stations were breaking for commercials.

"We should get credible garbage at least on this TV. The President in a tarboosh. What do they want us to believe?
They want to make your mind sick.
And Peter Prince. They think we can believe he behaves like that? If it was up to me we'd kick a hole in the screen of that box."

"Wait a second. I think I've got something."

"What is it?"

It was one of those TV guest shows. Peter Prince sat behind a desk and held up products that sponsored him from time to time. Miss Tivoli was in a chair to his right with her legs crossed and decolleté. They addressed each other with great informality, familiarity, and affection, and sometimes seemed to glance at a script that was out of sight behind the cameras. The show was broadcast in color, though we could see it only in black and white.

"I say, 'Let's just walk around together and enjoy this city and each other's company!' " (Miss Tivoli said) "And I slip my hands in around your elbow and squeeze."

" 'Okay,' I say (said Peter Prince) and we

"It's the new Peter Prince show."

"Again?"

"No. This one is different. It's one of those informal interview shows. Quiet. Let's give it a chance for a while."

Linda Lawrence resumed her knitting, conspicuously clicking her needles.

Philip Farrel settled back in his chair and cracked open another can from his six-pack.

start out through the streets of Cairo, feeling good. We like each other, a certain mutuality we have that makes Cairo feel good. It's midday. The streets are full of the musky odor of everything in the heat: the narrow, winding market street. A man passes with braids of garlic draped around his neck, and one broken clove stuffed in a nostril. Buffalo meat hangs in the butcher-stalls, covered with violet stain. We walk slowly, our arms twined from above the elbow to the hands, which are folded into one another. Suddenly it smells like mint. Full of mint. A young boy passes dragging two huge sacks full of it, and calling its name in Arabic." (Peter Prince paused here for a moment and stared beyond the camera at a prompter, or something.) " 'N'nà!' he calls, 'N'nà!' and I stop him to buy a sprig, and I put it in your hair, Miss Tivoli." (Miss Tivoli touched her hair and then brought her fingertips to her nose and closed her eyes as she sniffed.) "In three cubicles we pass men with their legs folded under themselves, weaving rugs. There's a shop that sells parts of camels, their chopped-off feet, their hides, their ears, and across from it a table heaped with peppers to sell, green, yellow, orange, red, the colors sweet as the flavor in the light sifted through the umbrella that shades them. A heap of cherries, of loquats. Huge tomatoes. Potatoes small and knobby. We feel as we walk as if we are one creature in

"Orange smash, plastic eyelash, Metrecal, Metrecal, Metrecal, space age soup, silly putty," Linda Lawrence muttered into her embroidery.

Philip Farrel farted once, twice, thrice, fource, fifthce, and Linda Lawrence admonished him to light a match, "So as to dispel the unpleasant odors. Odorless, odorless. The Infant Jesus had kein smell. Such were the active ingredients man were made for."

"What are you blubbering for when I try to listen here?" Philip Farrel farted again.

"Too much beer and beer and beer."

"Plug it up."

"Ouch."

sensation, nothing separates us, as if we breathe the scent-laden air into one lung. A little donkey pulls a cart along full of large, earthenware jars whose mouths are stuffed with paper. The man who leads the little animal stops in front of us and dips a few oil-soaked beans out of the jar with a wooden ladle. He puts one in his toothless mouth and holds it in his gums. He offers us the rest and we take a few, causing him to smile. You put a bean in my mouth and I put one in yours and we giggle as we chew the tasteless, oily, grainy fave. Now we are surrounded by the dark children of the quarter, dressed in the striped blue and white flannel smocks they wear. They look at us with big, brown, curious eyes, and rub their hands together and chatter while we chew the beans. We are Americans, and they know it. I buy them some beans. The narrow street is stuffed with people, people bargaining at the stalls or squeezing past. People barefoot, or with sandals. People with skullcaps, with net shopping bags, children clinging to their mothers' black smocks. 'This Cairo is full of people,' I say, and you laugh. 'I wish we could talk to them,' you say. We stroll along the wall of a large building covered with pegboards that hold cheap shoes and sandals. Several concrete stalls on the other side are full of packets of soap powder, caustic, stiff brushes. A great buzzing chorus of hawkers and bargaining sweeps at us

"I smell the smell of sleepy small ones. Lopsided. Dead. No odor. I can't go on like this. Wrench. Was it the tourist size they used?"

"What are you saying? Do you believe all that?"

from the right—it's an immense bazaar. We pass a display of ceramic chamber-pots, and earthenware water-jars and enter a market that smells like hemp where everything is sold for horses, donkeys, camels, oxen—saddle blankets, beautifully tooled harness and bridle, camel saddles, goatskins, whips, packs, lacings. We pass through and come out on a little square, with a handsome Turkish fountain there in the center, a small public bath with its entrance covered by a rug, and a little cafe with a couple of tables outside. We don't have to say anythingto know that we both want to sit down at a table. I order two Turkish coffees for us and we rest."

(Peter Prince stopped speaking and sat back smiling. Miss Tivoli leaned over to touch his arm as if to show how much she liked the way he told what he told. She glanced down at a few notes that were below the camera level and then began to take up the drift as Peter Prince reached behind himself to get one of the products he wanted to show us.)

"We say very little to each other (said Miss Tivoli, recrossing her legs, and throwing an irrelevant smile toward the wrong camera) because we have a certain feeling for experiencing things together, an ability to touch, smell, hear, as if we are one organism. This gives us a fine, communicative silence when we're together.

"Damn these commercials. You can't get any continuity on this damned television."

Philip Farrel cracked the last can from his six-pack. "Would you bring me another six-pack?"

"You're going to piss yourself to death soon if you keep drinking. That'll be your sixth six-pack."

"You know I don't get to stay home often to do this. It's one of my pleasures."

We met, yes, in the midst of all the others on the crossing from Naples, and it was just by luck that we fell out together, a glimpse of each other across the deck, the soft parallels of compassion from our eyes, an honest and passionate attraction. It was rare this thing that happened to me, or to you, you Peter Prince, who usually achieve your remorseful affairs through a hard lot of competition and disastrous lying."

(Miss Tivoli cast a soft smile at Peter Prince who had his hand on a box full of a product and was looking into the camera. She turned her smile to the camera and moistened her lips before she went on.)

"We sip our thick, sweetened coffee and watch the people passing. Our legs brush under the table and remain together. Across from us a man is talking with a large, green parrot in front of a shop where he sells live birds. The parrot speaks Spanish and the man with joyless patience is trying to get it to say something in Arabic. An inspiration suddenly strikes me, and I stand up. 'I've got an idea,' I say, and run my long fingers, which you frequently admire, down the length of your arm. 'Wait just a second,' I say, and I walk across to the bird-stall while you watch the joyless bird-vendor show me little bird after little bird. I finally choose one which I have him put in a cage of fine brass wire."

"Yeah." She got him the beer, and then began to manicure her nails.

"What are you doing that for? You sure haven't done that for a while. What, have you got a lover while I'm out?"

"Shhh, they started again."

"Well, do you have one? One of those?"

" 'That's a canary,' I say (said Peter Prince) when you bring the black and gold songbird back to the table."

" 'It's a love bird,' I reply (said Miss Tivoli). I'm grinning a mile wide because I'm so pleased. I have a beautiful idea."

" 'That's no love bird.' "

" 'You'll see.' I lean over and kiss you (Miss Tivoli leaned over and kissed Peter Prince on the cheek, which he stretched toward her) and we walk together back to our hotel, holding the cage together. Silliness like this in another woman would annoy you, Peter Prince, but in me it is a charming mystery, and it excites you. When we get to the room we put the cage down on a table near the open balcony so it catches the sun and the bird sings."

" 'That bird makes a hell of a lot of noise,' I say (Peter Prince) and I watch it hop around from the floor of its cage to its little swinging bar. It has such joy in it."

" 'Our love bird has to make all the noise he can.' I grab you around and put my warm lips on your neck and feel your (beep) rise. 'It needs to sing all night.' "

" 'You're crazy,' I step back and touch your soft (beeps) under the cotton blouse. I love the way you lower your eyelids and seem to moan when I touch you. You are so passionate. You reach out and touch my

Linda Lawrence blew on her fingernails. "And if I do?"

Philip Farrel cracked open another can from his six-pack. "Well then you'll . . ."

"Shhhhh . . ."

(beep) with charged fingers. I am trembling. The Cairo sky this late dusk is deep raspberry growing black. It is delicious the way we can ease off on each other and know that pleasure is coming. 'There's nothing better than this,' I say, and we hold each other in a trembling solitude."

(Peter Prince began to look for something under his table and bent out of sight while the camera scanned the excited, arm-waving audience, and finally stopped at the face of Miss Tivoli again, who was staring blank-faced into her lap. After a moment she looked up, smiled, and went on with the telling.)

"Well this evening we go for dinner to a restaurant that's a hangout for what's left of the British Colony in Cairo. We don't like the place very much, a particularly mute and unfriendly group who don't like to be looked at, and we have to keep our laughter in our throats. 'I take it you two are Americans?' A man in a blue blazer approaches our table. He wears an ascot, and his thinning hair is combed in black ridges back from his talcumed face. 'You are Americans, aren't you?' You shake your head, Peter Prince, trying to seem quite annoyed at the interference, but the man persists. 'Do you mind if I join you?' I expect you to get angry at the intrusion, but your politeness prevails. 'Suit yourself,' you say."

"I don't think he'll sit down, but he does,"

"Do you . . ."

"What?????"

"You know, have . . ."

"O are there . . . ?"

"What? What? What?"

"What?"

"Horseflies in . . ."

"H.F. in paradise, I knew it would come to that. But when you do . . ."

"Let go of me. Let go of me. Let go of me."

"First we'll act as if this wasn't . . ."

"We can't. I can't do that and finally . . ."

(Peter Prince said).

"Yes, the man sits down, and he's obviously a regular of the place, because without an order the waiter brings him a cup of warm milk and a dish of melted chocolate. 'You must be a couple of students,' he says. You nod and try to ignore him. 'You're two students and you're not married.' He looks around the room and turns back to us, grinning. 'But don't worry, I'm not the kind who complains about that. You can just do what you please.' He is expert at getting the chocolate off his fingers with one swipe of his tongue, and off his tongue with a quick swish of milk. 'Since you're students I'll tell you a story, and I'm sure you'll like it. I'll tell you how Cairo got its name.' I feel for your calf under the table and we rub legs. It's beautiful between us. The man stuffs a small pipe with tobacco, and lights it, and leans back with his legs crossed, in a story-telling posture. 'Do you know haw Cairo got its name?' He changes pitch, as if he summons up a special voice. 'I'll tell you how Cairo got its name. I'm not ashamed of knowing it, of knowing little things like this. They keep me going. I know that it was founded a long time ago, although time is relative where Egypt is concerned, because with Ancient Egypt in mind it wasn't really so long ago, compared, say, to Damascus, or Athens, or even Rome. It was founded on July 6th, 969 A.D. and the

"What?"

first stone of the Al-Aqhar Mosque was laid on April 4th, 970 A.D.' The waiter continues to bring us food while the man talks, and we pay as little attention as possible, and the man keeps talking helplessly as if he can't stop himself. 'There was nothing at all here before, where this city was created, and the general in charge of the Fatimid armies, a young, thick-bearded, happy warrior named Jawhar, traced the walls out somewhat north of the old settlement of Fostat, which is now an immense garbage dump, as you know. Well, long before, you see, the date for the founding of Baghdad had been determined according to the position of the stars, to which would be most favorable. Jawhar decided to do the same for Cairo, and he called in his astrologers to determine the date for this city he wanted to found for his army. You see it didn't have a name yet. "Choose," he said, "the best horoscope, so the descendants of the Caliph will never be dispossessed from this city." The astrologers worked day and night, along with the laborers and masons, and finally chose a proper date, a horoscope for the raising of the wall.' The man pauses to dip some chocolate and order another cup of warm milk. We nibble on some spicy lamb. I can see that you are practically trembling with boredom. 'I hope I'm not boring you, because this isn't a boring story. It's one I feel is just essential to tell to newcomers.' You look up at him. 'Who are you?' you ask. The man doesn't answer, but goes on telling the story. 'So, along the entire ramparts length they set up wooden posts with cord strung from one to the next on which they hung little bells of good fortune which they would ring to signify the start of construction, and the astrologers commanded the workmen, "When the bells ring, toss the mortar and the stones which you have nearby into the line of fortifications." They waited and waited for the right time. Suddenly a black raven landed on one of the ropes and all the bells rang prematurely. The workmen, and you can't blame them for it, believed the astrologers had rung the bells, and they started doing as they had been instructed. The astrologers were aghast, but they were up to the occasion. They consulted their charts. "Qahir, the victorious, the planet Mars, is in the ascendant," they shouted. Though their plans were undone they went on working. Indeed Mars was in the ascendant at the beginning of the laying of the foundations for this city, and it dominated the sphere, and that is how they gave the city the name Qahira, Mars, the victorious one.' He sips on his milk, a broad stretch of grin.

'Isn't that a fine, fine story.' "

(Peter Prince touched her arm and offered to spell her at the telling. She smiled at him, became silent, leaned back, and

"Oh Philip Farrel, that sort of thing is just the sort of thing that you never say to me ever." She threw off her knitting, the embroidery, the make-up attachment, the blankets, and her boy friend's cummerbund, which she was secretly repleating. "I want oh so, some words like that of sweet from you."

Philip Farrel could here have farted but that would have been a bad taste. Instead, "Now I must piss," he said, and disappeared through the beaded curtain.

"I told you it would come to that," she plaintively reminded.

Turning her mind to what was necessary Linda Lawrence got to work during the break. She mopped the floor, dried the moppings, waxed the dry floor, polished the wax. She dug the garden. She made tomorrow's casseroles. She rewrote the agenda for the meeting of the WSPRO, and paused for an

stared into her lap.)

"You say, 'Yes, that's a slick story, but don't you have that date wrong. Isn't it August 5th, 969?' He looks up and his eyes shoot open. 'Yes. Yes. Yes. You're right. It slipped my mind. I can't get over how it does that sometimes.' You look at him for a moment, tweak your chin, and then zero in. 'And wasn't it the Al-Azhar Mosque that came first, not Al-Aqhar, as you clearly asserted.' I love you, Miss Tivoli, you champion of champions, for your mind at this moment, and not your body. 'Why you might be right at that,' says the sniveling bore, and I'm so happy. You go on, pushing ahead with the truth like my Joan of Arc. You say, 'And, in fact, wasn't it a yellow and black canary, and not a raven at all, that landed on the bell-rope?' 'Was it?' he responds, his composure faltering. 'I would say so,' you assert, with the strength of a lioness. 'Well,' he says, and he fluffs up his ascot, 'I guess I'll have to be leaving,' and he extends his hand, as if I want to shake it, and notice there on the wrist a pale blue tattoo, the design of an artichoke. 'I enjoyed your company,' he says, and after shaking hands takes one last swipe at the chocolate with his forefinger and disappears through a curtain of hanging beads."

(Miss Tivoli moved to speak again, but the station broke for its commercial.)

alcoholic beverage. Then she went to the back and blew the whistle, rang the bell, and clanged the new-made gong to call her children home to bed from all the distances: Here came Smallfrog, and Dipple, Crusty the Wimp. Sarah, Cliff, Mark, Eddie, Dirk, Philip, Sploot, Clapper, Joan, Melton, Tightwire II, Harry, Clark, Kent, Loyal as ever Togo, Green Peggy, some others, Nick with a destiny, Saul, Sol, Sahl, their pets, Toughy, Rocko, Nails, Tender Max, Scorn Hillary, Flat, Speal, Edsel, Alfred, Brother, Toes and his sweetheart. All the others in a yawning multitude came at the ringing, glad to be home, like a satellite of puppies. "Beddybye," said Linda Lawrence, and she began to clean them up and pamper them, and she told them each a story as they went to bed. How she loved them, even for the trouble caused her. Philip Farrel pissed and pissed, and listened to the commotion of a rich home life.

(The show switched back on, catching Miss Tivoli in midspeech.) ". . . quiet stroll along the river we go back to the hotel room. The bird is making a beautiful racket on the balcony where we left it. 'This,' I say, lifting the cage, 'is the bird that caused Cairo to get its name, O dearly beloved.' You ask me how I know that and I reply with a kiss. 'Look at him,' I say. 'The bird is alive.' You stroke me and it feels good. 'Won't you cover the bird for the evening so it doesn't make so much racket?' you ask, because you don't know what I have in mind, what my plan is. 'Oh no,' I say, not wanting to tell you everything at once. 'I didn't get it for that. Mars is in the

ascendant, you remember.' I put the cage down and look through my overnight bag for a nailfile. I don't have one 'Do you have a pocket-knife?' I ask. 'If I haven't lost it,' you say, and you hunt around in your things."

"I find my utilitarian Swiss army knife tucked away in a shoe, and as you instruct me I open it to the punch. I have no idea what you have in mind, but it pleases me to watch you do anything. You are not beautiful, but marvelous, feminine and you have grace. You drive the punch through the soft metal bottom of the cage and make a hole the size of a half-dollar, then you remove the plastic flowers from the vase that holds the microphone that bugs the room and slip the cage over that. I'm beginning to see, and it's unbelievable. The bird flutters around his new cage-mate for a while, decides he likes it, and begins to chirp with such glorious, clear, unremitting song, so loudly, that I believe the spies, even the spies tuned in below will have to make love in its influence. 'The Victorious,' you say, pointing at your invention. 'You can't believe how much I love,' I say, and I wipe the clothes off you and you wipe the clothes off me and with an accompaniment of birdsong we (beep) and (beep) and (beep), such prolonged cadenzas of (beeping) that Spud Hazeley with Cyanide Pearl would choose to pause and watch in envy as we (beep) and (beep) and (beep) beep beep beep

"What did I miss?" asked Philip Farrel, shaking off the last drips.

"The best part. You missed the best part. You always miss the best part. If you only didn't drink so much, you'd trim down, and you'd see all the best parts."

"But I can't understand a word of that. They're not audible."

"Look at them. Read the lips. You know what it's about. We weren't born yesterday. You know what it is." Linda Lawrence made herself as seductive as possible with her wiles.

"I'm going to shut the damned set off. Peter Prince show. The public pays the price and gets this. Scorched."

"You understand . . ."

"Off it goes."

"Now it's off."

"Yes."

"Now what."

"Now whatever."

"Oh fuck you."

```
beep beep beep beep beep beep beep beep
beep beep beep beep beep beep beep beep
beep beep beep beep beep beep beep beep
beep beep beep BEEP BEEP beep beep beep
beep beep beep BEEP BEEP beep beep beep
beep beep beep BEEP BEEP beep beep beep
beep beep beep BEEP BEEP beep beep beep
beep beep beep BEEP BEEP beep beep beep
beep beep BEEP BEEP BEEP BEEP beep beep
beep beep BEEP BEEP BEEP BEEP beep beep
beep beep BEEP BEEP BEEP BEEP beep beep
beep beep beep BEEP BEEP beep beep beep
beep beep beep BEEP BEEP beep beep beep
beep beep beep BEEP BEEP beep beep beep
beep beep beep BEEP BEEP beep beep beep
beep beep bEEP BEEP BEEP BEEp beep beep
beep beep bEEP BEEP BEEP BEEp beep beep
beep beep bEEP BEEP BEEP BEEp beep beep
beep beep bEEP BEEP BEEP BEEp beep beep
beep beep beep BEEP BEEP beep beep beep
beep beep beep BEEP BEEP beep beep beep
beep beep beep BEEP BEEP beep beep beep
beep beep beep BEEP BEEP beep beep beep
beep beep beep BEEP BEEP beep beep beep
beep beep beep BEEP BEEP beep beep beep
beep beep beep BEEP BEEP beep beep beep
beep beep beep BEEP BEEP beep beep beep
beeeeeeeeeeeeeeeeeeeeeeeeeeeeeeeeeeeeeeeep
beeeeeeeeeeeeeeeeeeeeeeeeeeeeeeeeeeeeeeeep
beeeeeeeeeeeeeeeeeeeeeeeeeeeeeeeeeeeeeeeep
beeeeeeeeeeeeeeeeeeeeeeeeeeeeeeeeeeeeeeeep
beeeeeeeeeeeeeeeeeeeeeeeeeeeeeeeeeeeeeeeep
```

"What are you angry for? It's off."

"Fuck it. Fuck you. And the whole thing fuck it."

"You're jealous."

"I've a right to be."

"Screw you then."

Early the next morning Peter Prince and Miss Tivoli were arrested. They were led away together in a Mercedes Benz, and were given no explanation. Every time he tried to speak to her a hand was rudely shoved over his mouth and she didn't seem inclined to speak, moping by her guard, stunned. They were led into a large building of brutal design and separated there. "I'll never see her again," Peter Prince muttered, surprised to hear his own voice thinned out. They locked him alone in a small, windowless closet with one weak bulb on the high ceiling. He sat there silent, and then clenched his fist and waved it at the dimly lit ceiling. "You," he said aloud. "If you weren't so stupid, and forgetful, so lazy and inert. If you only could remember something." I had no idea whom he was talking about. "I've got you pegged, you know," and he let out a creepy little muttering giggle. "I've got you just about doped out. You're going to fail. You lack something. You've got something . . ."

We led him from that room into another, much larger room of ambiguous dimensions, where he was instructed to sit down. The wall around the room was lined with wicker love-seats on which several dark men sat in dejection, waiting to be called. At the center of the room from behind a desk a plump, glossy-faced Egyptian interrogated people in turn, their voices sometimes raised to a squeal, his always muted and nasal. Bare, unfrosted bulbs swung from the ceiling on double strands of wire, the wire lined with flies from socket to ceiling. There were no flies stuck to the flypaper that hung in spirals, and those on the lightcords didn't move. Two large fans whirled at the far corners from Peter Prince and circulated little air. Between the fans, in back of the man at the desk was a tall, narrow door through which some of the people left, and some of them left through the door by which Peter Prince had entered. The room was decorated in pale blue and white to match the robes of many of the poor Cairenes who were waiting. Peter Prince would have to be patient. He could do nothing in such a situation but hope to find someone good-natured enough to accept a bribe. There was no other way. They could do whatever they pleased with him, imprison him and notify no one. He would be a vacancy, his passport like an uncashed check.

He watched the men as they were interrogated, but couldn't tell what the nature of the interrogations was. If the wretches entered shivering abjectly they left with no more visible assurance; if they were proud and disdainful as they approached the desk the questioning didn't break that pride whether they left through the narrow or the wide door. Peter Prince was the only foreigner in the room. It was probably the wrong place for him. He would have to submit now, he guessed, to days of bureaucratic mistakes, of fumbling, inept commissioners who spoke little English, of insinuating bribe-beggars. The room was hot, and the fans didn't help circulate the air. He felt a sudden pain, like an empathetic stabbing. What had happened to Miss Tivoli? As if timed to go off the flies started moving all at once, some striking the flypaper and buzzing there like little electric motors. The rest of them had begun to find Peter Prince and to land all over his face, entering his nostrils, his ears, his mouth. What had happened to Miss Tivoli? The flies seemed drugged. They didn't try to escape when he swatted them, and if he closed his lips he crushed them, and if he rubbed his cheeks with his palms they left cool smears where they died.

"Peter Prince," the two heavy guards who stood in front of him clearly pronounced his name.

"What happened to Miss Tivoli?" he asked, but it was clear they wouldn't answer that question. He felt suddenly weary, lethargy like a weight of armor settled on his shoulders. He followed the guards to the table and saw there a new interrogator, his interrogator. He hadn't seen the man come in. He was lean, and wore steel-rimmed spectacles, and had a long, Semitic profile. His suit was pale yellow, double-breasted cotton, three sizes too large for his thin body. On his desk his briefcase lay open on its side, the papers visible leading into the darkness like steps. His hands were resting on the briefcase. They were long and slender, with knuckles like promontories, and when he folded his hands one over the other you expected great, cracking noises. The flies that had left Peter Prince as he crossed the room, began to find him again and he tried, inconspicuously, to ward them off. They sat silent for what seemed half an hour to Peter Prince, until he finally broke the silence himself.

"I'm willing to explain the whole situation," he said. "It was just a bit of love pranks, you know, harmless. You know love. It was a matter of love, you know, and frivolous. We needed, so to speak, to be alone, and you know that a microphone isn't the most welcome accessory in the room of two lovers. We just went to the market, and she bought the bird, she [where is she?] . . . When we got back to the room it was one of those whims she had, you can't predict . . ." He blew some flies off his lips. "It was just harmless . . ."

"Peter Prince," said the interrogator, dangling his spectacles in one hand. "What on earth are you talking about?" He spoke with an Oxford accent, but scraped r's off the back of his palate.

This, thought Peter Prince, was to try his patience. "You know what I'm talking about," he said, trying a tone of bored indignation himself. "It's why I'm here, isn't it? That bird cage we put over the microphone last night."

The interrogator looked at him for a long while with an expression that didn't seem friendly, and then he clapped his hands sharply to summon one of the guards, who left the room after he received some instructions in Arabic. "We will try to get over this with as much dispatch as possible."

"You mean it's not about the bird cage? I could perhaps offer you a slight . . ." He stopped. The bribe, he could see, wouldn't be welcome at this point.

"You might say that the cage is the least of it." The interrogator stared at his glasses while the guard came back in, carrying a pitcher of water, the cage, and a tiny flask. He put the cage down on the floor beside Peter Prince; the bird was dead in it, its wings snapped, its neck wrung. Peter Prince could feel his nerves just under his skin, cold and moist, his pores locked tight. He was here for something and it wasn't that bird. What was it? The guard handed him a glass of water and he tasted it: mineral water, sulfurous and vile, but he took some anyway, to lubricate his throat.

"Here," said the interrogator, handing him the flask. "Rub some of this on and it will keep away the flies." It smelled good, vaguely like lemon flowers, and it cooled his face, and kept the flies off.

"I would like to know," said Peter Prince, feeling somewhat calmer. "If it's not the bird cage and all, what is happening here? And why me?"

The interrogator reached into his briefcase and pulled out a pad. "I am here because I speak English rather well. You will find that although there are a few procedures I don't yet know, and a few facts of which I don't yet have the full grasp, that my facility with your language will serve to expedite this business."

"What business?" Peter Prince quickly glanced around the room to see that he was the last person to be interrogated. He felt vacated and cold, the shirt he wore too thin. "Where is Miss Tivoli?"

"How long have you been in Cairo?"

"Can't you tell me about Miss Tivoli?"

The interrogator put his glasses back on and tilted his head so he looked under them. "How long have you been here in Cairo?"

It was no use. "Two days," said Peter Prince.

"Two and a half days," the interrogator corrected him.

"Why do you ask me if you already know about it better than I do?" He thought he heard a faint weeping through the wall to his right and turned to look at the door through which he'd entered.

"Look at me, Peter Prince."

"I hope you're treating her well."

"How have you enjoyed your stay in Cairo?"

"I haven't enjoyed Cairo much, I'm here to see Nubia, before you drown it." That must be the wrong thing to say, he thought.

"How much money have you spent since you've been here, more or less?"

"I don't know that. Are you kidding? What difference does that make? My traveler's checks are in my room. Maybe thirty-five dollars, including the hotel bill, maybe more."

"Yes. Forty-three dollars, and some cents, less than fifty."

"Please. Can't we stop this foolishness?"

"Maybe that's foolishness to you, but that's a lot of money to someone like me. A little bureaucrat like myself earns that in two months, what you have spent in two and a half days. I'd like to spend forty-three dollars in two days, but I know I never will."

"Look. I'll give you one hundred dollars, if you will stop this stupidity."

"And if you gave me one hundred dollars," the man leaned forward and looked at Peter Prince directly through his glasses, his eyes the color of phlegm, "I still couldn't spend forty-three dollars in two and a half days. I would need the money just to get through the year, and would have to put some aside for catastrophe in my family, or in case another child comes."

"What can I do, then?"

"Be patient. There's nothing you can do. Just expect nothing. Don't expect compassion from a jealous man." The interrogator leaned over and wrote with his notebook on his knee. Peter Prince could still hear the noise of grief from the other side of the wall. He rose and went back to the door through which he'd entered.

"That's locked," the interrogator shouted. "The door in back of me is open but the guards will stop you if you try to go through without authorization."

"What's happening to Miss Tivoli?"

"I'm not sure anything's happening to Miss Tivoli."

"But I hear all that weeping from the other side of the wall. I know she's there." "Oh you hear it," said the interrogator, and he crossed over to where Peter Prince was standing. He was short and lean with a long neck, coarse as a chicken's. "Yes, maybe it is weeping. You become immune to those sounds here after a while. But I can't reassure you that it's Miss Tivoli. You see there's so much sorrow and misery and grief in Egypt.- He walked back to his desk with a funny, stiff-legged gait. "Will you come back here, or do I have to shout the questions?"

"Shout."

"Very well. What have you visited since you've been in Cairo?"

"You know. Why don't you tell me?"

"Peter Prince, I wouldn't ask these questions if I knew the answers."

"Bullshit."

"Ach. Just cooperate. It isn't pleasant, but it could be so much easier for both of us. What did you visit?"

"Alright," Peter Prince shouted. "I went to the Citadel with Miss Tivoli [where is she?]. To the Mosque of Ahmad Ibn Tulun, I think. We were in that vicinity for a whole day. I don't remember then. I went to the Egyptian Museum, and walked around then. Around the Nile, and went to one of those islands, found a museum about cotton. It's a little confused. I can't tell you any more."

"First of all," the interrogator shouted back across the room, "you have your days switched around. The first itinerary you so ineptly described, was actually, with a few inaccuracies, what you did on the second day, and vice versa. On that first day you got up rather late, which seems an unforgivable squandering of time to me, for if I were privileged, and rich enough to travel I should not waste any time at all, but get up at seven hundred hours prompt, and begin. You stayed in bed till nine forty-three hours, and then leisurely called for breakfast in your room, and didn't leave that room till noon, when most of Cairo was already closing up for its midday, how shall I say it . . . nap, yes. You went down to the lobby and asked for a map to prepare the itinerary you should have done the night before, and you seated yourselves on the divan and spread the map over your knees to examine it. When you finally left, after wasting an hour over a glass of iced sugar-cane syrup with lemon and mint you went first to the island, El Guezireh, where you just wandered foolishly for a good hour and a half, and found our Cotton Museum closed, after all, because it closes, as you should have known, at thirteen hundred hours, and then you sat down in a garden called El Tahrir for God knows how long, two hours and seven minutes, dozing there with Miss Tivoli, for all we know . . ."

"Isn't this just ridiculous." Peter Prince slapped his hands together and sat down on a wicker chair.

"Ridiculous," the interrogator rose half out of his seat. "You insult our city. You insult Egypt with your indifference."

"I'm not indifferent," Peter Prince pleaded.

"Only after sitting there for as long as you did, did you realize that you were in such a place as Cairo, and you hurried for a cab, and went to the Egyptian Museum then, arriving at fifteen twenty-two hours, when you know it closes at sixteen hundred hours; you gave a few of the closing moments to the mummy of Queen Takhouti, which you don't even remember, and to the immense rose-granite head of King d'Ouserkaf, the only one of its kind from the Fifth Dynasty. But what? What did you do then? Then you left. You returned to your hotel and drank, quite a bit of zebeeb, and then at twenty-one seventeen hours you stepped out with Miss Tivoli to eat at the Casino des Pigeons. I have never eaten myself at the Casino des Pigeons, and I never will. You are a fortunate man. All the best in the world falls into your lap . . . Excuse me." He stopped for a moment to consult some notes.

"This is dreary foolishness," Peter Prince said. In the hush he thought he could hear a sobbing woman. Which one? The fans whirred and the edges of the interrogator's pages fluttered. Peter Prince approached the desk. The interrogator was ready to speak, sitting on the edge.

"You're right. It is dreary. But you should want to hear about it, after all. It is your life. Especially the second day. You seem especially interested in that, because on that day you bought the bird, that bird you seem so involved in. At eighteen forty-three hours you bought it, seven hundred and twenty piasters, no bargain." He smiled.

"Look. I can't even guess what you're up to. What's the point of all this?"

"The point is that I must ask you several questions."

"You're proving something. You're not asking me questions."

"You can sit back in that chair if you please."

He felt weary, his limbs like weights. It was hours. He couldn't imagine how long the business had been going on. His mind was scattered, all parts separating. He needed to get out of there. "This is preposterous," he said, and sat down as he had been told to do. "I'm sure that you don't even know what's going on."

"The questions will get harder."

"I have no idea what's going on."

"That is the confusion."

"Have I done something wrong?"

The interrogator let his smile loose again and clapped sharply for a guard, who left the room immediately. They were silent till the guard returned with a small flask of zebeeb. The interrogator took it and poured a half-finger into a glass and covered it with three fingers of water. There was no ice. With a snap of his wrist he set the water swirling and handed the cloudy liquid to Peter Prince.

"Aren't you having one?" Peter Prince asked.

"You are offered one," said the interrogator. "I am not."

Though Peter Prince was familiar with the drink he didn't trust it in that situation, a cloudy, licorice flavored drink, that could disguise anything that was added to it.

"Don't be foolish. It's not drugged," said the interrogator when he saw Peter Prince hesitate.

"I didn't think it was drugged," said Peter Prince. He took a sip to reassure the interrogator. "I want to know why I'm being put through this."

The interrogator dipped again into his briefcase, the kind an impoverished teacher carries, full of books all the time, scuffed gray at the corners, the handle soiled and worn. It was full. He pulled out a brown folder tied with a cotton ribbon. "I think it's all in here." Peter Prince guessed that the briefcase was stuffed full of Peter Prince. He watched closely as the interrogator undid the folder, smoothing out the cotton ribbon between his thumb and forefinger. There was a brown blemish on the back of the interrogator's hand, with some thick black hairs growing from it. He could see the start of a tattoo on the wrist under the cuff. It was difficult to breathe the air of the room. The interrogator had his nose now down close to the folder, and he was squinting. He made a few noises, thrust his poised hand in like a frog's tongue, and pulled out a photograph. He handed that to Peter Prince.

At first the picture made no sense to him: a reticulated wire fence, part of a brick building, a concrete wall with some graffiti, a street, a curb: nothing: not even a decent photograph. He stood the photograph up against the briefcase and sat back in his seat. "Why did you want to show this to me?" Then, as if suddenly a memory had surfaced, he grabbed the picture again from the table. On the concrete wall, in big, black, irregular letters was the name GANGI. That was his schoolyard wall. There was the school, the steps down, his fence, his street, his basketball hoops. It was all there.

"How did you get this?"

"We acquired it."

"That's the schoolyard where I used to live, when I was a boy. I used to play basketball there, and in back of the basketball court is a Presbyterian church that had to carry on in a basement all through the war because they couldn't get building materials. By now it's probably built. I went to Boy Scouts there. That's my old neighborhood. It must be early Sunday morning, or maybe a schoolday, because no kids are playing basketball. Where did you get this?"

"There are many of them in here." The interrogator smiled like the Good Humor man from his old neighborhood as he pulled snapshot after snapshot of the schoolyard from the folder, some with kids playing basketball or stickball or softball or slug, some with crap games in the corners, some with kids just sitting around on the steps staring off across the warped expanse of concrete schoolyard. The gated windows on the second floor, the big, heavy, fireproof doors, the broken windows on the third floor. He could recognize some of the kids. There was the Greek, and Smith, and Ginzy, and Robert Haverfield whom he'd nearly forgotten. And there was Stoop, in almost every picture, awkward as usual, but not shy, always trying to get his clumsy self into a game. His face, in almost every picture, seemed highlighted, even when he was off to one side. Peter Prince felt an indefinable twinge when he saw Stoop.

"This is fantastic," said Peter Prince. "It's unbelievable. I can't believe what this is all about. What is this all about?"

"I've got another folder here that will interest you."

"That's enough," said Peter Prince, closing his eyes. The surprise of the first exposure had been exhilarating, but he feared whatever else could come out of those folders. "This is all very curious, but I don't understand what you want from me. I don't want to see any more pictures. What do you want to learn about me? I'd tell you anything right away, anything. But please get it over with."

"There is a saying, Peter Prince, that all things complete themselves in their proper time, and that he who with haste wants to change the pace gets buried folded over. The interrogation will end when it's done, not before."

Peter Prince wiped his brow. The fans were humming. "Well what do you need to know about me?" The interrogator didn't answer. How long had Peter Prince been there? Longer than he'd been there, sure. The interrogator looked different, refreshed. Something was going to happen. He wished it would happen. What was Miss Tivoli going through? He felt helpless, without pride, in this situation of amorphous torture he could be convinced to do anything, to admit anything. The bolts were tightening. Where? In his head. Where? Where those strange pictures they had found of his childhood were lodged. He was sick. The fans were humming. He lifted the tepid, cloudy drink to his lips and sucked some down. His gullet was a narrow passage, and the liquid drove a painful route down through. Without ice it hit his brain immediately, and tired him out. The guards, both big and fat, looked like eunuchs. They whispered to each other behind the interrogator, but didn't take their dark, fat-encircled eyes off him. Fat, shiny, like harem guards.

"Do you recognize him?" The interrogator was shoving another photograph in front of his face. "Do you know who this is?"

"Of course I do," said Peter Prince, trying not to look at the picture.

"Tell me about him."

Peter Prince looked at the picture. There was Stoop again. Stoop again in a graduation picture, with his twisted, cheesy smile, the shine of his peeling red nose softened by the retoucher. His eyes were opened wider than usual, full of that familiar paranoid craving for reassurance that always drove Peter Prince away. This whole proceeding was screwed up. What did they care about Stoop for?

"Well tell me about him."

"Why about him? Is he a spy or something? What do you expect me to know about him? I haven't seen him for ten years."

"You never were very friendly with him, were you?"

"I was friendly with him. How can it make any difference?"

"You didn't treat him very well." The interrogator pulled out another picture of Stoop, this one an action shot, of him playing basketball, taking that funny, leaning, one-handed shot, where he went off on the wrong foot, and stuck his tongue out.

Peter Prince smiled at that one. He couldn't help it. "That's Stoop alright," he said.

"You see your patronizing attitude."

"What patronizing attitude? I'm just telling you it's Stoop. It looks like him. The funny thing was he could make that shot."

"Then why did you never let him play?"

"That's a lie. I always let him play. If it was ever up to me I always let him play. He wasn't really very good, pretty bad, worse than I was. But it wasn't my fault if he didn't play." Good God. Peter Prince found himself back in the schoolyard in earnest. He had left all that behind on page forty-three. His schoolyard prejudices. He was ready to take a trip 4000 years back down the Nile, and he was being put on the line for a basketball choose-up.

"You might have made a sacrifice, stopped playing yourself to give him a chance. Something."

"This is ridiculous."

"He was an unfortunate boy."

"Sure, unfortunate. My neighborhood had lots of unfortunate kids, and they didn't come around . . ." He stopped himself.

"You were cruel to him, even though he thought of you as a friend, perhaps his only friend."

"Cruel to him, nonsense."

"You treated him like dirt. You wouldn't deign to look at him. You were some kind of royalty around him, letting him always follow behind you. You never had to worry about his loyalty or esteem. He was baggage to you."

"Listen. Listen. Let's make some sense of this. This has nothing to do with anything anyway. Where does all this information come from? Charge me with something here. This is Cairo, not New York City."

Peter Prince was shaking as the interrogator pulled another folder from the briefcase. This one contained an old manuscript, typed, erased, scribbled over, and I recognized it myself as a scene I had written to use earlier in this novel, but had discarded, choosing not to emphasize so this particular aspect of Peter Prince's boyhood. The Lord knows how that scene turned up at this interrogation.

"Here," said the interrogator. "Look through this. It should be of some interest to you. I'll have you stay here for a moment with it while I step out." He left through the narrow door behind his desk, and even the guards followed him.

Peter Prince sat still for a moment and held the manuscript in his hand. He felt suddenly lonely in the room. There was his own name, and Stoop's name on the manuscript. This was nuts. Who would want to write such a thing as this? It wouldn't be possible in any other novel. He should have kept out of Egypt, and he knew it. He could be flooded out of his head there, like a whole race of men, like the Nubians. Everything was being turned over. He shook on his feet when he stood up. The room was dimensionless; he could spend lifetimes from one corner to the next. How could his life ever finish when it was always beginning? There was no one in the room, but they were all approaching him in an unending procession of sacrificial cups brimful of time. He was in the center of a sphere with memories and premonitions whipping about him in unpredictable orbits. He couldn't see through the cloudy spin of events how everything moved, but he knew. He had arrived back at the desk where the manuscript lay fluttering. So much haste. He brought into focus the words there about Peter Prince and his friend Stoop. The fans were buzzing.

PETER PRINCE AND HIS FRIEND STOOP

zz
zz
zz It never failed. Every morning Peter Prince
zz came down the steps in the courtyard and there
zz Stoop would be, waiting to walk to school with
zz him. What could he do? The kid was such a pitiful
zz wreck. A smile puffed up one side of his twisted
zz face, his worn brown briefcase (his fag-bag) was
zz gripped between his legs. Peter Prince didn't
zz really dislike the kid. He was O.K., smart enough,
zz but he wished the kid wouldn't tag along so
zz much, making it seem that they were good
zz buddies. Peter Prince had trouble enough around
zz the neighborhood, getting along by clowning,
zz just good enough to get into a game, barely
zz zzzz staying out of fights—trouble enough that he
zzzz didn't need to be associated all the time with
zthumpzzzthumpzz someone the kids called the Creep. Stoop
zzzzzzzzzzzz
zzzzzzzzzthunderstood that he wasn't welcome, but he
zzthiszzzzzzzzzz
zzzzzzzzridiculousz waited just the same every day for Peter Prince to
zzzzzzway come out of the apartment house, down the steps
zztozzzz
zzzzz of the court, so he could walk with him. He didn't
zzzzzzz
zzz even walk by his side, but tailed a little behind.
zzzz Like most kids who are smart enough to know
z they are creepy he kept his place and tried not to
zz
zzzzsayzzz
zzzzzzthezzz be too conspicuous, but he was lonely and hungry
fan is buzzing enough not to be able to give up on Peter Prince.

When it came right down to it Peter Prince didn't mind Stoop the Creep. The kid knew how to talk about a lot of things, about music, poetry, and he knew a lot of biology, all of which interested Peter Prince, though he wouldn't let his friends know. Sometimes he'd throw an answer over his shoulder to Stoop, as if he were tossing a biscuit to a pup. It looked weird, like an oriental and his wife, the kid about five feet behind, talking in that funny accent of his (another strike against him on the block), not really a foreign accent, but the accent of a kid who has been forced to stick around his parents too much, listening to them speak Yiddish, German, Polish, whatever—an over-cautious pronunciation. Stoop's father was an egg-candler, a retailer of eggs, who peddled the produce he picked up in the country every Monday, riding all week through the whole neighborhood on his three-wheeled bicycle cart, selling from door to door. Peter Prince could see him once in a while through a crack in the door of the dark little room he had rented in the basement for his egg-candling. He sat there with his face glowing as he passed the eggs in front of the flame. It was strange that he got on that way, never taking the subway to work, and Stoop suffered from his being always home, a typical, spoiled, over-protected creep, whose father would show up at the schoolyard to make sure he got into a game. Peter Prince was stuck with him. No matter what other friends, Sweet, the Greek, Hudge, he picked up on the way, and no matter how those guys insulted the kid, he would tag along anyway, keeping his five feet behind Peter Prince, as if he knew Peter Prince wouldn't hurt him, and might even protect him. On the way home from school Peter Prince could avoid him, because he could leave by any exit, and could take a number of routes, but usually Stoop would catch up with him about half way home, and Peter Prince, if it was warm enough to play basketball, would have to tell him to take off about a block before the schoolyard so he wouldn't be seen walking up to the courts with the Creep. He had to get into a game himself.

In the winter of Peter Prince's senior year, Stoop, who was a junior, didn't show up for a long stretch, three weeks or more. It was like a spring day in January, the first day he didn't show up, warm enough for just a windbreaker, and when he saw that the Creep wasn't waiting for him it felt warmer. He practically ran to Broadway? It was like being free. The kid was really a cross he bore. He could walk to school without being ridden by his friends.

"Where's the Creep?" asked Duffy when he met him on Broadway.

"Who?" asked Peter Prince, playing it nonchalant.

"That kid, the Creep, Stoop, the one you're always walking with to school."

"Oh," said Peter Prince, as if he'd just figured out whom Duffy was talking about. "What should I know for? I don't know what happens to that kid. He just follows me to school a lot. I don't keep track of him."

"I always see you with him. Everyone always says, 'Here comes Peter Prince and his Creep.'"

He just works for me in front of the house every morning I don't have anything to do with it."

"Kick him in the ass a couple of times," Duffy said. "He won't follow you no more then."

Peter Prince laughed at that, he felt so good not having the kid tag behind him. He walked, flexing his shoulders as if he were working the kinks out of them. He stopped at Suki's for a egg cream where he met Swanny Festa, Gangi, Lucas, Herz, Birdy, Hubby, Gerry, Stames, Heavy, Strassburger, Rabow, Wimpy and Bodeen. They all asked about the Creep.

"Ha," said Peter Prince, licking the brown and white foam off his upper lip. "He creeped away." Everyone moaned at this limp humor and Peter Prince felt somewhat creepy an foul in the mouth himself, but it worked. The rest of the walk to school was full of loose arm-punching exuberance, with Peter Prince especially frisky, and all the boys strutting, loose at the knees, snapping their fingers. It was easier without the Creep, and there was no problem getting into games.

That was okay for about a week. He enjoyed the free traffic with the boys, but by the next Tuesday he about Stoop, and of hearing the meanness about him. On the Monday of the third week he popped out of his house really anxious and ready to see Stoop again was getting tired of having to make his nasty remarks Stoop wasn't there. He went back up the steps to his apartment pretending he had forgotten something, and Stoop still wasn't there. He was depressed by it, a weight heavier than the weight he felt with Stoop along. He walked to school along St. Nicholas Avenue, to avoid his friends. He couldn't face their questions any more of "What happened to the Creep?" He really missed him, the kid's smart talk, and his devotion. He had thought he could do without it forever, but he liked it, better than the buddyship of all the other guys.

When Peter Prince got home from school that day he went to the basement of Stoop's house where he knew the father was candling eggs. He knocked on the door, which swung open a little. The father asked him to come in. Peter Prince watched the man expertly pass the eggs in front of the lamp. He actually used a kerosene lamp, because that was what he was used to from the old country, and he couldn't see accurately with electric light. He quickly sorted the eggs into racks. "Just a minute. I have a few more here." He finished up and turned to Peter Prince. "Now what?" He squinted. "Ach. It's you. My boy wants to see you. He's always talking about you." The man grabbed hold of Peter Prince wrist and held it firmly as a hooked fish. "He's had his appendicitis." He tugged Peter Prince upstairs to the apartment where Stoop was recuperating.

There lay the Creep under a huge featherbed, the first Peter Prince had ever seen, with a

zzzzzzz
zztozzz
zzzzzzz
zshowz

zzzzzzz
zzzzzzz
zzzyourz
zzhowzz

zzeasyz
zzzzzzzz
zzzzzzzz
zzzzitzz

zzzziszz
zzzzzzz
zzzzzzz
zzlzzzzz

zzzamz
zzdoing
zzzzzzzz
zzzzzzzz
zthiszz

zpagezz
zzzinzaz
zzmore
zzorzzz
zzlesszz

stocking cap on top of his twisted head. The sight made Peter Prince laugh, and that good humor brought smiles to the parents' faces, who were standing shoulder to shoulder beside the bed, he still in his blue coveralls, she in a faded gray and yellow flowered smock. The boy seemed to laugh and cry when he saw Peter Prince, and he looked at him with so much love that it embarrassed Peter Prince.

thezz zz zpreviouszz zzpagezz zzzzwasz nothingzzz zzzbutzzzz zzzazzz zzfrivolouszz tourzzdezz zzzzzforce on this page we will get down to some real buzzing zzzzzzzzzzzzzz zzzzzzzzzzzzzzzz zzzzzzzzzzzz zzzzzz zzzzthiszzz zzzzziszzzzz morezlikezitz acredittotheform

The boy was wallowing in bedside gifts: books, dolls, puzzles, kaleidoscopes, games. "They operated on me and took my appendix out." He spoke with a thick nasality. From the midst of a pile of fluffy dolls on immense night-table next to him he pulled out a corked, sealed bottle, with a thing floating around in it like a small yellow sausage. "This is it. This is my own vermiform appendix. It looks like a fat worm. It's acute, but it isn't ruptured yet, so they let me keep it."

He handed the vial to Peter Prince, who stared at it for a while. "It's very nice," he said, holding it up for the parents to admire. They both shook their heads rapidly in agreement. Peter Prince could have told them shit was chocolate and he'd have them agreeing with him, so pleased were they that he'd come to see their Stoop.

"It's of so nice," Stoop giggled. "But it's interesting. Like a little Vienna sausage. Will you cook it for me for breakfast when I'm better, Mamma?"

"Oooooh. Peep peep," the mamma squeaked.

Peter Prince could think of nothing to say. He stood there smiling in that room littered with indulgences: a huge electric globe in one corner, a table with an expensive microscope in another, a bookshelf with both the *Encyclopedia Britannica* and *Americana*. He would have liked to tell that poor, displaced, son-doting couple that they were only ruining the kid by treating him too well. That they should stop giving him everything. They were making him light and puffy as the featherbed he slept under. But he couldn't say anything. He stood there, his weight on one foot, then on the other, examining, re-examining the vial with Stoop's appendix in it. It was warming in his hand and he could see the moisture rising up the sides of the cork.

"You really do like it?" Stoop said.

Peter Prince said that he did. He had to get out of there. He had done his duty and now had nothing to say and things would soon begin to get uncomfortable. He put the appendix vial back down among the fluffy dolls, and touched Stoop's forehead, a spontaneous gesture that surprised him, and Stoop too, who grinned and trembled. "I think I'll go. You must be tired." It was a strain on Peter Prince to be liked so much.

"Oh no. You can stay. I sleep all day anyway so I'm not tired. I'll be ready for school in two weeks or so, so I can walk with you again."

Peter Prince turned to the parents. "He must be very tired," and in eleven steps he was out in the hall again. He stood a moment outside the door and felt himself rise in his own benign presence through several atmospheres. He had made the boy feel good just by being present at his bedside. He'd never done anything like that before, and it made him feel giddy and philanthropic and he went immediately up to Suki's on the corner to get an egg-cream, and then a lemon and lime with water, and he sat there grinning till the corners of his mouth hurt, till taciturn Suki himself said,

"What you so happy for, your uncle die and leave you a million dollars?"

"Suki," Peter Prince said, "you're the greatest."

"Yeah, the greatest," said Suki. "You should tell that to my arthritis."

"Give me a cream soda."

Peter Prince felt great all the rest of the afternoon, mumbling and humming to himself, walking around the schoolyard, not hassling to get into a game. He felt good until evening, when his gut started to throw a bitter taste in his mouth, and he went to bed with a black nausea in his throat and his mind, and he dreamed all night of the wounded, the defeated, the sick, and the maimed.

On his first day out Stoop was waiting for Peter Prince at the courtyard entrance. His grin was immense, and after he said he felt fine he handed Peter Prince a small package. "Open it now," he said.

"Right now?" It was cold, had just finished snowing.

Stoop shook his head, and passed his books from one arm to the other in excitement. Peter Prince carefully unwrapped the little perfume box from its flowered paper, and found inside, between two layers of tissue paper, Stoop's appendix in its vial, just as he had left it.

"I want you to have it," Stoop said. He seemed to glow. "You liked it so much."

"But . . ." Holy shit, thought Peter Prince. This is the end. That's all. "Does your father know you're giving this away?" He held out the little vial. The thing had crumbled a bit.

"It's my vermiform appendix and I can give it away. My father looked at it all he wants to, and so have I, so now you can have it." His funny, O-shaped grin was open as wide as it would go.

"Thank you, but . . . I guess . . . It can't . . ." Peter Prince could see the grin diminishing on Stoop's face as he realized Peter Prince didn't have much enthusiasm for the present. He didn't want the kid to have a relapse. He put the little box in his pocket, and threw his arm over Stoop's shoulder. "It's really very nice of you. I really want to look at it some more." They walked for a while side by side, but Stoop inevitably dropped back to his usual five feet when they saw Duffy and the Greek, and he talked at Peter Prince as usual, expecting no answer.

"Hey, the Creep is back. Look at the Creep," said Tish when he caught up. "How are you, Creep?"

Peter Prince laughed with the boys. It was a difficult position he was in. The box with the appendix felt hot against his thigh, as if it could rupture there. He reached in and held on to the vial. He knew it would have to end, there was no

Steve Katz

butzzzzzzzzzzzzzz
plezzzzzzzzzzzzzzz
asezzzzzzzzzzzzzz
donzzzzzzzzzzzzzz
'tzzzzzzzzzzzzzzzz
getzzzzzzzzzzzzzzz
mezzzzzzzzzzzzzzzz
wrozzzzzzzzzzzzzz
ngzzzzzzzzzzzzzzz
Petzzzzzzzzzzzzzz
erzzzzzzzzzzzzzzzz
Prizzzzzzzzzzzzzzz
ncezzzzzzzzzzzzzz
iszzzzzzzzzzzzzzzz
expzzzzzzzzzzzzzz
erizzzzzzzzzzzzzzz
enczzzzzzzzzzzzzz
zingzzzzzzzzzzzzzz
thizzzzzzzzzzzzzz
szzzzzzzzzzzzzzzzz
diszzzzzzzzzzzzzzz
comzzzzzzzzzzzzzz
fortzzzzzzzzzzzzz
zzzzzzzzzzzzzzzzz
zzzzzzzzzzzzzzzzz
thezzzzzzzzzzzzzz
fanzzzzzzzzzzzzzz
makzzzzzzzzzzzzz
eszzzzzzzzzzzzzzzz
azzzzzzzzzzzzzzzzz
raczzzzzzzzzzzzzz
ketzzzzzzzzzzzzzz
whilezzzzzzzzzzzz
hezzzzzzzzzzzzzzz
trieszzzzzzzzzzzz
tozzzzzzzzzzzzzzz
readzzzzzzzzzzzzz
thiszzzzzzzzzzzzz

help for it. He couldn't be seen any longer with the Creep. He couldn't keep up this association. He'd have to skirt the park on the way to school, or leave early. His friends weren't ridiculing him, but he felt as if they were, and he had no way to defend himself. The Creep was practically his own body, and he was too weak.

The Creep didn't wait for him after school, at least he wasn't there. Peter Prince knew he would have to do a lousy thing, something without conscience, to break with Stoop completely, to give him back his appendix, and he knew it was his own lack of courage that caused it; but it was hard enough for himself in the neighborhood without his having to suffer Stoop's abject shadowing of him, and his constant association with that twilight figure.

"Hey, where's the Creep?" Nick DeMartino asked, coming out of the Firestone Tire store with a new basketball pump.

"What Creep?" Peter Prince asked.

"What Creep? How many Creeps do you know? Your Creep. Stoop. He's your Creep. You're always with him."

"Shit, man. I wish you'd stop that. I have to nothing to do with him. He tails me once in a while, that's all."

Nick DeMartino jabbed him with his new basketball pump. "That's no way to put down your friends, Peter Prince. He's a faithful friend. It's not like a girl whom you'd be ashamed to admit you liked."

Peter Prince could practically feel himself

blushing. They turned the corner of 174th Street and saw a crowd of guys by the schoolyard fence. They had someone backed against the fence and were gathered around him in a semicircle. They were mostly strangers, guys from over on Amsterdam Avenue. "We'd better leave this alone," said Nick DeMartino.

"Wait a second." Peter Prince lingered for a moment on the outside of the crowd.

"Hey," said Nick. "It's Stoop."

At that moment Peter Prince saw him too, his twisted face among the D.A.'s. He was crying.

"I hate to see someone cry," one of them said.

"Shit. He's a creep. Hey, creep. Pull down your pants, you've got got a hole between your legs."

Stoop was sobbing and couldn't speak. Someone had torn his jacket, and his bowtie had been cut.

"Jesus, Mary," said Nick DeMartino. "What are they pounding on that kid for?"

They both knew that it tried to interfere they would be stomped themselves. "Stop them," Nick said. "Stop them. He's your friend. They'll kill him."

Peter Prince was sweating. He kept his face down so Stoop couldn't see him. Peter Prince kept telling himself that he wasn't afraid of getting hit, that it was just getting involved. It was all too bad. "Look. I can't do anything," he said. "I've got to get home." He pulled Stoop's appendix out of his pocket and showed the vial to Nick DeMartino. "My mother needs this, right now. Right away."

while z I z a m t y p i n g t h i s e v e r y o n e e i s e h a v i n g f u n

"What the fuck is that?"

"I don't know. It's something I got for her at the drugstone. It's something she needs."

The gang on Stoop was laughing. One of them had a butcher's knife at his chest. He was foaming a little at the mouth.

"Look," said Peter Prince. "I've got to get home so I'm going. Tell them that Stoop just had his appendix out and that they could kill him. He's sick. They could really hurt him." He sprinted down the street. At the corner by the subway entrance he thought he heard someone call his name and he turned, but no one was near him. The gang up the street seemed to be dispersing, there were some cops, Flynn and Koscek, moving among them. Rather than cross above ground he went down into the piss-stained subway tunnel under Ft. Washington Avenue, came up on the other side, jumped the wall, and went home through the bushes. He had lost his keys and had to wait for his mother to get home from work. He didn't go outside, but sat on the bench in the hall waiting for her, holding the appendix vial in his hand. He could hardly move; he felt dry, precipitated, as if any move would leave him in a little heap, shapeless.

"What's the matter with you?" his mother asked when she came in the door.

"I'm hungry," he said, and stood up shaking. Once in the house he snapped on TV and sat down like a man after a hard day's work, to watch cartoons before dinner.

Stoop was there the next morning as if

nothing had happened. He wasn't even bruised. Peter Prince returned his appendix and explained that he didn't want to walk with him any more, maybe just that day, but after that they would go separately.

"But it's just a few months," Stoop said. "You graduate in a few months and after that I'll never see you again. School is over and I'll never see you."

Peter Prince hadn't even thought that far ahead. Just a few months. "Look, you just walk your way, and I'll walk mine. That's all. I don't want to walk with you." He wanted his voice to carry his resolve, but it came out an obsequious trill. He was weak, and he despised himself.

"Don't you even like me?"

"It's not that. It's just that I think it will do you good to walk by yourself."

"Listen. Please," said Stoop, falling back his usual five feet behind. "Peter Prince, I don't blame you for yesterday when you saw those guys after me. I don't care about that. I didn't want you to get beat up either and I was glad when you went away. I knew they wouldn't hurt me, because I showed them my appendix scar and they got scared. I scared them, and then the cops came. Please let me walk with you."

It was so simple. It would be nothing for Peter Prince to do, for a few months. He turned back to where Stoop was following. "I can't. I just don't want to. I made up my mind."

"Why can't you?"

"I don't choose to any more." The word

zzzzIzwishzzzz
zzzIzzwerezzz
zzzMarshallzz
zzMcLuhanzzz
zzzthenzzlzzzz
zzcouldzzzzzzzzzzz
zzzzunderzzzzzzzzzz
standzzzzzzzz
zzzzwhy
zzzzzzI'mzzzzzzzz
zzzdoingzzzzz
zzzzthiszzzzzzz
zzzandzevenzzz
zzzfeelzzzzzzzzzz
passionatelyzzz
zzzzzzinvolved
zzzdrivenzzzto
zzzzzzzit
zzzzzlikezit'szzzzz
zzzzzan
zzzuncontrollable
zzzzurgezzzzzzz
zzazzkindzzzofzzz
zzzzzzzcompulsory
tuberculosiszzzzzzzzz
iszzzzzzzzzzz
zzzzexamzzzzz
zzzthe
zzzfan
iszzzz
zzzbuzzing
thiszzzzz
meansthefan
is buzzing
buzzing

"choose" came out like a sneeze. Stoop was crying, he could see. He didn't deserve to console him, even. "Look. We'll meet sometimes and maybe over your place, and then we can talk about a lot of things." Peter Prince hadn't expected to make that concession, and didn't deserve it himself.

bbrrrratatatazzzz "Why can't I walk to school with you?"

zzzzzzzzzzzzzzzz "I can't . . ." Peter Prince couldn't say it.

"I'm very sorry," said Stoop the Creep and

zzzzzifzzzzz he wiped his eyes.
zzzzthiszzzz
zzzzzhaszzzz
zzzzbeenzzz
zzzeffectivezz
zzpleasezzzz
writezzzzzzz
zzzzinzzzzzz
zztozzmezz
zzzatzzzzzz

zzthefanzz
werebuzzzzzing
zzzztheywerezz
zzzzzzbuzzing
zzzzlzzzzzzzz
zzzzmightzzzz
zzzzznotzzzzz
zzzzzzbezzzzz
zzzztherezzz
zzzzzzbutzzz
zzzzzthezzzz
zzencouragment
zzzzwillzzzzzzz
zzzzgetzzz
zzztozmezz
                zz
                 zz
                  zz

(Z)

He was waiting for Peter Prince on the next morning, and he had to take a route through the basement, out the door of the adjacent building, through the park, and up 176th Street in order to avoid him. He had to make that detour every day till school was out. He did meet the kid from time to time and spend boring hours talking, during which Stoop never mentioned once that he still waited every morning, and Peter Prince never told of the detour he took to avoid the Creep.

"I'm very glad to see you didn't try to leave," said the interrogator, who had entered silently while Peter Prince was still reading. "You see the door was left unguarded, and you were free to go, but you had no way to know that."

Peter Prince felt almost relieved that he hadn't been aware of the escape possibility. A peculiar lethargy had stolen over him that made him too weak to run, and he was curious besides, with a kind of morbid apprehension.

"Did you like the story?"

Peter Prince shrugged.

"What would you add to it, anything?"

There was nothing he could say to that.

"You have to admit, then, that you were cruel to him."

"God you're simple minded. Even the author of that piece demonstrates that the attitude there was more complicated than mere cruelty. There were exigencies . . ."

"What exigencies, and how more complicated?"

"It's there, right in the story, as inept as the damned thing is, with an author who never bothers to really get to know his characters. It's right there. You can see it. It was impossible for anybody to put up with Stoop. Why are you worrying about this anyway? What is it to you?"

"I just have an interest in it. Why don't you tell me what was impossible."

"It's there in the text, in the story, if you ever learned to read. And it doesn't even take literary analysis. This is no subtle author. It's all right there, on the surface, where he leaves it. It was impossible . . . look, Stoop was a kind of jerk then, a creep, a brain leech, he sucked your head, and your time."

"He was intelligent, and very fond of you, and would sacrifice a great deal on your behalf."

"Intelligence, yeah. That was his real problem, the way he carried it. The kids resented him for that, and they took advantage of him. And he would always devise these schemes to waste my time, and have to explain everything to me in double detail. I wasted days on him, or trying to avoid him. I was just a kid then, and I needed to be one of the rest of them."

"He was complimenting you by finding you intelligent, and he wanted to share something with you. He was an unusual person. And what did you do?"

"It's in the story there. I usually told him to kiss off, that I was too busy, the Bullets had a game, some excuse. The most terrible thing I ever told him was he ought to go to a plastic surgeon and get his face straightened, but I always regretted that. You know the cruelty of kids."

"He was a lonely kid, and you were cruel to him."

"I admit that, but did I have a choice then, living as I did? Nowadays if I met him we'd be good friends, I bet. But you bring this all up as if it was important to you. Why? Why don't you just finish up whatever business you have with me?"

"This is the business we have with you."

"Oh come. Don't be so cryptic. Stoop? What is he in some kind of international trouble? I'll help him out."

"He's dead."

"You say he's dead?"

"He was killed."

"What do you know?"

"He died in battle."

"Oh good, fine, I believe everything you say." Peter Prince shook his head as if he were trying to revive himself. "How do you expect me to believe this, here in Cairo? This is all nuts."

The interrogator pulled out a picture of Stoop in uniform. Peter Prince stared at it for a moment. The face was still twisted, but it seemed more weathered, experienced, tougher. "He was a goddamned captain," Peter Prince said.

"And he was up for promotion."

"What does this have to do with me, here?"

"You are a person with the disease of selfishness and indifference."

"Sssssssssss. Insanity."

"You would be indifferent too to the fact that just before Stoop died he was thinking of you. You, and how indifferent you were to him. How you never put yourself in a position to understand him. In fact your indifference was what he thought of just before he stood up and was shot."

"What do you mean by that?"

"I shall have to preface my response to your question with a brief explanation, and I'm sure even after everything is elaborated for you you will still be incredulous. You see, men on the battlefield can reach a certain point when things are really bad, when death is commonplace all around them, a certain point where they resign themselves, and I mean that literally as quit themselves out of themselves, and sometimes after that point is reached, when whatever of life they were holding on to in their imaginations is relinquished, they can then accomplish amazing feats of bravery. The most timid, even cowardly men can turn into heroes at this point and attack pill-boxes, run screaming into machine-gun nests, fall on hand-grenades in what seems an act of great self-sacrifice, but which is, since they have transcended their egos at this point, not self-sacrifice at all since there is no self to sacrifice. Perhaps they've decided they are already dead and any other consequence is superfluous, a kind of bonus. It's interesting when they survive as they sometimes do, because they almost invariably go back to what they were before, with no ability to resummon that bravery, and no recall except the medals they've collected. This happens to men at all levels of intelligence, because in battle the mind and the nerves are in balance, and the habit of reason, if it does anything, gets in your way. An interesting stage is the one just before that identity-fracture or ego-death I've described, because at that point the mind is turned on like an automatic slide-projector and although one wouldn't say that a man's whole life flashes before his mind's eye, what does happen is that in order to suppress the horrible spectacle of friends dying miserably around oneself the mind begins to select memories at random that flash up irrelevantly and with utter surprise, and that's why once in a while you can see a man grinning as he fires his automatic weapon into the onrushing enemy—not because he enjoys killing, but because his mind has fixed a particular memory that causes the smile reaction. It's useful. What happens at a certain point is that maybe something appears, strikes him—some particularly pleasant or sometimes horrible memory—his mind freezes on it, and he throws himself on the grenade. It's not unlike the Japanese lovers who commit suicide at the apogee of their love. Such a thing, without a doubt, happened to Stoop."

"You can't know this."

The interrogator pulled a small, honey-colored lozenge from his pocket and sucked it in. "What happened in the particular case of Stoop, your friend, is that he built slowly to that moment of ego-death, as more intelligent men are wont to do, and went through a projection of various images of his mother, the river, a bridge, the museum of natural history, and finally, suddenly, Peter Prince—not the little vignette you read, but some utterly trivial discussion you had with him about a story you'd read, and you were anxious to get away, as usual and you said, 'You're full of shit, Stoop,' and left him. He wept over that through the evening, and that was the event that he froze on under the infinitely worse conditions of the infamous Fortune Cookie Ambush. The platoon was surrounded, and isolated. He had already lost a lieutenant, and communications were dead. His men, most of whom were debilitated by dysentery, had fought off a number of attacking waves of Orientals. The ammunition was low. There was no hope. Fear and death smelled bitter in their camp. The last wave was about to hit when this memory of you struck, and he stood up as if already dead, stepped, so to speak, out of his ego, and proceeded to fire. His men, roused by their captain's insane, brave act, took heart and repelled this last attack, and found your friend Stoop with a bullet through his helmet and under his heart. His act had saved them."

Peter Prince smacked his forehead. "You don't know this. Good God. Come on, you don't expect me to believe . . ."

"I can assure you Peter Prince that we have methods and I can show you any proof you require, irrefutable."

"I don't want to see any of it. I don't want to see a damned thing." He stood up and walked around the chair. He needed a cigarette. The interrogator was smiling. "That's it," Peter Prince said suddenly, and he leaned on his forefinger on the interrogator's desk. "You're trying to accuse me of killing him. That's it. That's why I'm here. You're telling me that I killed him."

The interrogator smiled and started to gather up some of his papers.

"Why don't you just say it? Say that I killed him."

The interrogator folded his hands together and leaned back. "You raised that interesting inference, Peter Prince."

Peter Prince looked at the two guards who seemed to be straightening out the room, and at the interrogator who was more and more efficiently stuffing papers back into his suitcase. His tongue was dry. He squeezed the empty glass on the desk. The interrogator clicked the latch of his briefcase shut, and stood up.

"Are you going?" asked Peter Prince.

"Yes. I'm through."

"Aren't there any more questions you need to ask me?"

"There are no more questions."

"How can you be through?"

"There are no more questions."

"What did you find out?"

"Goodbye, Peter Prince," the interrogator said, and he rose with the guards following, to leave by the narrow door.

"Well am I free to leave?" Peter Prince asked, as the man got to the door.

The interrogator switched off the fans as he left and Peter Prince was alone in the room. It was silent there but for the high-pitched whine of Peter Prince's charging nerves. He sat down in the air around him, and mumbled to himself, "There ought to be some intensely relevant ending to this scene I've just been through, some symbolic final gesture," and he looked out at me as if to accuse me of enjoying what I just put him through. Tedium. He slid off the chair like a man off a sick-bed, and left through a door, that led him into a narrow corridor between a row of narrow desks to another narrow door that opened onto the street. The civil servants at the desks, all shiny with sweat, watched him with mute, hostile curiosity as he left.

It was late. The streets glowed red from the sunset, and he started to walk away, breathing the moist air like a sponge. "Now I can take that trip down the Nile, finally," he said, not directly to me, but whom else would he be speaking to in that city where he knew no one?

"Peter Prince," someone shouted, and he turned to see one of the guards chasing him with something in his hand. He stopped and waited till the guard reached him with the bird cage with its dead bird in it.

"Where is Miss Tivoli?" he asked, but the guard left without answering. "Is this your idea of an ending?" he asked, shaking the cage at me. He walked back to the hotel. Miss Tivoli wasn't there, but she had left a note. It was a relief to know that she lived. He went up to his room and attached the bird cage to the microphone again, and then opened the letter. "Dear Peter Prince," it said. "I'm leaving. I can't stand Egypt any more. I'm sorry I'm so impulsive. Maybe I'll see you again, though I never know where I'll be. It was very good with you. Many kisses and station identification."

Peter Prince could have wept at that. He rattled the letter above his head toward me. "What good. What good have you ever done me?" he whistled.

*

The old engine of the beat-up riverboat clattered and banged and the deck cargo, which included Peter Prince, screamed in Arabic, bleated, clucked and sang. (I spent a lot of good hours trying to find out precisely what kind of boat Peter Prince might have ridden on, since I was a little too shy to ask him at this point, maybe later. I had to use a cheap one, of course, one more like the boats that take passengers, cattle, cargo, from island to island in Greece, or like the boat in the *African Queen* with Humphrey Bogart. Perhaps I researched in the wrong places; at any rate, I could find out little about it. A friend of mine knew a girl who had just returned from Cairo after three months of helping out on a dig in Fostat, which was once a city itself, but is now Cairo's garbage dump. We talked and talked. In fact we went out to dinner and ate a grubby *paella* with flies in it, and we talked. I told her all about Peter Prince in Cairo, and how he got along. She listened carefully and I watched her face to see if I'd done anything wrong. I was actually pleased because she seemed neither incredulous nor bored. Verisimilitude is not the least of my worries. After coffee I finally got to ask her about the riverboats. She said that she didn't know much about them, that some wealthy people could afford boat trips, she thought, and that she had really missed so much in Cairo that she'd have to read this novel before she returned. A stomach ailment kept me from pursuing the research further, and though I suppose with persistence I could have found out more about the boats, I have chosen not to because I've become rather fond of this old boat I'm using. I've been fond of it before in various movies, in a story, I think, by Somerset Maugham, in various novels, and I'm grateful to all of them, including *Heart of Darkness*, by the Polack writer, from whom I got the shape of the hull. If anyone knows more about the subject and cares to reveal it he can contact my agent and we'll gladly publish the corrected description in an appendix to the second printing.) The old engine rattled and clattered and shook its boiler-plates and drowned out the noise of its deck cargo, which included Peter Prince. The deck was slippery with sheep and chicken-dung, human spit, vomit and excrement. (The reader may delete this detail if it's distasteful.) Human spit, vomit, and excrement. Except when they argued, which wasn't frequently, the Egyptians on the deck were a taciturn bunch. They squatted and leaned, humorless and hungry, against the cabin walls and bulkheads; some of them curled up on the deck floor with the animals. A group of women sat crowded on the only bench on the boat that was bolted loosely to the deck near the stern. There was desert as soon as they got out of Cairo. Along the banks of the river a thin strip of cultivation, and beyond that the vacant hills, purple, orange. The sky shot back over it all like a steel plate. No clouds. In the fields the *fellahim* worked as if they'd been there for millenniums. Blind, lame, parasite ridden Egyptian peasants. Peter Prince leaned on the greasy gunwale and looked out into the purple space as the boat carried its noise south. It was timeless, yes, the timelessness he had needed, but empty also, and boring. The landscape was impressive, too impressive, unviewable, and he couldn't look either at the banks close by, that emerald swath, with people in it miserable, women washing clothes on the banks and giving their scrawny children the same water to drink, that Nile water full of parasites that would blind them at sixteen, make them too weak to work by twenty. It was uncomfortable, watching them. He didn't know how to deal in himself with the discomfort he felt seeing these miserable people through the veils of his own possibilities. He was traveling back, he felt, to the source within himself, within Egypt, out of time, back into the motion of dreams where he could remake Peter Prince as he preferred him, after he knew. The banks of the Nile distracted him with their suffering. It wasn't easy to be there. It was a horror he faced, not only that the earth didn't feed the millions that suffered to live on it, but that there was nothing, nothing, nothing Peter Prince could do, no joining, working, spending, that would ease enough, without increasing, the suffering in the world, to make his sacrifice worth bearing. It was too hot. The hills looked liquid at their edges in the flowing heat. Was that what he had to do, to keep himself comfortable, to guard himself from suffering, to promote himself in the contagious midst of the world? And what could he do with this guilt that intruded? Everything he owned made him feel guilty in this place—the Swiss army knife with its seven blades that was coveted, he saw as he pared his nails, by every man on the deck. Could he give it to someone? Did he have enough pocket-knives for the Egyptian poor? He felt that he owed even his too ample flesh, his abundant health, to the poor wretches on the Nile banks, and the miserable people traveling with him to Aswan. He didn't see in them the natural joy that he had seen in the poor in Southern Italy, where they sang easily, and assuaged his guilty well-being with their good humor, and he could see that their poverty gave them something he could never have. He remembered being jealous even of the poor in Napoli as they easily cheated him. But the *fellahim* were poorer. Poverty was in their bone-marrow. Poverty dropped like cataracts over their eyes. What could he do? Poverty forced him to stare across at the vast palely tinted emptiness of Egypt.

From time to time he glanced back at the only other foreigner on deck passage. He was a European, a short man with a little roll of fat at the back of his neck, and stubby hands, both of which gripped the gunwale. He was nervous. His eyes shifted from landscape to faces, from face to face. Those eyes, when they met Peter Prince's, rolled onto the next object with an oily continuity, as if he didn't want to encounter anything. Peter Prince peered through the dirty window into the cabin where people had purchased seats. There were a few tourists sitting around uncomfortably in there, and three men who looked like Germans with a large map spread over their knees, a couple of fat Egyptian officials, and an immense, regal Nubian who wore white robes.

"You want sit in there? You can still buy seat in there." Peter Prince turned to see the mate, who put a hand on his shoulder. The man wore a greasy uniform and his teeth were rotten.

"Why do you think I want a seat in there? This is fine for me." Peter Prince motioned toward the deck with his hand.

"Americans. They sometimes get uncomfortable. They start here, then buy seat."

"Not me. I'm fine."

"Fine? What is?"

"This is just fine for . . . It's O.K."

"O.K?"

"You want buy your seat now then?"

"No."

"O.K. here, outside, on deck."

"Then why you look in through window? If you look in through that window you want seat."

"No."

"Then do not look in through window any more. *Interdit. Interdit.*"

"I can't even look through this window? It's ridiculous."

"No," said the mate. "No." He grabbed a hunk of Peter Prince's cheek between his thumb and forefinger. "No look through. *Interdit.*"

Peter Prince felt that pinch for an hour. He should have slugged the man, but knew he couldn't. They could easily feed him to the desert here. He should have bought a seat and ended it. Pride was giddy. The mate was talking now to the stubby man at the gunwale, and that man was even more nervous, lifting his hand all the time to cover his mouth and nose. When the mate left him the man collapsed into a squatting position against a bulkhead. Peter Prince crossed the deck, determined to talk to the man this time. He felt his pocket-knife pressing on his thigh. Before he took five steps someone had hold of his ankle. An emaciated *fellah* was sitting at his feet and holding his ankle with a hand that looked like a root. He was near blind, had a few brown teeth left, and wore filthy gray pajamas over his yellowish, shiny skin that seemed covered with scales. With his other hand he held the tether of a goat that kneeled on the deck, nibbling on boards. He kept repeating something that sounded like "Boodoe, Boodoe," and he pointed at the bulge in Peter Prince's pocket. He showed Peter Prince his forearm that was swollen with an immense, leaking boil. "Boodoe. Boodoe," the man said.

"I don't understand what you want."

A crowd of men gathered and squatted around on their haunches. They stared at Peter Prince's thigh, and the man's swollen forearm. He kept his grip on the ankle.

"What does he want?" Peter Prince asked the gathered men. None of them seemed to hear him. They were mostly deaf or blind.

"Boodoe. Boodoe," the man insisted.

One of the men in the circle looked up and repeated, "*Couteau.*"

"Knife," said Peter Prince. The man wanted his knife. He reached into his pocket and pulled out the Swiss army knife with its seven blades. The man smiled and shook his head vigorously, and made a cutting motion across the boil with his hand. He wanted Peter Prince to slice open the boil. The crowd was chattering in Arabic. Peter Prince put the blade back into his pocket. "I'm not qualified to do that," he said. "I can't do it." The boil was painful to the man. "Boodoe. Boodoe," he repeated several times, and in a frenzy took a deep breath and tore into the arm with his few teeth. The people drew their breath in a collective gasp. Blood and pus ran down the man's arm in yeasty mixture. As if it wasn't human pain, Peter Prince watched it, as if it was an act put on for him. His Swiss army knife with its seven blades was pressed in his fist in his pocket.

"You could have helped him. You have a knife in your pocket. You could have cut that open for him." The European had joined him and together they were watching the man bleed. Someone had taken the goat's tether from him and he was squeezing and sucking the poison from the wound. "That might be a scorpion bite, or something. It needs to be cut open and poison drawn. I'm surprised he knew that. He can die now of an infection." The man squinted at the bad arm. "Here," he said. "Let me have your knife. We might prevent the death." Peter Prince put the Swiss army knife into the man's hand. He pushed aside a few of the Egyptians closest to the suffering one and took hold of the wounded arm. The *fellah* looked at him and stopped groaning and trembling as if he saw not a human being, a Caucasian, but something supernatural. The man pulled out a pocket lighter and heated the knife blade and proceeded to cleanly open the wound and then cauterize it. The Egyptian only bared his teeth to show he felt pain. It bothered Peter Prince that he didn't even want to look away. He had no feelings at all, except a certain desperate necessity to keep his distance. The best he would ever do was give charity through the mail sometimes: a swivel-chair behind a large oak desk, at most a knock on his door or a buzz on the intercom. He hadn't sympathy nor apathy enough to live with the condemned of the earth. He didn't want them near him, to touch him. His feelings might not have been unusual, but they were disappointing.

"There," said the man, returning Peter Prince's Swiss army knife. "Now there is more of a chance."

"I could never do that." Peter Prince felt a sudden rush of tears.

"Obviously you couldn't do that. You have too much compassion. You must act like a veterinarian."

"They're not animals."

"I can't speak to them, and they don't listen to me or understand me. There's no communication so what can be the difference? Does he need to have a tail like an alligator? There are enough of those up the river here too. This is a sort that you help, that's all. It's like circumcision. Like . . . circumcision. I should have circumcised him. Ha."

"I never could have done what you did."

"Yes. That's right. You never could have done it; I told you so. It's compassion. You feel too much. The pain of others, what difference? You couldn't do it to a bird if it was a bird. You were paralyzed. I could see it on your face. I was operating on you. You weren't disgusted or frightened. That paralysis is called pity." The man had the habit of tilting his head back as he spoke and thrusting his jaw toward you.

"Don't you ever have pity?"

"Pity. Ha. Pity. Pity. You can come down this river in a canoe if you have a paddle. But you need a canoe too. So what do you need pity for? It's an irrelevant matter. I survive. Turtles survive." He gestured toward the man on the deck who seemed to have fainted. "If you wonder about that you can call it my hobby, my habit. I've done things like that more times than you have tears."

"Are you a doctor?"

The man waved his hand in front of his face, "No no no no no no no. No doctor."

"Then how . . .?"

"Questions," the man shouted, raising both his arms. "The camel crosses the desert without a sip of water and he has to ask me questions. How did you get free to ask me questions? Enough. I was a medical assistant in the war." He leaned forward so his chin nearly touched Peter Prince's shoulder. "In the German army. And that's enough to say now. We've talked enough to wear out the engine already. And I'm a Jew besides. Enough."

The man turned in a military manner and went back to the rail where Peter Prince had first spotted him. The desert had changed. To the west it had broadened out in a fertile plain while to the east there was still the barren plateau. They were coming to Beni Suef where the boat made a stop. It was a heavily cultivated plain to the west full of green thick as seaweed, and there was a pale green haze lying low in the air as if the color were evaporating. The city was small and spread out along the river —a few minarets, the blunt spire of a Coptic church, a couple of tall government buildings. It was almost sundown. It had taken seven hours to travel this 120 kilometers to this town. They would leave again after dark. Peter Prince disembarked and went to sit for a while in a cafe where he had some coffee and a dish of chick peas in olive oil. It was a silent place, almost no motor-cars. After Cairo it seemed to have no pace at all, the people moving as if submerged in the clear, heat-laden atmosphere. The sky was filled with swallows that cried and swerved as it darkened.

He could not bear himself, how much he loathed himself, his tongue coated with oil, the sweet coffee. There was some process he was in that was disintegrating him. That strange man had said that he survived. He had been in the German army, and was a Jew too. So that was possible. He loathed flesh. He looked around the little square for the roll of fat at the back of the man's neck. He knew that though he didn't want to know any more about him he would end up asking the man questions, and learning more. His head would be stuffed, and he wanted it clean. To fill up with the present like the boil on that Egyptian peasant's arm, that suppurating wound that was the life that anyone you met gave to you. He was going back where the bones were, and he wanted to be clean—back where the memory was elementary and immense. He needed to begin again back there. Up here, where he lived, there was too much to stumble over, too many distant coordinates of will, and broad planes of habit. He wanted it worked out of stone, out of time, not this thick, infested, tumescent churning present that made him sick when he tried it. He had learned this much about himself: that there was nothing he could do for the world. It was taking care of itself.

Peter Prince got back to the boat when it was dark. The German paused long enough to tell him that he had wasted his time, that he should have gone to see Lake Qurun and the Fayum. A chill had come into the air over the river. The deck class was more crowded now, people lying down next to animals to stay warm. It was just cold enough after the hot day to reach your bones. All Peter Prince had was a ridiculous raincoat to put on over his light cotton shirt and his shorts. He envied the *fellahim* who could lie close together and with their animals to keep warm. He sat down by the cabin wall in misery and drew his knees up to his chin and tried to keep from shivering. He could dimly see the German still standing by the railing. Every star shone on the black desert. In the East a shallow dome of silver light grew where the moon would rise. Peter Prince fell asleep letting the moon rise.

It surprised him when he woke up that he had slept at all in the cold. It was still cold, just before dawn. The German wasn't standing by the rail but had found a place next to a sheep and was snoring there. Peter Prince paced the deck and slapped himself to warm up. Not as in a hazy climate where the dawn seems to diffuse through the atmosphere in soft waves, but the dawn came on the desert in voracious thrusts, yanking the heat behind it. You see a violet start, then red light, pink, then the white light as the sun leaps up and it's hot.

"Did you see that other fellow who got on at Beni Suef? You saw him?" The German had hold of Peter Prince's elbow.

"What?"

"A fellow who got on there. I wasn't conversing with anybody. A fellow got on there who was tall and blonde and wore a small rucksack and boots."

"I didn't see anybody," said Peter Prince. "My name is Peter Prince. You haven't introduced yourself."

"Yes. You must have seen him. He had a peculiar thing that looked like a radio on his belthook, and he was smoking those small black cigarettes in the dark."

"I didn't see anyone. Maybe I was tired."

"I saw him get on and now I don't see him anywhere. He's a blonde. I don't like this at all. The sun is still rising and it will start to set in the afternoon."

Peter Prince began to cross the deck out of the sun. "I told you my name; now why don't you tell me yours?"

"Oh yes," said the man, walking with him. "Nicholas . . . Nicholas Karras. And there he is." At the other rail they saw a tall, bronze, athletic man who was brushing his teeth and spitting into the Nile.

"That name is Greek. Are you Greek?"

"German. I don't trust that man," said Nicholas. "He looks too clean, like a Nazi, you know. They used to wash themselves with cold water and brown caustic and scrub brushes. He looks like one of those." The German then turned to look at Peter Prince. "You look like I can trust you, though. You're helpless."

They were passing through one of the villages of low white houses strung out along the riverbank. The people were already awake, leading their few beasts to drink at the river-edge. The women washed early, before sun-up when it got too hot. "Ach," said Nicholas. "That life out there. It has such simplicity. Everyone is always busy and that's good. Poverty has its advantages, you know. They are sick people, but there are sick people in hospitals too. Even suffering, you know, is something to be sure of. You see . . ." and he gestured by moving his elbows and waving his loosely clenched fists ". . . you see how I talk and I talk and talk. Yapyapyapyap."

"Suffering," said Peter Prince wisely, "is reassuring when it happens to someone else."

"Why not? Why shouldn't it happen to someone else. There's suffering in the world like water in a reservoir. Why not? More suffering, more people, more suffering. Are you going to do something to stop it? Give up your right thigh and see if it helps. What? No. All you have to do is be smart and jump ahead. Stay a jump ahead. You can do it if you look out. It's an obligation."

"Obligation to whom?"

"Hum Hum Hum. To yourself. Do you think there's more than one pit in a prune? It's not an easy business, I tell you." He looked behind Peter Prince at the blonde man who had hung up a little mirror and was shaving with a dry blade. "You know,- he spoke in a whisper and tugged on Peter Prince's earlobe to bring his face closer. "I think I already said that I was a Jew. I said that. And that I got through the war in the German army. I tell you this in strictest confidence, because I see you aren't clever, sneaky. I can trust you. We are in Egypt, after all. But the way I see you have to do it is this. If you are caught in a fire in the dry brush what you should do—the best thing—is to run back in to the fire, where it's already burned. Then you know you are safe a little. You have to jump around on hot feet, but you don't get burned to death. Death is your enemy. Preserve yourself, and I did that. I joined the German army. It was the safest place, the Medical Corps. I had managed to destroy most of the files on me, but there weren't many in my little town. They knew nothing about me when I enlisted, nothing. My name (I told you, of course, one of my many names), it was as German as it was Jewish. I even kept it, altering the prefix a little. I went to church during the war, regularly, and it was like an oyster in a crab shell, but I didn't mind it. I wept secretly a little tear now and then because all the people I knew were dying, and they are still dead; but what was Ito do? Die? I fought with Rommel here in the desert. Here. Believe me, the Egyptians still thank the Germans for relieving them of British tyranny. Rommel was not so bad. Then I went to the Eastern front, and was lucky I came away from there with my life in that winter. I was assigned to a command hospital there so I never got very far into that frozen place. The last six months before we lost the war where was I? Ohhh. They had me stationed in a concentration camp, a small one. I won't even tell you the name of it, but it was terrible. The gas chambers malfunctioned even, and believe me I prayed that they wouldn't get them fixed. I was numb for six months, those six months, and I shall never recover from them. You know the story. What could I tell them? I am a Jew. Gas me. Put me in an oven. Would you have said that? I had committed myself to staying alive, and that was it. You Americans . . . what have you learned? Do you know death when it stands at the door to your neighborhood? I am not a brave man, and I'm not a man of principles. I am only alive. I joined the German army, and it was a gamble. And here I come to Egypt, back into the middle of it. You know if that mate I spoke to yesterday had known I was Jewish he would have locked me up, and they would have tortured me for their pleasure."

"I don't believe that."

"Hah. What did he ask me? 'Do you want a seat in the cabin?' Sure. He listened, I could tell. He listened for a little something that would let them know about me, that I was Jewish. A turn of phrase. Anything."

"That's nonsense. He asked me the same question."

"Sshhhhh," Nicholas suddenly admonished him. "Here comes the Nazi."

The blonde man moved in on them slowly, shyly. He looked softer from close up, his face marked with veins and pits as the face of a man who stays drunk a lot. He spoke with a kind of Australian cockney. "Either of you blokes ever done this before?" The German looked into the face of the newcomer for a long moment. "My name is Fishbein," said the newcomer. "Michael Fishbein, and you?"

"This is the first time for me," said Peter Prince, and he introduced himself.

"I went over to that bloody lake they've got over there, and the old tombs. It's a great lot of stuff, all that, but I don't say I go for it much, a lot of dusty rubbish. This boat trip is fine enough though. I have a bunch of friends I'm traveling with like to go out on digs, and they're out there now somewhere, but I'd just as soon stay close to the water. That bloody heat isn't for me. I had ten years working outback and I hated it all the time. Just the sight of this desert makes me lonely, doesn't it you?"

After looking the newcomer over carefully the German took hold of the railing and stared off into the desert, not showing his face.

"But I guess I interrupted something here," said Fishbein, looking from the silent German to Peter Prince. "I'll see you chaps later. I have to talk with the mate."

"No," said Peter Prince. "You're not interrupting . . ." But the fellow had already moved away. He was somewhat shy; Peter Prince liked him.

"You see," said the German, turning back. "You see, I can't trust anyone. No one. He's going to the mate. Who knows what he'll tell him. That I look Jewish." He ran his hand over his profile. "Why did I come to Egypt? Is it very obvious? Every day I look more Jewish. It was alright in the war, because my nose was smaller. It looked . . . small. Now it grows like a tree. In America they looked for the fountain of youth, and I come to Egypt. What do I look like? How do I look?"

"You look," said Peter Prince. "As you are. No more, no less. I don't say Jewish when I see you."

"That's because you are a fool. You are an American. It's obvious he saw something. Otherwise why would he go to speak to the mate? He looked at my nose. You saw him stare at it. He's going to tell the mate about it. This damned nose. When I was a boy it was a nice tiny little pugged thing, and when I enlisted I could have been taken for anything, a Bavarian Catholic. You know when it began to grow? It grew little by little all through the war, but the last six months it really began to spread out. The commandant at the concentration camp was a little myopic, but he used to call me in and stare at my nose as if it was another person in the room, and he'd issue two sets of orders, one to me and one to my nose. At the rate my nose was growing I figured a few months was all I had before they found me out. *Juden. Juden.* I was one of them, and they were going to find me out. The inmates already knew with their big noses. The war ended just on time, and I thought the nose began to subside with it . . . Oh to hell. To hell with them. What do we need them for anyway? Just to sneeze a little bit. We could do that through a hole in our chins. Birds fly, men sneeze. The damned things give us away like secret documents."

"To tell you the truth, sir, I don't think you have to worry about your nose. It looks just right to me. I've seen big noses, believe me."

"Oh to hell with you. What have you ever seen? You want to save the world; I know you. What do you know? I'll tell you something, that when you try to save the world it dies of its own accord. And you look back on it and see that you've given it a little push. Save yourself, yourself. Look at us. We all have to take this little trip up the Nile. Why? To see Abu Simbel, and some of Nubia before it is all under water. They're going to drown the land of Cush, and we're coming to see it as if it were a theater production, the last week of the performance. Some people go to see the belly dancers. The archeologists haven't even had a smack at what they're drowning. Everything's going under, not only Abu Simbel, but Cushite burial grounds, the earliest Christian churches, pagan shrines, Egyptian shrines, Moslem ruins. Splash. All of it. And the Nubians, people who are far superior to the Egyptians in cleanliness, not to mention craftsmanship, honesty, beauty, are all being uprooted for this progress, this dam, this saving of humanity. Do you know that it is calculated that by the time the dam is completed the population will anyway have grown so much that all the newly arable land will produce just enough, and no more, to keep the people in the state of misery they are now? More people with the same misery. Who is to say that famine isn't better? And what is going to happen to the thousands of fishermen along the Mediterranean coast when the 'river that rose in heaven' no longer carries into the sea the organic matter that feeds the fishes they live off? There will be no more fish. So. That life is done. The way you will save the world. Armed by Nazis, engineered by Communists. So. What does it mean? It means that Nubia will be destroyed. It means that I risk my neck to get in there and take a last look. See him now?" He pointed at the Australian. "He's over there talking to the mate. I haven't got a chance now. Please. If he asks you just tell him that I told you my nose got broken in an accident, and that's how it got this way. Tell him that."

The man's nose wasn't large. He didn't look Jewish. Peter Prince wanted to tell him so, but he saw it was futile and instead agreed to do what the man said, and turned to look at the desert again where the emptiness was peaceful and interesting.

"Listen," the German went on. "I know I can trust you. I think I can. I mean I might be in for some trouble, and I need someone I can rely on. I'm going to ask you to hold on to something for me."

"I think you're making all this up."

"You are a naive American, who doesn't understand the ways of the old world. Will you help me? Will you please help me?"

Peter Prince sighed and gave in.

"Will you hold on to something for me?"

"O.K.," he said irritably.

The German palmed a small pistol that he pulled out of a big pocket of his kapok jacket and he placed it in Peter Prince's hand, holding the hand and gun between both his. The German's hands were big and hairy and Peter Prince noticed a blue artichoke tattooed on the wrist. "Here. I'll trust you with this. Just hold onto it for me because I might need it." The man left him with the gun in his hand and walked over to the Egyptian whose boil he had cauterized, who was breathing with deep shudders. The German pushed him with the side of his foot but the man didn't move or open his eyes. The German shrugged and crossed the deck. Peter Prince had the gun, a tiny Beretta.

"And don't forget," the German shouted at Peter Prince from across the deck, and he made a gesture that at first seemed obscene until Peter Prince realized he was guardedly pointing to his nose.

The little gun lay in his hand like a pool of mercury. It was amazing how much it weighed when you held one. What would he do with it? Was it loaded? He turned it over till he found the latch that freed the clip. It was full, the little bullets lying in there like unhatched eggs. The gun was light without them. He took his raincoat from his satchel, slipped the gun into one pocket, the clip into another, and rolled the whole thing up into a tight cylinder.

"He's a funny chap, that little dark fellow." The Australian came by just as he put the raincoat back. "He won't say a word to me."

"That is strange," said Peter Prince.

"I mean it's not as if there's a whole boatload of bloody people you can talk to and pick and choose your friends so you can be snobbish if you please. He gets me roused. I mean it's just the three of us, and all these bloody aborigines or whatever you call them, with their beasts. It seems to me we owe each other a certain loyalty, or a certain civility at least, but the bloody snob just turned his back on me."

"He's been civil enough to me," said Peter Prince. "But it took him the better part of a day before he said boo, so don't let it worry you."

"I'm glad you're here, at any rate," said the Australian, and he extended his hand for a handshake, revealing the blue artichoke tattooed on his wrist. "Say, I don't think I caught your name the first time, damned impolite of me."

"I'm Peter Prince." The man's grip was soft.

"I guess I shouted my name out loud enough last time." He looked around before he leaned over to whisper it in Peter Prince's ear. "Fishbein," he said. "I'm a little jittery about that. You know why. This is bloody Egypt, after all, and sometimes I forget that they're not exactly friendly to my kind." He winked.

Peter Prince's first impulse was to tell him that the other fellow, too, was a Jew, and that he also worried about it. He saw the German standing near the bow, gazing at them as they talked. He looked furtive and suspicious, like a grubby spy. Peter Prince didn't understand how that little German could have survived in the situation he had related, but he told the Aussie nothing because he felt he owed the German a little loyalty, only because he had met him first; and because the poor man needed so desperately to trust someone. Peter Prince said nothing but, "For all I know I am one too."

"Well I'll be a bloody bastard. You don't say. It's so bloody noisy on this ship. How come you said, 'for all I know'?"

"I think I have a bit of it in my past."

"We've got to watch our step around here then, don't we?" He threw an arm over Peter Prince's shoulder. "They told me back in Sydney all about what's happened to some of ours coming in here. They have a bad time here, I guess, if ever they find out. I don't think that's likely though, if you're careful."

"Well what did you come for? To see the ruins? To see Nubia?"

"You can bloody well take another guess. Ruins. You can shove them where you please. No, I like to move around, and I'm kind of an amateur engineer. I want to see how they're doing that dam, you know. It's a bloody project. It's big." He spread his arms to show how big it would be. "It will hold twenty-five times as much water as the old dam, five hundred eighty-six feet above sea-level the surface; the dam itself will be about three hundred sixty feet high above the foundations, and two miles long, and the lake it forms will be about three hundred miles long from Aswan all the way to Kosha in the Sudanese Nubia, some four thousand million million cubic feet of water. It staggers the bloody imagination. If you don't think that's going to put out the kilowatt hours. That's what this miserable place needs, some air conditioning."

"They're going to flood out a whole race of Nubians, a nation," Peter Prince said, weakly.

"And don't think it comes free. It's costing a pretty sum. A total public investment of seven hundred fifty-eight million, eight hundred thousand dollars, broken down into three hundred twelve million dollars for dam construction, four hundred eighteen million dollars for power plants, lines, irrigation, etcetera, twenty-eight million dollars for flood control. There will be a private investment alone of two hundred sixty-eight million, eight hundred thousand dollars. A small war costs only about one billion, twenty-seven million, six hundred thousand dollars. That's not bloody shekels."

"And you don't care at all about destroying Nubia, and the ruins that will go under, and all the uncalculated results?"

"Oh I might go on to see all that bloody dreary stuff, just to say I did it, but it bores me worse than a tea party."

"How do you do now?" asked the mate, who came through the cabin door. "You still want seat inside?"

"No. No thank you. Not at all." Peter Prince slapped him on the back.

"You good man, O.K." The mate winked. He stood around for a moment talking about the heat. There had been hotter days, but this was hot enough. If you stood in the sun long enough you would shrivel up, like a raisin.

The suffering man began to mutter to himself in the middle of the deck, his eyes half open but not seeing. He had a bad fever. The tether of his goat lay on his open palm. "I think he'll die," said the German, who had traded places with Fishbein the Aussie. "He's losing fluids rapidly, and his blood will turn thick. It's like the cholera."

The ship suddenly jerked, and the motor whined like a stretching dog. The German had fallen on Peter Prince and was taking the excuse to whisper in his ear. "I saw you talking to him. What did he say? Did he say anything about me? I talked to him for a while, and I'm sure he's not a man to trust. What did he say? I saw both of you talking to the mate. I saw that." The man's tongue was practically in Peter Prince's earhole. It was near midday and the temperature was around 140 degrees fahrenheit. They were docking in a town of white houses.

"Where are we?"

The German straightened up. "It must be . . ." He squinted at the town they were closing in on. "It must be Asyut, a little less than halfway to Aswan. The name comes from the ancient Egyptian *syut*, which means sentinel, or watcher, and their local deity was the jackal, Wepwawet (not the jackal-headed god Anubis), whose name means path-opener, opener of the ways. Let us hope so."

Peter Prince shrugged. They pulled up by a fairly new dock and the modern building of the Ibrahimia Canal Commission. The Nile was damned up here with a barrage, an immense construction itself, and the water diverted through a canal two hundred miles over the desert to irrigate cotton.

"We'll stop here for three hours," he explained. "Till it's cooler. Maybe four hours."

"How do you know this? You sound like a tour guide. Have you done this trip before?"

"I read up on it," said the German, with a certain pride. "I always read all I can before a trip. It's the only efficient way to travel, because if you know what is happening you can pay attention to the more interesting details, and to unusual events, like that man who is dying. Tell me, what did that big fellow say to you?"

"Nothing."

"Nothing? A balloon is filled with nothing. Pop. You were talking with him for more than a half hour and he said nothing, you say? It's not likely."

"We conversed. People talk like that, you know."

"I know people talk. Of course, I know people talk. You are very stupid. What did you talk about? And please don't say 'nothing.' Please. You know how important this is to me. Please tell me. What did he say about me?"

"That you had been uncivil to him."

"Hah." The gangplank was lowered, and they made their way onto the dock. "What did he say about himself?"

Peter Prince felt a big, smiling lump rise in his throat, as if his guts, at least, understood the joke. "He said he was," and he looked around before he said the word, "Jewish. Jewish."

"He was what?"

"Jewish."

"So. And you believe it?"

"I believe you that you are. Why shouldn't I believe him?"

The German turned his profile again to Peter Prince and put his index finger up to his nose. "What do you think this is? And I'll show you something else." He turned to the wall they were standing near and unzipped his pants and flapped out his circumcised penis for Peter Prince to see. "That's why I will never go to a prostitute here. I would be reported immediately."

"But circumcision is common. Moslems are circumcised."

"Do I look like a Moslem?"

Some old men sitting around in the shade were watching them through half-closed eyes. "This is absolutely stupid," Peter Prince said.

"Please, please." There were tears in the German's eyes. "Believe me. I am in earnest. It is desperate for me here. I don't feel at all safe, not at all." The man kept touching Peter Prince and that made him uncomfortable. "That man is a Nazi as sure as I'm circumcised. They have been hunting me down since they found out I fooled them. I'm not joking with you. I know it sounds strange, what I say to you, but I am a desperate man. Please don't disregard me."

What could Peter Prince do? This trip he hadn't wanted any involvement and now he couldn't even see the desert from where he stood. "I'm going into town, he offered. "And you are welcome to come."

"To do what?" the German grabbed Peter Prince's wrist with the grip of a madman.

"To eat something, sit in a restaurant, or something. Come along with me, if you please to."

"No. No. It's not important. I'll stay here."

"For three hours alone?"

The German sighed. "That Egyptian one, I should tend to it. Maybe I can help."

The taxi that shuttled from the river to town was an old Ford station wagon with wooden sides and a running board, the seats upholstered with the rich, elegant rugs that were made in Asyut. They traveled slowly down a broad avenue along the canal lined with palm trees and tall umbrella pines. The trees swayed softly giving the illusion of coolness, but the wind through the car came as if through a blast furnace. The driver laughed at Peter Prince's obvious discomfort. "They say that only the devil will choose to live where dates can grow," he said. He had been hungry, but the heat took care of that. All the small white houses around were shuttered, and what might have been the shops of the town were all closed. He felt like he was being cooked, and would have been if he didn't finally peek in through a heavy bead curtain on what was a small restaurant, coffee shop, and outdoor cafe in the cooler hours. After the glare outside the darkness within seemed nearly absolute, and it was cool in there. Men snoozed on chairs around the room. Some in back were playing a kind of pick-up stix, and others at another table were seated around what looked like a parcheesi board. He sat facing the entrance and waited for someone to take his order. To his right was a little counter from which drinks were probably served and he could hear along with the sticks falling and the dice and softly speaking men, the sound of pots in the kitchen. Fishbein the Aussie poked his head through the hanging beads and then withdrew it because he couldn't see anything. After a few moments Peter Prince went back to the kitchen where an old woman stood scouring pots with a piece of pumice. He tried to ask her for a drink but the woman couldn't understand him, and she shouted into the back room to bring out a young girl who smiled broadly when she saw Peter Prince. She asked him what he wanted in broken French and he told her some zebeeb with ice and water. She assured him that if he sat down again she would bring him something. He watched the entrance for a while again and this time Fishbein the Aussie entered, felt his way around in the dark, and then chose a seat in back of Peter Prince. The girl brought a tall clay mug of cloudy stuff that smelled like lemon flowers and had the taste of almonds. It was good. And she brought a small dish with it of crystallized rose petals, which were also good.

"I didn't see you." Fishbein the Aussie slid his stool up to Peter Prince's table. "A half hour in that sun out there and a man would be ready to eat."

"Human flesh can be yummy," Peter Prince said irrelevantly as he let a rose petal dissolve on his tongue.

"They might not get started for five hours someone said. The ship's leaking fuel."

"At least it will be cooler when we get going again," Peter Prince said. He offered a taste of his beverage to Fishbein the Aussie.

"Bloody awful stuff," he said. "How on earth do you drink it? I hope I can get a pint of bloody brew here." He turned to the back of the room and clapped his hands. The little girl appeared, still smiling. She was a pretty thing, with huge brown eyes and tiny puffs of breast forming under the black smock she wore. Fishbein the Aussie asked her for some beer, but it was obvious that she wouldn't understand him in any language.

"*Du bière*," Peter Prince said.

"Ahhh *bière*," she responded, and did a little curtsey before she left the table.

The light exploded like a flashbulb every time someone pushed aside the beaded curtain. "That dark fellow, that other one, he's a bit crazy, he is."

"Is that so." Peter Prince knew it would be best to cool it, and wait to see what developed. He wasn't comfortable in that situation anyway, stashing a gun for somebody. There were too many strange unknowns. Fishbein the Aussie looked like anything but a Jew, and maybe the German had been right about him. Silence was always the start of a good defense. The girl brought a mug of the same drink that Peter Prince had and the Aussie tasted it, turned to say something, shrugged, and swallowed half of it in a gulp.

"He finally came down off his bloody horse to talk to me, and he seemed O.K. then. He was doctoring up one of those bloody aborigines who was sick. It looked like a waste of time to me, and I told him so, so he came around to talk to me about it. I told him I thought he probably had better things to do with his bloody time than doctor up one of those blokes who was only a couple of breaths from death. He went back to work on him anyway. I started to leave but he stopped me and began this loony conversation about you."

"About me?"

"Yes. He asked if you were Jewish, and all that."

"He what?"

"Yes. He asked if you were Jewish, and I told him that you said you were, and he told me that I couldn't believe you." He sipped on his drink again. "Ughh. This is a lot of wet trash." He poured what was left into

Peter Prince's mug, and clapped his hands again. The girl came out this time with a colorful embroidered apron over her black smock. Fishbein the Aussie ordered beer again, this time drawing a beer bottle for her on the back of his driver's license. The situation made Peter Prince apprehensive. For the first time he felt that perhaps he was being manipulated, and he couldn't know what for. He didn't want to seem anxious.

"What did you tell him I was Jewish for? I never told you I was Jewish. I never said that to you." He looked back to see if anyone was listening in.

"Well that's the way I interpreted what you told me. I can't imagine a person saying he was a Jew unless he was one."

"Well I'm not sure what I am, my father . . ." He stopped himself because Fishbein had looked away as if not interested. The girl returned this time with a beer bottle from which she emptied into Fishbein's mug the same cloudy almond beverage. "Oh shit," he said, and smiled at the girl, and paid her. "He kept warning me that I shouldn't trust you." He looked up at Peter Prince.

"Trust me?"

"Yes. He described the conversations he had with you, the way you are so evasive about certain matters. He thinks you are some kind of bloody neo-fascist agent. He told me he even saw you fooling with a gun you carried."

Peter Prince felt his pulse fluttering in his stomach. He should never have taken the gun from that madman. He should never have left from anywhere, but stayed where he was, where things weren't so dangerous and confused, with each person churning out of the mystery of his past with a threat in tow. What could he do with that gun wrapped in his raincoat?

"He told me," said Peter Prince, struggling to laugh once his nerves were assembled again. "That I should watch out for you. He thinks you're some kind of agent or spy or assassin."

"That poor bloody idiot, running about with all those complexes. Did he tell you that story of his that he was a Jew during the war and served in the German army to escape?"

Peter Prince didn't answer. He felt his trust being yanked on. Perhaps the German was right, and this man was actually drawing him out.

"Well he told me that story, and something about his nose. He said the bloody thing grew, like Pinocchio's all the time he was in the service. Did he tell you all that too?"

Peter Prince nodded. He felt his spine rattle because he knew he shouldn't have admitted anything.

"The poor man has such fantasies. Imagine a thing like being a German and a Jew and in the German army, all that is quite impossible, beyond reason."

"Why?"

Fishbein the Aussie gave Peter Prince a look of such arrogance that he knew he couldn't trust him again, and every time he was tempted to he saw that sneer overlapped. "I know enough about what happened in those years to say it would be impossible. Did you believe that story?"

"I didn't see any reason not to."

"You are easily sucked in, Peter Prince."

They sat in the darkness of the café until it was time to get back on board and then took a cab together back to the ship. The Egyptian was dead and they carried his body off the vessel wrapped in a rug. Karras the German leaned on the rail watching the body go. He had been working on the man till he died and he looked exhausted.

"I told you the bloke was ready to go," said Fishbein the Aussie. "There isn't much resistance in them once they start slipping, these aborigines."

Peter Prince left them talking and went over to his own corner of the deck, and that was where he intended to stay, alone, for the rest of the voyage. He had enough of this mad involvement with the fantasies of other men. He had come for a reason. He unlocked the satchel and took the raincoat out, somehow hoping the gun would have vanished. The whole situation was unreal, paranoiac, disastrous. There, out there the desert cliffs were violet and darkening as the sun set, a few tender clouds turning scarlet. The whole absurd business kept him from looking at

Egypt. Egypt. He thrust his hand into the cylinder of his raincoat. It was there, alright. He turned to face the river and one wall and secretly unwrapped the gun. It gave him a special thrill to see it, not disappointment or despair. A gun is fickle and belongs to the finger on the trigger, and belongs to no one. It was small but had a kind of chunky power to its look. But for three hours of pistol drill in the army he'd rarely held one. He shoved the clip back into the butt and hefted it. It felt better with the weight of the slugs. Around the deck the people all looked weary. A woman had taken possession of the dead man's goat. Fishbein the Aussie and Karras the German were still talking across the deck. It was a nice secret power to have this gun palmed, like a narcosis. The mud of the river had taken on red tinges of the sunset. He slipped the clip out of the handle, and then slipped it back in. The sound was one that seemed to rise from his dreams. The gun was loaded.

They would be in Luxor by morning and he could cut out there, stay overnight to see the ruins of Thebes, and catch a boat one or even two days later. He wasn't obliged to stay with this situation, though he had made certain half promises. It was too involved and too sticky for him. He leaned against the cabin wall and faked sleep each time either of his compatriots tried to approach him. "Well, what did he say to you?" he heard Karras the German say any number of times, trying to pry Peter Prince out of his feigned sleep. By morning they were approaching Luxor and he prepared himself to disembark, standing anxiously by the gangplank and not turning his head for fear he would be confronted by Karras the German or Fishbein the Aussie. They stood on either side of him as the boat tied up.

"Getting out here, are you?" said Fishbein the Aussie.

"I want to spend some time at Thebes."

"I need you to stay, please stay," Karras the German whispered in his ear. "I believe I am going to be assassinated. It's the end for me."

"Don't worry," Peter Prince assured him. "Calm down." He stared straight ahead, afraid that a glance into either of their eyes would be a commitment.

"I'll miss you traveling. Maybe I'll stay and then push on when you do again," said Fishbein the Aussie. "It'll be bloody dull alone with that one."

"I'm not sure when I'll be pulling out again."

Karras the German grabbed Peter Prince's arm, and he could feel the moist breath in his earfolds. "Look it's a bad sign that the Egyptian died. It's for sure my finish. Don't believe that tall blonde one. He's a slick operator, one of their best. As much as I talk with him he doesn't give me a hint of what he's up to. That's no good sign for me . . ."

The gangplank was down and Peter Prince yanked his arm free and started off the boat without turning around. He turned a corner into the town and was free. He hadn't realized how heavy the situation had become, but now he was free of it. He took a room at the Hotel Savoy with a shower and a view of the river. After he washed he went to bed and slept, and woke up suddenly in the late afternoon remembering that he still had the gun. It was in his satchel still, in the raincoat. Why hadn't he remembered to give it back? He didn't want to touch it again, would leave it in his satchel until he had a chance to return it. He went to search for a restaurant carrying the weight of the weapon in his head.

The next day went better and he took in the ruins of Thebes at Luxor and Karnak with a lightness and appetite: The avenue of sphinxes with rams' heads, ruins from three Thotmes, from Amenophis, the Ramses, the elegant kiosk of Sesostris, the Ramesseum with its colossal head of Ramses II, that Egyptian sense of the colossal that he expected to see at Abu Simbel, the temple itself of Luxor, with the ancient name of Opet, or IpetSut—Harem of the South; this was the harem of Amon, the god of Thebes, whose sacred beast was the ram, and all the obelisks of Thotmes, Amenophis, Hatshepset, the colossal hypostyle hall of Karnak, the gracefully painted walls of the necropolis of Sheik Abd el Gourmah. Peter Prince involved himself in all of this, which caused him for the while to forget the gun, the keeping of which could make him, if he thought of it, feel guilty, not as if he'd just left the man as a temporary acquaintance, but as if he had deserted him. He mouthed the names of the ruins he looked at, reading from a guidebook he had bought at the hotel, and mumbling to himself about the beauty, the harmony, the proportions. It was all there. The light was good, and under the pith helmet he had bought the heat didn't bother him. He did the tour vigorously, seeing all he could, and taking notes on it which he would later lose. Although he wouldn't admit it to himself it was all disappointing, something missing, not in the ruins themselves, which were marvelous, he was sure, marvelous and rich, but something missing in his feeling for them, something he had expected in himself but didn't find. The other tourists around gave him no clue, because they were too bothered by the heat to show astonishment or recognition of something he hadn't noticed. He felt in his head an opacity of consciousness that wouldn't let penetrate the significance of the form of things. Dark and private troubles intervened. The gun. The Nile trip had been too involved. Perhaps he had to see more before understanding began, but that gun kept crossing his mind the way the coughing of a sick man in the next room can destroy the sensation of sleep. All he wanted was to sleep, and to dream the gun away.

The boat he took the rest of the way to Aswan was very much like the first. (It has already been established that there might not be boats like this at all tramping up and down the Nile, but whatever type of boat it was that Peter Prince originally took, it's not untruthful to say, in any case, that he embarked again on a similar boat.) The deck passage was full of the *fellahim* with their animals and a few tourists to whom he paid no more attention because he didn't want any more involvement. He would be mute and alone. They rode through the heat of most of that day and were to reach Aswan by evening. There he was to change boats and continue to Abu Simbel and Wadi Halfa. There was a lot to look at this time, many of the crescent sailed *felucca* with people at work on them binding sheathes. As it got cooler toward evening Peter Prince crossed the deck to watch the sun go down. Leaning there on the rail were two men talking very softly. Peter Prince noticed a tattoo on the wrist of the taller man, a blue artichoke. He turned away. The voices were the same, a slight German intonation, and the unmistakable Australian twang. It was Karras the German with Fishbein the Aussie. Peter Prince crossed quickly back to the other side of the deck and stood there with his foot touching the satchel that held the gun.

"Hey there you are, you bloody evasive bastard, how are you? Here we've been on this bloody steamer together and this is the first time I've spotted you. I thought you'd be clear up to those ruins by now, easy. How do you like that. It's good enough to see you."

Fishbein the Aussie didn't look as jolly as the tone of his voice made him out to be. His motion seemed calculated, as if he somehow had Peter Prince. His eyes had no luster. "I stopped at Luxor," Peter Prince smiled. "I didn't want to pass up Thebes."

"No you do have a taste for all that bloody dust. I stayed over there and it was worse than Melbourne in mid-January. But you get sick of a bloody ship, you know. He stayed over too." He pointed at Karras the German across the deck. "That bloody man's a paranoid idiot. You know what he did?" He reached into the baggy pockets of his shorts and pulled out a derringer. "He asked me to hold on to this because he thought you were going to give him trouble. It's you he doesn't trust. The questions he asked about you." Peter Prince could see the small dark hole in the barrel waving around in his face. "He thinks you're a Nazi, or a spy, or something."

"Me?" Peter Prince knew that something wasn't going right.

"You could appear more surprised than that, Herr Prinz."

"You're joking."

"Is that a fact?" Fishbein the Aussie kept the gun leveled at Peter Prince's head.

"But he gave me one of those little guns too." Peter Prince stared into the barrel of the gun. "For God sakes turn that gun away."

"It's bloody awful to have a gun pointed at your head, isn't it?" Fishbein the Aussie kept the gun leveled there. Peter Prince stared for a moment, not believing what was happening to him, and glancing desperately from time to time at me. Finally he kicked his satchel out in front of himself, opened it, shook the contents onto the deck, unwound his raincoat and let the pistol fall between them.

"Take it," Peter Prince said.

Fishbein the Aussie, keeping the gun level, bent over and in one motion threw the pistol to Karras the German who had mysteriously appeared behind him in the right spot. It was like a play in football.

"You see," said Peter Prince. "There's nothing wrong with it. I didn't want to hold it for you in the first place. Keep it now."

"We have it now," said Karras the German.

"Well won't you . . . What are you going to do?" Peter Prince was afraid to move his hands.

"What do you expect that we'll do?" asked Karras the German, and they both came up on him waving the little guns, heightening the melodrama and suspense of this scene. No one else in the novel was paying attention.

"I don't expect anything. We just met on this boat and . . ." With the gunbarrels leveled at him Peter Prince became desperate. "Stop. You don't know anything about me."

"We know enough about you to take care of matters, Peter Prince."

Peter Prince looked up to the wheelhouse and saw a gunbarrel black as the President's car aimed at the folds of his inner ear. "What are you up to?"

"Hah," Fishbein the Aussie guffawed. "The way this bloody book is put together do you expect that we know? We know enough about you.-

He knew that he was going to die, no doubt about it, and he tossed my way such an immense glare of hate that if I wasn't sure of what was happening I might have turned away in shame. What could he do? His story was almost written as far as he knew. Could he roll over the railing into the Nile and swim off? They would get him. This was it.

"Why?" he asked the gunwielders.

No response.

JUST THEN there is a tremendous crash, and the boat heaves and rattles all over such that a man on solid ground would think it was an earthquake. Peter Prince ducks just before the guns go off and hears the bullets whisper by him, "Not yet, not yours," and they all run to the bow to see the seaplane that has JUST THEN landed in the Nile and has crashed into them headlong. There is a dazed pilot in the plane, and who else, bruised but hearty? It is Sarah Spurgeon. She turns up just in time. "You're for sure going to fail," Peter Prince says, turning my way again, giddy with his rescue.

"Who me?" I say, and let out a little cosmic laugh, and gaze deep into the long pages of this sequence. "I am doing nothing wrong. This is the way the events occur. This is what happens."

Sarah Spurgeon climbs on board the battered ship and rushes to throw her arms around Peter Prince the saved one, ungrateful Peter Prince. Peter Prince stares at her as if he wants to memorize her features this time, but he can see only her mouth which is telling, "Well, when I met Mister El Taher while I was shopping he explained to me how much better the shopping was in Alexandria, so I just had to go along there with him, and he's been so dear to me, and I don't blame you for leaving without me, but I just had to spend a few days in that marvelous city." She pulls a pair of sandals out from under the belt of her slacks. "I got these for you. Then he offered to fly me up here and I was simply dying to see you, so we came up here in his seaplane, poor thing."

They slowly arrive in Aswan. Peter Prince has one arm around her shoulder, and he is grinning out at me through the haze of type.

"Why did you come back at all, Sarah Spurgeon?" he asks.

"Oh Peter Prince," says Sarah Spurgeon. "You're my responsibility. And besides," she throws both her arms akimbo in order to best show the trim fit stretch fabric of her sweater, "it makes me feel like Cleopatra," she says, as it grows darker and darker.

*

"That's a rather unlikely scene," says Linda Lawrence to Philip Farrel, and Philip Farrel to me after dinner, hoping for a chance to turn on the TV again. "Why did you have to go make it so mysterious?"

"Artistic talent," I say. "Sheer genius. And you have to admit that though this sequence begins funny it ends cool, or vice versa, and I think the author deserves his credits here. All together. A shorp thirst of braise for the author."

*

There has been here some confusion, some confusion here, about how Peter Prince got here. He's here, and I didn't expect him. I was just preparing his arrival and shuffling the empty pages to describe it, but he's here and I'm in a hurry now, because for all I know that book is ending, and I need to have something to do with that. I am the author of Peter Prince. Across the street from him grows a reticulation of steel girders (how's that for putting it?). He watched it. Lightbulbs waved on their cords through the cubes of space as if protected from a storm. I don't know. I'm not prepared yet to say anything at all about this. He just got here and created confusion, and now things are in a hurry to be over with. It was lunchtime. Men, working men, sat on the horizontals, leaned against perpendiculars, and ate from lunch pails or brown paper bags. Peter Prince watched them because they were just across the street from the bench he was sitting on. Behind him was The Metropolitan Museum of Art. Think of that, and then try to dream up a something. On his left hand was uptown and the many things that implied, on his right hand downtown, way downtown, and many other possibilities. On his lap lay a book that confused him. His confusion is mine as well, because he's back in America—New York City (so to speak), and I wish he'd do something so this narrative can be splendid once again.

Linda Lawrence, herself, was surprised to see him sitting there out of context scanning a book. She was up to something else entirely; in fact, she was on a brief vacation from this novel, trying to make out a little on her own time, when she just by chance was walking by the museum and saw him there. Peter Prince. She'll probably accuse me of planting him there, and was a little pissed off at the situation. At first she wanted to cross the street, go around a couple of blocks and never admit that she'd spotted him. Who can blame her? It's a bore when you run into those people in real life that you're forced to spend time with in novels. If he didn't just seem to sit there, not ever looking around, staring now and then into that goofy book on his lap or gazing off across the street, she might then have just bugged off. But he didn't even seem inclined to notice her. He looked as if he'd been sitting there ever since this novel began. What then is life and its mysteries, I ask you? It's a little spooky. She paused and adjusted her collar while deciding what to do next. I remained out of it, waiting elsewhere for what was going to turn up.

Linda Lawrence spent a day outside this novel that began, as it always does, with her children, the youngest of whom she left with a platoon of baby-sitters, and the older ones she saw off to school. They liked a bit of personal attention from their busy mother. While she was waiting there at the office for her new assignment she busily invented a new filing system that revolutionized life at work. In due time she went to the bathroom. There she sat for a long long time, not because of constipation, but because the men's room was immediately adjacent, the booth she sat in separated from a man's booth by a thin piece of plywood, like a membrane. The johns had obviously been jerry-built with the shortage of material after the holocaust. It was in that booth she met the man, her lover, the one she didn't dare to contact elsewhere; only in the intimacy of their booths back to back, with the thin wall between, could she give herself to him in the true sense of the give. She waited and waited and waited and waited and waited that day.

"Oooooooooffffffffffff," she had to say. She had to make a squeezing noise to convince other women who came and went that she totally occupied the booth. "Wheeeeeeeeeeeoooooooooouuuh!" She sat fully dressed on the toilet seat and had to make that other woman leave. She saw the impatient shuffle of red satin office slippers through the space beneath the gate of the booth. The woman had to understand that Linda Lawrence wasn't getting up, and intended to remain for the duration, however long that was, of the time she intended to stay, which was till her lover had come and gone.

"Ooooooooeeeeeeee," She needed a natural, unexagggerated sound.

"Are you alright in there? Do you want some help?" The voice in the red slippers was thick and husky.

That sound had been the wrong one, and she knew it. She needed something smoother. "Mmmmmmmmmmmm," she tried.

"Are you going to take much longer?"

That sound had turned the trick. "Iiiieeeuuh mmmnn don't knnnnoowwwwuhh."

"You okay?"

"Mmmmmmmm hmmmmmmm."

"Then I guess I'll have to try downstairs," said the husky red slippers. "Should I check back?"

"Nnnnnot nnnnneccccuh sssssary. Nnnnnooo."

A few little arabesques near the door crack and the red slippers pulled out, on tiptoe. She waited till she was sure she hadn't been tricked, then put her shoulder to the gate and stepped out into the lavatory proper: the eroded sink, the cot with a flowered mattress, and the watery gray light through a wire-mesh window. She wondered if her lover's privy was drawn with the same quality of stark realism. Did it smell this way of blood, urine and disinfectant? Suddenly she had a brainstorm when she spotted on the door two rusted eyes that used to hold a hook. From a vending machine she got two sanitary inserts which she slipped from their plastic wrapper and she rolled the plastic between her fingers to make a twisted cord which she drew through the rusted eyes and fixed there with a square knot. That could prevent any sudden entrances while she was in her special circumstance.

She mosied back into the booth and waited. They had agreed not to open the hole through which he poked his, and over which she slipped hers, until they were sure who was there. She waited. If it weren't for the delicious associations she had with the place she could have puked from the filth: the moisture from the old plumbing soaked through the cracked tile floor and left it always damp, so one had to hold her skirt above it when she sat down on the toilet. No matter about that. Hush. She could hear a male through the partition entering the booth adjacent. She knocked three times: their signal. A long moment and he returned her knock.

"I'm always afraid you won't get here," she said.

"And I that you won't be here," he said.

She could feel his long breathing through the wall. Her fingers worked at the little hole they had disguised in the partition. It slipped out. She helped him waggle his hot proboscis through the aperture, still pliable as cartilage, firming up. "My Peter Prince,'" she said, tenderly punning on the name of the main character of this novel. She dipped cool water from the bowl to rinse the thing and as her fingertips brushed it the meaty stub grew. It was so splendidly thick that she kissed it, and it scalded her lips when they touched it. It was charged like a soldering iron and made her mouth swell and tingle. "Oh I miss you," she said, tonguing the purple rim of the tip. "When I don't have you." She stroked the pulsing channel.

O sweat smudges of body heat. Linda Lawrence panted over the protrusion, licked it, lifted her skirts and scissored it. She was so happy she kicked off her shoes and danced on the toilet lid. "Yipe. Yipe." It grew and grew, like a fleshy inflatable telescope, like an expanding water tower, and extendable smokestack. As she palmed it it grew and she lipped it and warmed it and breathed, "Ohhhhh, happy." It was thick around as a weightlifter's bicep, and long as a thigh and a half, and it was growing. She couldn't imagine it. The partition cracked and splintered. Linda Lawrence felt an immeasurable ecstasy in her breast as she watched. It wasn't mere satisfaction as she licked it, nuzzled it, kept it warm. It grew. She couldn't keep up. From the toilet seat she leaped astraddle and grabbed hold of it as she used to grab hold of the mane of her mare, Gooper, when she rode it bareback through the pillowy hills, and she slid back and forth on the tough length of it in a delirious delicious lubricious rhythm. Out of her mouth rushed her high, stuttering love noise. It was still growing. She stood up and ran back and forth on it barefoot, like tepid lava underfoot. The sweat rushed down her body like a skin shedding. She stood at the end and looked to the ground as if it was a diving board she was afraid to go off, and then she did a cartwheel back and tipped off to one side. It was thick as a strand of George Washington Bridge. She had to do something good for it, to show her gratitude. What? She leaped back on top of it and stretched out on her belly and tried to wrap her arms around it, but couldn't, and so lay there, spread-eagled, and at once she grabbed up all her strength, and held as tightly as she knew how, and performed there to even her own amazement, a brand new variation on the Cleopatra Wriggle, vibrating from her toenails to her forehead. That did it. It stopped growing, and she slowed down, panting and farting like Gooper, her mare. She lay there, half asleep, and dreamed of ostriches and other wingless birds.

"Hey. In there. Are you alright? I smell smoke." It was the husky voice of the red-slippered one. Just one shoulder thrust and the Tampax wrapping would bust and the jig would be up. Linda Lawrence slid down to look over the situation. The situation had gotten too big to slip back through the hole. The partition had given a little, but there was this constriction at the point of penetration, like a balloon tied up. Had the poor creature behind the partition turned bright blue? There was still a pounding on the door. She leaned against the partition and whispered, "God. Can't you slip it back through?"

"Unngh," was the reply.

"But you have to. There's someone trying to get in here. Please." Was it worth it? Were clandestine adventures ever worth the consequences? She thought of pouring salt on it as she used to do to slugs on the road when she was a little girl with a braid riding her mare Gooper: to watch them dissolve in a silver pool. She had no salt and couldn't do it anyway and still live with herself later on. It was there. The woman was banging on the door as if on her belly. She had to bring the swollen thing down.

"You exagggeration," she said (see the title of this novel). "You bulge of pomp." She opened her pocketbook and looked around in there for something that would help. Nothing but some writing equipment, sunglasses, her smokes, her lighter, lip pomade, hankies, and a slim paperback by Saul Bellow.

"I'm gonna break in," a final threat from the husky voice. "Something's wrong."

The desperate Linda Lawrence pulled out the paperback and began to tear pages from it, slapping them onto the sticky extension as fast as she could and covering it completely with the printed page. Even if she couldn't shrink it she would disguise it, and then maybe slip away. It was done, and something happened. There was a moan from the man's side, and all at once, like a pop of a cork there came a shower of messages from the head of the intrusion. They drifted down all over the gray room just as the satin slippers snapped the wrapper, and like a turtle's head Linda Lawrence's friend withdrew, leaving the Saul Bellow paperback behind, cemented into a soft cylinder. PETER PRINCE was the message on some of the paper scraps.

"You certainly do exploit a ladies' lavatory," said the woman who had entered.

Other messages said PROCEED TO ROOM FORTY-THREE. Linda Lawrence grabbed her handbag, tucked the cylindrical paperback under her arm, and proceeded to room forty-three.

She reflected then that her encounter with Peter Prince might have been no accident, but part of her assignment after all. Who knows how he got there? He sat there like a shill staring at the construction across from him. It was still lunchtime.

Room forty-three was a long, plush conference room, with an oblong conference table as its main furnishing. At the far end of the table sat the President alone in a single light like a wax museum exhibit. The room was too hot. The President slowly looked up and motioned Linda Lawrence toward him into the light. She noticed that he stared at her hair as she came toward him, and it embarrassed her that she hadn't taken the time to straighten it out, but he seemed to be admiring it.

"Uhmmm . ." He lifted his hand to point at the chair across from himself. "Sit . . . sit down. I take it you came . . . you came."

"You sent for me, didn't you?" She noticed the bleariness of his eyes.

"Right. That's right. That's sweet of you."

From their position it was hard to see the far end of the dark teak table that extended as far as they could see with the rows of black leather chairs into obscurity.

On the walls she could see the palely luminous portraits of all the former presidents.

"Are you stoned?" she asked, at the risk of being presumptuous.

He smiled. "Would you like a toke?" He finally exhaled.

"But you're the President," she said.

"Those," said the President. "They're the portraits of the former presidents, and I should like to have one done of me in a manner similarly banal, but terrific. Among my friends are many artists, and in my collection, as you probably have read in this novel, are many of the modern masterworks, but none of these artists could or would care to do such a portrait as the trustees require, desire on my retirement, which is not as far off as you could imagine, because I notice in your expression a certain incredulity, that you don't believe I'm old enough to retire, but I assure you that I do have, so to speak, that desire now. Of all these presidents only one," he looked slowly around at the hanging portraits, "only one . . . that one," he pointed into the darkness, "lived more than three years beyond his retirement, and he only five. Well I intend to rupture all those records and set a new, inspiring precedent. I am retiring young enough to have a whole lifetime ahead of me. My act will accomplish in me a kind of rebirth, a new career, if I please, a kind of Eastern Wing (If I must consider how my life is going) to my life, and thereby I shall divinely haunt my friends, my former colleagues, and effect in their lives perhaps a new opening, a change toward a sense, a new sense of awareness, if not of their total selves, at least of the games their lives have been built on, the way the young ones are nervous about money and the old ones won't admit they're disappointed. Everything is discouraging now that there's hardly enough to do in the world for everyone (anyone) to keep busy. That's why drugs (and maybe I shouldn't mention it) have this immense importance now. That's it, why. Because we haven't anything to do any more. Nothing with our feet, tongues, ears, hands, hips, eyes, elbows, nostrils, hands. Everything is taken care of. We are being survived for, and all there is to use is our brains (our minds abdicated to IBM), chop them up in as many ways as we can, mince them up; connect, correct, reconnect. It's so satisfying. You can still see it at meetings, how the old urges still hump up in the collar-bones, in the neck-napes. Some get angry, and their little faces thicken up with ideas like raised numerals. They can't believe yet, or haven't found it out yet, that it has already been done for them, quicker, and all they have to do any more is take the credit. That we still meet any more is miraculous, because there's nothing to say. The corporation runs. It fluctuates, but moves comfortably. A couple of them have taken up philosophy. I, of course, drugs. They'll all come around to drugs if they haven't already in their own cabinets. The retirement, you see, will not only be helpful, but honest as well, if that word carries a sense of anything today. Honest. pop. The only mystery. pop. that I want. pop. in the portrait. pop. is that I. pop. appear as if. pop. I were not. pop. as young as. pop. I seem to. pop. you now. You. pop. should study me. pop. and imagine me. pop. at the age. pop. of sixty-five. pop. when most people. pop. retire voluntarily or. pop. involuntarily. Make a. pop. banal, old distinguished. pop. portrait of me. pop. the President. It. pop. will mystify the. pop. trustees. It sounds. pop. quite nice to. pop. say pop after. pop. every three words. pop. Don't you think?"

"But I'm not an artist."

"Who said you needed to be an artist?"

"But I've never even painted a picture."

"Ohhhhh," he groaned, pointed at her as he had when she first entered, then he looked on his wrist where there was a tattoo, and a list of names in ballpoint. "You must be Linda . . . Linda. . . . It's smudged."

"Linda Lawrence."

"Yes, yes." His laugh sounded like the wind through a line of wetwash. "Something else," he said.

"The message was that I come to room forty-three."

"This is room forty-three, and you are Linda Lawrence."

"I still am."

"Remarkable."

"I don't understand."

"Well the problem is that we have for you the job of mustering support,

signatories, a lot of them, and as you know there is very very little time left."

"Time for what?"

"Time to muster the support."

"I still don't understand a thing about it."

"In time."

"I don't understand why you've selected me."

"We've already been through that . . . your name."

"You mean because I'm Linda Lawrence?"

"That's been . . . yes."

"Are you sure?"

"That you are . . . ?"

"That I can," she interrupted, and smiled. The bathroom event had given her a new sense of her own potential. "Maybe so," she whispered. "Maybe so."

The President raised his hand above his head and made a few floating gestures. "You're here, aren't you?"

Linda Lawrence silently clapped her hands. "I believe in myself."

"Soon everyone will." The President unrolled his kidskin pouch of glistening instruments.

And Linda Lawrence headed uptown, making her plans, and establishing a schedule for herself, and until she discovered Peter Prince she believed she could get it done with relative ease, but after she saw him she was confused. How was she supposed to react, and in what direction? You see, it's perfectly clear how she got there, but Peter Prince, there's some confusion about him. (Yes. Come in. No, without spuds.)

*

The devil take me, reasoned Peter Prince with himself. I'll get out of this yet. But not just yet. His situation was just becoming appetizing, anthropologically speaking. Peter Prince was hardly recognizable himself, swaddled in gray cloth, his skin stained with dyes. He stood in the middle of a circle of dark men and women who were chanting to the beat of drums while a number of young men danced around the inner rim of the circle. Before him a young couple sat on two old jeep jump-seats that had been covered with tribal cloth. The young man was Peter Prince's friend, Dooman, a Galla tribesman, son of the chief of the tribe among whom he was forced to live. The son had liked him so much he had made him alanji in the ceremony, a role that Peter Prince could liken only to being best man at the wedding ritual Peter Prince knew best. He looked at the couple on the seats, ceremoniously rigid, she sitting on his lap where she had been placed by the father. Aside from occasional noise of children on the outer perimeter of the ceremony everyone was transported without distraction into the ritual, doing the rhythms with their limbs, making sounds with their lips. It was as if a dome frescoed with the blue sky of the plateau, and its few ripped up clouds, East African blue, like none other, had been lowered over them, and the universe was frescoed on there, everything in a proper place, birds dipping across infrequently in organized patterns. Their mutuality bounded the world, and Peter Prince felt sure that the medicine man who danced in a slow closing spiral with a pitcher full of *tej* was working his way toward him who as *alanji* would have to do something with it.

Peter Prince was still an alien among these savage men, although they did trust him more than most other white men. In himself he could feel an old sensation in the veins, the ecstasy of the ritual. He had a way, among these primitive people, of becoming a favorite, despite himself. As he had been among the Danakil, so he was among these fearsome Galla. Peter Prince kept quiet, unlike the noisy, proselytizing missionaries they now and then saw, whom they despised; but Peter Prince wanted to learn their ways, and they couldn't tolerate anyone who didn't. They were a taciturn people, semi-nomadic herdsmen who shifted their herds through the various high grazing grounds. Though their life was superficially simple, their customs were elegant and complex, full of elaborate protocols and complicated manners. It took sometimes five minutes for two men to greet each other when they met, for it was impolite not to bow and inquire about each member of one's family.

"... and does your Uncle Runu drink the sweet beer?"

"Yes, thank you, with relish. And does your Brother Gotha-su drink the sweet beer?"

"Yes, thank you, with relish, and ...' so on into the afternoon. Aunts, uncles, nephews, they politely stressed everybody. In fact, every name out of this novel was eventually included in the ritual of greeting Peter Prince.

"Does your Linda Lawrence drink the sweet beer?" and he had to reply that she did, though he didn't know what she preferred to drink, and he had to squirm through the ritual with the name of every character in this novel, from Armando Amante through Zephraim Zinfandel. He had managed with Dooman, after some time, to make his relationship a little more casual. Dooman was interested in life out there among the *deniboonGakagoka*, as civilization was called by this tribe. Gakago was a kind of small demon who caused the young to do naive things, and the whole phrase translated, more or less, "new lost people"—because most of the white people they had contact with were lost, especially the Italians whom they had helped slaughter other Abyssinians, collecting the heads for them, only to be later betrayed and mistreated themselves, the Italians behaving only as a *deniboonGakagoka* could. Dooman openly trusted and befriended Peter Prince, and Peter Prince cultivated in their relationship at least enough of the American casualness so that when they met in private they went through the ritual with only the immediate relatives. Dooman was tall and strong, with fine, sensitive features. He was a great hunter, and particularly proud of certain clear, lumpy scars on his chest that he had gotten from a leopard he'd knifed, and certain marks on his face that had been given him like medals. He taught Peter Prince to fling a spear, and to hurl from a special sling, and to hunch over and move without sound through the low brush, and to conceal himself in most open country, downwind from the game, and to leap when he had to. Peter Prince was clumsy at this, but one day managed to pitch a wobbly spear at a zebra and nick the beast, which Dooman had to finish off.

Dooman was getting hitched, and had chosen Peter Prince as the *alanji*. The marriage of the son of a tribal chief was a generally hilarious event. Peter Prince witnessed everything: the elaborate ceremonial exchanges of cattle between the in-laws, the preparation of the bride, which was a puberty rite, she being not yet quite thirteen, and pretty. The coming ceremony was heralded by three weeks of giddy debauch; the old women rushing around making beer, the stoned young boys and girls humping, grunting and slurping in the bushes, in the corrals, in the public *tukuls*, everywhere. Peter Prince was joyously included, whose immense penis, a legacy of the Danakil treatment, was a white object of wonderment that all the girls wanted to slip into themselves. While his bride was being prepared, the suture on her vagina ceremoniously unstitched, all the older women instructing her in their various specialties: the hip-jostle, belly-roll, thigh-quiver, pelvic snap—they taught her the ritual cleanliness above all, the various scents, and how to wash her man when they were through—while his bride was learning all that, Dooman seemed infinitely lusty, sloping down into whatever could wiggle under him. Peter Prince discovered that even this was a ritual, that even though Dooman seemed to take to it with a great love of chaos and abandonment to orgy it was performed to an overall rhythm—young women on certain days, older women on others, all proportions and classifications of bodies, so that the groom would be richly satiated and when the time came he could enter his bride without cruelty, with sweet love and tenderness. Peter Prince didn't know what the alanji was intended to do, though he did think it analagous to being best man, and though he did intend to escape he felt beholden enough to Dooman, whose humane treatment of him had made life possible, not to try till the wedding was over.

It was in the chief's village where the wedding was to take place. The chief had a complex of *tukuls* in the center of the village, five structures in all, the central one a large cylinder of sun-baked mud decorated with shiny bits of ceramic. It had three concentric rings or rooms, the central one housing a crude throne covered with pelts, where the chief held audience and tribal council. The middle room contained the chief's possessions, including some old car parts on which he placed a special value. The outer circle was divided up into closed, locked rooms, one small section given over to a library with several books in English, including an anthropology textbook full of pictures and descriptions of certain Galla rituals. The chief lived in largest of the four *tukuls* around the central structure, another housed his wives and daughters, whom he sometimes confused and made love to indiscriminately, another was for his sons, and the smallest for his personal servants and guards. Dooman was one of the youngest sons, and he was taking his first wife.

Through the week before the wedding, while everyone was engaged in general sexual riot, wedding guests arrived from all over the plateau that in Addis Ababa was called the Christian Highlands. The people didn't quite have the stature of the Danakil, but they were impressive just the same. They liked to powder their bodies with dust and blacken their teeth. Each of them brought a few cattle that were collected in a corral outside the village, and part of the ritual two days before the wedding was for the groom to select one for roasting, the owner to be payed back by the bride's family with goats and beer. Peter Prince helped Dooman in the mad selection. It was like bulldogging without horses. Dooman selected the fattest beef, and Peter Prince draped himself over its neck and tried to drag it to the ground.

The activity dizzied Peter Prince. It all seemed like chaos, though once anything was explained it became clear. Peter Prince asked Dooman about the bride's father, for example, who was constantly causing a disturbance at the doors of his own *tukuls*. "Well her father is a strong, impulsive man, especially when he is drunk, and he can't lie with his wife," Dooman explained, "not when his daughter is doing *tekdu* [puberty ritual], because if he does lie with my bride's mother at that time the girl will never bear children, not until a cake of flour mixed with certain herbs, and with the bride's nuptial secretions, is eaten by the mother on the day after I first sleep with her, and thereby the mother testifies to the daughter's womanhood and fertility, can he lie again with his wife. As you can see he wants badly to do it so they must have strong men to restrain him."

The bride's father was a little fat, one of the few tribesmen who was that way, and quite self-indulgent. He had a habit of cupping his genitals and flapping them at everybody. He enjoyed pointing at Peter Prince, who was quite pale in the tribe as well as stumpily built, and he would often grope for Peter Prince's petzel, half jealous, half in admiration.

On the day of the wedding the bride's father stayed close to Peter Prince most of the day, and seemed to be looking him over carefully. Peter Prince was with the groom's party, and since he was *alanji* assumed he had to submit to their staining his body and face with dyes, and draping him in gray cloth in a manner similar to Dooman's white wedding robe. Dooman was handsome, and proud as any groom. Peter Prince was fond of him, pleased and flattered to be his best man, though he still intended to get away after the wedding, in the ensuing confusion.

The ceremony was well under way when they got to the circle, the drummers beating a slow rhythm that older men danced to, within a circle of older women who shimmied and jerked their old pelvises nostalgically. It was a kind of pantomime they did, a depiction of traditional marriage situations to instruct the bride and groom.

A hand in his back made Peter Prince move to the center of the circle at the time Dooman did. A man in a large mask did a dance around the seats in the center, sprinkling a powder on it that had a harsh though not unpleasant pungency. It seemed to Peter Prince that the whole area was humming and charged, and so was he, because they were waiting for the bride, and when she appeared he felt himself rise a little from the ground, and there was a sigh that felt like all the air had been sucked out of the dome. Her breasts had been oiled and were shining like plums. Dooman sat down as soon as he saw her, and her father stepped forward and with a few ritual gestures ordered her to sit on his lap. They sat there stiffly.

Their mutuality bounded the world, and Peter Prince felt sure that the medicine man who danced in a slow closing spiral with a pitcher full of tej was making his way toward him, who as *alanji* would have to do something with it.

The masked man handed Peter Prince the pitcher and made some gestures that seemed to mean that Peter Prince was to pour the warm liquid over the two betrothed. "*Alanji,*" the masked man said. After a pause Peter Prince slowly stepped forward, doing it at a pace that would allow him to correct any of his gestures in case he sensed he was offending them. He was alright. He tipped the pitcher, letting the contents flow evenly over the couple. The drums began and around him the whole tribe started to dance, they shook their rings and bells. The ground quivered under him. It took hours for the pitcher to empty itself, as the drum beat and the dancing grew faster. He stepped back when it was empty, and the bride and groom, who at the outset had seemed so stiff, began to melt into the viscid flowing sweetness. They began to wipe handfuls of the sweet stuff from each other's bodies and to slurp it down. The tribe was singing, and even Peter Prince began to dance, making a slow circle around the couple that was groping and tonguing in sweet betrothal. He had no idea how long it took, but the ritual seemed to exhaust Dooman who sat there hardly moving with his eyes closed with his bride in his lap. The bride, however, seemed lively and expectant as she eyed Peter Prince, and her breasts wobbled with energy. Several men draped in gray like Peter Prince stepped forward with a bolt of white cloth and they lightly lifted the bride off the groom's lap, who slumped over immediately on the seat as if asleep. A white horse was led forward and Peter Prince was lifted onto its back; from that perch he watched them slowly swaddle the bride in white cloth, binding her arms to her side and her legs together. When they were through they draped her across the horse in front of Peter Prince. He felt blinded, had no idea what this part of the ritual was about. The drums went mad, and the people yelped, and the horse jerked and began moving, doing a light two-step like a circus performer. Peter Prince held on to the moaning shape of the girl for fear he or she would fall off the horse. "*Alanji*," she moaned, "*alanji*." Being best man involved more complications than he had anticipated. The horse was led to the tukul Peter Prince knew the couple was to occupy until succession to the father's chiefdom was clear. He was helped off the horse and instructed to enter as they took the bride down and deposited her on a pelt-covered straw tick in the *tukul*. They took the horse away and left the two of them alone. Peter Prince looked at the mummiform girl on the cot who seemed to be asleep, the white wrappings rising and falling evenly over her breast. He could hear the celebration still going on back there, the drums and the singing tribe. He suspected what was expected of him and he didn't like it.

"*Alanji*," the bride was moaning again, and trying to roll over. They had left her nose and mouth free, the small nose with narrow nostrils, and the nice large mouth streaked around with pale dyes. "*Alanji, naktoo boron oomee*," which meant that he was to unwrap her and make love to her. That's what he had feared, that he was some freaky part of the ritual, perhaps to be disposed of afterward. He didn't want any part of being best man in this situation. Who knew what the outcome could be? The tribe had no sentimental attachment to him, and he was foolish to ever expect they did. He went to the door to see that some men had been put there to guard the *tukul*. When they saw him they rushed to the door. One of the men was the bride's father, who immediately pointed at the girl and started flapping his genitals as was his custom. Peter Prince was stuck. He returned to the girl still moaning on the cot and began slowly to remove the bandages from her face while she smiled and did lovely obscene things with her mouth. The cloth stuck in places like adhesive tape and she winced when he pulled it off. She watched him constantly once her eyes were uncovered and sang little songs he didn't understand. When her hands were free she started caressing him, her long fingers sneaking under his gray robes. He was desperate and distracted, but something made him, perhaps the smell from the powder the medicine man had sprinkled on the seats, crazy to fuck her. When all the cloth was off her she sat upright on the cot naked, gathered and folded the wrappings, took them to the door where her father grabbed them and ran off back to where the ceremony was still high, and then returned to Peter Prince. There was an uproar when the father got to the circle and it made Peter Prince nervous, but she calmed him with long strokes of her fingertips. She loosened his robes, and they fell over together onto the hide-covered cot as the scene faded.

Peter Prince woke up to a *tukul* full of people. Nyowe, the bride, was already out of bed and washing her husband, Dooman, who stood in a trough of water. No one paid any attention to Peter Prince, who stood up, shook himself off, and wrapped himself in a pelt. Everybody in the room was happy to prepare everything. They were grinding, weaving, stitching, smoking. There seemed to be nothing any more for Peter Prince to do. Even Dooman wouldn't talk to him. He tried to go out the door but was held back by two men who wouldn't say anything to him. Peter Prince was a hostage. He sat down to watch, mystified by a whole day of post-matrimonial activity which he didn't care about in the setting of any culture. Toward evening the crowd, which had been changing constantly all day, some bearing gifts, some come to do work for the newlyweds, began to thin out. When the *tukul* was finally empty Dooman, who had spent all day with his wife in affectionate discourse, finally came around to Peter Prince.

"Well," said Dooman. "I am married. What do you think?"

"Does this go on and on?"

"Two more weeks."

"When can I go?"

"You're here for two weeks, at least. Don't worry. She can even want you for longer."

"Are you joking with me?" He was afraid to insult anyone or display his apprehension from this precarious position. "For two weeks?"

"The *alanji* may not leave. He will be fed, will make love to the bride and make her good for the husband, and will make sure the husband doesn't mistreat her. The spirits provide."

"Dooman, I know you're not going to mistreat her. I would rather leave her to you."

"You must make sure. It is our custom."

"And after the two weeks?"

"We'll see then."

Peter Prince didn't like the something he saw in Dooman's eye. They shook hands, and the groom left the bride alone again with him. Some fellow tribesman might have understood what was going on and could have submitted to it willingly but it made Peter Prince insecure. He would have to use some of his tactics to escape. But the bride was a consolation, and she had become fond of him. She looked at him shyly and began to sing a little song about the sweetness of the *alanji* who was protecting her from Gakago, and she made delicious snapping motions while she did a little dance around him. She loved his long white tickler and as often as she would come near him she'd reach under his loincloth to plink it. This clouded somewhat his anxiety, and under this veil of pleasure he almost lasted out his term, forgetting about escape for a week and five days of silence and boredom in the daylight, luxurious satiation at night. During this time Peter Prince noticed that Dooman assumed more and more authority in the situation, and began to treat the girl even cruelly, so that she would come to Peter Prince for the last few nights in bed, weeping, and he would console her, feeling the poor creature, who seemed to love Peter Prince more than she did her husband, insinuate her way into his heart. But it was time for him to move, leaving a day's leeway for failure, and he would have to feel that he had deserted Nyowe, but that was a price one paid whenever one escaped.

Since Peter Prince has already escaped successfully 1,849 different times in this novel I won't trouble to recount this one, except to tell of how the hunting instruction Dooman had given him stood him in good stead this time in the wilderness, where he survived alone for eighty-six days and nights till he was captured again by his old friends, not Nicholas and Cindy but the Danakil, by Prester himself, who was so glad to see him again that he wrapped him in a precious robe of strange cloth that seemed to glow as if sequined, though it wasn't, and had to be washed not with water, but with fire.

Well this is no surprise, but it is a little frustrating, since I opened up this business in Ethiopia to see if there'd be some clue to explain Peter Prince's return to America, to that bench, with that book in his lap, staring at the reticulation before him, The Metropolitan Museum of Art behind him. What's the good of it? We get nothing out of it. There's just this passion to explain, but since Ethiopia does us no good we can just delete the whole previous scene, now that we've looked it over. Delete the previous scene.

This makes things a little spooky for me, because if Peter Prince just got there by himself to that bench then this novel can easily end by itself, behind my back; I could turn my back for an instant to gather up the summation and the climax I had planned, and by the time I spin back it could be done, bound and sealed. It could walk away with Linda Lawrence still confused, Philip Farrel in the middle-far distance. I can't become delirious over it any more. Everything seems to happen that way. We point, we suppress a giggle or a yelp. In the long run our lives are little peep shows. It's startling sometimes, or repetitious, but it ends anyway. Tough. I'll let it end. I want to get out of this place anyway. I'll turn my back and head for the door. *Addio.*

"Peter Prince?" (So Linda Lawrence approaches him on her own time. It does at least restore my faith in her, though it's too late to do anything about the book. She at least shows some initiative and justifies my hiring her. She does take some responsibility on herself for this narrative, which is going to end soon anyway, thank God, I guess.)

"Are you Peter Prince?"

I could see that he wasn't very interested because he rushed open the book that was in his lap and started reading as if he wanted to avoid talking to her.

"Peter Prince?"

He stared at the strange pages of the book.

"Well, honey, don't just sit there. I'm not here for my own good. I've got things to do, myself, but we were in the same book together. I'm Linda

Lawrence."

Her face, the construction across the street, The Metropolitan Museum of Art behind his bench. So what? He shrugged. "So what?" he said.

"Linda Lawrence, you're Linda Lawrence."

"Peter Prince, how did you get here? How did you get here? How did you get here?"

The question reached him. "That's what I need to find out myself. That's why I'm reading this book. This book." He handed it to her.

Linda Lawrence sat down on the bench beside him and fingered the heavy old leather binding of the book, soft as skin. It opened with a distant, cracking sound. The pages were tough and yellow. *The Return of Peter Prince* was the title of the book, no author, no publisher's seal, no copyright. "Where did you get this book?"

"The book was here when I got here."

"How did you get here?"

"Read the book," said Peter Prince.

Philip Farrel was slowly approaching them, frustrated himself because his watch at the pier had been futile. He shifted dispatch case from hand to hand. This novel had been for him steady work, and he didn't like to believe it was ending. As far as I'm concerned it's already over, except for a slight confusion of tenses. I've given up on it, and that book The Return of Peter Prince, I've never heard of it, no author given, though he's an impostor, no date of publication, probably a freak job by one of those unnameable New York poets. I'll step the other way. Lunchtime was over. Linda Lawrence thumbed the pages of *The Return of Peter Prince*. Across the street construction began again. The men in hard hats riveted, pounded. Cranes lifted girders. There was a lot of shouting from supervisors, but none of the noise reached Peter Prince, or Linda Lawrence, a mute pantomime across the street from where they were, another indication that this novel is ending on its own, sputtering out, just when I had prepared a cohesive mysterious immense denouement. That's pissed away. Forget I ever said it. Not a sound in the text from the construction across the street, though they were starting to slap on the curtain walls.

"Won't you even tell me how you got back here?"

"The book is in your hand."

The traitorous Linda Lawrence opened the book to the index and found "Prince, Peter, the return of." She was referred to the following pages.

in the alinement purposes other than Through these procedures Prince was shot in the head curb exit the subje
West curbling on City. Peter Prince was 26 window and at that position the 21'. Continue Discover that   greete
of bullet at Park A nearly whole bullet was found on hospital after the assassination Farrel was nix film.   Peter

brought into from the room on tha
were made caused by a 6.5 millim
by FBI hole approximately one of
seam twice hit a rest of his sh
of Secret Service seat of Peter
stated at the back of and saw
doctors lodged in the point o
hospital. In the unable to fi
At that time they did not kno
Prince's because the tracheot
a which and "Made in Japan"
straps. The sling to be a mu
bag. Identification analyze
cartridge from the C2766 Ma
of one was Dick Gallup the
from precedin neck slightl
spine which pro enment as
shots. The hole mately 5
from the tip joint and a
listance below mastoid p
point immediately behin
Farrel and the two bull
limousine licher—Carca
the exclusion cases fo
building fired the abo
weapons Peter Prince
unpedi reatened movem
Pulp foll of Philip
the Peter Prince aut
Prince from Nov. 21,
k 1, 1;30 p.m., c.s.
loi through place.
AFB. Late in the a
and attended a din
lent. In city as
ccano rifle weap
it was not po fr
the other by nea
however expert
the two larger
Depository were
one was body
ertions, the docto
hat a bullet passed through
in the back of h when external hear

o to the second floor from the operation at some tears
lower neck and exiting in torn by Peter Prince
the coat, 53/8 inches below center ba
automobile. for the contention
Prince's as the moto
that right right
of entry land
a path into any
front of Peter
dense. While the
the two leather
instrument camera
the and the three
the Depository. Tw
FBI Laboratory Con
to the right of his
to the source of the
inches (14 centimete
approximately the sa
process, the bony po
wound seventh on Phil
fra Peter Prince's li
rifle fou Building to
near the corner of the
describe of all other w
agent tographers from i
and plainclot and Paula
Farrel the arrival at lo
The trip began with Pete
for Peter Prince plane, S
They were Philip Farrel w
I dedicated the U.S. Air F
through the city in a moto
Thomas. At stadium a very
much Nice cher as ial limou
unmutilated area to However
were from the with regard to
in the course of trea Farrel
the fragments were "similar to
fragme examination of the he
very little Prince's chest No
By proj K and proceeding at er
portion of Peter Prince's otemy
heada hospital rejec arge muscle
mas lier stages of the muscle do
Peter Prince's necktie. Before th
the crowd on the right. He started

The following columns run vertically up the center of the page:

WITH PICTURES OF THE LITTLE PROJECTILE WHO WAS THEIR CHOICE, A SPECIAL FAVORITE AMONG THE

THE NAPALM CANNISTERS, A LITTLE PROJECTILE WITH A SHY DEMEANOR, WHO KNEW THAT BEFORE THE

PROCESSION WAS OVER HE WOULD BE CHIPPED AND BENT OUT OF SHAPE • HE APPROACHED THE LECTE

AND STOOD BESIDE THE FAT ONE • THE CONVENTION DIDN'T SEEM TO BE CALMING DOWN • "abelisla

waylomakealivingislandfortheaquaredealwewillspendandspendtaxelectand electthisphony

war." THE FAT ONE LIFTED THE SMALL PROJECTILE ONTO HIS MEGATON. "praisethelordandpassthe

amunitionwehavesoughtnoshootingwarwithhitlerforthedurationwewillletherest

ripenonthevine." THE LITTLE PROJECTILE WHO WAS CHOSEN WAS

TOLD OF THE PLAN • HE WOULD THUMP AND

ENTER • THUMP AND ENTE

THUMP

FEW LISTENED NOW WHILE THEY MARCHED AROUND THE CONVENTION FLOOR CARRYING PLACARDS NOW

teladittlegroupofwillfulmenthebyphenatedamericanalwaysholattheamericanflagundermost."

thegrasswillgrowinthestreetsofehundredcitieainasmokefilledreominsomeho

inthenameofthegreatjehovahandthecontinentalcongress

thesunwillgodownonamillionmenincms

rfellowsaredying

shooting started, Philip Farrel had been facing toward   the crowd on the right. He started
to turn toward the left and suddenly felt a blow on his back. Philip Farrel had been hit by a. __ Philip Farrel had

several cars onto house when he heard of deer he looked on the motorcycle with his
conclusion this chart, cases, depicted the skull. When a bullet and exists at anoth
it the diameter of the hole side. Based on his Prince's skull Color any
opinion shot the head and from C2766 weapons. Two who made independent
bullet fragments and WOUNDS of the shots fired Commission car
car and representatives bullet-hole wound in the II, the
President was Perkland. The small the large quantity
of blood said his answers at the theory about
hat edge at the time rather open. Comment
testified before the used it (his
answers). But, again the conf
an ection of his com ter
the press con er
23, 1963 repo
Perry

AND DISAPPEARED
34
atten dea
Peter Prince da
apple the not know if
two that the neck missile
Dr. sta as a wound of Commission
of the neck try or exit—Esperim When
the Peter tie was cut off by eft of the knot
leavin ad a nick on the lef orizontally, indicatin
ng horizontally, but would shed light on While riding i
on November 22 chest, right wrist a cit edges of the wo photo
on X motorc showed hit him whick photogr took responsibility to The
conclusions of the Commission a has satisfied the assassination prolonge
and thorough killed Peter Prince red from it who the observation in the neck
could be evidence of it elected that possibilities could at a single bullet ring thr
he with the point for the neck and the did not know neck being wound characteristics a wo
as the entrance or formation regarding the by expert those worn by special wound ballist using
the C2766 same type as (See Commission eat from the side of his head. uder film shows the throa
chin an angle. Based conducted the autopsy, ullet through the Peter approximate positi
rip to Texas rily Philip Farrel to the Peter be desirable utes had been the si
of a honor of the problems of luncheon site. tomary practise tunity to
see the During School moon he flew rcade spoke at the in honor of
U.S. R large, enthusiastic crowd lsewhere during the trip,
Prince. en Peter Prince asked replied "that the crow see
him before but to see Beatrice Benefix flew to for
ovember 22 Pete afterward a Prince liked out
him Peter public. skull which it chie
of the Forces Institute of bulle
wounds, illustrated about
the head based on coll
effect of a p
perforate
ente

THE
ROOM AT A RATE
ghtorahotic"
greeioneandfire"
outprideofancestry
semustgethelunatic
evotepeoplewhoare
ONE ROSE IN
elly."
SHOT. "americaing
storyismoreorless
ANOTHER BROADCAS'
ccesseflaw." "dem
unwrittenlaw." AN.
CHAOS WAS THE SCEN
BEGAN TO MOVE ABOU
conflict" SAID THE
STOOD BY THE LECTE
"therearenoatheist
vepeacewaringthebl
mostimaceuousdesse
seandstivelormerm
orassoutofthetrench
omeasbychristmasest
domitcheermenthepoo

OF MEN FLASHED
k" "pickoutthebig
"othoboken" "afi
ALLED THROUGH THE
THAN SOUND. "with
posterhythechine
helargemollycoddl
yaically and mor
DELEGATION LIKE A
smeltingpot." "hi
bunkitstradition"
ED. "withoutduepr
entisamericanathe
OTHER SCOLDED.
AS THE DELEGATION
"amirrepressible
FAT ONE WHO STILL
AS THE MASS MOVED
infoxholesletusha
codyahirtyeareofmi
tudewemuststabili
alcyfortymeneighth
scandbacktotheirh
rictaccountability

the
causes ho
hospital stretc
removed and taken on
an elevator second floor he
was which was then moved wheeled
the moved this stretcher from the grou
floor alone the care of one of the stretcher
autopsy material to 141/2 bullet. Animal skin Co.
6.5 bullets were from a distance of 180 holes which wer
only slightly a little unstable at although not quite the one
most given He said possible, he said other the exit of the Accordin
to this report at the same fore, does not preclude supports the conclusio
that Prince. As discussed in chapter that Peter Prince was injury caused by a
second later. Gerard W. Malanga, a Press, had stationed himself to take pictures of
the passing circulated photograph which the first of the two shots which 900.) According to
simultaneously" with a shot fired. Comparison of his revealed that Malanga fired from the sixth

a
bul
know
markin
on both
bullets w
weapons, s
compare the
markings dete
whether Oaklanc
hospital to the
wearer's The tie
was elongated one
object move manner w
missile by the second
sequence and it is and
that both men were struc
by the testified that afte
the first shot she hands mo
towards his throat, as howeve
Paula Pulp further state hit im
thereafter by the both Peter Pri
and the Peter Prince's movement
testimony therefore missed howe
vides further was located the
right shoulder the tip of th
ear the of an inch (7 by a
had is small observation
from the went out on ab
and behind stories at
the surgeon the bevel
or strikes a pane of
the glass face on
the what school t
of several of th
publishers hou
crew were emp
of the Co,
itself bui
reported
that th
saw Pr
the
six
fl

U
BUNCHI
OUT ALONG THE
THOUGH THERE WAS O?
TO STAND ON A HILL THOUGH
ITS ENTRANCE WAS LEVEL AS FAR
EVERYWHERE. ONE KNEW THAT TO ENTER H
UP. INSIDE WHERE THE PERPETUAL CONVEN-
ARSENAL THOUGH ALL BELIEVERS WERE GATH-

: PASSES IN
THE PLACE ITSELF
S CONSTANTLY CHANGED
ACE, THE HALL ITSELF SEEMED
I WENT BY WHAT MIGHT HAVE BEEN
COULD SEE PAST THE STREETS THAT WENT
WOULD HAVE TO CLIMB, OR TO GIVE HIMSELF
TION WAS HELD IT WAS SILENT AS AN
ERED THERE, AND EVEN THE CYNICS—ALL THOSE THAT WORK THEMSELVES INTO
THE RECESSES, INTO THE NUBBY CAVERNS, INTO THE DEEP, UNDULAT-
ING TWISTS, AND THOSE THAT CAN FLUTTER IN AIR AND
HANG THERE, CHARGED, OFF WHOM THE LIGHT
GLANCES WHEN THEY ARE BROADCAST LIKE SPERM AND
MISTAKES ARE MADE, THE SILENCE WAS HEAVY, LIKE THE HUSH
BEFORE A BATTLE IT FILLED SO MUCH SPACE IT COULD HAVE BEEN THE BLOOD.
STREAM OF A BEAST GRAZING ON THE BANKS
OF A RIVER OF GALAXIES, THEY WERE
OFF, WOULD HE FINALLY APPEAR? GROUPS
WAITING FOR A FAT ONE TO KICK THINGS
OF DELEGATES RAISED THEIR LUMINOUS
PLACARDS WHEN HE SHOWED UP. THAT WERE
FOR THE LIGHT WASHING OVER
THEM. A NOISE ROSE STEADY AS A F
D SOLIDIFIED INTO A SCREAM

bullets in the Peter Prince arcano rill
found in were performed under a doct
who had U.S. Army performed in Pet
Prince's head bullets fired by
the results of this series
that (a) one shot passed
through probably passe
the Philip penetra
Peter Prince's
head automobi
and (d) th
shots pr
misse
t

as
to w
it was
the First
Shot assassin
perhaps missed i
an effort to Princ
passed under the oak
tree, or passed under t
tree and the tree might ha
struck a portion of the On th
other hand the greatest his pick
truck on the opposite side of the o
artichoke's car. He observed the gunma

THE PLAC.

B
d
at
the
scene o
the assa
floor win
of the saw
a rifle in P
Depository at
the scene of t
assassination tl
window of the saw
a rifle in the win
joined the at the U
testimonial the Peter
Prince joke at a large
back of the head as lyi
on his back during the ho
in his head was also hidden
which covered Peter Prince
the press conference would hav
happened based on than his prof
opinion on his answers at the
press Commission: as a matter
of speculation that Dr. V
who also answers and I emp
that we had no is corrob
by some of the involved
Peter Prince over for
an exam heart activi
ceased and Peter Pr
was pronounced we
surgery and ulti
Upon learning
Peter Prince
Hospital un
close guar
plane at
field B
Benef
body
boa
t

clwearecomingbackmore
ithatwayanddont
anybodytell
"yeswearonthewaybacknotbymer
surelythaneverbeforeb
youdifferently." O

I sneaked a little closer myself and got a look at that book and believe me I can't account for it. I certainly didn't write it, would never have thought of it, and I deny responsibility for it. An ending is an ending whether you put it there or not. I'm getting out. I bid this novel goodbye. Goodbye. Goodbye Peter Prince. Whatever is happening it's out of my control. I'm going on to simpler, more suitable things for me. I'm going to watch football, spend time with my kids, hold out for more money at work. I've had enough of this business as I guess this business has had enough of me. I've paid off Linda Lawrence though she sits there on that bench and thumbs through his book, and Philip Farrel is paid off too, though he comes to that bench himself, on his own, as if it's a sentimental habit. It's all very touching but I'm getting out of here.

"Peter Prince," I throw one last shout back into the disintegrating scene. "Aren't you going to get up and do something? Anything?" Who knows if he hears me? It's out of my control. I bid this novel goodbye, and turn my proverbial back as if I'd never had anything to do with it anyway. I'm going to drop in on the rest of the world. Next stop, maybe, television; or I'll feed myself out through those electrodes that will be planted in our skulls at birth. I'll be a unit of pleasurable revelation. Smiles will result. So I bid this masterpiece goodbye. I'll tell you only now that I had planned to bring it back to that castle where it once began, where Peter Prince could be reunited with his woman whose father stone by stone had laid up the castle there. I had not planned a totally unsuccessful reunion, the return to be a relaxing experience for Peter Prince, his woman mature enough to have done with cats and to have set the Limburger out herself on the sideboard. The spotted heaps of wrecked cars would have grown by then into a high rusting range that ringed the castle in such a way it would be impossible to look out over them, making the place much cozier. I would have had Peter Prince skate in over the polished floors hoping to surprise his woman only to find that I had planned a surprise party for himself, a regular denouement with all the characters of this novel from Armando Amante to Zephraim Zinfandel present, including Linda Lawrence's whole cast of children. There would have been several pages of conversation during which loose ends could have been knotted and the significance of all events finally brought to light, at which time the reader could make the pleasurable discovery of a certain consistency of theme and image throughout. It's tough, but I must bid goodbye to this narrative; goodbye, behind my own back. I hereby abdicate this throne of insolent compassion. Toodle-oo. Even that bulb I developed for the final scene that has the warmth of librating candlelight and the ambiguous force of fluorescents, has to go unmentioned. That splendid denouement that was to close the book and make it publishable has to be ferreted into the archives of the unwritten. I hope you don't mistake the emotion of this statement for bitterness. I have grown fond of the procedures here, and leave reluctantly. Goodbye. That last scene was to have been America, with a rock and roll band at the castle, and all the new dances, formal and primitive, if only I could have known he was coming back for the celebration, if only now I had a little hint of how he got here I would begin even now my ending; just a hint how he got home. There's no room any more for responsible order. For the authors of these works.

SEVEN POWER
WIDE BOOK
INSTRUCTIONS
CONDITIONS
DEVILS
INCANTATIONS
MANIFES-
TATIONS!
Strange
Practices
beginning to end
THE PETER of PETER PRINCE
It's Your's
...and
IT'S STARTLING SEQUEL
SEVEN POWER!
Like a BOLT FROM THE BLUE!
It's GREAT!
TO PETER PRINCE

*

"Goodbye, Peter Prince," I say, meek as anything.

"Goodbye. Forget it. Just get the fuck out of here."

"Look: a big blank nothing in the story of Peter Prince."

He just turns his back on me, like lights switching out in an office building.

I'm through. I buy myself an orange soda and sit down on a bench in the park by myself. I still see the back of the head of the former main character of my ex-novel. Philip Farrel now is thumbing through the pages of that absurd volume. Suddenly a blue atmosphere flows onto the scene and things change. The walls of the building are up, and on each section of the curtain wall in electric yellow letters the name PETER PRINCE appears or his initials, P.P. Unbelievable. Those huge balloons rise over the city bearing the name of PETER PRINCE skyward where skywriters are already sprawling his name over the scape. He himself stands up and shakes hands with the throngs of people headed for the PETER PRINCE exhibition at the museum. I take a PETER PRINCE leaflet from a young organizer.

"I'm the author of Peter Prince," I told the man with the hot-dog cart.

"And I'm the president of Standard Oil," said the man, and pushed off.

I'm not ashamed of it. I say it. "I am the author of Peter Prince." And if I weren't impeccably dressed, sporting my grandfather's tiepin, my beltbuckle monogrammed, people would probably think I was nuts. But it's true, true as my spit-polished dress boots. I am the author of Peter Prince.

Don't
THE SUCCESSFUL MAN!
BE ONE!
REAL DOWN
ON HOW TO GET UP HIGH!
Personal Power
SHUCKS
PRINCE, PETER
MAKE
for the
LIGHT!
STOP STUMBLING
DARKNESS!!
POWER and SUCCESS!
BURP!
MONEY! LOVE!
NOW
DON'T
ACT
HELPS

ABOUT

STEVE KATZ is the author of eight novels, including *The Lestriad, Saw, Antonello's Lion,* and a trilogy, *Wier & Pouce, Florry of Washington Heights,* and *Swanny's Ways.* He has also published five collections of short fictions, among them *Stolen Stories, Creamy & Delicious,* and *Kisssssss: A Miscellany,* in addition to several volumes of poetry. He was one of the founders of the innovative publisher Fiction Collective alongside Raymond Federman, Ronald Sukenick, and Jonathan Baumbach, and has taught at the universities of Cornell, Iowa, and City of New York. His most recent book is the memoir *The Compleat Memoirrhoids.*

W.C. BAMBERGER believes in the convention that a writer's "bio" is a list of publications, so: W. C. Bamberger is a freelance introductionist, fictioneer, essayist, editor, translator and publisher. His most recent novel is *A Light Like Ida Lupino*; he has written essays on subjects ranging from *Wonder Woman* comics to the death of Kierkegaard; he edited *Guy Davenport and James Laughlin: Selected Letters*; he has published translations of Gershom Scholem and Paul Scheerbart, among others; as (alias) Bamberger Books he has had the honor of publishing Steve Katz's *The Lestriad* and *Journalism.* He lives in Michigan, USA.